Sea, Sun, and Scallywags

Daphne Neville

Copyright © 2015 Daphne Neville

All rights reserved, including the right to reproduce this book, or portions thereof in any form. No part of this text may be reproduced, transmitted, downloaded, decompiled, reverse engineered, or stored, in any form or introduced into any information storage and retrieval system, in any form or by any means, whether electronic or mechanical without the express written permission of the author.

This is a work of fiction. Names and characters are the product of the author's imagination and any resemblance to actual persons, living or dead, is entirely coincidental.

ISBN: 978-1-326-18311-0

PublishNation, London
www.publishnation.co.uk

CHAPTER ONE

1967

A warm, south westerly sea breeze gently blew around the sheer, craggy cliffs and across Trengillion's beach where Ned Stanley slowly ambled across the wet sand and shingle, carefully treading to avoid the tumbling waves splashing close to his sandalled feet.

Considering it was early in the month of August and the school holidays, Trengillion's beach, in comparison with previous years, was quiet, for the Torrey Canyon disaster during March earlier in the year had left its scar and patches of oil were frequently found amongst rocks and clinging to seaweed washed up with the ever changing tides.

Ned sighed. It was hardly surprising that sun bathers were fewer in number, for the prospect of attempting to remove oil from clothes, shoes and skin was not a job to be relished by even the most dedicated of cleaning fanatics.

A seagull circled overhead as Ned stopped and cast his eyes across the broad expanse of rippling, dark blue ocean shimmering beneath the rays of the brilliant summer sun. What a contrast to the scenes in early spring, when stinking, dark brown, waves of scum, frothing like the head of fermenting beer, had tumbled onto sand and shingle, already buried beneath several inches of thick, glutinous, reddish brown sludge.

One hundred and twenty miles of Cornwall's beautiful coastline suffered contamination during the invasion of the massive oil slick, and as it flowed, unhindered, from the broken tanker towards the shore, fifteen thousand seabirds and all marine life, including seals, perished in its path.

Ned, headmaster of the village school, thought of the children he taught and the distress they'd experienced over the death of so many helpless creatures. Images on television showing oil-drenched birds gasping for breath, tugged at their innocent hearts as they tried to understand why their willingness to help could do little or nothing to ease the tragic situation.

Yet, amidst the doom and gloom, arose a huge of amount of excitement and much debate regarding the government's handling of the situation. Speculation followed, regarding any remedy which might bring the unfortunate episode to a satisfactory conclusion. Hence, as off-shore action unfurled, Trengillion's inhabitants watched with interest in large numbers from the cliff tops, thrilled to witness the main topic of national news bulletins.

Every effort was made to ease the situation. Firemen and Royal Navy personnel attempted to disperse the oil with detergent. Foam booms were brought in but progress was slow and they broke up in rough seas. Nothing it seemed, worked, and eventually the Royal Air Force and Royal Navy dramatically bombed the ill-fated ship in an endeavour to send it to the bottom of the ocean.

It was a memorable sight. Fires raged out at sea beneath the thick wall of heavy, black smoke, eerily darkening the early spring skies. However, exceptionally high tides extinguished the fires and the operation failed.

The following day the bombing mission continued and eventually the Torrey Canyon, battered and broken, succumbed to the onslaught and sank ninety eight feet beneath the waves to its final resting place.

Ned half-smiled. Events of those memorable times would inevitably dominate the smoke filled bars of the Cornish pubs for many, many years to come.

But for all the pollution, a considerable number of people had still made Cornwall their holiday destination: not all were sun worshippers. Many visitors were simply curious to see for themselves the county where tragedy had struck and others came to enjoy the beautiful scenery. For surely the coastal paths winding over the Cornish cliff tops and beyond were some of the finest to be found in the British Isles.

Ned and his wife Stella had decided to stay at home for the duration of the school summer holiday, having been persuaded to do so by their two daughters, Elizabeth and Anne. For both girls were keen to remain in the village, as Gregory Castor-Hunt and his younger sister, Lillian, were to spend the holiday at their second home, Chy-an-Gwyns, prior to the family moving to Florida for two years towards the end of August.

Ned smiled. He was very fond of the village children, most of whom he had taught since they had first started school as shy infants not wishing to be parted from their mothers. He found his job both satisfying and rewarding and was proud and privileged to observe at close hand the development and making of a future generation.

Ned tucked his hands into the pockets of his corduroy trousers and slowly ambled across the beach towards an old bench dedicated to Denzil Penhaligon, a fisherman who had drowned back in 1950. He sat down. Where had all the years gone? His forty-first birthday was fast approaching and the world it seemed was a much different place; many of the innovations had occurred since he had first set foot on Trengillion's soil back in 1952. For the Swinging Sixties were well and truly established and it seemed the old ways were gone forever. Nearly every house had been up-dated with modern kitchen appliances and the smallest bedrooms converted into bathrooms. Only three houses in the village had outside lavatories still in use, with no facilities to flush other than buckets filled with water from solitary taps inside kitchens, unmodernised, with china sinks and old coppers tucked away in dark corners.

Ned turned and looked towards the village. From almost every rooftop, firmly secured against chimney stacks, serried ranks of television aerials dominated the sky-line, and discussions regarding favourite television programmes viewed the previous evening on the three channels was a popular pastime with friends and neighbours whenever they met.

Ned chuckled, recalling the previous summer's highlight: 1966, when England hosted and won the World Cup. Almost everyone in Trengillion had watched and enjoyed the final match with unbridled patriotism, even Ned himself, who considered football to be a futile game of very little interest.

The clock on the church tower struck the half hour. Behind it lay a field once owned by Frank Newton, landlord of the Ringing Bells Inn. Now it belonged to the village, a gift from Frank, which boasted a slide, three swings, a see-saw, a roundabout, and was fondly known by all as the Rec. Beyond the Rec, lay a paddock and stables, home of two old horses, Winston and Brown Ale, owned by Frank, but looked after by Meg Reynolds who taught infants at the village school.

The sound of Scott Mackenzie's *San Francisco* drifted through the airwaves. Ned grinned. Yet another dramatic change, the frequent sound of lively pop music blaring from gardens, fields and public places: its source, the ever growing popular, transistor radio.

Yes, things had changed beyond recognition and most would say for the better. The dark days which followed the War were now but a distant memory. Britain was booming and the National flag was a symbol of the nation's pride, both, commercially and through government sources.

Ned threw back his head and laughed. Some things, however, had not changed. His mother's love of colour for instance, and it seemed to him now that the fashion designers and trend setters, who in their wisdom inflicted their bizarre outfits on every man, woman and child, shared her love of vivid, outrageous garments, for never in a hundred years would he have imagined himself wearing a shirt of floral fabric. Although such an item would not be in his wardrobe had his mother not been up to London recently for a trip to the Royal Albert Hall during which she purchased the garment, a memento from a visit to Carnaby Street.

Ned looked at his watch. Time to return home to The School House for lunch. He rose, left the beach, walked up the incline and strode past the Inn into the village. As he reached the gate of his garden, Cyril Penrose drove by in his new Land Rover. Ned waved. Cyril tooted in return, a huge grin stretched across his rugged face. He was after all a man of property, occasioned by the death of Charles Penwynton in December the previous year.

Ned grinned as he walked up the garden path. Poor Cyril, he had been distraught when first he'd heard of the old man's death, but all had turned out well in the end. The estate was split into separate lots, and as a reward for being loyal tenants for over thirty years, the Penroses were offered the chance to buy their home, Long Acre Farm, for a very favourable sum. And Cyril, rejuvenated by his good fortune, vowed he would not retire a day before his seventieth birthday.

To date, the only property on the Penwynton Estate not sold was the large house itself in which generations of the Penwynton family had lived ever since they'd had it built in the sixteenth century. It was, however, up for sale and there was much speculation as to the fate of the house due to its neglected condition.

The children of Trengillion, as on every dry day since the beginning of the school summer holidays, were gathered together inside their den, deep in the heart of Bluebell Woods, beneath a large elm, fondly known by generations of children as the Cuckoo tree. Nearby, the ivy covered trunk of a fallen tree lay close to the stream, its demise having created an opening amongst the canopy of tall trees thus allowing the sun to peep through and provide warmth for the daytime campers.

"I wish the summer would go on for ever and that you didn't have to leave us. It's an awful long time is two years and you'll forget us all in that time," grumbled Susan Collins, taking a bag of toffees from her pocket and offering them to her friends.

Lillian Castor-Hunt agreed. "I know it is and I don't want to go away one bit. I wish my father was a fisherman like yours then we could stay in one place and not keep moving from one house to another. It's alright for you lot though, you'll still have each other while we're away, but Greg and I will have to make new friends and it seems so pointless when it's only for two, silly years."

"I don't think I'll mind that," said her brother, thoughtfully. "I think it will be quite exciting and travel does broaden the mind, Lily. We're very lucky to have a house here in Cornwall as well as one in Surrey, and the weather in Florida should be utterly superb. Although, I will of course miss you all and these last two weeks have been the best ever."

Lillian Castor-Hunt and her brother Gregory were staying at Chy-an-Gwyns, a large house high on the cliff tops overlooking Trengillion and the sea. Their father, Willoughby Castor-Hunt, was an architect, hence for most of the year they lived in their home in Surrey. Tabitha, their mother had given up her career shortly before the birth of Lily due to ill health, and because she was still weak nearly eleven years on, the doctors had recommended lots of sun and warmth, hence, the family had decided to go to America to aid her recovery and Willoughby had taken early retirement on his sixtieth birthday in May to ensure his young wife had his undivided attention.

"While you're away, does it mean your poor house will be empty?" asked Graham Reynolds. "My dad says houses get damp if they're left empty for too long."

Gregory shook his head. "No, it won't be empty, not all the time, anyway. Father has let the place to Mrs Rossiter who doesn't want to be on her own now that her children are all away at university. She'll only be there until Christmas though, and then she'll go back to her proper home. And then next year it will be a holiday place because Father has put it in the hands of a letting agency."

Anne Stanley frowned. "Who's Mrs Rossiter?"

"She's someone Father knows: well, he knows her husband, anyway, although they only met recently when Mr Rossiter started going to Dad's tennis club. Apparently, he's in the Royal Navy, Captain Henry Rossiter, and he's currently away at sea."

Elizabeth was impressed. "A sea captain's wife. Do you know what she's like?"

Greg shrugged his shoulders. "I've no idea because I've never met her, nor have I met Captain Rossiter."

Diane Reynolds wrinkled her nose. "That doesn't make sense. If Mrs Rossiter's children are away at university and her husband is away at sea, then she'll still be by herself at Chy-an-Gwyns, so how can she be coming to Trengillion to avoid being on her own?"

"Oh, I think she's bringing a friend or a relation with her for company, something like that. I don't really know as I've not been told. I'm only going on what I overheard the other day when my parents were talking about it. They won't be of much interest to you lot though as there'll be no children with it being term time, and as I said they're grown up, anyway."

"I think it will be quite exciting to meet up again after such a long time," said Elizabeth Stanley, dreamily. "We'll all be grown up then. I'll be fifteen and even my baby sister will be a teenager."

"I wish you wouldn't call me your baby sister," grumbled Anne. "I start the big school next month and I'm not the youngest here, anyway. Graham and Lily are both younger than me but you wouldn't dare call them babies."

Elizabeth ignored her sister's remark and suggested a game of hide and seek to build up an appetite before they ate their picnic lunches.

After a process of elimination, Susan Collins was declared to be *it,* and whilst she hid her eyes, crouched inside the den and counted to twenty, the others dashed off in different directions to hide in an obscure a place as was physically possible.

"Com-ing," shouted Susan in a sing-song voice, as she withdrew her hands from her face.

The woods were eerily quiet as she timorously emerged from beneath the large elm. Beside the fallen, ivy covered tree she stopped and listened for twigs snapping in the undergrowth or whispering voices, but only the gentle sound of trickling water wending its way through the trees on its journey to the sea disturbed the silence. With no indication as to the whereabouts of her friends she ambled down to the pathway used by walkers which ran alongside the water's edge. There she stopped. In which direction she should go? Left, right, or over the stream where the trees were less dense?

Decisively Susan followed the stream until she reached stepping stones on a bend where the stream was narrow. There she crossed, with a backwards glance, constantly feeling she was being watched.

She continued her walk, timorously looking into every possible hiding place as she went. Jumping each time she heard a rustle in the undergrowth and wishing, continuously, that being alone in the woods did not make her nervous.

When the remains of a tumbledown building, part-hidden by thick ivy, came into view, Susan stopped. She heard a giggle and with heart racing, peered behind the wall. Crouched amongst the rubble, both Anne and Lily hid with their cardigans pulled over their heads.

"Found you," laughed Susan, with much relief. "But you're not supposed to hide in the same place as each other."

"We know, but we were too scared to hide separately", said Anne, brushing earth from her skirt. "The woods seem a bit scary today. Don't tell the others, will you?"

"Of course not. Come on let's go and find them, my tummy's rumbling and I want my lunch."

They found Diane and Graham Reynolds without much difficulty further up-stream. Elizabeth, they might not have found at all had a rook in the trees up above not startled her, thus causing her to scream. The only person left unaccounted for then was Gregory and try as they might, the six friends could not find him anywhere.

"All right, Greg," shouted Susan, twirling around as she looked in all directions. "We give up. Where are you?"

There was no response to her call. Lily cried out to her brother, but again Gregory did not respond. In desperation they split up, but for reasons of safety, kept within sight of each other as they trod the woodland path relentlessly calling Gregory's name.

Beneath a horse chestnut tree Diane stopped to tie the lace of her plimsolls. She jumped when two, spiky, green, unripe conkers fell from the tree and splashed into the stream. Intrigued, she looked up. Above in the branches, Greg sat dangling his legs from a sturdy branch, part hidden, amongst the thick leaves high in the tree. He grinned smugly as she called the others to her side.

"You cheat," shouted Lily, cross, but relieved that he had been found. "It's not fair if you hide up there."

"Why not?" said Greg, niftily climbing down and jumping the last few feet. "We're allowed to hide anywhere in the woods and that's what I did. But actually you'll probably be interested to know what I could see from up there. There's a lorry parked outside the old Lodge House at the foot of the drive leading to the big house, and men are busy putting up scaffolding so it looks like someone must have bought the old place and they're going to start doing it up. Shall we go over that way and have a look?"

"Oh yes," said Graham, with interest. "Let's go now."

"No," said Elizabeth, emphatically. "I think we should eat our lunches first. It's past one o'clock and I'm feeling hungry."

They took a vote on their next move which was won by the girls. The boys conceded defeat and all headed back to the den where lunchboxes were hidden in the undergrowth to avoid detection by anyone following the woodland path.

"Who do you think has bought the Lodge House?" asked Lily, climbing onto the trunk of the fallen tree.

Susan shook her head. "Search me, I didn't even know it had been sold."

"I don't know either," said Elizabeth, removing tin foil from a cheese and piccalilli sandwich. "But I heard Mum and Dad talking about it ages ago and Dad said he hoped the new people would have children to help swell the dwindling numbers of pupils in the school."

"Well, whoever it is they must have a bit of money, that place is a wreck, the roof's fallen in and it's in a worse state than the big house," said Greg. "I could see the roof clearly from the conker tree."

When all sandwiches and cakes were eaten and the empty lunchboxes were back in their hiding places, the friends followed the path through the woods towards the edge where the Lodge House stood at the foot of the driveway leading to Penwynton House.

A dry stone wall bordered the perimeter of the woods and in front of it, hydrangeas smothered with huge blooms in shades of pink, white and blue tumbled onto the grass edging the winding driveway.

To avoid detection and keep out of the builders' way, the children hid on top of the dry stone wall behind the hydrangeas.

Several men were busy erecting scaffolding, and from the back of a lorry a cement mixer was being unloaded onto a spot beside a stack of slates. The boys watched the activities with interest but the girls were more interested in the builders themselves as several were quite young.

Diane pointed to a dark haired lad standing on the back of a lorry. "Isn't that Steve Penhaligon?"

Susan nodded. "Yes. He went into building straight after school. Dad said he wanted to be a fisherman but his mum begged him not to. It's a shame really, but it's probably for the best."

Lily was confused. "Why didn't his mum let him go fishing? I think that's pretty mean if it's what he wanted to do."

Susan shook her head. "Not really. His dad was a fisherman, you see, and he got drowned. You know who his dad was, don't you? We often sit on his bench when we go to the beach."

"Oh, you mean Denzil Penhaligon! No wonder his poor mother doesn't want him to go fishing then. But Steve must have only been little when he died, because it was a long time ago, wasn't it?"

"1950, I think," said Elizabeth, thoughtfully. "I know it was just before Christmas. I've read the inscription on the bench enough times, so yes, Steve would have been a baby. How horrible, never to have known your dad."

As they spoke, a handsome young man with thick, shoulder length blond hair emerged from the side of the house. The girls ceased their chat and stared open-mouthed in disbelief.

"He's the spitting image of Danny Jarrams," squeaked Elizabeth, when she could find her voice. "You don't think it is him, do you?"

Graham laughed. "Don't be daft. Why would Gooseberry Pie's bass guitarist be helping put a roof on a tumbledown place in Cornwall? I mean, it's a long way from the bright lights, isn't it? And I shouldn't think he needs the dosh."

Elizabeth drooled. "I don't know, I guess it's just wishful thinking."

"Oh no, I've lost my watch," cried Anne, grasping her wrist. "It must have come undone when we were playing. I know the catch was lose."

Elizabeth glared at her sister. "Then stop whining and go and look for it. Really Anne, you're so careless. Retrace your steps, it can't be far away."

"Will you came with me? I'm too scared to go on my own. Please, Liz."

"No," snapped Elizabeth, emphatically. "You lost it, so you can find it."

"I'll go with you," said Lily, jumping down from the wall and taking Anne's arm. She turned to the others. "We'll not be long, I hope."

"Little sisters!" groaned Elizabeth. "They always manage to spoil things, now I expect I'll have to go and help her because I feel guilty. It's not fair. I'd much rather be here watching Danny."

"That's cos he's gorgeous," whispered, Diane, wringing her hands. "I think we must come here every day now and see how progress at the old Lodge House is coming on."

Jane giggled. "I second that. Perhaps we ought to move our den further over this way. I know he's not Danny, but do you think he might be his brother or something like that?"

"Danny Jarrams doesn't have a brother," Greg airily retorted. "Only an older sister and she's a nurse. I was reading an article about Gooseberry Pie in my pop magazine only yesterday."

"Well, I shall pretend he's Da..." Jane's remark was lost by a piercing scream from inside the wood.

"Oh no," gasped Elizabeth, scrambling down from the wall. "That sounded like Anne."

Without speaking the friends ran back into the woods calling Anne and Lily by name. They found the girls huddled together in a small clearing in a dip between two banks of earth. Both were sobbing.

"What's the matter?" cried Elizabeth, falling on her knees and hugging her little sister tightly.

"She saw a strange man looking at her through the bushes," said Lily, trembling. "He didn't hurt her but he frightened her badly."

"But what was he doing?" asked Gregory, casting his eyes in all directions. "I mean, did he approach you or anything like that?"

"No," said Anne, wiping her eyes with a handkerchief. "He just stood there staring at me, but I didn't like the look of him and he didn't smile or move at all until I screamed and then he just disappeared."

"Did you see him, Lil?" asked Gregory.

"No, we'd split up so that we could cover more ground. I didn't see him at all, but I wish I had."

"Anyway, I found my watch," said Anne, attempting to smile. "So that's something. It was lying where we are now. It was after I picked it up and put it back on that I noticed the face looking at me."

"Would you recognise him again?" asked Susan.

"Probably," said Anne, "but I only saw his head so I couldn't give you much of a description. Except that his hair was longish and he had big ears."

Elizabeth scowled. "How do you know he had big ears if his hair was longish?"

Recalling the image, Anne shuddered. "Because his hair was tucked behind his big ears."

"I think we must keep our eyes peeled from now on when we're in these woods," said Graham, who would never admit he was frightened. "I expect the bloke is quite harmless but it doesn't pay to take risks."

"Are we going to tell our parents?" asked Diane. "I mean, I think we should."

"What! But they'll stop us from coming here," said Susan, horrified, "and that'd be terrible, especially now we've discovered Danny."

Jane nodded. "You're right and after all the strange man didn't do anything wrong, did he? But from now on we must always stick together and listen out for any gossip about dodgy looking men with long hair and big ears."

They returned to their den in silence, each keeping a watchful eye out for the mysterious stranger who had invaded their orderly lives and created an unpleasant atmosphere.

CHAPTER TWO

Sitting at the kidney shaped dressing table inside the largest bedroom of Rose Cottage, Molly Smith carefully secured her best black hat into position on top of her honey blonde curls. Until three years before she had regularly dyed her hair black, but on reaching the grand old age of sixty she had decided it was time to let the dye grow out and revert to her true colour. Molly, however, was unable to live with the white hair which gradually covered every inch of her head. "I look like an old granny," she had groaned with humdrum persistence to her family and friends, until finally her husband, tired of hearing the grumbles and witnessing the bouts of depression, insisted she paid Betty a visit to arrange for her hair to be dyed a subtle colour which would complement her aging complexion. Hence, thanks to Betty's advice and skills, Molly was a blonde and she loved her hair to distraction.

"Aren't you ready yet, Moll?" called the major, impatiently, from the foot of the stairs. "We'll be late if you don't get a move on. It's ten to eleven already."

"I'm just coming," she replied, dabbing face powder onto her cheeks before rising from the stool.

In the full length mirror on the landing she checked that her skirt was hanging evenly, and when finally satisfied her appearance was acceptable, she descended the stairs with confidence.

Arm in arm, Molly and the major left their cottage and walked with haste down the road to the church where they quickly took up their pew on the left hand side of the aisle. Molly felt a little choked. The organist was playing slow, mournful music. Tears prickled the backs of her eyes. Funerals always made her want to cry but she must refrain from making a spectacle of herself, for the major would not approve and Mabel had, after all, lived a long and full life. For ninety one was a good age by anyone's reckoning.

When the service was over, the mourners gathered outside in the churchyard for the internment, and as Mabel was lowered into the earth, Molly cast her eyes along the row of recent graves, where flowers nodded their heads in the August breeze beneath the headstones of people she had known and whose friendship she had lost during the fifteen years she had lived in Trengillion.

Next to Mabel's final resting place alongside her late husband, Godfrey, lay Flo Hughes, who had died following a heart attack late the previous year. Beyond Flo, lay Pearl Ridge, the vicar's disabled wife, who had died when complications arose following an operation on her back. Beyond Pearl, Harry, the builder's mother, Ethel Richardson lay. Molly had only known her since she had started to attend the Over 60s Club every Tuesday in the village hall. And over in the far corner, a gleaming, newly erected marble monument towered above the tops of more modest grave stones in memory of Charles Penwynton, who lay in the large family plot, its boundary edged with heavy black chains draped between equidistant granite pillars. Molly sighed. The trustees of the estate had organised the stone but no family members remained to lay flowers on the grave and mourn, and it seemed sad that after so many years of prominence, no-one in Trengillion now bore the name Penwynton.

The major nudged Molly, aware that she was not paying full attention. The vicar was no longer speaking, and Frank, followed by Godfrey's two, white haired sons and their wives, were in turn pausing over Mabel's grave and dropping rose petals onto her wooden coffin.

Molly and the major stepped forward to join the small procession of mourners, each slowly passing Mabel to pay their respects and say the last 'goodbye'.

Afterwards they left the churchyard and walked round the corner to the Inn where Dorothy had made sandwiches for the mourners; a farewell lunch to her husband's late aunt.

"That was a nice service," said Ned, clutching a pint of cider, to his mother. "The vicar didn't go on too much and it wasn't too sad with Mabel being very old and all that, although I would have thought there would have been a better turn out, but then I suppose most of her contemporaries are long gone."

Molly smiled. "She may have been old, Ned, but she still had her marbles. I shall miss her; she was the life and soul of the Over 60s Club, even if she did have a sharp tongue.

Annie Stevens served on the bar with Dorothy, as Frank thought he ought to play host, being the only relative of Mabel present, and especially as neither of her adopted daughters was in attendance; for both were well into their sixties, one was in poor health and the other had no-one to look after her cats!

"You look tired, Frank," sighed Doris Jones, helping herself to a salmon and cucumber sandwich. "I think it's time you thought about retiring, you're not as young as you were and you work far too hard."

"Funny you should say that, Doris. Dot and I were talking about giving up this place only last night, cos between you and me, we rather like the idea of buying Godfrey and Mabel's bungalow and retiring there. Neither of Godfrey's sons are interested in living in the village, and it's them as will inherit it. As you know, they've both got their own places and families in town. What do you think? I've always admired that bungalow and it'd suit us down to the ground."

"I think that's a very good idea. It's a smashing place, the garden's a good size too, not that that would appeal to you. Dot has green fingers though so I'm sure she'd enjoy a spot of gardening. It's secluded as well; you couldn't really do much better in my opinion."

"Good, cos I've had a word with Godfrey's sons and they're going to let me know when it'll be theirs to sell. As for the garden, I rather fancy learning a bit of horticulture, pruning roses and suchlike. I've never had time for stuff like that before, but I reckon with a bit of tuition I'd be quite good."

"Looks like the weather's likely to be fine this weekend," said George Fillingham to the major as they sat in the snug bar chewing the fat. "Shame about the rain last Sunday, it rather spoiled the game."

"Couldn't agree more. The wretched damp seems to get to my joints these days. I'm beginning to think golf's a young man's game, but I'll be damned if I'm going to hang up my irons yet."

"Good heavens, you mustn't even think of giving up for a year or two," laughed George, draining his whisky glass and offering the major a cigar. "I mean, if you did, whatever would you do all day long?"

"Can't imagine," said the major, taking a cigar from the proffered tin. "Thanks, George. Another drink?"

"Well, it's a little early, but go on, yes, you've twisted my arm. I don't expect Bertha will be in any hurry to leave as she has plenty of her chums here to chat with."

"Those shoes are the same style as your white ones aren't they?" commented Bertha Fillingham nodding towards May Dickens' footwear. "You know the ones I mean, you got oil on when you played with your grandson on the beach last Whitsun."

"May laughed and held up her foot. "How observant of you. Actually they are the white ones I got oil on, but because the damn stuff wouldn't come off I decided to dye them black and I'm jolly pleased with the way they've turned out. I couldn't bear to chuck them away, you see, they cost a pretty penny and they're so very comfortable too."

"What a brilliant idea. I've some cream shoes that are beginning to look a bit shabby and I did intend to send them to the next school jumble sale, but on second thoughts I think I'll take a leaf from your book. Where did you get the dye?"

"Woollies," said May. "Can't remember exactly how much it was but it was only a few bob. Make sure you wear rubber gloves if you do take the plunge though, the dye's horrible messy stuff if you get it on your hands. In fact that's why I'm wearing my leather gloves today."

"Oh dear, poor you, and I'd imagine the dye is worse to get off your skin than the oil. Still, never mind, I suppose it'll wear off in time. Meanwhile, if I were you, I'd abandon the twin-tub and do a bit of washing by hand. That should do the trick."

May grinned. "Funnily enough that's what Molly said. So I think I'll look out my old washboard when I get home."

"Where are the children?" Molly asked Ned, as he handed her a gin and tonic.

"Bluebell Woods I would imagine; that's where they spend most of their time."

Molly sighed. "Oh, to be young again!"

"Hmm, they were telling us last night that work has started on the old Penwynton Lodge House. Have you any idea who's bought it?" Ned loosened his black tie and undid the top button of his shirt.

"Oh yes," grinned Molly, exultantly. "Fred Stevens has bought it for his retirement. Well, that is to say his parents have. If you remember, his mother and father live in Newquay where they have a small hotel and they've bought Fred the Lodge on the understanding that he must find the money to do it up. There's no rush as he won't be retiring for eight years or so, but this summer he's getting the roof done and the outside made water tight, then he'll do the rest himself piecemeal, but not the plumbing and electrics of course; he'll have to get professionals in to do those jobs."

"Lucky old Fred," said Ned. "I've never seen the Lodge close up. I've just had glimpses of it through the shrubbery, but what an idyllic spot for anyone wishing to commune with nature. Is Annie pleased?"

"Delighted," said Molly. "It was she who said she wished they could afford to buy the place, and that was enough incentive for Fred to tap up his parents for some money. He's an only child you see, so he'll inherit all they have, anyway."

Jim Hughes, standing close by rolling a cigarette, heard Molly's comment. "I always fancied living in the Lodge when I were a lot younger. It's got a nice big garden, you see, so there's plenty of room for growing all the veg you'd ever need and room for a couple of pigs too, and o' course a few chickens." He replaced the lid on his baccy tin. "Trouble is you'd most likely have trouble with foxes if you lived up there. Bleedin' things."

Ned nodded. "Yes, I've heard Madge saying they're a curse up at Home Farm."

Jim slipped his baccy tin into his pocket. "They're a curse everywhere. Still, they wouldn't have bothered me too much as I'd have had me gun handy, though the pesky things usually come out at night, so often by the time alarm bells have rung it's too ruddy late and the damage is done."

Molly looked shocked. "Oh, Jim, tell me you'd never really shoot a fox. I know they're naughty but they've such dear little faces and they can't be that much of a nuisance, surely?"

Ned nudged his mother. He thought it unwise to encourage a discussion regarding the morals of shooting creatures with a retired gamekeeper.

"What about Penwynton House itself, does anyone know if that's been snapped up yet?" Ned asked, in order to veer the subject into safer waters.

Molly heeded the warning. "No, at least I've not heard that it's sold. In fact when Doris was telling me about the sale of the Lodge, she said she'd heard that the big house has been taken out of the hands of local estate agents in Truro and is now being handled by a London firm because the trustees think there's more chance of finding a buyer up there. So if that's true, goodness only knows who might end up buying it."

Jim picked up his half-full pint glass of bitter and took a sip. "I'd heard the same. It's too much money for local folk, anyhow, 'though some of the farmers are a lot better off than they'd ever admit. But having said that, none of them are likely to be interested in buying a damn great place like Penwynton House."

"Humph, it'll probably end up as a hotel," said Ned, disapprovingly, "or, God forbid, the home of an over paid pop star. Oh well, we'll just have to wait and see."

Molly cast Ned a quizzical glance. "So what would you like to see happen to it? I mean, if you don't like the idea of it being a hotel or the home of an over paid pop star you must have some other preference."

Ned scowled. "Actually, you've got me there because I can't think of a satisfactory answer unless it were something that would benefit the community."

"A hotel would benefit the community," said Molly, emphatically. "It would provide employment and bring tourists to the area, both of which would boost the local economy."

Jim lit his cigarette. "I dunno about that, the economy down here seems to have done alright up until now."

"Maybe, but the population is growing and with mining no longer a viable option and with fishing in decline, some other sort of employment needs to be thought of. A hotel would employ women too, and with more and more women wanting to work that has to be a good thing."

Jim opened his mouth to say women should be content to stay at home and bring up their children but he thought better of it. After all, things had altered since he was young and the Swinging Sixties with its women's liberation movement had dramatically changed opinions.

CHAPTER THREE

"I want you both to tidy your rooms this morning before you go out. Auntie Rose and Uncle George will be here by tea time, so you'll not have time to do it when you come in," said Stella, to her two daughters as they ate their breakfast in the kitchen of The School House.

"Oh, but Mum, can't we just shut our bedroom doors then they won't be able to see inside," groaned Elizabeth, with shoulders slumped. "The weather's much too nice to be stuck in inside, and anyway, Greg and Lily will be calling for us in half an hour."

Stella folded her arms. "Then either they will have to wait for you or you will have to work very quickly. Closing doors is not an option. Remember, Auntie Rose used to live here, so naturally she'll want to wander around the place. She always does. Now come on, chop, chop."

Elizabeth and Anne stamped up the stairs muttering to each other about unreasonable parents.

"I don't know where they get their untidiness from," tut-tutted Stella, piling breakfast dishes onto the draining board. "It's certainly not from you or me. Although I suppose it's probably my father. Mum was always tidying up after him as he never put anything away."

She turned to Ned whose head was firmly buried inside the morning paper. "You must pop down to the churchyard, Ned, and trim Reg's grave. Rose is bound to take him some flowers while she's here and I noticed at Mabel's funeral it was looking a bit overgrown. Oh dear! The lawn needs cutting too and the windows could do with a clean. Ned, are you listening to me?"

"Yes, dear," said Ned, dropping the paper onto the floor, "and I think you're making too much fuss. Rose and George are coming to see *us* and Cornwall, they're not coming down to judge us in The Tidiest House Competition. But I will trim Reg's grave as I've been meaning to do that for some time."

"I suppose you're right, it's just that Rose always kept this place spotless and that's the way I'd like her to see it today. Would you like another cup of tea before I wash up?"

"Yes please. But remember that Rose didn't have two untidy children when she was here and so had no excuse for not having an immaculate house."

"You're right. Nor did she have a husband when I first met her, but she did have a dog."

Ned smiled. "Freak, what a strange looking creature he was. It'll be the first time she's been to Cornwall since he died."

Stella filled the kettle, switched it on and then sat at the table to wait for it to boil.

"Poor Rose, what a shame she was never able to have children, she would have made a lovely mother and it would have stabilised their marriage too. Childless couples are more prone to drift apart if there are no commitments to tie them together."

"Do you think we might have drifted apart then had we not had the girls?" Ned impishly asked.

"Goodness no," laughed Stella, rising to make the tea. "I think you and I were made for each other. Don't you?"

Ned grinned, rose and gave her a hug. "You know I do, even when you nag. Now, pour that tea, and then I'll pop down to the churchyard before I cut the grass."

George and Rose arrived in Trengillion just before four o'clock having made an early start straight after breakfast. Ned and Stella greeted them warmly for it was two years since they had last shared each other's company. The previous summer, George and Rose had taken their fortnight's holiday at the home of Rose's parents in Blackpool.

"Did you have a good journey?" asked Ned, greeting them in the hallway.

"Not bad," replied George. "It's a pity the Cornish roads are so primitive though as it takes ages to drive through this county. Gosh, you're getting quite grey around the ears now you old bugger. I think it's time you took a tip from an old friend and tried the Grecian 2000."

"So, you do treat your hair," said Ned, giving George a friendly push. "Last time I saw you, you emphatically denied it."

"Well, a chap has his pride, squeaked George, in a feminine voice, "and one has to compete with the beautiful people now we're in the Swinging Sixties."

"Hey man, love and peace," laughed Ned, flinging his arms around George and slapping his back. "Love and peace."

"Cool, Neddy baby," cried George, returning the slaps. "It's real groovy to be back in your pad, man. Let's chill out while the babes make us tea."

"What is it with those two?" Rose whispered to Stella, as they walked down the hallway. "As soon as they get in each other's company they revert to childhood."

Stella slowly shook her head. "I don't know but they've always been like it, haven't they? Sometimes it is a bit of a worry though."

Ned and George seated themselves in the living room while the women went into the kitchen. "So what was Blackpool like?" asked Ned, reverting to normality. "I know you have a tendency to believe the weather up north is always grim."

George laughed. "I know, and it proved me wrong; we didn't have one spot of rain all the time we were there. We've been before of course and I quite like it. There's plenty to do, so we're able to go out every day. The first year we went I was dreading it might rain all the time and that we'd be stuck indoors with Rose's parents, but it's such a busy place that things don't come to a standstill even if the weather is wet. And don't laugh, but last time we actually went to a discotheque."

Ned raised his eyebrows. "What on earth would an old timer like you be doing at a discotheque?"

"Hey, less of the old, Ned. It was fantastic, grooving the night away, in fact we went more than once. Rose is a good dancer and she had a brilliant time. Needless to say we were the oldest couple there, but damn it, why should the kids have all the fun? I wish we had had the music of today when we were young. I was born twenty years too soon."

"Jamie Stevens has approached the Village Hall Committee about holding a discotheque here for the kids starting in September. Some of the committee members were against it saying it might bring in trouble makers from elsewhere, but most, including Mum, were all in favour, so it looks as though even Trengillion will be up with the times."

George frowned. "You'll have to remind me who Jamie Stevens is because I've forgotten."

"You know, his parents are Fred the village bobby and his wife, Annie. He's twenty now and works in the Midland Bank, but he also plays the guitar and is really into pop music. In fact, he and some of his mates from the bank have started their own group and they're going to perform this year at the village drama group's annual show. They call themselves, Thistles and Thorns, would you believe?"

"Oh well, I suppose it's no worse a name than some of the top groups. I mean, surely, never before, can there have been an era for crazy names and song titles as there are today. How's my admirer, Gertie, keeping, by the way? Her twin boys must be teenagers now."

Ned nodded. "They're fourteen and young Susan's twelve. I don't know where all the years have gone."

George agreed. "Me neither. That reminds me, have I told you that old Gabby will be retiring this Christmas?"

"What! Mr Gathercole, the headmaster?" asked Stella, pushing a hostess trolley as she and Rose entered the room. "Surely he can't be nearly sixty five."

"Yes, he'll be sixty five on December eighth. We'll be starting a collection for him next term, so if either of you wishes to contribute, then now's your chance."

Stella parked the trolley in front of the fireplace. "Of course, we'll make a contribution. He was very good to us when we told him we were leaving to come to Cornwall, wasn't he, Ned? I know some people thought him a miserable stick-in-the-mud, but I liked him."

The front door swiftly opened and closed. "Coo-ee," called a voice from the hallway. "It's only me."

"We're in the front room, Mum," shouted Ned.

As Molly entered the room, George and Rose both stood and gave her a hug.

"I saw your car, so knew you'd arrived safely. How lovely to see you both again, you've not changed one bit."

"Would you like a cup of tea, Mum" asked Ned.

"No thanks, love. I'm not stopping, I only popped in to say hello, and I'm sure you've lots to talk about, anyway. I'm on my way to the post office, you see, so I must dash as they close in five minutes." She turned to Rose. "Do pop round and see me soon as I want to show you Freak's grave. I've planted a lovely red rose on it and it's blooming beautifully at the moment. Must go, see you soon."

George laughed and nodded in the direction of the door. "How old is she now?"

Ned sighed. "Sixty three. You'd never believe it, would you? I swear she has more energy than me. The girls think she's brilliant because she always knows what's number one in the charts and listens to pirate radio stations, but only when the major's out of course."

"What is number one at the moment?" asked George, taking a packet of cigarettes from his pocket. "Is it still *All you need is love*?"

Ned wrinkled his nose. "I think so, but I wouldn't stake my life on it."

Stella grinned as she handed out mugs of tea. "Just as well. It's Scott Mackenzie's *San Francisco*. I watched *Top of the Pops* with the girls last week when you were out."

"I liked Molly's dress," said Rose, dropping an artificial sweetener into her tea. "It's very trendy. Did she make it herself?"

Stella nodded. "Yes. It's a copy of one of Maggie Nan's designs. She didn't use a pattern of course, but just made it with the aid of a picture she saw in a magazine. And the fabric is slightly different from the real thing too. The dots are smaller because that was the nearest she could get in Helston."

"It's brilliant," said Rose. "I wish I had her gift for sewing, it'd save me a fortune. I've been tempted once or twice by these cut-out-and-ready-to sew outfits offered in women's magazines but I've never actually sent for one."

Stella nodded. "Same here, but I usually dismiss them because they're quite plain."

"I agree, but then I'm not too keen on Maggie Nan's designs as they're too flamboyant for my taste. Having said that, I liked what Molly was wearing today."

George turned to Ned. "Hey man, do you like your chicks to wear Maggie Nan or do you prefer Zandra Rhodes?"

Ned wrinkled his nose. "Neither, I'm a Vivienne Westwood type o'guy. Zandra's stuff is okay, I suppose, but Maggie Nan's gear, well, I just don't dig it."

Stella cast a withering look in the direction of both men.

Rose giggled. "Okay we get the message. No more fashion talk, although it has to be said that I think it's unlikely Maggie Nan will be doing much designing for a while, anyway, cos her popularity has dwindled badly since her face lift, hasn't it?"

"Face lift?" said Stella, her face contorted by a confused frown. "I didn't know she'd had one."

"What! You can't read the right newspapers and magazines then; it's been hot gossip in London for the last month. Rumour has it that she went to the States at the beginning of July for the operation, although it was claimed by her agent she was away on business, but when she came back she was wearing huge sunglasses and a large hat and refused to speak to the media. Anyway, someone snooping from the branches of a tree overhanging her back garden saw her and said she looked dreadful. And then last week she was seen at Heathrow catching a flight back to the States where the press claim she's gone to get her face sorted out, even though her agent said she's there on business again. But the media are adamant she's in for more surgery and they're trying to track her down."

Stella tut-tutted. "Silly woman. Whatever made her think she needed a face lift? I always thought she was rather attractive for a woman of her age. How old is she? Forty five, forty six?"

"Forty eight," said Rose. "She's the same age as me, that's how I know, and the media claim she wants to look younger to compete with all the young glamorous models her husband photographs. It must be tough at the top. I'm glad I'm just me."

"Why are women so vain?" asked Ned, rising to reach the ashtray on the sideboard. "Why can't they just accept their faces and bodies as they are? I get fed up hearing about diets and hairstyles, but then I do live in a house with three females."

"It's human nature to want to be attractive," said Rose. "Which reminds me, is Betty still hairdressing?"

Stella nodded. "Yes, and she's doing very well. I think nearly everyone in Trengillion goes to her. All the women anyway, and even a few of the men. She's had the old wash room on the back of the cottage converted into a salon and it's really nice."

"Good, I must go and see her whilst I'm here. She's half the price of the hairdresser I use in London and she does just as good a job."

"Are she and Peter still in the same house?" asked George. "If I remember correctly their placc was part of the Penwynton Estate, wasn't it?"

"That's right. They got it to rent through Betty's dad who worked on the estate. They're laughing now though, cos like nearly everyone else who lived in Penwynton properties, when the old man died, they were offered the chance to buy it, and so they did. They're the only ones in our set with a mortgage. I think they've done really well, especially as the house is actually in the village. Most of the Penwynton houses are on estate land, or were. It's all been split up now of course."

Rose pointed to the corner of the room. "You've some different furniture. I've not seen that writing desk before. Is it as old as it looks?"

Stella rose from her chair and pulled down the front of the desk. "Oh yes, and it's not just any old rubbish, it came from Penwynton House. We paid a fair bit for it but we consider it an investment, don't we, Ned?"

"Hmm, and there are a few other bits we bought upstairs in our bedroom. Needless to say the girls think our treasures are dreadful. They prefer the modern stuff, but I'm afraid we're a bit old fashioned and consider contemporary stuff to be rubbish."

"So how come you have things from Penwynton House?" George asked. "Did they have a sale?"

"Yes, didn't we tell you?" asked Stella, returning to her chair. "They had an auction back in the spring. Nearly everyone from the village went and it was a smashing day out. The weather was glorious which was perfect as the sale was held outside in the driveway. I think nearly everybody in Trengillion has something as a memento from the big house now. The paintings weren't sold though; they're all on loan to one of the big art galleries, but they'd have been far too big for the average house, anyway."

"Are you still happy with your new job, Rose?" asked Ned, remembering they had not seen her since she had started working as a police telephonist. "It must be right up your street, a bit of mystery and crime."

"I love it, in fact if I were a lot younger I'd think about joining the Police Force. I've become fascinated with gossip ever since I've lived in London, although, of course, I have to be discreet in my job. Having said that, discretion isn't necessary most of the time as a lot of calls are about really trivial things, like my cat's gone missing or my neighbour is playing loud music. We do get serious calls as well, of course, and only last month we had a bank robbery on our patch which made the BBC Evening News."

"Is it anything like *Z Cars*?" asked Stella, with a laugh. "I mean to say, are any of your policemen like Jock or Fancy?"

"I'm sorry to say no," giggled Rose. "I wish they were."

"BD to Z Victor one," laughed Ned. He and George then pretended to be driving as they hummed the theme music to the popular television drama, *Z Cars*.

CHAPTER FOUR

Willoughby and Tabitha Castor-Hunt happily opened the doors of Chy-an-Gwyns to welcome in the children of Trengillion who had befriended Greg and Lily during the years they had taken their vacations in Cornwall. It was the last time the children would play together for two years. The Castor-Hunts were due to leave in the early hours of the following day to return to their Surrey home prior to flying out to Florida on September the first, and they wanted to make the children's last gathering a memorable occasion.

As the weather was fine, tea was served outside on the front lawns and sandwiches were followed by every type of cake, pastry and cream bun imaginable. Strawberry trifle, chocolate mousse and lemon ice cream made by Tabitha, finished off the tea party which delighted the young guests, who savoured the delicate, tongue tickling flavours which tantalised their taste buds. The choice of drinks, served straight from the fridge, included, lemonade, dandelion and burdock, ginger beer and Tizer.

The contented children ate until they were full, and then to burn up the calories played games of hide and seek, sardines and postman's knock. When they felt weary they sat down to rest and played a quiet game of I-spy in the shade of a very old apple tree which seldom bore fruit as the blossom was always lost in late spring during the strong south-westerly winds which seemed to blow every year without fail. During the many passing years since Willoughby Castor-Hunt had first purchased the house in a state of poor repair, he had vowed to fell the tree due to its lack of fruit, but he never had the heart to carry out his threats, feeling perhaps the tree had as much right as he to occupy its little bit of Cornwall.

Before the best of the daylight had faded and it was time to say their last goodbyes, Elizabeth Stanley, who had celebrated her thirteenth birthday the previous month, fetched from the kitchen her Kodak Instamatic camera, a present from her grandmother and the major. She then asked everyone to prepare themselves prior to grouping together in order that she might take some pictures as a keepsake.

The children rose from the grass and brushed down their clothes.

"You must comb your hair, Tony, it's been ruffled ever since you got stuck beneath the hedge."

"Does it matter, bossy boots?" grinned Tony, pushing his fingers through the loose, thick curls he'd inherited from his father.

"Of course," retorted Elizabeth, primly, "everyone must look their best." She then sent the other children inside to tidy up their appearances and wash their hands.

Tabitha smiled to herself. Elizabeth reminded her of how she had been as a girl. Headstrong, firm and downright bossy. But Elizabeth was able to get away with her domineering manner; the other children always obeyed her commands, even the boys, although that no doubt was due to Elizabeth's attractive features and especially her large, dark eyes.

When everyone's appearance met with Elizabeth's approval, they all left the garden and filed out onto the cliff top where they sat on a patch of grass. Behind, the sparkling blue sea and cloudless sky, made the perfect backdrop.

"Shall I take the pictures for you, Elizabeth?" Tabitha asked. "It would be a shame if you were not in them too."

With a toss of her long brown curls, she handed the camera to Tabitha. "Yes, please, that would be lovely. Thank you very much. I'd like you to take six if you would be so kind, then there'll one for each family."

Rose and Stella called at Fuchsia Cottage to see Betty and arrange for Rose to have her hair done. They were let in by her husband, Peter, just back from sea, and found her sweeping up curls after May Dickens's trim when they entered her salon at the back of the cottage.

"You look a little flustered," smiled Stella, as she closed the door. "Have you been busy?"

Betty wiped her brow on the back of her hand. "Just a little. It gets a bit hot in here when the driers are all going. Jane usually gives me a hand when I've a few booked in, that's if she's not at school of course, but today she's up at Chy-an-Gwyns with the others so I've been on my own."

Stella pulled aside a chair from the path of Betty's broom. "Yes, of course. It's a shame the Castor-Hunts are going, they all get on so well together, they'll be sorely missed and we'll miss Willoughby and Tabitha too. Still, I believe they intend to live down here permanently on their return home from America as they're selling their house in Surrey, and two years is not that long, is it? After all it seems like only yesterday our children were in nappies."

Betty reached for the brush and dustpan. "Don't remind me. We're all thirty five and over now and forty is hammering on our doors."

Rose winced. "Oh, to be forty again. I shall be fifty in two years' time. Half a century, now that is a worry."

"Well, you certainly don't look it," said Betty with earnest.

Stella agreed with a nod.

"Thank you. I'm pleased to say I don't feel it either."

Betty stood still to catch her breath. "I suppose those days back when you worked at the Inn seem forever ago now."

"Yes, they do, and I hear that Frank and Dot plan to retire soon. Their leaving will be a great loss to the village, although I can understand why, and I think both of them, and especially Frank, have done well to keep smiling for as long as they have. It's damn hard work running that place, especially taking in guests as well."

Betty tipped May's grey hair clippings into the bin. "Do you miss Trengillion? It must be so different to life down here living and working in London."

"It is different, inasmuch as it's exciting and alive, but yes, I do miss Trengillion, in fact I miss Cornwall in general. It's lovely to see the sea again and breathe in the clean fresh air, and you've no idea how much it broke my heart seeing the state of the beaches on the telly earlier this year. All that oil! Dreadful!"

"Can't believe that was even this year," said Betty, stifling a yawn. "It seems so much longer ago than March. Anyway, it looks a lot better now, in fact the untrained eye probably wouldn't even spot any oil, whereas us locals can spot a blob a mile away."

Rose laughed. "We went to Blackpool last summer to visit my parents and although we had a good time it wasn't the same as being here, oil or no oil. It gets very busy there, you see, but then I hear there are a lot more caravan parks springing up in Cornwall now."

Betty looked heavenward. "Don't bring that subject up when in the company of some of the old timers. They don't approve at all which I think is sad. As you say this is a beautiful county and we should be happy to share it with others. Everyone deserves a holiday and the season is not really that long, is it? And I always enjoyed meeting people when I worked at the Inn."

"So, do you miss the conviviality of the Inn?" asked Rose. "I did for a long time after I left."

"Sometimes," said Betty, "but then I meet plenty of people hairdressing too, that's one of the perks, although, of course, they're not usually holiday makers. I'm certainly in touch with what's going on in the village though, especially if Madge has been in. She does go on a bit about how much weight she's lost, but it's made her look a lot younger, so I can hardly blame her for crowing. She talks a lot about food too, and that always makes me feel hungry, but then I suppose talking is a substitute for eating, and she is a good cook. I've heard lots of people say so and she often helps Dot out at the Inn. Her apple pies melt in the mouth, apparently. It's funny really, Madge has lost weight and Albert's put it on. Would you both like a coffee and one of Jane's rock buns? I've half an hour off now 'til my next appointment?"

"Well, yes that would be lovely," said Stella, and they followed Betty through to her kitchen.

"Who does the waitressing at the Inn now?" asked Rose, as Betty filled the kettle and they sat down at the table. "When I was last here it was, oh, I can't remember her name. You know, Harry and Joyce Richardson's daughter."

"Jill," said Betty. "She's gone now. She got married last summer and has moved to Plymouth. Alice Penhaligon is the main waitress now. She left school last year and told her mum she wanted to work in the village, so her mum had a word with Frank. Frank of course was only too glad to take her on as he's had a soft spot for the Penhaligons ever since the tragedy."

"Sally Stevens helps out too," added Stella. "She needs the money as she's still at school doing her A-levels."

Rose groaned. "Oh God, I remember her when she was born and it seems like yesterday. So what does she want to do when she finishes school?"

Betty placed a plate of rock buns on the table. "Join the Police Force like her dad apparently. Her mum was telling me when I cut her hair last week that she's really serious about it. I don't think I'd like to do that myself or have my children do it either. I'd imagine it could be quite dangerous, especially if you end up up-country somewhere."

"Oh, I don't know," said Rose. "Not everyone up-country is a criminal, I can vouch for that. It's just that the newspapers only report the grim side of life. You know, dog bites man is of no interest, but man bites dog, sells papers. Who was it said that? I can't remember."

"John B Bogart," said Stella, "Editor of the New York Sun. He said, when a dog bites a man, that is not news because it happens so often. But if a man bites a dog, that is news."

"Still the same old school ma'am," laughed Rose. "I don't know how you remember all those quotes."

Frank Newton pulled out a chair from beneath the table in the kitchen of the Ringing Bells Inn and sat down. "They're coming out to see us tomorrow afternoon."

"What time?" asked Dorothy, taking a bottle of milk from the fridge and pouring some into two mugs of tea.

"Between half past two and three. I said it's no use coming before as we'll be tied up with the lunch time opening, although of course you could show 'em round the rest of the Inn. It'll be a James Godson coming apparently, according to the young lady I spoke to on the phone, and she said they should have no difficulty in finding us a buyer as there's quite a big demand for pubs and inns, especially freehold. Oh dear, it looks as though we could well be gone by Christmas, Dot."

Dorothy refrained from making comments about relaxing and taking things easy, for she could see by the look on Frank's face that was not what he needed to hear. She returned the milk bottle to the fridge.

"Everyone will miss you, Frank, when you've gone, even the non-drinkers. You'll always be called Landlord, even when you're pruning your roses and someone else is behind that bar."

"They won't just miss me, Dot, they'll miss us both, and the way we've run things. We've been head of a good team over the years but it just worries me that whoever's here next might make some silly changes."

"Well, I hope they won't make too many and destroy the charm and character of this old place, 'cos I think if they do they'll have a rebellion on their hands and a lot of un-sold beer in the cellar."

Frank smiled. "I dunno whether I'd be able to face coming in here with someone else in my place, so if I fancy a pint in the future I'll probably have to drive over to Polquillick."

"You can't drink and drive, Frank, those days have gone. You'll have to get yourself a bike."

"But, I've never ridden a bike in my life and I'd most likely fall off on the first corner I had to tackle."

"You've never ridden a bike!" exclaimed Dorothy, surprised, as she sat down at the table. "Well, that'll have to be one of the first things you learn. You can't live in the country you know and not ride a bike."

Frank chuckled. "Why not? I've done so for over thirty years and it's done me no harm."

"Because there are too many cars on the roads these days," said Dorothy, emphatically. "Country lanes should be quiet and peaceful like they were when I was a girl. You need to be able to hear the birds sing and admire the flowers and scents in the hedgerows, and the lanes between here and Polquillick are very beautiful, especially in May. Oh dear, I can see I shall have my work cut out, but one way or another Frank Newton I'll make you a country boy yet."

CHAPTER FIVE

Rain, gentle but persistent, fell from the heavens in the early hours of Saturday morning as Willoughby Castor-Hunt loaded up the car with suitcases containing clothes and the most treasured possessions of his family. The previous day, whilst the children had enjoyed the company of their friends in the gardens under the supervision of his wife, he, with the help of Ned Stanley, had moved many of the family's belongings into the loft for storage ready for the house to be occupied by Mrs Rossiter and eventually holiday makers.

Tabitha woke Gregory and Lillian just as the sky began to show the first hint of daylight. With yawns and groans they rose from their beds and ambled downstairs for breakfast, but neither could eat, the hour was too early and their spirits too low. Lily sat sombre faced and watched the milk in her dish disappear, greedily swallowed by two Weetabix. She hated the prospect of two years in Florida and every night had prayed that her mother's health might take a miraculous turn for the better thus enabling them to stay in England and continue the life she knew and loved.

When her parents announced it was time to leave, Lily ran round the house and said goodbye to every room and then clutching her favourite doll, reluctantly left the house and ran through the garden, beneath fuchsias dripping with raindrops and into the waiting car.

As they pulled away from the back garden and drove across the field towards the lane on the hill leading into the village, Lily looked back at Chy-an-Gwyns. Beyond its outline the sea, grey, like the sky, gently rippled beneath the bleak horizon. With a heavy heart she fought back the tears. When next she would see that view she would be a big girl of twelve. Her heart thumped loudly. Two years hence was a lifetime away.

The car, with father at the wheel and windscreen wipers thudding through bouncing raindrops, reached the lane and veered right towards the cove. At the foot of the hill they passed the beach where waves tumbled onto the deserted sand. Beyond the two beachside cottages they turned up the incline into the village, past the Inn and past Fuchsia Cottage, the home of Jane and Matthew. Past Coronation Terrace where Diane and Graham lived, and then further along, past the home of the Collins family, Susan, Tony and John. Next they passed the post office, home of Stephen and David Pascoe, and finally they passed The School House, home of Elizabeth, and Lily's best friend, Anne. She blew a kiss to all her friends, and watched through the back window as the village became a speck in the distance, blurred by the raindrops trickling down the tinted glass pane. Lily pulled a handkerchief from the sleeve of her cardigan, wiped away her tears and stifled a sob, and when they turned a corner and a glimpse of the village was no more, she curled up on the seat and reflected on the good times Trengillion had bestowed upon her and the cruel unfairness of life.

By mid-morning the rain clouds had dispersed, the sun was shining brightly and outside the Inn, visitors were packing up their belongings ready to return to their respective homes. Meanwhile, in the Inn's kitchen, Dorothy Newton made coffee and tea for the band of helpers who came in every Saturday to help her clean the rooms ready for the new arrivals, and on this particular week every room needed doing as all guests were leaving on the same day.

"Oh dear, I don't know where the bloomin' time goes," said Frank joining the ladies in the kitchen. "No sooner have guests arrived and I've got to know their names than they're off and I have to start all over again."

Dorothy grinned as she screwed the lid back on the coffee jar. "The next lot shouldn't be too difficult to remember, Frank. We've a family called Brown, a single man called Short, a single woman called Pringle, another single man called Tucker, and two sisters called Gibson."

Frank scowled. "How do you reckon that'll be easy to remember? It sounds most confusing to me. And are the single folks single, as in not married, or just on their own?"

"They're all simple names, that's what I meant. There's nothing unpronounceable. I always worry about strange names, as I'd hate to cause offence. And when I say single, I mean they're on their own, although the single lady is unmarried because she's a Miss Pringle. I don't know about the marital status of the single men though, but I'm sure we'll find out in time."

Frank groaned. He did not like change-over days.

The Inn's new guests arrived at various stages throughout the afternoon. Dorothy greeted them each in turn and memorised their faces as she ticked off their names in the register.

"From what I've seen of today's guests we should be in for a trouble free time," said Dorothy to Frank, having just shown the latest arrivals, the Browns, to the family room. "So far they're all very pleasant and polite."

Frank nodded his approval. "Well, let's hope it stays that way. I can't be doing with folks as are impossible to please. How many are there in the Brown family?"

Dorothy picked up her knitting from the sideboard in the living room where she and Frank rested in the afternoons. "Four, and you'll have no problem remembering them as they all have brown hair and they're the only ones with children this week."

No sooner had Dorothy finished off a row on the cardigan she was knitting for herself than the sound of the doorbell rang through the building.

"I'll go," said Frank, rising from the chair. "You sit down and rest for a while, you've been on your feet all day."

Frank was rather taken back by the apparition he found standing on the doorstep and for a fleeting moment, because of the length of hair, was not sure whether to greet the new arrival as sir or madam. His dilemma, however, was quickly remedied, when the person in question offered a friendly hand.

"Hi man. I've a room booked here. My name's Freddie, Freddie Short."

The two men shook hands.

"Err, yes, come in please, Mr Short and I'll show you your room. I'm err, the landlord of this Inn. Frank's my name. Frank Newton. Err, did you have a pleasant journey?"

"Groovy, man, the scenery around here's pretty cool. Hey, but don't call me Mr Short, Frankie, call me Freddie. Everyone calls me Freddie, even my kids."

"You have children then," gasped Frank, with surprise.

"Yeah, but they're not with me, they're home with Trish."

"Oh, I see," said Frank, nonplussed, as Freddie Short crossed the threshold, carrying two large carpet bags containing his luggage.

"Say, this place is real quaint, Frankie," said Freddie, glancing around the dimly lit hallway. "How old do you reckon it is? I'd say it was early eighteenth century. Am I right?"

"Spot on," said Frank. "As far as I know it were built in the 1740s around the same time as Penwynton House cos it was part of the Penwynton estate at one time, you see. But they sold it off after the First World War."

"But you've not been here since then, surely," drooled Freddie.

Frank laughed. "No, I'm not quite that old. I came here in the thirties. I bought the place for a song, as it were very run down. Lots of dry rot and woodworm. It took several months, well, nearly a year actually, to get the place habitable and a fair bit of cash too, but over the years the old place has paid for itself over and over again."

"Has it always been an inn then, do you know?"

"Yes, and it's always been the Ringing Bells Inn and I wouldn't change its name for all the tea in China."

The two men climbed the stairs. At the top they passed a freshly painted half glazed door.

"That's the bathroom in there," said Frank. "There's always plenty of hot water so you can take a bath whenever you want, or a shower if you like. We had one fitted back in the spring and lots of folks prefer it cos it's quicker than filling the old tub."

"Fab," said Freddie, as they walked the entire length of the landing to the room on the end.

"We've put you in here," said Frank, opening the door. "I hope you like it. Dinner is at seven o'clock."

Freddie stepped into the room and enthusiastically threw his luggage onto the bed. "It's groovy," he said, clutching the iron rail at the foot of the bed. "I dig the sloping walls and the uneven floor, and wow, who's this old guy hanging on the wall?"

"That's Claude Gilbert, an old smuggler-cum-fisherman," replied Frank, fondly patting the old picture frame. "I never knew him, of course, a bit before my time, but I knew his nephew, he lived with us for a time, in fact he died here in this very room."

"Wow," Freddie exclaimed, waving his arms and looking towards the ceiling. "Does his ghost walk here?"

Frank laughed, "Not as far as I know, but the old place has witnessed a few ghosts in its day. I hope you enjoy your stay."

"I will man," said Freddie, with exuberance. "I will. I'm sure I shall love every minute."

"Was that another of the guests?" asked Dorothy, as Frank returned to the living room and took his chair by the hearth.

Frank chuckled. "It were, and I certainly won't have any difficulty remembering that one's name."

Later, that evening, Alice Penhaligon carried a tray of prawn cocktails from the kitchen into the dining room ready for her first encounter with the new guests. The first table she approached was in the bay window where two ladies sat opposite each other deep in conversation. At first glance, she thought they were mother and daughter but when she looked closer she realised they were of a similar age and were in fact sisters, namely Sharon and Lynne Gibson, who proudly told Alice they were down for a fortnight to take a holiday and combine it with a family wedding due to take place the following Saturday at the Lizard.

Alice smiled sweetly. "How nice. I hope you enjoy your stay with us."

On the next table sat the Brown family, and in the corner a woman alone who Alice assumed was the charming spinster Dorothy had spoken of. Pauline Pringle was her name and she was taking her first holiday for many years, having recently lost her elderly mother whom she had nursed and cared for since she was a young woman of twenty one.

Beside the fireplace sat a man alone. Alice knew he would be either Edward Tucker or Frederick Short. When he smiled but said nothing she realised he was Edward Tucker, for Dorothy had told her that Mr Tucker was a man of very few words.

Alice glanced around the room holding the tray, empty, except for one prawn cocktail, as she pondered where the last guest might be. Her curiosity was short-lived, however, for someone was singing as they descended the stairs. She watched as the dining room door opened to the gentle tinkling of a bell. Through it Freddie Short sauntered bringing with him a waft of *Spook* aftershave. In the middle of room he stopped and bowed to the dumbstruck waitress.

"Hi, babe," he grinned, straightening the rows of beads hanging around his neck and entwined with a black leather boot lace from which dangled a cow bell. "Where do you want me to sit?"

Alice pointed to the only empty table. Freddie sat down and winked as she placed the prawn cocktail in front of him, unable to think of anything to say. For Freddie Short looked like no-one she had ever encountered before. Certainly she had seen people dressed in a similar fashion on *Top of the Pops* and other television programmes and she had read an article about tie dying in a magazine, but to see such a vision in Trengillion was a new experience and something that would inevitably fuel up the tongues of many a gossip.

Alice headed towards the kitchen, eager to tell Dorothy about the new arrival and as she passed the Gibson sisters' table she heard Sharon ask Lynne. "Do you think he's one of those hippie people?"

"Looks like it," whispered Lynne, glancing at Freddie's bright orange bell-bottomed trousers. "And I've read that such people are rather promiscuous when it comes to, well, you know what."

Sharon frowned. "What on earth are you talking about?"

"Hanky-panky," whispered Lynne. "You must know what I mean. They believe in free love and such like so we must make sure the door to our room is well and truly locked every night."

Freddie, not knowing the nature of the sisters' conversation, winked and waved to them as they glanced sideways in his direction.

"See what I mean," said Lynne, with thick eyebrows raised. "We must stick close together at all times. I sense trouble with that one."

CHAPTER SIX

"How would you like to spend your birthday?" grinned Stella, as she handed Ned his present.

"Thank you, I really don't mind. What do you suggest?"

"Well, I was thinking it might be nice to go that new Chinese restaurant in town. Meg and Sid went there recently for their wedding anniversary and they said it was really very good."

"Okay, yes, that sounds fine to me. You'll join us of course, won't you?" asked Ned, turning to George and Rose, both preoccupied with film loading instructions for Rose's new camera."

"Absolutely, we often have Chinese when at home," said George, taking the film from its packaging. "I think it takes a lot of whacking, although I'm very partial to a nice hot curry too."

Ned removed the wrapping paper from Stella's gift. "Well, we can't have curry as there isn't an Indian restaurant in town yet and I expect it will be a year of two before there is. Although Cornwall's doing its best to catch up with you lot in London, and I reckon at present, we're only a couple of years behind."

"Perhaps we could make an evening of it and go for a drink at the Inn beforehand," suggested Rose, pulling the camera from its case. "We've not been in yet and I should like to see everyone again, especially Frank and Dorothy."

"Of course, but I think it might be better if we ate earlier and then went for a drink afterwards," said George. "It's a bit risky to drink and drive now they've brought in this damn breathalyser thing."

Ned nodded. "You're quite right, for although there's very little risk of being breathalysed in Trengillion it might be a bit different in town and you know what coppers are like when they get a new toy."

"Brilliant," said Stella, rising to her feet. "I'll just give your mum a ring, Ned, and make sure she's alright to keep an eye on the girls tonight and then I'll ring the restaurant and book a table."

Meg Reynolds, glad to be outside after a morning cleaning out the kitchen cupboards, strolled down to the beach and sat on Denzil's bench. There she watched the tumbling waves splashing gently onto the shore, glistening beneath the sun's golden rays.

Deep in thought she didn't hear the sound of approaching footsteps and was unaware of anyone's presence until she heard a gentle cough.

"Excuse me, may I join you, please?"

Meg sat up straight. Standing beside the bench was a tall man with a head of thick, dark hair, a holiday maker, she assumed.

"Yes, of course." She moved along to the end of the bench and the man sat down.

"Thank you. I wouldn't have troubled you but I've been out walking and it's such a beautiful day that I don't really want to go indoors yet."

Meg smiled. "Have you walked far?"

"Over to Polquillick. I walked there by road and came back by the coastal path."

"Good heavens, that's a fair distance, you must be dead beat."

"A little but I'm a keen walker, in fact it's just about all I have done since I've been here."

"I take it you're on holiday."

The man nodded. "Yes, I arrived here on Saturday and I'm staying at the Inn. The name's Tucker, by the way. Edward Tucker."

"And I'm Meg, Meg Reynolds."

"I take it you're a local, Meg."

She nodded. "Yes, born and bred."

"Good, then perhaps you can answer a few questions for me, like who owns that fantastic house up there on the cliffs." He pointed to Chy-an-Gwyns.

Meg smiled. "That's a question frequently asked. It belongs to a Mr and Mrs Castor-Hunt. They're not there at present as they're spending a couple of years in Florida."

Edward Tucker's drew his breath and whistled. "Florida! It's alright for some."

"They've gone because of Mrs Castor-Hunt's health. Doctor's orders and all that."

"I see, but surely the house isn't going to be unoccupied for two whole years."

Meg shook her head. "No, it's being let out. In fact a couple of ladies are due anytime soon and they'll be there until Christmas."

"I see, and what about Penwynton House. I've not seen it of course, in fact I don't even know where it is, but I heard people talking about it in the bar the last night. They were discussing its size, condition and the possibilities of likely purchasers and I was intrigued."

Meg nodded. "Yes, we're all keen to know what will happen to it. It's on the outskirts of the village and tucked away down a long driveway. It's huge and needs a vast amount of restoration."

"So I gathered. I noticed dozens of Penwyntons are buried in your churchyard and one of them quite recently. Is it being sold to pay off death duties?"

Meg shook her head. "No, but sadly Charles of whom you speak, was the last of the Penwyntons and the estate, including, house, farms, cottages and land has been left to a distant relative in Canada. He doesn't want to live here though and so the whole lot is being sold off. The farms, farmland and cottages have already been bought by their sitting tenants and the house is now up for sale on the open market."

"I take it the house is empty then?"

"Hmm, the furniture was all auctioned off earlier this year and the huge family portraits are on loan to an art gallery."

"Very interesting." He leaned back on the bench and looked up towards Chy-an-Gwyns. "I wouldn't mind staying up there, the views must be quite spectacular, both out to sea and inland." He turned to Meg. "Do you live in the village or out in the sticks?"

"In the village quite near to the school. I teach at the school, you see, so it's very convenient."

He pointed to her wedding ring. "And your husband, what does he do?"

Meg grinned. "Sid's a newspaperman. Only at a local level but he loves it."

Edward Tucker's eyebrows rose. "Hmm, interesting but I shouldn't think you get many headline grabbing stories around here."

Meg laughed. "You'd be surprised. The village has witnessed a few dramatic events even in my lifetime and only this year we had the Torrey Canyon disaster."

It was almost dark when Ned, Stella, Rose and George left the Chinese restaurant and walked through the quiet streets to the car park by the library.

"This is the first time we've been with you for your birthday since 1953," said George. "I hope we won't get anything like the events of that evening happening at the Inn tonight."

"God forbid," said Stella, clutching Ned's arm to steady herself on the uneven pavements. "I can still see that awful apparition in the fireplace even now. Which reminds me, do you ever hear from Elsie these days?"

"Ouch! That's a bit harsh," laughed George. "But no, we haven't kept in touch. Rose and I have moved a couple of times since we got married and as I've not the foggiest idea where Elsie's living, it'd be damn near impossible anyway. I've heard she has a couple of kids though so hopefully she's content and all that."

Business was brisk as they walked though the Inn door just before half past nine. Behind the bar, Frank and Dorothy were assisted by Annie Stevens, who worked two nights a week to give her life a little purpose, for her two children had grown up and she felt surplus to requirements, even though both Jamie and Sally still lived at home and provided her with plenty of washing, cleaning and cooking.

Ned went to the bar to get the first round of drinks while the others lingered beside a table in the snug where holiday makers collected together their empty glasses in preparation to leave. When Ned took out his wallet to pay for the drinks, Frank refused the ten shilling note proffered.

"On the house," he insisted. "I'm really glad you've all come in. I've been wanting to see Rose, and George too, of course. I must find time to have a chat with them before you go because next time they come down for a holiday we'll most likely have gone."

Ned nodded. "Of course, we'll be here 'til closing time and I know Rose is keen for a chat with you too."

From beneath the counter, Frank produced a small tray. As Ned placed the glasses on it he cast his eyes over the Inn's patrons.

"You've a good crowd in tonight, it's hard to pick out familiar faces amongst all the strangers."

Frank chuckled. "But you'll notice that one of our guests well and truly stands out amongst the rest." He nodded in the direction of Freddie Short wearing a bright orange, tie-dye tee shirt tucked into purple, crushed velvet, bell bottomed trousers neatly fastened around the hips with an ornate, orange, suede belt. Tied around his head was a twisted narrow scarf. From its top peeked a small posy of orange marigolds and round his neck dangled two strings of beads and the cowbell.

"Look at that chap over there with the long hair. He's staying here and I think I've heard more comments about him these past few days than I've heard about all my other guests over all the years put together. We all reckon he's one of those hippie people, but if he is I hope he's not taking drugs or anything dodgy like that."

Freddie Short stood by the door chatting to Pauline Pringle who was perched on a high bar stool. They looked an odd couple, for Freddie was loud both in dress and manner whereas Pauline was quietly spoken and dressed subtly in a cream coloured twin set and light brown pleated skirt.

"So what made you come to Cornwall for your holiday?" Ned heard Freddie ask Pauline, as he slowly carried the drink's tray towards the snug. "Have you ever been here before?"

Pauline blushed. "No, but several years ago my auntie and uncle spent a couple of weeks in St. Ives and they brought us back a Cornish calendar. I spent hours looking at the beautiful pictures and kept it for many years, long after it was out of date, in fact I still have it. Anyway, I vowed that one day I'd come here and see Cornwall for myself. After Mum died my friends said I ought to go somewhere where I'd meet lots of people. Somewhere like Butlins, but I thought I'd be even more lonely surrounded by families, than I would be here on my own."

"Well, if ever you want someone to chat too, honey, I'm all ears."

"Thank you, Freddie, you're very kind. It's not easy facing the big wide world after years of being tied indoors looking after Mother."

Ned moved quickly on realising he had stopped in the middle of the bar causing a hold-up, solely for the purpose of eavesdropping. On his arrival in the snug, once seated, he relayed what he had heard to Stella, Rose and George, to justify his lengthy absence.

"You are a nosey bugger, Ned," laughed George. "Why on earth should you be interested in the conversation between a weirdo and some old maid?"

"I don't know really," he conceded. "I think it's a flaw of character I've inherited from my mother."

"Except that your mum would be a lot more subtle," said Stella, glancing through the doors of the snug into the public bar where Pauline was in the process of climbing down from the bar stool indicating she was about to leave her companion and retire to bed.

As Pauline left the bar for her room, Freddie cast his eyes around for someone else with whom he could converse. He caught Sharon Gibson's eye and winked lasciviously. Sharon blushed and took a large swig of her lager and lime to conceal her embarrassment, and delight.

"I saw that," said Lynne. "Really, Sharon, you shouldn't encourage that sort of thing. I've told you what he'll be like."

Sharon giggled. "But I think he's rather cute and he's got a lovely bum."

Lynne cast a horrified look at her sister and picked up the cardboard drinks mat to fan her flushed face.

"Oh, for heaven's sake," said Sharon, perplexed by her sister's over the top reaction. "I'm only speaking the truth and if you weren't such a prude I think you'd agree with me."

"I'm not a prude, "snapped Lynne.

"You are," retorted Sharon. "If you're not careful you'll turn out like Mother."

Thereafter the two sisters sat in silence and watched as Freddie, having caught Stella's eye, responded with a smile, went to the bar, refilled his glass and then swaggered into the snug to introduce himself to her.

"Do I know you from somewhere, sweetie?" he pointedly asked Stella, pulling up a chair to the table where she sat with Ned and her friends.

"I very much doubt it," she blurted, amazed at his audacity. "I live here and have done for the past thirteen years, and you, I believe, are on holiday."

"You live here! How fascinating. So what do you do to pass away the time?"

"Look after my family and my home," said Stella, somewhat haughtily. "This is my husband," she said, waving her hand in Ned's direction. "And these are our friends. My husband is headmaster of the village school."

"Really! That's cool. I teach too, at college. Art's my subject."

Stella half-smiled. "Then you're in good company. I used to teach English before I moved down here and George teaches too, but up-country."

"So, where do you teach?" asked George.

"London," said Freddie. "Putney to be precise and I wouldn't be anywhere else. How about you, are you far up the line?"

"We live in West Kensington," replied Rose. "So we're nearly neighbours."

"So, um, you're from London too," said Freddie, with an uneasy laugh. "But you're on the north side of the river so that makes you foreigners in our eyes." He turned to Ned and Stella before she could answer, "So, what's it like living down here? I would image it's alright in the summer but it must be pretty dead and a bit of a drag in the winter."

"It's no different from any other country district in the winter," scoffed Stella. "Except of course we have the sea on our doorstep and that can be just as satisfying on a stormy winter's day as any day in summer."

"Hmm, as long as there are no oil tankers out at sea leaking filthy oil," said Ned.

Freddie flicked a stray strand of hair from his face. "Oh, yeah, I read all about that and saw it on the telly. Was it as grotty as it looked?"

Ned answered. "Probably much worse. Television didn't give a true picture and of course it wasn't able to convey the sickly smell."

Freddie nodded. "And of course the telly showed it all in black and white."

"Well, that was the colour of the oil slick," said Stella. "Or at least black and brown. It was horrible, and I think we'll be finding random patches of oil for many years to come."

Freddie laughed, picked up his glass and took a large swig of beer. "Well, it won't stop me taking a dip in the old briny. I reckon salt water's good for the skin, talking of which, what do you make of the latest news on Maggie Nan? Or does such gossip not interest you?"

Rose leaned forward. "It interests me. What's the latest then, I've not heard anything since I've been down here."

"Good gracious, my dear girl, you must have heard. She's been kidnapped. I heard when I phoned a mate of mine after dinner. Apparently it was on this evening's Six o' Clock News. She's been kidnapped out in the States, but there are suggestions by people in the know, that it might be a hoax and she's playing for time to recover from her horrendous facelift. You must have heard about that, babe?"

Rose nodded. "Of course, and I knew she had gone out to America too. She flew out with her agent, didn't she? I read all about that, but this kidnapping is all news to me. So when did it happen?"

"Not sure, a couple of days ago, I think. It gets a bit complicated with the time differences. I don't know whether to believe it or not. I mean, why would anyone kidnap her?"

"Well, money's the usual reason," said George, confused as to why anyone should think otherwise, "and her husband has plenty of that. I believe he's one of the richest men in the country, what with the dosh he's made from photography and the load he's inherited from the family. Lucky sod!"

Johnny and Milly ambled into the snug and sat on the opposite side of the fireplace.

"Why do I recognise that bird's face?" whispered Freddie, watching Milly's legs as she neatly tucked them beneath the table.

"She's the post mistress here in the village," replied Stella, wincing at hearing Milly called a bird. "And the young man with her is her husband."

"Hmm, pity. There seems to be a shortage of unattached females down here. Still, I suppose it's just as well. Trish wouldn't approve if the place was crawling with dolly-birds."

"Trish?" questioned Ned.

"My girlfriend," said Freddie. "She's back home with the kids. I tried to get her to come down here with me but she wouldn't cos the youngest gets travel sick. Still hey-ho. I'll buy them each a stick of rock and send them a postcard."

"Err, where are you staying?" asked Rose, feeling someone ought to speak to break the awkward silence which had followed Freddie's last statement.

"Here, at the Inn. I've this really cool room at the back and there's a portrait of this fab old guy hanging on the wall. I can't remember his name, but Frankie tells me he died in there so I hoping to see his ghost."

Sharon Gibson, eavesdropping, squeaked on hearing his comment and promptly turned an unflattering shade of cerise. Freddie amused by her embarrassment, winked again and blew her a tantalising kiss.

"George and I know your room well," said Ned, trying to ease Sharon's discomfort. "We've both stayed there on separate occasions in days gone by. The chap on the wall is called Claude Gilbert."

"Hey, that's right," laughed Freddie. "I remember the name now. I leave my door unlocked all the time so his ghost is free to come and go as he pleases, that is of course assuming he has a ghost. What do you think?"

George answered without hesitation. "I think you should lock your door for a start. You never know who could be around."

"No, there's no need down here. Why, I see folks everywhere with flowers and vegetables for sale outside their houses with just a tin can or dish to put the money in. I reckon Cornish folk must be pretty honest."

"Well, yes, you're quite right, and Reg and I only ever locked our door when we left the village and last thing at night. But I can't see the point in leaving a door unlocked so that a ghost can open it, as they're supposed to be able to go through walls and doors, aren't they?"

"Ah, but can they?" asked Freddie. "I mean to say, have you actually seen one do that?"

Seeing that her sister still looked flushed, Lynne Gibson stood and opened the window to let in some cooler air, this promptly had a strange effect on Freddie. He stretched his neck, twitched his nose and glanced towards the open window. Outside four young men sat on a bench in the light that shone from the bar, smoking and laughing.

"Anything wrong?" asked Rose, puzzled by his actions.

"Grass," he muttered, picked up his beer. He then rose, excused himself and disappeared causing the bell around his neck to jingle as he vacated the snug.

CHAPTER SEVEN

On Tuesday morning, a gleaming, yellow, Lotus Elan glided through the village of Trengillion, turning the heads of school boys and men as it drove down the main street before stopping outside the Inn. From it, a woman wearing a pink paisley design headscarf, removed her sunglasses and called to a young woman emerging from inside the Inn.

"Excuse me, dear, are you able to point me in the direction of Chy-an-Gwyns?"

Sally Stevens, having just finished work on the breakfast shift, pointed towards the coast. "It's the big house up there on the cliffs, but I don't expect you can quite see it from where you're sitting. It's easy to find though, just carry on down to the cove and then you'll be able to see it quite clearly. To get to it, just follow the lane up towards Higher Green Farm. You'll find the entrance about half way up the hill, on the left of course. Just look out for a green five bar gate. The name Chy-an-Gwyns is on a brass plaque. After that just follow the track across the fields and you'll be there."

"Thank you," said the driver, with a sweet smile.

"My pleasure," said Sally. "You must be Mrs Rossiter."

"Good heavens, how did you know that?"

"It's common knowledge that the Castor-Hunts have let out their house to you until Christmas and that your husband is in the Navy and away at sea."

Mrs Rossiter's eyebrows rose and touched a loose blonde curl peeping from beneath her headscarf. "Really? I'm flattered."

Feeling scruffy, Sally rolled up the sleeves of her dress to hide the cuffs, damp after washing the breakfast dishes. "I hope you'll enjoy your stay here. I think we're coming up for the best time of the year. I love the autumn and always have."

"So do I, dear. I adore the warm colours, the rustle of fallen leaves, the early morning nip in the air and the smell of bonfires burning away summer's lifeless debris." She smiled. "May I ask your name?"

"Of course. I'm Sally, Sally Stevens. My dad's the village policeman, so needless to say, I live in The Police House."

Mrs Rossiter replaced her sunglasses. "Well, thank you, Sally for your help. And as news obviously travels very fast in Trengillion I shall have to behave whilst I'm here and that way I won't encounter the wrath of your father." She gave a girlish giggle and released the handbrake. "Good bye, dear." And with a roar headed down the road towards the cove.

"Who was that?" asked Frank, with brush in hand ready to sweep the cobbles, a job he did every morning unless it was raining.

Sally smiled. "Mrs Rossiter. That car will make Jamie drool when he sees it, although I'm not too sure he'll like the colour. She seemed nice anyway, if you were about to ask, but she was on her own and I thought she was supposed to be coming down with a friend."

"Probably got someone joining her later," said Frank. "If she's here 'til Christmas there's plenty of time and that car wouldn't really hold enough luggage for two. Not enough for two women, anyway."

News of Catherine Rossiter's arrival at Chy-an-Gwyns travelled fast, although probably more for the car she drove than the lady herself. But nevertheless her residency, albeit short term, created a stir of excitement and she became the subject of many conversations. For that reason, her first visit to the Inn the following evening caused several ribs to be nudged as muffled whispers met with eager ears. She entered the bar alone, head held high, immaculately dressed and not a single hair out of place. After closing the door she walked straight up to the bar where she placed her expensive leather handbag beside a half filled glass ashtray.

"Frank," she smiled, with eyebrows raised as she offered her soft, slim, manicured hand. "I am Catherine Rossiter."

Frank warily took her hand, surprised by the manner by which she chose to introduce herself, much like she was announcing she was the Queen of England.

"How come you know my name?" he asked, his forehead wrinkled by a puzzled frown.

She laughed. "Your name, Mr Newton, is written above the door, and as you are the only male present I shrewdly put two and two together and guessed that you are he. I take it I'm correct in my assumption?"

"Well, yes, I'm Frank Newton and this here is my dear wife, Dorothy."

Dorothy smiled feebly. "Welcome to Trengillion," she muttered, though not convincingly. "I hope you enjoy your stay here. It's a very beautiful spot and Chy-an-Gwyns is a lovely house."

"I'm sure I will. Now my dear Frank, may I have a large gin and tonic please with a slice of lemon and a little ice?"

"Of course, Mrs Rossiter. One gin and tonic coming up."

"Oh, Frank, please, do call me Catherine, after all I'm sure we shall be seeing quite a lot of each other. Having said that, I don't think I shall be out quite so much when my friend arrives as she has very little appetite for socialising."

Catherine mingled with the locals and holiday makers with complete confidence and most were charmed by her personality and pleasant manner. Dorothy, however, had her doubts, and Alice Penhaligon, also working on the bar, agreed.

They watched Catherine glancing around the bar on her return from the Ladies with, they assumed, a critical eye. After her inspection of the public bar she walked into the snug where she reached up and touched the plates. She then wandered briefly into the sports bar. When back in the snug, she stooped and looked into the empty fireplace.

"I reckon she's looking for dirt," spluttered Dorothy, choked with indignation. "Well, she's out of luck 'cos I don't think she'll find any."

"She's certainly up to no good, that one," said Alice, tight-lipped. "And it's not right her flaunting airs and graces like she does. She makes me feel clumsy and stupid."

"She doesn't mean it," said Frank. "It's just the way people like her are. I reckon she's alright, at least she's trying to be sociable and that's more than a lot of folks do."

"Well, I won't have a problem with her as long as she keeps her hands off you," muttered Dorothy, annoyed that her face was flushed. "But if she oversteps the mark I'll be ready for her, airs and graces or not."

Frank laughed. "Women fighting over me. Now that's a first!"

"Don't you get too big headed, Frank Newton," scoffed Dorothy. "And you can take that smug look off your face. There's definitely something not right. You know as well as I do that it's very unusual for a women to go into a bar without a man, unless, as is the case with some of our ladies, they're paying guests."

As she spoke, Freddie appeared from upstairs where he had changed from the clothes he had worn for dinner into a knee length kaftan and sandy coloured jeans. His feet were bare. A strand of honeysuckle rested behind one ear.

Dorothy gasped as he paraded into the bar. "Oh my goodness, whatever next! He looks like he's wearing a pair of his grandmother's old curtains, and he's borrowed her old knitting bag as well."

Frank laughed. He had never before heard his wife say a critical word about anyone other than herself, yet in a very short space of time she had found two people whose manner or appearance displeased her. Still grinning he caught Catherine Rossiter's eye. She winked.

"Blimey," he mumbled as he turned to serve a holiday maker standing at the bar with several empty glasses. But he felt unsteady and accidently knocked over the pint of bitter Alice had placed on the bar for Cyril Penrose.

Rose and George returned from a shopping trip in Helston just as Stella put the kettle on.

"That was good timing," said Ned, sitting at the Kitchen table checking his bank statement. "I assume you'd like to join us for tea."

Rose eagerly sat down at the table and kicked off her shoes. "Yes please, I'm parched, and my feet are aching. We went for a walk all around Helston after we'd done the shopping as I wanted to see it for old time's sake."

"And did you find it much changed?" Ned asked, as he put away the bank statement in its folder.

Rose nodded. "Yes, we walked from the boating lake right up through the town and into Station Road. I can't believe they've closed the branch line. I loved that little station. It looks so sad now."

"I heartily agree," said Ned, "because I, like many others, had hoped that one day the railway would go all the way down to the

Lizard. But that wasn't to be and now we have to travel to Redruth or Penzance to catch the main line train. I suppose that's what you call progress."

"Humph," scoffed Stella, "progress, my foot."

Ned grinned. "Yes, maybe an unfortunate choice of word."

Stella poured boiling water into the teapot. "It's criminal if you ask me and I don't think Doctor Beeching would be very welcome if he were to take a holiday down here, even though we're all getting used to having no branch line now."

"When did it actually close?" George asked, hanging his jacket on the back of a chair.

"It closed to passengers on November the fifth 1962 and to goods from the fifth of October 1964. Gwinear Road Station closed that same day too. They began lifting the track in April 1965 and by the end of the year the British Oxygen Company had removed all the metals."

George laughed heartily. "Yes, I remember it was already closed when we were last down but we didn't get to see the aftermath for some reason or other. And if I might say so, Ned, you reeled off those dates like a true professional."

Ned rose to help Stella lay out the tea cups and saucers. "I'm very familiar with the dates because the juniors did a project on the railway closure last term. They loved it. We drew maps of the track routes and the children brought in old photos. One of them even had an uncle who used to be a signalman. It was very interesting, and liking trains, I think I enjoyed it as much as the kids."

Lynne and Sharon Gibson, both unmarried and still living at home with their elderly parents, had for several months relished the opportunity of two weeks' freedom in Cornwall where they could do as they pleased without being conscious of their mother's watchful eye. For both girls, if indeed girls they could be called, were in their early forties and although both had had brief relationships with various men during their adult years, none of these dalliances had amounted to anything as the suitors were constantly put off by the girls' reluctance, in fact refusal, to introduce them to their parents. Hence, when the invitation arrived for the family to attend a wedding in Cornwall, the girls were delighted to accept, knowing their parents would never undertake such a mammoth journey covering nearly three hundred miles. And from that day on, they blessed the summer their cousin Norman had taken up with a girl from the Lizard whilst in Cornwall where he visited the Goonhilly Satellite Earth Station with his work colleagues from the GPO.

"Did you bring a needle and cotton with you?" asked Sharon, as they lay on top of the cliffs overlooking Trengillion beach one sunny afternoon, their disagreement a day or two earlier having long been forgotten.

Lynne, watching clouds through half closed eyes as they drifted across the azure sky, turned her head towards her sister. "Yes, but only black or white. Why?"

"Cos I'm going to take up the hem on the green suit I'll be wearing on Saturday. It's far too long and I've got nice legs, so why not show them off."

Lynne, aghast, sat bolt upright. "But you can't. Whatever will Mum say? Oh, please don't start being rebellious again."

"Stop trying to make me feel guilty," snapped Sharon, rolling onto her side. "I've thought it through and Mum won't say anything because she won't know, because I shall let the hem down again before we go home. Not that I really need do that as I'm unlikely ever to wear it again. In fact, I won't just take it up, I shall chop several inches off first so that I can make a better job of it, and I'll get some green cotton next time we're in the post office since you only have white or black. Damn it, I'm fed up with being told what I can wear and what I can't. Why don't you do the same with your suit?"

"Well, I, umm..."

"...Oh, go on, Lynne, we agreed we'd do as we pleased this fortnight. Stop being so boring and let's make a proper job of it."

"But my legs aren't as good as yours, and what if Uncle Cecil and Auntie Beat decide to go to the wedding after all. They're bound to tell Mum and Dad, you know what Auntie Beat's like."

"They won't even notice," said Sharon. "Come on, be realistic, Lynne. All the other women, especially the younger ones, will be wearing short skirts so we'll not be alone. Besides, I don't think they'll be there. You know how Uncle Cecil hates driving on unfamiliar roads. Anyway, you want to look nice don't you?

Remember, our cousin Phillip will almost definitely be there and you've always rather fancied him."

"Yes, you're right," said Lynne, conscious her face was burning. "But actually, I've got an even better idea. Let's go into town and each buy a new outfit, that way we can take our old suits home, untouched, and Mum will be impressed that we've kept them so clean. I mean, it's not as if they were bought especially for this wedding, is it? They're at least five years old cos we had them for Peggy's wedding back in either sixty one or sixty two."

"Brilliant idea, yes," cried Sharon with delight, patting her sister on the back. "Welcome to the Swinging Sixties, Lynne. We still have a couple of days left so we'll give lots of thought to what we want and then go shopping on Friday straight after breakfast. And as the weather's looking good I'm not even going to buy a suit I'm going to wear a dress, a brightly coloured, short dress, something flashy like the ones Maggie Nan designs and I shall have a fabulous new hat to match."

"Hmm, I doubt if you'll be able to get anything at all Maggie Nanish in Cornwall."

"I think you'll be surprised. I saw some pretty fantastic looking outfits in a shop called Abbotts when we were in Helston the other day so we must go there first."

"Shall we buy new shoes, as well," said Lynne, thinking of their cousin Phillip. "Unserviceable, impractical shoes or sandals all strappy with high heels which will make my legs look slimmer, and of course handbags to match?"

"Absolutely, and do you know what? I'm even going to wear false eyelashes. I've looked at them time and time again in Boots but I've never been able to bring myself to buy any knowing I'd not be able to wear them without Mum noticing. But on Saturday she won't know as she'll not be there to inspect us before we go out."

Lynne was shocked. "I'm not going to go that far. I think false eyelashes look tarty, but then my eyelashes are a lot longer than yours, anyway," she laughed. "I reckon you must have been in the back row when God handed them out."

"Oh, don't mention God, Lynne, it makes me feel a little guilty and we haven't even done anything wrong yet. Not that it's wrong to want to look attractive anyway."

Lynne took a deep breath. "No, but it is wrong to be deceitful and I do have a punishing conscience."

"Perhaps we ought to forget the whole thing and wear our suits," teased Sharon. "But I don't want to and I know deep down you don't either."

"No, we'll not wear our suits and we shall have new dresses. It's up to us what we do with our own money. After all we work hard enough for it in that wretched factory, and do you know what? I reckon it was divine intervention that fixed the wedding date slap bang in the middle of the factory holiday fortnight. It was meant to be that we should attend this wedding and therefore it's our bounden duty to make sure it's a success."

Sharon laughed. "I think you're being a bit economical with the truth there. But sod it, yes, we'll do as we please."

"Sharon," gasped Lynne, in disgust. "Please watch your tongue. The use of foul language is a step too far."

CHAPTER EIGHT

As Gertie passed the post office on Thursday morning, she observed a notice in the window advertising for a lady to do a few hours' cleaning a week. Anyone interested was to apply in person to Mrs Catherine Rossiter at Chy-an-Gwyns. Gertie stopped and considered the advertisement. A few extra pounds would be useful and it would only be until Christmas anyway. She wondered if she ought to consult Percy before taking any further action but decided if she were to dither for too long then the vacancy may well be filled and the opportunity lost. For money was not the real reason for Gertie's enthusiasm, nor was it a desire to get out of the house. The job would simply allow her access to Chy-an-Gwyns and the opportunity to explore and find out more about Catherine Rossiter of whom she had heard a great deal. With her mind made up, Gertie went into the post office to buy some sugar even though she had a bag, unopened, in her kitchen cupboard.

Pat Dickens was just leaving the shop and dropping a packet of twenty cigarettes into his pocket as Gertie walked through the door. Milly was behind the counter totting up figures on a piece of paper.

"You're looking nicely tanned, Gertie," she smiled, on looking up. "Have you been sun bathing or working outdoors?"

"A bit of both. I seem to have a lot more time on my hands these days with the children growing so fast and they've not exactly been a handful this summer cos most of the time they've been down the woods with the others."

Milly smiled. "I know, we really appreciate it and it's good to know they're safe. I do up a lunch box for Stephen and David each morning then I don't see them again 'til teatime. I was a bit concerned at first about letting Stephen go as he's only seven, but Elizabeth and Diane are both thirteen now and they insist they'll always look after him. I think it does kids good to have a little independence."

"Absolutely, my boys often join them too and I've always believed there's safety in numbers," said Gertie, glancing towards the window where the back of the advertisement was clearly visible. "Anyway, I'd like a bag of sugar, please."

Milly took a bag of sugar from the shelf and placed it on the counter. "Anything else, Gertie?"

"Err, well, I know I shouldn't, but I'll have a quarter of Bluebird toffees please and a Rowntree's Nux bar."

Gertie felt a pang of guilt. She had been working in the garden hoping the exercise might help keep her weight down and so the sweets would rather negate her efforts. Still, if she got the cleaning job that would give her some exercise especially if she walked up to Chy-an-Gwyns.

"Has Mrs Rossiter's advert been in the window long?" Gertie asked, casually.

Milly tipped the toffees onto the weighing scales. "About half an hour. Why are you thinking of applying?"

"Probably. What's she like?"

"Very nice. Charming in fact. She's been in a couple of times now, once to arrange a newspaper delivery and today with the advert and to buy some ham and cheese. You'll like her, I should go for it, two people can't make much mess, can they?" She screwed the lid back on the glass jar and returned it to the shelf.

"Is her friend here now, then?" said Gertie, counting out the right money into Milly's outstretched hand.

"No, she's arriving at the weekend, apparently, so Mrs Rossiter said she won't need any help until after she's arrived."

"Thanks," said Gertie, picking up her purchases. "Very interesting. Regards to Johnny and I'll see you next week at Drama practise."

"Gosh, yes, that fortnight's gone quickly, hasn't it? It seems like only yesterday that Joyce and Harry went off on holiday. The kids will be back at school before we know it."

Gertie nodded. "Yes, I suppose they will. I must try and remember to ask them tonight if they have any homework, cos I know what they're like. They leave everything until the last minute and then get all stressed and bad tempered because it's not done."

Milly sighed. "Oh dear, I suppose I've got all that to come. Although to tell you the truth I always left my homework 'til the last minute."

Gertie giggled. "So did I, but the children must never know."

Inside their den in Bluebell Woods the children of Trengillion discussed how best to spend the day. They had already been over to the Lodge House to spy on Danny but to the girls' dismay he was not there.

"I hope he hasn't gone off and got another job or something like that," complained Susan, venting her frustration on a twig which she snapped it into several pieces.

Elizabeth shook her head. "I doubt it. Remember he was here yesterday and I don't think he'd start a new job in the middle of the week."

"I expect he's got a cold," said Jane. "I'm sure I heard him cough several times yesterday and his voice sounded rather husky."

"His voice always sounds husky," said Susan dreamily.

John laughed. "Come on, girls, cheer up. It's a lush day and I don't want to spend it listening to you lot whining about darling Danny's absence."

"I'm hungry," said Matthew. "Let's have lunch."

Elizabeth looked at her watch. "We might as well, it's already half past twelve."

They each picked up their respective boxes.

Anne shivered. "I'm cold. Can't we have our lunch somewhere sunny? These woods feel rather chilly today."

Tony scrambled to his feet. "I agree. Come on, everyone up."

"But where shall we go?" Diane asked, replacing the lid on her lunch box.

Anne was quick to answer. "Let's go to the field where all the buttercups grow. It'll be lovely and sunny there."

The Buttercup meadow was part of the Penwynton Estate and lay below the gardens of Penwynton House. It was a sheltered spot once used to graze sheep with a ha-ha to protect the gardens from the animals. But over the years the sheep herds had dwindled until all had gone; the neglected pastures then became unkempt and eventually overgrown with an inevitable crop of buttercups.

The children stood on top of the ha-ha wall and gazed down at the field of golden flowers.

"Wow, they look so pretty," said Anne. "I'd love to paint them."

"They're weeds," said Elizabeth, tossing her hair, clearly jealous of her sister's artistic talents.

Anne frowned. "They're not, they're wild flowers."

"Same thing," scoffed Elizabeth.

Susan giggled. "My mum says weeds are wild flowers that grow in wrong places, so I guess you're both right."

Matthew jumped down from the wall and pointed. "Come on, let's race to that hedge at the bottom."

Clutching lunchboxes they raced across the fields and collapsed, laughing and breathless before they even reached the hedge.

"What have you got in your sandwiches today?" Susan asked, pulling hers apart. "I've got egg."

Tony and John both nodded. "Same here, but then Mum's hardly likely to do us all something different."

"I've got cheese and piccalilli," said Diane.

"Me too," said Graham.

"Mine are ham and mustard," said David, "and my brother's will be the same."

Elizabeth and Anne both had cheese and tomato.

"Let's swap," said Susan, "then we can all have a bit of each."

Everyone agreed and so sat in a circle and placed their sandwiches in the middle on the up-turned lids of their lunchboxes.

After eating and drinking, they lay on their backs and watched the clouds slowly drifting across the pale blue sky.

"Have you seen that bloke staying at the Inn with the long hair?" asked Susan. "He looks dead cool and I reckon he's a real hippie. He's not as handsome as Danny of course, and he's too old anyway."

"Too old for what?" John cast a quizzical glance at his sister.

"Well, to marry of course."

Tony laughed. "Is that all you empty-headed females ever think about? There's more to life than marriage, you know."

"Dad thinks he's a bit dodgy," said Anne. "I don't know why but I heard him refer to him as Freaky Freddie."

"Humph! That's because Dad's dead old-fashioned," snapped Elizabeth. "He couldn't differentiate a cool person from a square, nor could Mum for that matter."

Diane rolled onto her side. "I don't think your parents are old-fashioned. They both look young and wear really nice clothes. My dad's older but even he tries to be fashionable. Bless him!"

"It must be really difficult for our parents' generation," said Jane, thoughtfully. "Difficult to know how to dress, I mean. When they were young, fashion was for older folks but now it's really for the under thirties. The music they had was pretty dire too. One way or another they've really dipped out."

"And they lived through the War," said John. "We shouldn't forget that."

"And food rationing," said Susan. "Imagine, life with no chocolate, sweets and cakes."

"Trust you to think of food, you pig," teased Graham.

With their holiday fast coming to an end, Rose and George decided to chance the risk of oil and spend the day on the beach, for the weather was warm and the opportunity to top up the sun tan seemed too good to miss.

"Come with us," said Rose to Ned and Stella, as they cleared away the breakfast things. "You don't need to stay all day if you don't want to."

Ned frowned. "You know I'm not one for sun bathing and I certainly don't want to go in the sea. But damn it, yes, we'll join you, that's if you want to, Stella."

"Of course," she said. "I've nothing else to do. Nothing that matters, anyway, and the children won't be back before tea time unless it rains and I don't think that's likely to happen."

While Stella made a flask of coffee, Ned went to the garden shed and to the amusement of everyone else came back with a large sheet of polythene.

"I think we ought to lay this down beneath the blanket, just in case there is any oil lurking beneath the sand. It's not easy to know without digging up the whole area of beach you want to occupy."

"Were you a boy scout, Mr Fusspot? George teased. "I mean to say, you seem to be prepared for anything."

Ned shook his head. "No, I wasn't. I'm just practical and I ruined a pair of perfectly good trousers sitting on a rock earlier this year.

But then you up-country buggers wouldn't understand the misery oil can cause."

There were quite a few people on the beach and several in the sea. One of them was Freddie Short, waist deep in water, he waved and beckoned them to join him.

"Come in, the water's quite warm," he shouted, as they spread out the polythene sheet and the blanket.

Ned promptly sat down, but George, Rose and Stella, each with swimwear beneath their clothing, quickly removed their outer garments and ran into the falling waves.

"Christ, it's freezing," screamed Stella, shivering as the water splashed heavily around her knees.

"Not if you're completely submerged," said Freddie, advancing to drag her under. Stella, however, was too quick and ran back to the blanket and Ned.

"Humph," muttered Ned. "I think you've rather taken our druggy friend's fancy. Put your top back on, Stell, I don't like the way he looks at you."

Stella pulled a towel from the beach bag and began to dry her legs. "Oh, Ned, don't be so pompous. He's only being friendly. Look, he's dragging Rose in now and George isn't making a fuss."

"Well, George wouldn't, would he? Because George is George," said Ned, stiffly. "Whereas I am what I am and the thought of losing you terrifies me."

"Oh, does it?" said Stella, tossing the towel on the blanket and snuggling up to his side. "Well, your jealousy is quite unfounded, my sweetheart, because nothing would entice me to leave you for the likes of Freddie or anyone else for that matter."

Ned put his arm around her shoulder and kissed her gently. "I'm sorry. I promise I'll not be possessive in future, but I can't help it if I mistrust your hippie friend."

As he spoke Rose returned from the water and wrapped herself in her towel, shortly followed by George.

"Too cold for you," asked Ned, surprised by their early return.

"Yes and no," said Rose. "We've come out cos we're going to have a game of rounders with Freddie. Won't you join us? The more the merrier."

"Rounders," said Stella, putting on her cardigan, "Count me in. It's my favourite game."

"But you can't play with an odd number," said Ned, watching Freddie run away from the beach. "It wouldn't be fair and where's Freddie going?"

"Girls against chaps," said Rose. "I know that means you'll outnumber us but it doesn't matter cos we'll still beat you."

"Freddie's gone back to the Inn for a bat and ball," George added.

Ned wrinkled his nose. "Right, I'll join you, but I must warn you I used to be very good at cricket." He stood up and glanced along the beach. "Actually, I don't think it's fair to expect you two women to take on us chaps, as good as you might think you are." He pointed across the beach. "Ask those two ladies over there sitting on Denzil's bench if they'd like to join us. I don't know their names but I've seen them around and they're about the same age as us."

Freddie returned with bat and ball as they were deliberating whether or not to ask the unknown females if they would like to join in. When asked his opinion he grinned from ear to ear. "Brilliant idea. I'll go and ask them."

Lynne and Sharon were eating ice creams and discussing the wedding outfits they were hoping to purchase the following day when they saw Freddie approaching. Lynne frowned. "Christ! His bathing trunks couldn't be skimpier, could they? They're almost obscene."

Sharon giggled as she straightened her hair.

"Hi girls," said Freddie, mischievously winking at Lynne. "Fancy a game of rounders with me and my new buddies?"

Lynne blushed. "Well, I don't really think…"

"…Yes please," said Sharon leaping to her feet having quickly eaten the remains of her choc ice. "We could do with a bit of exercise."

"But I've not finished my ice cream," Lynne whimpered, playing for time.

Freddie leaned over her and licked the contents of her cornet.

"Every little helps. Come on, girls, follow me."

The sisters followed Freddie across the beach to where *the buddies* were marking out the pitch using shoes for posts and a folded towel on the spot designated for the bowler. When everything was in place, the game began. The chaps won despite being outnumbered by the girls, for neither Lynne nor Sharon had done any running since their school days other than to catch the factory bus and neither Stella nor Rose fared much better.

After the game, George, warmed due to the excessive exertion, ran across the sand and plunged into the waves to cool down. Ned returned to the blanket where he removed his pullover and rolled up the sleeves of his shirt. Rose and Stella gathered together the shoes and sandals. Sharon, also feeling warm, removed her tights, pushed them into the pocket of pinafore dress and waded into the oncoming waves. Freddie threw bat and ball towards his knitted shoulder bag and ran into the sea. As he passed Sharon he slapped her bottom.

"With legs like yours you should be in a bikini, sweetheart, not that cumbersome dress." He leapt into the waves. "And we should play games more often."

Sharon giggled and hitched up the hem of her dress a little higher.

Lynne, with no desire to paddle gazed longingly at Denzil's bench. She was tired and wanted to sit down. After bidding a brief farewell to Ned, Stella and Rose, now all on the blanket drinking coffee from flasks, she turned to walk towards the bench. But as she passed Freddie's tasselled bag laying on the sand she noticed a shiny metal object part protruding from the open top. With curiosity roused she purposely walked close by to take a casual glance. A sturdy pair of handcuffs, fastened to a chain, glistened in the sun. Without uttering a sound, Lynne fainted.

"What's up Dot?" said Frank as they sat in the kitchen of the Ringing Bells Inn enjoying a cup of tea before Dorothy started the dinner. "Something's on your mind, I can tell, you're miles away."

Dorothy leaned her head to one side. "It's Pauline, Pauline Pringle. When I look at her I see myself as I was before I married you. She's dowdy and frumpy and no-one should be frumpy these days, not with all the bright colours in the shops. And Frank, her hairdo, it's awful, far worse than mine ever was. You'll no doubt say I'm interfering and perhaps I am, but you see, I'm trying to think of a way to do something about it, subtly of course." She took a deep breath. "I know it's not cricket, but do you think it would alright if we fixed the raffle at the Barn Dance on Saturday night?"

Frank groaned. "Fix it. How do you mean?"

"Well, if we could fix it so that she could win a prize giving her a free hair-do at Betty's salon, she'd be able to improve her looks without knowing we'd had a hand in it. Betty always donates a voucher for a hair-do so all we'll have to do is make sure she wins it."

Playing for time, Frank opened up his tobacco pouch and slowly filled his pipe. "But what makes you think she'll be going to the Barn Dance?" I mean to say, I wouldn't think it'd be her cup of tea at all. Poor soul, I bet she's never danced in her life."

"I daresay she hasn't but that's not a problem. I'll buy a ticket and pretend one of the locals gave it to me because they're unable to go. I'll say they wanted me to pass it on to someone I thought might like to use it. I'll be going, anyway. You said I could, and I'll get Molly to help too of course, as I expect she'll be doing the raffle. What do you think, should I do it or am I just being an interfering old busybody?"

Frank chuckled. "Well, your heart's in the right place, Dot. There's no doubt about that. Yes, go ahead. You have my blessing if you think you can get away with it, and such a plan will be right up Molly's street."

Dorothy jumped up and gave him a quick hug. "Thank you. I'll pop round and see Molly first thing in the morning after breakfast. I need to see her, anyway, as I intend to donate that hideous gonk I won in the Whist Drive raffle at Polquillick last summer. It's been sitting on the dressing table long enough, I shall be glad to see the back of it."

"Really! I've always thought that gonk looked a bit like me."

Dorothy nodded. "So have I and that's why it must go. There's something unnerving about having a husband with gonk-like features."

"Fix the raffle!" said Molly, putting on the kettle to make coffee, "I like that idea. It always seems to me that the prizes go to someone unsuitable. At last month's Whist Drive for instance, Jim Hughes won a beautiful hairbrush and comb which is no use to him now poor Flo's gone."

Dorothy laughed. "Well, I wasn't planning that you should fix the whole raffle, just the hair-do for Pauline, and I think you'll find Jim's hairbrush prize wasn't wasted as he gave it to Doris."

"Really, she didn't tell me. Do sit down, Dot. How do you know?"

Dorothy pulled out a chair from beneath the kitchen table and sat down. "Because Jim told me one night when he was in for a pint. He said he'd won the brush and didn't know what to do with it, so I told him to give it to one of his lady friends and he decided on Doris cos he's known her since they were young 'uns."

Molly sat down to wait for the kettle to boil. "Well, that's good then. Anyway, how are we going to fix this raffle? I take it we're not going to let folks choose their own prizes like at some events, cos if we do Pauline won't go for the hair-do, will she? Oh dear, but not letting folks choose their own prizes goes against everything I just said about people winning unsuitable things."

Dorothy frowned. "Hmm, you're quite right. Perhaps the hair-do could be a separate prize for the best dancer or something like that."

Molly laughed. "But we don't know whether or not Pauline can dance or even if she will."

"Damn, anyway if we did that we'd need a judge which would mean telling him or her of our plan."

"I know. How about having a prize for the lucky numbers on the tickets. That way it'd be a doddle to make sure Pauline won."

"Excellent idea. I take it the tickets are numbered."

"Oh yes, and we can use an old book of cloakroom tickets to enable us to put the corresponding numbers into the hat."

"Brilliant! That's such a weight off my mind."

Molly stood as the kettle came to the boil. "That's settled that then. Just one other thing. How can we be sure Pauline will be there?"

Dorothy reached for her handbag and took out a ticket. "I shall see to that by giving her this spare ticket which I just happen to have. It should be easy enough to catch her and persuade her to go as she usually goes for a walk in the mornings and spends the afternoons reading in her room or out the front on the old bench. I think she'll like the idea anyway as she's keen to get out and about and meet people even if she is quite shy."

Molly made two mugs of coffee and sat back down. "Excellent. So, when it comes to drawing the lucky ticket number for the hair-do, I'll make sure I have concealed in my hand Pauline's ticket number. You'd better hold the tin up quite high though, Dot. We don't want anyone's beady eyes noticing our deceit." Molly giggled. "Now I've something to look forward to. Not that I'm bored at all, far from it, but it's always nice to have little plans and schemes to put into operation."

Dorothy sipped her coffee. "You should pop in for a drink more often, we don't see much of you these days and it's always good for Frank and me to see familiar faces. After all, we'll be gone soon."

"Oh don't, I can't imagine the Inn without you and Frank. I dread to think what the next people will be like. It's a horrible thought having strangers run the place. I'm sure I won't like them."

"Oh, don't let Frank hear you say that, Molly. He's very hesitant about going, but he must. It's too much for him now, he needs to relax more. Anyway, we'll still be in the village for the rest of our days."

"You're quite right, of course, I'm being selfish, and we will be going to the Inn a bit more soon, but this time of the year the major spends a lot of time at the golf club, which is nice for him as the winters can be very long."

Dorothy nodded. "Especially if they're wet and windy. I must admit I half expect the roof of Chy-an-Gwyns to fly off with some of the gales we get."

Molly giggled. "That reminds me. What's this Catherine Rossiter that I've heard so much about, like? Is she really a man-eater? According to some of the gossip I've heard she's after anything in trousers."

Dorothy raised her eyebrows. "Well, I can't say that I'm too keen on her, and she certainly speaks to Frank in a manner which I find irritating, but it's probably just her way. I think she looks on us all as country bumpkins."

"Oh, she does, does she? Well, we'll have to get in soon then so that she can meet the major. He'll soon be able to tell whether she's genuinely classy or if it's all a front. He's very good at figuring people out."

"Hmm, I shall look forward to that. And before I forget, I'd like to donate something for Saturday's raffle." She reached for her bag and handed the gonk to Molly. "I won this at a Whist Drive in Polquillick last summer."

"Good heavens! Don't tell him I said so, but it looks just like your Frank. How uncanny."

Dorothy sighed. "Oh dear, so you can see the likeness too. That's the reason I'm happy to pass it on. It gives me the creeps."

Molly dropped the gonk into a box with other raffle prizes. "Well, I'm sure someone will be happy to give him a new home. I must confess I'm none too fond of them and I can't really see why they've caught on."

Dorothy nodded. "By the way, I keep meaning to ask. Are you going to dress up for the Barn Dance tomorrow? I mean, are you going to wear checks and so forth. I'm not quite sure yet what I'm going to wear."

"Oh yes, definitely. I've made a couple of skirts especially for the occasion, but I'm not sure which one to wear. Let's go in the sitting room and then I'll go and get them and you can help me decide."

Dorothy sat down on one of the two fireside chairs. From upstairs she could hear Molly humming *Marie's Wedding*.

"When Molly returned she spread both gingham skirts over the back of the settee. "What do you think? Whichever I choose I shall wear it with a white blouse so there's no problem with matching."

"Hmm, I really don't know," muttered Dorothy. "They're both lovely and green's my favourite colour, but I think red is much more you. It's no good, you'll have to choose."

"Right, I shall wear the red and you shall wear the green."

"What, oh no, I can't possibly borrow your brand new skirt…"

"…of course you can," interrupted Molly. "It'll fit you because the waistband is elasticated. Anyway, you must wear it; that way I can be sure I won't be the only one dressed up 'country style'."

Dorothy stood, picked up the skirt and held it in front of herself. "Well yes, I'd be thrilled to wear it, at least it's not too short." She laughed. "Really, it shocks me sometimes, the sights I see at the Inn. I mean, I don't think anyone should wear short skirts if they don't have nice legs. I'm all for showing off one's assets but flaws should be covered up."

"Well, I agree to a point, but it's very unfortunate for those not blessed with perfect legs and the mini skirt is just so fashionable these days. I expect it'll all change before long. I see already more and more females are wearing trousers."

"Yes, I suppose things are always changing, but I think it's unhealthy the way everyone seems to have become slaves to fashion. What I mean is, I don't quite know what to make of people these days. It seems that the children, especially girls, no longer want to be children, they drool over pop stars and long to wear fashionable clothes and make-up. Meanwhile adults want to be young again, especially women, so they grow their hair and shorten their skirts, feeling they've missed out. The whole population it seems to me is aged between sixteen and twenty nine."

"There's nothing wrong with that, Dot," said Molly, sitting down on the settee. "We're none of us looking forward to being thirty."

CHAPTER NINE

Lynne and Sharon Gibson wearily sat down in The Coffee Bean café each with a cup of tea and a thick slice of Black Forest Gateau.

"This probably isn't a good idea," Lynne sighed, unenthusiastically cutting into her gateau with a fork. "My new dress is rather clingy and these extra calories won't do anything to help conceal the unsightly bulges."

Sharon didn't share her sister's concern. "Don't fuss, your new pantie-girdle will hold everything in. Eat your cake and enjoy it."

"Hmm, I suppose you're right, but I'm beginning to wish I'd bought the yellow, empire line dress rather than the blue mini with the fitted waist."

Sharon shook her head. "No, you made the right choice and remember Dingles didn't have any hats to match the yellow, and the colour made you look pallid anyway. Blue suits you much better, Lynne, and it matches your eyes too. Which reminds me, I haven't got my false eyelashes yet."

Lynne groaned. "Does that mean we have to walk all the way back up to Boots?"

Sharon glanced across the road to Woolworths where people were coming and going through the two sets of double doors. "I might be able to get them in Woollies," she said, pointing to the store with her dessert fork. "But having said that, we have to go back up through the town anyway to get to the car park, and I distinctly remember seeing a couple of chemists on the way down here."

The sisters had a second cup of tea after the gateau and then collected together their purchases and wandered up the street. As they approached the traffic light Sharon pointed across the road to Wakeham's the Chemist. "Let's go in there for our cosmetics."

They crossed the road. After going through the Chemist's door they stepped down into the shop.

Sharon bought a pair of Mary Quant false eyelashes. She also bought false nails and turquoise nail varnish to match her chiffon shift dress.

"While we're here I'm getting a new bottle of perfume," said Lynne, glancing around the shop. "Nothing expensive, just a spray bottle of Yardley Flair. One of the girls I work with wears it and I rather like its smell."

From a shelf she lifted a blue box containing the favoured bottle. Sharon, liking the idea of something new, selected a turquoise box containing a bottle of Sea Jade simply because it matched her outfit.

Delighted with their purchases the sisters walked up through the town towards the car park, tired but excited, both in very high spirits and giggling more like school girls than mature women.

Once back with their car, Sharon unlocked the doors and they packed dresses, hats, shoe boxes, cosmetics and toiletries safely inside the boot.

"Smashing view from up here," said Lynne, glancing across the valley to open countryside as Sharon closed the boot.

"Hmm, no wonder we're knackered walking around with all these hills and so forth. I'll be glad to get back to the Inn and put my feet up."

"Me too. We don't want to be tired tomorrow."

"Definitely not, although I suppose the first thing we really ought to do when we get back is try on our entire outfits, but not with painted nails and eyelashes of course."

Lynne felt her knees weaken as a vision of Cousin Phillip flashed across her mind. "Yes, we must do that. I really can't wait until tomorrow. It's going to be fabulous."

"Fingers crossed."

Simultaneously they opened their car doors but before either had time to climb in they heard voices calling their names. Surprised, they turned. Their jaws dropped. Walking across the car park, furiously waving their arms, were Auntie Beat and Uncle Cecil.

On Friday evening, Ned and Stella went out with George and Rose for a farewell drink at the Inn, for the summer was fast coming to an end and teachers everywhere were fully aware that a new term and academic year lay just around the corner.

The day had been hot and the evening was warm, and so they chose to enjoy their drinks outside until darkness fell and a chilly breeze forced them to return indoors. Inside, both bars were busy as holiday makers mingled and chatted with locals, especially the public bar where voices were tuning up ready for the singing to break out, a frequent occurrence on Friday nights, usually started by the fishermen. With no seats free in the public bar, Ned, Stella, Rose and George went into the snug where they were just in time to grab a table vacated by Lynne and Sharon Gibson, who wanted an early night in preparation for the wedding they were to attend at the Lizard the following day.

In spite of the vibrant atmosphere, Rose seemed very subdued, she sipped her drink quietly, her gaze frequently falling on the singers visible through the open double doors of the snug. Ned noticed and squeezed her hand.

"Don't look so glum, Rose," he whispered. "I know how you feel. I can still remember the lump in my throat and that empty feeling as I left Trengillion the very first time to return to London. But you know you are both welcome to come and stay as often as you like. In fact, why don't you come down for Christmas? It'll be just us this year as Stella's folks are going to her sister's."

Rose half smiled. "I'd love to, and I know George would too, but we've agreed to go to my parents this year. We went to George's last year and so it's only fair."

Ned sighed. "Of course. Well perhaps next year, you'll both have done your duty to your parents then and it'll be our turn to entertain you."

Rose laughed. "That's forever away, but yes, we'd love to join you then. Christmas 1968. Oh dear that sounds such a long time into the future."

"It'll be here before you know it," said Stella, topping up her gin with tonic water. "But you must come back before then, anyway. How about for Frank and Dorothy's last night? I should imagine once they've found buyers then the new people will want to be in by Christmas, so it probably won't be that far away."

George put his arms around the shoulders of his wife. "That sounds a good idea and if it's on a Saturday evening then we can leave straight after work on the Friday and travel overnight as the roads will be a lot quieter then. But we'll only be able to stay for the weekend as we'll have to be back for work on Monday morning, unless of course it falls at the beginning of half-term."

Rose smiled. "That is a lovely idea; I should definitely like to be here for that, but I don't think it will be a very happy occasion. In fact I should think most people will be downright miserable."

"I hardly know anyone in here tonight," said Stella, trying to brighten things up. "The locals are far outnumbered by holiday makers."

"There are quite a few locals in the other bar," said Ned. "Down at the far end. It's just that you can't see them from where you're sitting."

"Does anyone know who that chap is sitting near the door over there?" asked Rose, nodding her head in the direction of the person in question. "I know his face for some reason but I can't think where on earth I've seen him before."

Ned shook his head. "He's not local. Not from Trengillion, anyway, I'd put money on that. But I've seen him around here recently so he's probably staying in the village."

"It's not from here I think I know his face. Oh, this is so annoying, I'll not be able to sleep tonight now for trying to work out where I've seen him before."

As they each made suggestions as to possible locations where Rose might have seen the stranger causing her dilemma, Sally entered the snug looking for empty glasses. To keep Rose happy, Ned asked the identity of the man puzzling her.

"Oh him," replied Sally in a hushed voice. "That's Edward Tucker. He's staying here at the Inn but doesn't say a great deal unless it's to ask question; he doesn't mix with people much either. I think he's a bit odd and we're sure his hair is a wig."

Stella smiled. "Why do you think that? His hair looks perfectly natural to me."

Sally quickly glanced over her shoulder and then continued. "Oh yeah, his hair looks natural enough but it's not the same colour as his eyebrows. Take a closer look when you next pass him and you'll see they're very fair, almost white, whereas his hair is very dark, nearly black."

"He probably dyes it," said Ned. "Lots of chaps do now, don't they, George?"

"Well, maybe he does," said Sally. "But I think if he was going grey his hair would be thinner."

Rose looked puzzled. "But surely you don't consider someone to be odd just because they dye their hair or wear a wig."

Sally giggled. "No, of course not. We think he's odd, or at least I think he's odd, because he watches people all the time and continually looks over his shoulder. I've even seen him jump once or twice when voices have been raised or when the Inn door has opened, noisy like."

"Where's he from?" asked George.

Sally glanced back at Edward Tucker who was listening to the singing. "Up London, but that's all we do know about him. He's pleasant enough, polite and all that, but there's definitely something troubling him."

"Perhaps he's on the run," grinned Ned facetiously, "and he's a criminal of some kind. There you are, Rose, you've probably seen him on a Wanted poster in one of your police stations."

The colour drained from Sally's face. "Oh, no, you don't think so, do you? Has he been acting odd tonight?"

Rose laughed. "No, not at all, poor chap, he's hardly spoken to a soul. It's just that I feel I know his face from somewhere, and if he's from London then there's a slight possibility I've seen him somewhere there, but I don't think it was on a Wanted poster. And London is a big place so I don't think I'd remember his face from just passing him by in the street. Perhaps he's been on the television, but then if he had you'd all recognise him too."

Sally picked up four empty glasses. "Well, sorry I've not been much help. I'd better get back to work as I see another load of people have just walked in."

"She's a lovely girl," said Ned, watching Sally scurry back into the public bar. "She's a credit to Fred and Annie. Jamie's a nice lad too. I hope our girls turn out as well as them."

"Of course they will," said Stella. "Once they get past the adolescence stage. It can't be easy growing up in these liberated times. Oh, shush listen, this is one of my favourite songs, it's saucy but it always makes me laugh."

Behind the bar, Sally washed the glasses she had collected and then reached for a tea towel to dry them. On finding both towels were very damp she slipped away from the sink to fetch clean ones from the drawer in the kitchen. As she walked along the passage the phone rang. Sally picked up the receiver and was asked by a politely spoken, but loud man, if Fred Short was in.

Sally replied in her best telephone voice. "Yes, he is. If you'll just hang on for a moment, I'll go and fetch him."

Sally found Freddie sitting outside in the dark with a group of young people staying at Cove Cottage. All were quietly singing folk songs in the light of a candle burning inside a jam jar. Accompanying them was a bearded, ginger headed man strumming a guitar. When she told Freddie of the phone call he thanked her and quickly dashed inside the Inn. Sally followed for she still had fresh tea towels to fetch, but when she heard Freddie speaking she was very surprised and something made her hide in the dining room doorway and listen to his conversation. For Freddie was not speaking in his usual manner, his voice was soft, cultured and devoid of the laid-back hippie jargon everyone associated him with. Furthermore, the words he spoke sounded serious, and intuition told Sally he was receiving instructions, although she had no idea what they might be. Sally continued to listen, mesmerised by his words, until he put down the receiver and returned to the bar tapping his fingers along the top of the dado rail as he went.

As soon as Sally heard the bar door close indicating the coast was clear, she ran to the kitchen, grabbed two tea towels from the drawer and turned to dash back to the hallway eager to return to her duties before Frank or Dorothy noticed her over-long absence. But in her mad rush she failed to check the passage was clear and outside the kitchen door she collided heavily with Edward Tucker who was loitering at the foot of the stairs. The impact caused him to stumble and fall backwards onto the floor. Apologising profusely Sally helped him to his feet and asked if he was hurt. He informed her he was fine. She smiled sweetly to hide her amusement for without doubt his hair was a little askew.

Sally returned to the bar, shaken but relieved no bones had been broken, and as she dried glasses and returned them to the shelves, she pondered over the conversation she had heard. She decided, however, to say nothing, as Frank and Dorothy might not approve of her spying and eavesdropping on their guests. She put the last glass on the shelf. Frank was pulling a pint for Sid Reynolds and Dorothy was busy pouring a round of drinks for Ned.

"Oh, Sally be a dear, please," said Dorothy, "and fetch a couple of lemons from the kitchen while I finish off this round, we seem to have got through rather a lot of it tonight."

Sally nodded. Still feeling a little unsteady, she was glad of a chance to escape the noise and heat.

She left the bar and returned to the hallway but paused when she heard the voice of a man speaking in hushed tones. She tip-toed down the passage and peeped around the corner. Edward Tucker was now on the phone and talking very quietly. She crouched down afraid to let herself be seen as she tried to get the gist of the one way conversation. "Well, look into what I've told you and while you're about it find out what you can about Fred Short and I'll try and do the same at my end. That call I heard him make tonight makes me think he might be onto something and I want to know if he's one of us. Can't let him get in first. I'll ring you tomorrow."

He then slipped up the stairs and into his room.

"Gran," said Anne to Molly, who was babysitting. "Do you think Elizabeth's skirt's too short? Dad says it is."

"Well, it is a little on the short side, but then that's the fashion so she's not the only one exposing a lot of bare leg. You ought to sit a bit more elegantly though, Elizabeth. It's not very ladylike to lay sprawled out over the chair's arms as you are."

"But I always sit like this" said Elizabeth, attempting to pull down her skirt as she peeled an orange. "It's the only way I can get comfortable. Anyway, I once saw you sitting with your feet in the chair, Gran, and you'd got your slippers on too."

"Yes, but you wouldn't have been able to see my knickers whilst I did so, which is just as well as they're probably much the same size as your skirt."

Both girls giggled causing Molly quickly to change the subject.

"Your mother told me you've painted a picture of Penwynton House, Anne. Would you care to show it to me?"

Anne jumped up. "Yes, I'll go and fetch it." She eagerly left the room and ran up the stairs.

"It's not very good," said Elizabeth, scornfully. "So don't get too excited, Gran."

"Elizabeth, don't run down your sister's efforts. You should encourage her more. She looks up to you and you're very lucky to have a sister. I was an only child and I'd have loved someone to share things with."

"Humph, that's what Dad says, but she's so annoying and babyish. Really, she drives me mad and Mum and Dad always make such a fuss of her."

"She's growing up fast, dear. And once she starts at Grammar school she'll develop even faster. Then you'll look upon her as an equal and I hope a friend as well as a sister. You're very lucky, you just don't realise it."

Anne entered the room waving a folder full of her work. She placed it on the table, removed the picture of Penwynton House and then lay it down on her grandmother's lap. Molly picked it up.

"This is really very good, Anne. I've only ever seen the old house once and that was when we all went there for the auction, but there's no doubt that anyone who had seen it would recognise it from your picture. Well done!"

"That auction was dreadful," sneered Elizabeth. "At least the things that Mum and Dad bought are. I mean, look at that awful desk thing, it's so old fashioned, it's embarrassing. I have to tell my friends it'll be worth a fortune one day so they don't laugh at it. And as if that's not bad enough, upstairs in Mum and Dad's room they have this grotty chaise lounge thing. It looks like it came out the Ark, but thankfully my friends don't ever go in there so they won't see it."

Molly laughed. "But Chy-an-Gwyns is full of beautiful old furniture, so Gregory and Lillian wouldn't laugh, and I'm sure your other friends in the village wouldn't either."

"Well, no, but I wasn't thinking so much about them as Marianne at school. Her parents have a brand new house, you see, and all the furniture is brand new and modern. We *all* envy her, she's *so* lucky. Dad's such a square. He says modern furniture is rubbish and held together with staples. Well, maybe it is but at least it looks really cool."

"Would you like to see the rest of my paintings, Gran?" asked Anne eagerly.

"Of course, dear," said Molly, holding out her hand.

Anne passed the folder to Molly who went through the pictures one by one.

"They're lovely, Anne. Very realistic. You've obviously inherited your mother's keen eye and artistic talents."

Near the bottom of the pile Molly came across the picture of a man with longish hair tucked behind his big ears. "So who's this?" she asked, trying to identify the face. "I don't think it's anyone I know."

"Oh you won't know him because he's no-one in particular," said Anne, quickly, forgetting she had done a sketch of the mysterious stranger and not wishing to explain the incident in the woods. "I was just doodling. Would you like me to paint a picture of your cottage? It always looks so pretty, especially in the summer."

"I would like that very much," said Molly, moving on to the next picture. "Meanwhile keep this painting of Penwynton House in a safe place because after it's sold it might look very different."

"Who do you think will buy it, Gran?" asked Anne, as she gathered her art work and returned it to the folder. "We're hoping it'll be Danny Jarrams. Do you think it will be?"

Molly smiled. "What, that handsome young chap in Gooseberry Pie? I very much doubt it, sweetheart, but you can always dream that he will. In fact you can get anything you want in dreams."

"Do you still dream about things you want then, Gran?" asked Elizabeth, thinking her grandmother's words sounded as though she might be about to burst into song. "I mean, you must have most of the things you want by now."

Molly nodded. "Yes, I have, and I'm very grateful for that. All I want now is for you all to be happy and live long, healthy and useful lives and to be kind to others. Which reminds me, are your mum and dad taking you to the Barn Dance tomorrow? It is after all for a very good cause."

"Mum's taking us," said Elizabeth, "but Dad doesn't want to go even though Mum's bought him a ticket, so I expect he'll make an excuse and stay at home or go down the pub."

"He doesn't want to go!" spluttered Molly, aghast. "Well, I shall have to have words with him when they all get back from the Inn. Why, even the major's going."

CHAPTER TEN

On Saturday morning, as Dorothy said goodbye to the Browns who had reached the end of their week's stay at the Inn, she heard the frivolous laughter of women on the landing above, hence, immediately after the door closed following the departure of her guests, she turned with intrigue to see who was responsible for the high spirits. She was surprised, therefore, when the Gibson sisters descended the staircase in a waft of strong perfume. Dorothy, mesmerised by the transformation of the two dowdy girls, was overwhelmed with admiration over their bold efforts and felt compelled to say so.

"My, how glamorous you both look. I wouldn't have even recognised you had I bumped into you in the street. You're beautiful and very colourful."

Lynne giggled. "Thank you, Dorothy."

"Yes, thank you" said Sharon as she searched through her handbag for the car keys. "It's very sweet of you to be so complimentary."

"Not at all. I really mean it, and I hope you'll both have a lovely day. The weather's certainly on your side. Hot although I noticed earlier there's quite a fresh wind blowing."

Lynne pulled at the hem of her dress in case Dorothy was comparing her legs with those of her sister. "Oh bother, if it's windy we might have to hold on to our hats."

"You will, but it'll be worth it because as well as being very attractive fashion accessories, the wide brims will also protect your faces from the sun." Dorothy looked at her watch. "So, what time is the wedding?"

Lynne caught sight of her reflection in the mirror and smiled, the image pleased her. "Twelve o'clock. It's at the Lizard. We've not been down before, but we've looked at the map and think we've allowed plenty of time."

"You should be alright as long as you don't get stuck behind a tractor. That can be a bit of a nuisance, especially this time of the year, and the roads to the Lizard are very bendy in places."

"Right, we'd better go then," said Sharon closing her handbag with car keys in her hand. "It'd be really embarrassing if we were to arrive late at the church."

Dorothy opened the door for the girls and watched as they walked past her. "You've done the right thing choosing to wear thin frocks. Everyone in a suit will be sweltering hot today."

"They will, won't they?" giggled Lynne, as they waved and dashed towards the car.

"Good old, Dorothy," said Sharon, as she climbed into the driver's seat. "She's given us a reason to have changed our outfits. Now if word should get back one way or another to Mum about our dresses, we can say the weather forecast predicted a very hot day and we couldn't face getting hot and sticky in our thick suits, which were after all bought years ago for a winter wedding."

Lynne half smiled. "I wish I could share your optimism but knowing Auntie Beat and Uncle Cecil will be at the wedding has rather spoiled it for me."

As they drove through the village they passed The School House where Ned was helping George load up his car with luggage. On the garden path, Rose was saying goodbye to Stella.

"Oh God, it's going to be awfully hot stuck in the car all day," groaned Rose. "Especially if we get held up in traffic."

"Well, you could always stay for another couple of days," said Stella, "and hope the weather cools down in the meantime. That way you'd be able to go to the Barn Dance too."

"That's awfully sweet of you but we really must get back as I have to be back at work on Monday morning. Still, never mind, perhaps it's just Cornwall where the weather is hot."

"Blimey, that was a lucky escape for you," whispered Ned to George. "You nearly got roped into the wretched Barn Dance just then."

George grinned. "I shall think of you doing the Dosey Doe when we get back home. We'll probably go and see *You Only Live Twice* tonight, that's if it's still on in the cinemas. But if it's not then I'm sure we'll find something else to suit our tastes."

As George and Rose drove off, Cyril Penrose came up the hill from Long Acre Farm on a tractor pulling a trailer loaded with bales of straw. Its destination, the village hall.

"Oh no, tell me I don't have to sit on one off those ghastly things," groaned Ned, as he watched it drive by. "They're alright for kids but I would have thought adults would prefer something more comfortable."

"Like the sofa here or the seating in the pub?" Stella snapped. "Really, Ned, if you really don't want to go to the Barn Dance, then please don't go. Because if you're going to moan all the time I'd rather you stayed at home, anyway. What's happened to your enthusiasm for community spirit? You're usually very keen and supportive of fund raising events."

"I don't like dancing," said Ned, flatly. "You know that. Perhaps I'll go and show my face and then slip down to the Inn to keep Frank company. Should be nice and quiet down there with all the cackling women competing with each other as to who is the best dancer."

After lunch, Ned walked through the lichgate into the churchyard clutching a pair of garden shears and a bunch of brightly coloured dahlias picked from his mother's garden. As he ambled along the gravel path he was aware that someone else was in the churchyard, a woman he had never seen before. She was walking slowly along the rows of graves and thoughtfully reading the headstones. Ned knelt down, quickly trimmed the fresh growth of grass on Reg's grave and replaced the faded asters, put by Rose during her stay, with the dahlias. When the task was completed, he stood to admire his handy work. The woman was near to him. She smiled sweetly.

"It's very beautiful here. Did you grow the dahlias yourself?"

"Ned laughed. "Good heavens, no, I don't have green fingers. They were grown by my mother."

"They're beautiful. I love flowers and gardens, and this churchyard is very much like a garden, is it not? I don't recall ever seeing one quite so neat and tidy. The sexton here must be very conscientious."

Ned was overcome with pride. "Thank you on behalf Arthur Bray our sexton and campanologist. I'll pass on your compliment when next I see him."

"Please do." She looked up at the trees, swaying beneath the fast moving clouds and the pastel blue sky. It's so peaceful here, one feels one must speak in hushed tones so as not to drown the gentle murmur of the sea and the sweet songs of the birds. As Dorothy Frances Blomfield Gurney so eloquently put it: *One is nearer God's heart in a garden than anywhere else on earth.* Do you not agree?"

Ned smiled, amused by her poetic nature. "Yes, and I used to know someone with similar sentiments, about gardens, that is. But sadly she's no longer with us."

"Oh dear, and who was that?" asked the stranger, her head gently tilted to one side.

"Sylvia, she used to be landlady at the Inn; she was Frank's first wife. Frank's the Inn's landlord, in case you didn't know."

A broad smile crossed the stranger's face. "Yes, I know to whom you refer, the gentleman and I are acquainted. And are those flowers for the lady in question?" She waved her hand in the direction of Reg's grave where the dahlias nodded beneath the headstone on which she was unable to read the inscription due to the angle at which she stood.

"No, no, this is the grave of a friend. Sylvia's not buried here. Her ashes are scattered up on the cliff tops beside the old mine." Ned's face reddened. He felt uncomfortable discussing Sylvia with a complete stranger.

The stranger sensed his mood and held out her hand. "My name is Catherine Rossiter and I'm staying here until Christmas in the house on the cliff top."

With a smile, Ned took her hand. "Chy-an-Gwyns. You must know the Castor-Hunts, then. They're good friends of mine and my family."

"I don't know them very well at all, they're really acquaintances of my husband, but I have met them once or twice. I take it you live here then. But you're not Cornish, are you?"

Ned laughed. "No, I'm not Cornish, but I do live here and I'm very lucky to have the job as the village school's headmaster."

"Really, how nice. I would imagine teaching young children is very rewarding."

"It is," said Ned, glad the topic of their conversation had changed. "I teach the juniors and the infants are taught by Meg Reynolds who is a good friend of mine, both inside and out of school."

"Oh, I see," smiled Catherine. "That sounds conveniently cosy."

"No, no," gabbled Ned, realising she had misinterpreted his remark. "Meg and I really are just good friends. I'm married and have two daughters and Meg is married too with a son and a daughter. Her husband works on the local newspaper."

Ned was intrigued when he heard Catherine wince. She, however, said nothing but turned and pointed in the direction of the Penwynton graves.

"May I ask who the Penwyntons are? I see from the new headstone that one of them has recently passed away."

Ned nodded. "Sadly the Penwyntons are no more. Charles was the last. He, and they, lived at Penwynton House across the valley and they owned lots of land, several farms and many of the houses in and around Trengillion. I'm afraid I don't really know much more about them than that, and I saw Charles Penwynton only on very rare occasions."

"What a shame. I suppose now the house will be sold."

"Yes, its sale is in the hands of London agents. All the houses on the estate have already gone. Most were bought by the tenants who lived in them."

"Hmm, I think I shall take a look at the house while I am here, I've rather taken a fancy to Cornwall. Not, I'm sure, that we could afford a house as gracious a dwelling as I would imagine Penwynton House to be."

"It's huge as well as gracious," said Ned. "Although I've never been inside. I also hear it's in a very poor state of repair."

"Still worth a look though," smiled Catherine. "I adore large houses, whatever their state of repair."

On Saturday afternoon the children of Trengillion met on Denzil's bench as prearranged where they found Stephen and David Pascoe excitedly holding a brightly coloured kite. It was David's birthday and the kite was a present from his grandparents, Madge and Albert Trelaor of Home Farm.

David leapt from the bench when he saw the others approaching. "Can we go and fly this, please? Dad said he'd help but he can't leave the post office until later cos Mum's having her hair done."

"Yeah, that'd be great," said Graham, "I've not flown a kite for years."

John looked up at the clouds scurrying across the sky. "Not here though, the wind's blowing from the north west so it'll blow it out to sea."

Tony nodded in agreement. "Let's go to the Rec."

John grinned. "Great idea, brother."

The Rec was empty when they arrived and so while the boys prepared the kite for flight the girls each took a swing.

The kite, in colours of red, white and blue, its pattern that of the nation's flag, flapped and fluttered above their heads, its long tail swishing and swirling behind. The girls stopped their swings and watched as David, with Tony guiding his hands, controlled the long string. The rest of the boys sat on the motionless roundabout.

After a while the kite took a nose-dive and collided with the top of the slide. Elizabeth who was nearest the slide ran up the iron steps and released the tangled string from the safety rail at the top. As the kite fell to the ground, John nudged Tony, watching Elizabeth as she sat on top of the slide ready to take the easy route down. Susan noticed. "Hey, what are you two up to?"

They both laughed. "You'll see."

Elizabeth unaware of the mutterings below let go of the frame. The girls stared in amazement as Elizabeth, screaming, whizzed down the slide at an amazing pace, flew off the end and landed on her bottom several feet from the end of the slide. In a daze she picked herself up and brushed grass from her skirt. "What on earth's happened there?"

"Dunno," said Tony, grinning from ear to ear. "Perhaps somebody polished it."

"Polished it," repeated Jane. "Who on earth would do that?"

Tony put his hand inside the pocket of his jeans and pulled out the stub of a worn down candle.

"You," laughed Susan, "I might have known. When did you do that?"

Tony pushed the candle back into his pocket. "Last night. Mum's got a bag of old candles under the sink which she keeps in case of power cuts in the winter. I got the idea from a mate at school who'd done the same in his local rec. It's a hundred times better than it was before. Isn't that right, Liz?"

Elizabeth frowned. "Yes, I'm sure it would be if you're prepared to travel at a hundred miles an hour."

John gave her a quick hug. "We're sorry if your landing was a little hard but your face was a picture. I wish I'd had a camera with me."

While they were talking Graham and Matthew, both eager to try out the slide, climbed to the top and Matthew who was in the lead, was preparing for take-off when Graham nudged him. "Look down there in the hedge. What do you reckon that bloke's doing?"

Graham peered towards the boundary of the Vicarage. "Search me. Bird nesting perhaps."

"What, in August! Don't be daft."

"Well, perhaps he's lost something."

As he spoke the man pulled back from the hedge and in doing so caught his hair on a twig and to the amazement of the boys his hair was ripped from his head.

"Christ, he's been scalped," said Graham, beckoning to the others to climb the slide to witness the spectacle. Crammed together on the slide, eleven children gazed, open mouthed as the man plucked his detached hair from the bush and placed it neatly back on his head.

Sharon and Lynne Gibson drove back into Trengillion just after ten o'clock; both were in very high spirits following several flutes of champagne and numerous glasses of port and lemon. They slowed down as they passed the village hall, their attention taken by the loud music, rhythmic clapping and laughter emanating from the Barn Dance, indicating the event was still in full swing.

Outside, sitting on a bench, Freddie Short sat smoking a cigarette, deep in conversation with fisherman, Percy Collins.

Sharon tooted. Lynne, exuberant, because Cousin Phillip had called her 'Gorgeous', shouted, and both waved from the swerving, swaying car. Freddie, amused by the antics of the clearly inebriated sisters, waved back.

The Inn was fairly quiet as Sharon parked the car in a higgledy-piggledy manner on the cobbled area in front. As she stumbled from the car she cast a quick glance around to make sure the village bobby was not on patrol, for it suddenly occurred to her that she'd had far too much to drink.

"Looks like nearly everyone's gone from the Inn already," giggled Lynne, peeping through the window of the public bar. "Look, there's only a handful of people in there and they're all the boring old timers."

"Well, they said it'd be quiet tonight," slurred Sharon, propping herself up on the window ledge beside her sister. "All the locals must be at the Barn Dance cos they were making an awful row, weren't they? And if you remember, even Dorothy said she was going."

Lynne removed her high-heeled shoes to avoid their heels slipping between the cobbles. "That Barn Dance sounded nearly as much fun as the wedding."

Sharon giggled. "The wedding was fab, wasn't it? And I shall never forget seeing Auntie Beat and Uncle Cecil dancing the Conga, legs kicking and all. They were nearly the life and soul of the party."

"Auntie Beat was sloshed if you ask me."

"Hmm, she was. Any idea what she was drinking?"

"Cherry B. I was taking pictures near the bar when Uncle Cecil was buying drinks, that's how I know."

Sharon patted her sister's handbag. "I hope the pictures you took come out. Not that we shall show the ones of Auntie Beat to Mum, cos we promised. Fancy her wearing a suit with a skirt short enough to show her knees. She must be in her sixties now."

"She's sixty one cos she's five years younger than Mum. Anyway, we'll be able to show Mum the pictures of Auntie Beat where the length of her skirt doesn't show. It's only fair."

With arms linked the sisters teetered across the cobbles. When they reached a flat area and the side door of the Inn they crept inside and closed the door making as little noise as possible. Not an easy task considering the state they were in.

"We must keep very, very quiet," Lynne tittered, licking her red port-stained lips, "or we might wake the Brown children."

Sharon sat down at the first tread of the stairs and giggled. "We'd have to make a lotta racket to do that, silly. They went home this morning so they're millions and millions of miles away by now."

Lynne slapped her hand across her mouth to stifle a laugh. "Oh yeah, I'd forgotten that, but we still must be quiet cos Pauline Pringle always goes to bed early."

Sharon unsteadily rose to her feet. "Yes, but she might not be here cos she's probably gone to the Barn Dance."

Lynne frowned. "Doubt it. I can't imagine Pauline dancing, unless your darling Freddie insisted she went and took her. But she wasn't with him when we saw him just now, was she?"

They reached the top of the stairs without causing a disturbance and crept along the passage towards their room. Outside the door, Sharon took the key from her handbag and pushed it onto the lock, but as she turned the handle both girls jumped, startled by muffled noises which appeared to emanate from Freddie Short's room.

Shushing her sister to remain still and quiet, Sharon put down her bag on the floor and tip-toed along to the end of the passage. Outside Freddie's door she lowered her head and listened, attempting to identify the cause of the sounds, for both girls, having seen Freddie outside the village hall, knew he was not inside. After listening briefly, Sharon, none the wiser, returned to Lynne's side. With fingers to lips, the sisters slipped into their own room afraid to speak.

"It sounds a bit like someone opening and closing drawers," whispered Sharon, kicking off her new shoes.

Lynne removed her hat and wearily sat down on her bed. "Phew, that's a relief. I had a sudden image of a scantily dressed female handcuffed to the bedrail."

Sharon giggled. "You never know, that still might be the case, but then no, the noises definitely sounded like drawers opening and closing."

"But it couldn't be drawers. I mean, if it was, what on earth could anyone be looking for?"

Sharon shrugged her shoulders. "Money, do you suppose?"

"Hmm, possibly but I reckon it's more likely to be drugs."

Sharon reached for her bag of toiletries. "I think I'll go along to the bathroom and clean my teeth, but I'll leave the door slightly ajar so if anyone goes by I'll see them. Meanwhile, you stay here and keep watch through our keyhole."

Lynne nodded. "Alright, but if I had to make a bet I'd say he's got a woman in there."

"You could be right and she was probably looking for the handcuffs."

Lynne gasped. "No, do you think so?"

Sharon shook her head. "No, because he wouldn't have left her on her own if he had. Especially to go to a barn dance."

"Maybe it's his mum."

"Even more improbable."

A look of horror crossed Lynne's face. "I bet it's a ghost. There must be hundreds of floating around in an old place like this."

Sharon turned pale. "A ghost! Yes, of course. It'll be the ghost of Gill Claudebert or whatever he was called. You remember we heard Freddie telling that headmaster chap and his friends about him. He said there was a picture of him on the wall and he died in there. It's bound to be him."

Lynne wrinkled her nose and sighed. "Yeah, but a ghost wouldn't open and close drawers, would it? I mean to say, there couldn't possibly be anything inside them that a ghost would want."

"Phew, yes, you're right. We're over reacting. He must have a dog."

"A dog! No, we'd have seen it if he had, and we'd have heard it bark. I mean, we've been here a week now. Anyway, dogs can't open drawers."

Both girls fell onto the floor laughing at the image of a dog on hind legs going through Freddie's unconventional clothing, but their laughter promptly ceased when they heard the click of Freddie's door open and then close. Without speaking, they fell to their knees and crawled across the carpeted floor towards their door. Together, holding their breath, they quietly opened the door and nervously peeped into the dimly lit passage, just in time to glimpse a figure dash into one of the other rooms. The sisters looked at each other in disbelief. For without doubt, the person they saw was quiet, unassuming, Edward Tucker.

CHAPTER ELEVEN

On Monday morning, after her children had gone out for the day, Gertie left her house in Coronation Terrace and set off for the walk up to Chy-an-Gwyns to start her new job. Mrs Rossiter had agreed to pay her three shillings and sixpence an hour, which Gertie considered a generous sum as the job would not entail any heavy work, just dusting, vacuuming and general tidying up. She would not be required to make up fires in the colder months, or clean bedrooms as Mrs Rossiter and her friend would look after their own rooms, neither was she expected to clean windows inside or out, so Gertie felt she had fallen on her feet and the job would be money for old rope. What's more, she liked Mrs Rossiter from the very first moment she met her when she had nervously walked up to Chy-an-Gwyns to ask about the job.

When she arrived at the house she went to the back door as instructed and let herself in. She found Mrs Rossiter in the kitchen making up a tray of tea, grapefruit, and buttered toast.

"Good morning, Gertie, you can start where you want and plan your own routine, but I'll ask you on this occasion not to vacuum for a little while. Margaret arrived late last night and she's not yet up, so I don't want her disturbed by unnecessary noise before she's had time to wake properly."

"Of course," said Gertie, hanging her jacket on the back of the kitchen door. "I'll leave the vacuuming 'til last. Is Margaret your friend?"

"Yes, and the poor dear has not been well of late. I think the drive down was probably a little too much for her but she insisted on doing it and she's old enough to make decisions and look after herself."

Gertie grinned. "I'll start in the bathroom if that's alright with you, Mrs Rossiter."

"Oh please, Gertie, do call me Catherine. Would you like a cup of tea before you start, there's one in the pot."

"Yes please. It's thirsty work walking all the way up here. Still, hopefully it'll have burned up a few bloomin' calories."

"Dad," said Elizabeth in a voice which Ned knew meant she was about to ask for something. "Dad, do you think I could have a pop magazine every week? It'd only cost a shilling and it'd make me really, really happy."

"Would it," said Ned, carelessly. "And what's in this particular magazine that would make you so happy?"

"Oh, everything," said Elizabeth, with enthusiasm. "Lots and lots of coloured pictures of the grooviest groups, and news of the latest fashions, plus all sorts of other useful things."

Ned smothered a smile. "So what's this fantastic magazine called?"

"*Fabulous 208*. The 208 bit is to do with the frequency of Radio Luxemburg."

"I see, but surely if this magazine means so much to you, you could buy it with your pocket money."

Elizabeth shook her head. "I would but I'm saving up for a real suede skirt and I still need another thirty shillings to buy it."

"That's fair enough, but if you have a magazine then Anne will want one too."

Elizabeth knelt by Ned's chair and clasped her hands. "No she won't because she can read mine when I've finished with it. Oh, Dad, please, please say yes."

"Alright, but you must sort it out. Go and see Mr or Mrs Pascoe at the post office and get umm, Fabulous whatever added to our order."

"Thanks, Dad, you're the best," said Elizabeth, jumping to her feet and hugging him tight. "Now all I need is for Mum to wear her skirts shorter and for you to grow your hair and then everything will be just perfect."

"I'm not growing my hair, young lady," spluttered Ned, running his hand over his head. "And your mother's skirts are quite short enough, thank you very much."

"But, Dad, your hairstyle is so square and don't say you're too old to have more hair because Susan's dad has long hair and he's about the same age as you."

"Actually, Percy Collins is a few years younger than me, furthermore, he's always had long hair. At least he has for as long as

I've known him. So with him it's not a fashion statement, just personal preference."

"But couldn't you grow it just a teeny-weeny bit?" pleaded Elizabeth. "Please!"

"No," said Ned. "And if you still want that magazine you must stop harassing me, now."

Elizabeth gasped and left the room mumbling an incoherent 'sorry'. When Ned heard her bedroom door close he rose and looked in the mirror. As he was doing so Stella entered the room, returning from outside where she had been hanging out the washing.

"What's the matter, Ned?" she asked, hooking her peg bag on the back of the pantry door. "You've a puzzled look on your brow."

"Hmm, nothing's wrong but I was just thinking. Oh, I don't know. The thing is, do you think my hair's too short? I mean, does it make me look square?"

Stella laughed. "A little, I suppose, but then you are in your forties now."

"I know, but I don't want the kids at school to think of me as an old fuddy-duddy. I might grow it just a little bit to see what it looks like."

Stella raised her eyebrows. "Have the girls been nagging you by any chance?"

"Good heavens, no," snapped Ned, with unjustified indignation. "Of course not."

"Good, because as you always say, we can't be dictated to by the younger generation. Now, if you'll excuse me I must get on with my chores. I've a busy sewing day ahead of me as I think it's time the hemlines of my skirts and dresses went up an inch or two."

"Did any of you have the News on tonight?" asked Gertie, as she hastily removed her coat and hung it on the back of a chair in the village hall on Tuesday evening.

Meg nodded. "I did and I bet you're going to comment on Maggie Nan's kidnapping."

"Oh, what's the latest, then?" asked Stella, sitting beside Meg. "I missed the News tonight because I was in the bath. Has anything exciting happened?"

Gertie sat down with her copy of the play on her lap. "The police think it's genuine and so does her gorgeous husband, cos a television company in the States has received a ransom note from her kidnappers demanding fifty thousand dollars in used notes. Can you imagine that amount of money?"

Betty joined in. "And her husband is flying out there to get the ransom money sorted. I saw it too."

Stella laughed. "I bet Rose is over the moon. She loves anything like this and just couldn't believe it when Ned and I told her we didn't even know Maggie had had a face lift."

Joyce Richardson tut-tutted. "Oh dear. When I saw it I guessed that story would have you all going tonight. Now I expect if any of you have learned your words then they'll have gone clean out of your heads."

"I've learned mine," said Sally, with pride. "Mum's been testing me on them all week."

"Well done. How about the rest of you? It's nearly September, you know, so we only have about six weeks until the concert."

Everyone else sheepishly confessed they didn't know their words and all made excuses about no peace due to the school holidays and noisy children all over the place.

Joyce smothered a smile. "Alright, you can use your books tonight, but it's the last time. Next week you must do without and I'll get Doris to come along and prompt. I've twisted my husband's arm and he'll knock us up a stage again. How are the backdrops coming along, Stella?"

"I've finished one, but I'm finding street scene a bit difficult. I drew the shops too big then couldn't fit them all in so I've had to start that one again, but I think I have it sussed now."

"Excellent, then I think if we're all here, ladies, it's time we made a start."

Since the Barn Dance, Dorothy had patiently waited to see Pauline Pringle step into the bar with a new hair-do, and thus far she had resisted the temptation to satisfy her curiosity by asking Betty for when Pauline had made an appointment. For to do so would probably entail admitting to Betty that that particular prize had been fixed and she and Molly had agreed that it must be kept secret for all time otherwise no-one in Trengillion would ever trust them with a draw again. By Wednesday, Dorothy was getting a little concerned, Pauline was due to go home the following Saturday and if she left her transformation much longer then she and Molly would not be able to witness the change it would make to the middle-aged spinster's life.

On Thursday afternoon, Dorothy's hopes were raised. As she fried onions in the pan in preparation for the evening's casserole, she heard someone walking down the stairs. Simultaneously another person entered the Inn through the side door. Leaving the cooker, she stepped across the kitchen floor to eavesdrop on the muffled voices of the guests as they met in the hallway. To her delight she believed one voice was Pauline. The other, without question, was Freddie. Dorothy strained her ears to listen but much to her dismay was unable to make out any of the conversation. She was, however, able to confirm Pauline's identity by her girlish laughter, no doubt in response to Freddie's deep, cheerful banter. After the voices had faded, and the two persons had gone their separate ways, Dorothy stepped out into the hallway. A huge grin stretched across her face, for without doubt, the strong scent of shampoo and hair lacquer lingered in the air. Dorothy was ecstatic and rubbed her hands with glee, there was no question as to who the persons in the hallway had been. Pauline had obviously just returned from the hairdressers and Freddie was leaving the Inn for Penzance where he was going to see some band or other. Dorothy knew of Freddie's movements because he had told Alice at breakfast that he would not be in for dinner. Delighted that her plan had worked she picked up the phone to ring Molly to report mission accomplished.

When she arrived for work, Alice was delighted to find Dorothy in a very ebullient mood, although she had no idea of the reason behind the high spirits. She was, however, a little surprised by the continuous barrage of questions each time she returned from the dining room regarding the guest's welfare. Do they all seem happy? Are they all there? Is Miss Pringle looking well? Alice was baffled and informed Dorothy that the guests were all fine, as usual. Dorothy was annoyed. Alice must be blind, either that or she was so wrapped up in her own life that she could not see further than the end of her nose.

When the evening meal was over and the clearing up done, Dorothy hastily washed and changed ready for an evening on the bar with Frank. Normally there would be no rush as Frank always employed an extra pair of hands during the height of the holiday season to enable Dorothy to take her time and even have a short rest if she so desired. She found the bar busy as she eagerly cast her eyes around looking for Pauline. Pauline, however, was nowhere to be seen. But then Dorothy heard her laugh emanating from the snug. Dorothy cursed, for she could not see in the snug from behind the bar.

"I'll just pop out and collect a few glasses," she casually said to Frank. "I can see quite a few empties."

With haste she slipped out from behind the bar and headed for the snug, but as she passed through the double doors she stopped dead. Pauline was there as expected and talking to the Gibson sisters, but her hair was just the same, mousy, greyish brown, straw like and pulled back tight in a hideous pony tail. To say Dorothy was disappointed would be an understatement. Her jaw dropped as she carelessly picked up a few empty glasses from the window sill. Without doubt, Pauline's hair had been washed, for it shone a little in the light from the lamp near to her head.

Dorothy wandered back behind the bar in a state of confused bewilderment and poured hot water into the sink to wash the glasses. Pauline must have had her hair done and then when she got back to the Inn, decided she preferred her old style and yanked it back in that hideous elastic band. Dorothy muttered beneath her breath. "What a stupid, silly woman!"

"Are you alright, Dot?" asked Frank as he watched the glasses crashing around in the sink. "Someone's not upset you, have they?"

"No, not exactly. It's Pauline. Have you seen her hair?"

Frank frowned. "Well, yes, but I didn't notice anything different about it. Are you cross cos she hasn't had it done yet?"

"That's just it. She has had it done, Frank. I heard her come back from the hairdressers this afternoon, but she's put it back in her old style. Molly's going to pop in tonight for a peep. She'll not be impressed. That prize could have gone to a much more worthy cause."

A little later Dorothy found the ice bucket nearly empty so went to the kitchen to get some more from the freezer. As she was leaving, the side door of the Inn opened and Freddie waltzed in singing at the top of his voice.

Dorothy stood mouth gaping wide open and stared. But it was not Freddie's singing that surprised her, or his early return from the concert, or his outfit. It was his hair. Still long, but a little less so, and largely increased in volume due to a huge mass of frizzy curls.

"I can see you like my hair, Dot," said Freddie, twirling around and patting his head. "Isn't it fab? Betty did it for me. She's a real cool chick. Pauline won a prize hair-do at the Barn Dance but she gave it to me cos she has a nasty skin allergy. I paid a bit extra of course because Bet permed it too, but I love it. It's groovy, man, groovy."

Dorothy racked her brain for something appropriate to say, but instead felt a deep desire to laugh. "It looks err, very nice, Freddie. Very nice indeed."

CHAPTER TWELVE

Gertie was standing in her stocking feet on the large dining table in Chy-an-Gwyns flicking one of the two chandeliers with a feather duster and repeating her lines for the play, when she heard a car pull up at the back of the house. Intrigued as to who it might be, she climbed down from the table and peered from the window into the garden where she saw a man whom she did not recognise walking along the path. Puzzled and curious she crept out to the hallway and listened for him to knock. As Catherine answered the door, Gertie peeped around the corner to try and establish the reason for his visit. She watched as the man nodded politely, raised his hat revealing a balding head fringed with dark grey. After replacing his hat he pulled from his pocket a card and showed it to Catherine.

"May I introduce myself?" he said, with a self-confident smile. "My name is Teddy Tinsdale and I would be very grateful if you'd spare me a little of your time for an interview?"

"No," said Catherine, with unreserved vehemence. "No, most certainly not, and if you'll excuse me I'm busy. Please leave and don't trouble me again."

With a crash she slammed shut the door and swore beneath her breath. Gertie was flabbergasted and fled back to the dining room before she was seen, where from behind the curtain she watched the car drive away, and then, just in case Catherine should come in her direction, she leapt back on the table and continued to dust. Catherine, however, went upstairs and Gertie could hear her talking angrily to Margaret in the room above, although it was not possible to make out what was being said. Gertie was puzzled. Who was Teddy Tinsdale? And why on earth did he want to interview Catherine Rossiter?

"I think next time you dye my hair I'll go a shade lighter and then perhaps the grey won't show through quite so much. I can't believe how much the condition of it has improved over the years. As Milly was saying the other day, it's twice as thick as when I first came to live in Trengillion. You're a clever young lady, Betty. I would never have realised that being blonde was detrimental to my hair and brown suits me so much better, anyway."

Betty smiled as she fastened the cape around Madge Treloar's neck. "Thank you, it's always good to hear positive comments from a satisfied customer. Do you want the usual amount trimmed off?"

Madge held out a strand of hair. "Yes please. I'd have left it 'til my next perm but it's just beginning to get to that irritating stage where it looks a bit messy and it's also annoying when I'm outdoors and the wind blows it in my face."

Betty reached for some clips and began to pin up Madge's hair. "Your young grandsons tell me they love helping you out on the farm. I expect you're getting quite busy now."

Madge sighed. "We always seem to be busy. Albert and the lads have started to get the spuds in now while the weather's dry and I've been helping sort the little blighters. I have to wear gloves though. I can't bear getting earth beneath my nails and they get broken easily too. My nails that is, not the spuds. I'm determined not to let age get the better of my appearance, you see. Not that I've ever been much to look at. But I think it's only right that women make the best of their good points and I've always had nice nails and a fairly good complexion, and now, thank goodness, I've a fairly decent figure too. I'd never have a face lift though, not like that silly Maggie Nan woman. Fancy spending all that money on something that makes you look worse. If you ask me, she and her poncey husband must have more money than sense."

Betty smiled. "So, what do you make of the whole business regarding her kidnapping?"

"I think it's utter tosh and her husband is in on the whole thing. It's a big publicity stunt to try and regain her popularity. Not that I ever saw much in her so-called works of art. I like dresses to look like dresses and not like over-elaborate wedding cakes. What do you make of it, Betty?"

"I'm not so sure that I agree with you. Rumour has it that her husband was having affairs all over the place with some of the models he photographs and that he was waiting for the right moment to tell her he wanted a divorce. That's what I read, anyway, and of course if that is the case then he's not going to be involved with a kidnapping plot, is he?"

"Hmm, I'd not heard that bit of gossip. But then if that's the case why has he gone racing off to America to pay the ransom money? Surely having her kidnapped would be the perfect solution for him, if he wanted shot of her."

"He's probably gone because he believes her life is in danger and even though he no longer loves her he doesn't want to see her hurt or worse still, killed."

"That sounds a bit too romantic to me. Still no doubt we'll hear more. But I wouldn't be surprised if she's not living the life of Riley somewhere, enjoying watching the drama unfold on American television."

Bertha Fillingham and May Dickens liked to take a walk together every Friday afternoon providing the weather was favourable, for both were feeling the effects of advancing old-age. Bertha had recently celebrated her seventy fourth birthday and for May her sixtieth was fast approaching. They usually met at the Ringing Bells Inn where they had coffee whilst deciding which route their weekly excursion should take.

"There's hardly a breath of wind today," said May, who lived at Higher Green Farm on the cliff tops not far from the Witches Broomstick. "So we don't have to worry about walking in a sheltered spot. The world is our oyster; we can go anywhere."

Bertha took a seat beside her friend. "Yes, I had noticed and I'm feeling fighting fit. I reckon it must be the vitamin pills Doris recommended. Let's go for a stroll along the coastal path to the old mine, we've not been that way for ages and I really should make the most of my fitness before I'm too damned old."

May patted the hand of her friend. "You'll never be too old. Neither you nor George have aged one bit since you retired down here. How many years is it now? Thirteen?"

"Fifteen," said Bertha. "If you remember we were looking for a place when they found the body of that poor girl, Jane Hunt. That was in either February or March 1952, just after the King died. And then we moved here in the June. George says he never dreamed retirement could be such fun and he's a dab hand at golf now in spite of his gammy leg. Has Pat thought anymore about selling the farm and retiring?"

"Well, he mentions it from time to time, but I think he'll keep going for a few more years yet. Now that Cyril Penrose has said he'll not retire a day before he's seventy it's got Pat feeling he must do the same. But then Cyril's not a dairy farmer so he doesn't have to contend with the early mornings. Not that they bother us that much now, it's become a way of life."

Dorothy entered the bar with two cups of coffee. She smiled. "It always seems to be Friday. So where are you off to today?"

"The cliff path towards the old mine," said May, moving her purse to make way for the cup and saucer, "and then back along the lanes."

"Well, I should take a bag if I were you, I hear there are lots of blackberries around this year, at least there are on our farm according to Madge. She's made several jars of bramble jelly already."

Bertha, produced a large paper bag from her jacket pocket. "I'd already thought of that, but I'm not intending to make anything edible I was thinking about having a go at blackberry wine. Doris made some for the first time last year and she's very pleased with the results, although she said it's not as good as elderberry."

Dorothy chuckled. "Doris and her wine. Jim was in the other evening and he told us he went round to visit her the other day and she got him trying some of her latest concoctions. He said he felt quite drunk when he walked home and it took him twice as long as usual. Poor soul, he was worried Flo might not have approved, but I told him Flo would have been amused. She always had a good sense of humour. God rest her soul. "

Bertha nodded. "Poor Flo. She was the same age as I am now when she died. It makes me wonder how much longer any of us have, but it's just as well we don't know, I suppose."

"I must get back to the kitchen," said Dorothy. "I've started making tonight's dinner and I don't want it sticking to the pan."

She left the bar to return to the kitchen just as Freddie entered the side door of the Inn with wet hair and a towel tucked beneath his arm.

"Hmm, something smells good. So what's for dinner tonight, Dotty?"

Dorothy was taken back. She had never been called Dotty before in her life.

"Err, chicken, bacon and mushroom pie," she stammered.

"Yummy, yummy, my favourite. You're cooking is too good, Dotty. I shall have to go on a crash diet when I get home."

He passed by her and ran up the stairs whistling *All You Need is Love*.

Dorothy grinned to herself and reflected on the contrast there was between the guests of 1967 and those of 1952 when she had first started to work in the Inn.

She returned to the kitchen, stirred the meat and onions in the pan and made a mental note to make sure Freddie had an extra big portion of pie for his dinner. It was after all the last time she would feed the guests apart from breakfast the following day, for already their fortnight's holiday was coming to an end and Dorothy had to admit that of all the guests leaving she would miss Freddie the most.

"I'm sure this cliff path is steeper these days," May panted, as she helped Bertha up a sharp incline.

"Phew, I agree and the policemen nowadays should still be in short trousers. Except Fred, he's the only grown up one left."

"And Dick Remington over Polquillick," said May." He's no chicken either." She stopped to get back her breath. "Let's sit down for a minute on that patch of grass over there behind that rock. We're not in any hurry, are we?"

They left the path, walked towards the edge of the cliff and sat down with their backs against the rock.

"Heaven!" whispered Bertha, closing her eyes. "Who could ask for anything more? I wouldn't swap my life with anyone else in the world."

"Me neither, and it doesn't matter how many times I look out to sea, I just never tire of it. And the smell! I love it!"

Berta nodded. "And the cry of the gulls." She opened her eyes. "But I'm not so keen on those bloomin' things." She pointed in the direction of a helicopter flying along the coast. After it had passed and all was quiet again she took her hands away from her ears.

"Ah, but it would be a very welcome sound to anyone who had the misfortune to be in trouble or have fallen from the cliff path."

Bertha shuddered. "What a horrible thought. You'd have to be pretty careless though to get into such a predicament, wouldn't you? Falling from the cliff path, I mean."

"I suppose so, but there do seem to be a lot of silly folks around these days. Come on, let's make a move before I nod off."

They left their resting place and ambled on past a row of derelict Coastguard cottages and on in the direction of the old mine.

"I hear they've all been bought by a property developer," said May, glancing at the eight forlorn houses. "I expect when they're sold on they'll be holiday homes."

"Yes, but then it wouldn't be very practical to live up here all year round, would it? They're a long way from the shops and the coastal path's a bit slippery in the wet winter months. So they'd be best as holiday homes."

"But they have access from a little lane going through Cyril Penrose's land. You've probably never spotted it before as it's very overgrown. It's only a fifteen minute walk from here to the village, or less if you're fit. Look, the lane leads off from that gate over there."

Bertha put both hands on her hips. "Well, you live and learn. I've never noticed that gate or the lane before and I've always thought of myself as observant."

"All houses on the cliffs have access from somewhere or other," said May. "They'd have needed it for them to have been built in the first place."

"Of course. Silly me. Talking of houses on cliff tops, what's our new neighbour like?"

"New neighbour?" said May, puzzled. "Who do you mean?"

"Mrs Rossiter," said Bertha. "Up at Chy-an-Gwyns. Young Alice Penhaligon reckons she's after Frank cos she always makes a fuss of him when she's goes to the Inn. Have you met her? I haven't."

May smiled. "I've seen her out and about but not to speak to. But I've heard nothing bad about her. Pat's seen her once or twice and he thought she was very nice. He said she's cultured, but then I suppose she would be being married to a Navy captain."

Bertha laughed. "Well, if she's cultured I can't see her making eyes at Frank. Not that there's anything wrong with Frank. In fact a nicer man I couldn't wish to meet, but he's not exactly Richard

Burton, is he? That's the trouble with youngsters today, they read too many silly magazines and it puts daft notions in their heads."

"If Frank was Richard Burton I reckon I'd be an alcoholic by now," laughed May. "Did you see him in *The Sandpiper*? He was gorgeous!"

"I most certainly did. In fact I saw that film twice. Once with George and then again when he was out for the day playing golf. I caught the bus into town and watched a matinee. Of course I never told George, he wouldn't have understood."

"No, men aren't too keen on weepy films, are they?"

Bertha frowned. "No, but going back to Mrs Rossiter, whom I've not even had a glimpse of, I'm told young Milly thinks she's very nice and I know Gertie likes her too. You know she's working up at Chy-an-Gwyns now. Gertie that is, not Milly."

"Is she? No, I didn't know that. What's she doing up there?"

"Just a bit o' charring, but she says it's a doddle as Mrs Rossiter and her companion don't make much mess. In fact Gertie's never even seen her companion."

"Good grief. Talk of the Devil," said May, stopping dead. "That's her. That's Catherine Rossiter, up there by the old mine."

Not wanting Catherine to know of their presence they crept a little closer and hid behind a group of prickly gorse bushes.

"Ouch, what's she saying?" said Bertha, attempting to get comfortable. "I can't hear. Is she talking to herself?"

"I don't know. I can't see anyone else unless they're lying on the ground. And I can't hear what she's saying either."

They watched as Catherine paced back and forth on the cliff top before she finally walked to the cliff edge where she threw up her arms and then started to sing.

Bertha gasped. "She's mad! Normal folks don't do things like that."

May grinned. "Perhaps she's been to see *The Sound of Music*."

"Oh, yes, now that's another good film, and Christopher Plummer can blow his whistle for me any time he wants."

Attempting to suppress the desire to giggle, both women watched as Catherine fell onto her knees and peered over the side of the cliff and onto the waves below.

"Good God! Do you think she's going to jump?" asked Bertha.

"We must startle her and let her know we're here," said May, preparing to rise. But before she was able to stand, Catherine sprang to her feet, brushed grass from her knees and then with a spring in her steps walked off along the track towards the overgrown lane leading back into the village, unaware as she passed the gorse bushes that behind them hid two dumbfounded ladies.

That evening, members of the Drama group assembled in the village hall for another rehearsal. They usually met just once a week on a Tuesday but as Joyce Richardson had been away for a fortnight on holiday, she had asked the ladies to squeeze in an extra rehearsal as they all agreed they needed it.

Gertie felt she was in an awkward predicament. She was desperate to know who Teddy Tinsdale was but could not ask anyone directly because they would want to know why, and she was unwilling to confess to eavesdropping for fear her indiscretion might get back to Catherine. So instead she conjured up a story.

"I was walking to work this morning when a car stopped and the driver asked if I knew whereabouts in the village Teddy Tinsdale was staying. I said I'd no idea. Have any of you lot heard of him? I mean, might he be staying at the Inn, Sally?"

Sally was bent double straightening her tights which had wrinkled around the ankles. "No he's not. I know all the guests and there's definitely no-one of that name amongst them. Having said that he could be one of the new arrivals expected tomorrow."

Gertie frowned. "Oh, and has no-one else heard of him?"

No-one had. Gertie was disappointed but then conceded if he was not staying in the village then he must have come to Trengillion specifically to see Catherine, otherwise he would not have known where she was staying. Gertie was annoyed, she had drawn a blank and knew she would just have to sit back, wait and keep her ears open to see if the name cropped up again.

CHAPTER THIRTEEN

"So, what does it feel like to be able to earn your own money again?" Betty asked, on Saturday morning as Gertie took a seat in her friend's hairdressing salon ready for a trim, shampoo and set.

"Brilliant, though it's not exactly a fortune. But Percy says I must keep it all for myself as fishing has been quite good this summer. That's why I'm splashing out on a new look."

"Well, your hair won't cost you anything even if you are earning now. You know I don't charge you and I never will. You are after all my oldest friend and I used to practise on you. Remember?"

"Yes, of course, but it doesn't really seem fair, Betty. You've always done a smashing job and I would like to pay my way."

Betty tied a waterproof cape around Gertie's shoulders. "Alright, another time you can pay a little to cover the cost of the shampoo, conditioner and the electricity, but today it's a present, a birthday present, so no arguing."

"Okay, I'm happy with that, but you've already bought me a present so I shouldn't have another. I'm being spoiled rotten today. I know I've already told you we're going out, but guess where we're going? Percy told me this morning. Apparently he's booked us a table at the Talk of the West in St Agnes for the cabaret. Isn't that sweet of him? I'm really excited as I've never been there before."

Betty was impressed. "Wow, neither have I, that's brilliant. I hear it's really good, so your hair-do must be extra special."

"Well, I'll leave that up to you, you've so much more imagination than me. Whatever it's like I'll not complain, you know that."

As Gertie laid her head back into the wash basin, Jane emerged from the kitchen with clean towels and put them in a cupboard.

"Oh, thanks, love," said Betty, turning on the taps. "Now would you be a sweetheart and pop the kettle on and make Auntie Gertie and me a coffee."

Jane sighed. "Alright, but then can I go and call for the others? Diane's invited us all round to listen to her new Troggs LP. She's been saving up for it for ages and only got it yesterday."

Betty nodded. "Yes, of course, you've been a great help this morning and Auntie Gertie's my last customer until after lunch, anyway. But have a bite to eat before you go, there's a fresh piece of cheese in the fridge. I only bought it yesterday."

"Okay, I'll make a sandwich then. Shall I make one for Matthew too while I'm about it?"

"No, he's alright. He's staying at the post office 'til teatime and having lunch with David and Stephen."

"Is he? Okay then. I'll be in with the coffee as soon as I've made myself a sandwich."

"She's so grown up now," sighed Gertie, as Jane left the room. "But then they all are. Oh dear, sometimes it's a job to keep up, but I mustn't dwell on age or time, not today. Instead you must tell me all the latest village gossip, Bet."

Betty rubbed shampoo into Gertie's hair. "Hmm, well, let me think. It's been a bit sparse this last week, probably because Madge and Albert are busy with potatoes, harvest and suchlike, so they've not had time to sniff out any local scandals."

Gertie giggled. "They really are a prize pair, aren't they? When it comes to gossip, that is."

"Absolutely. But the last time Madge was in, all we talked about was potatoes and Maggie Nan's kidnapping. Everyone else has been much the same. You know, they mention the weather, Maggie Nan of course, oh, and Freddie from the Inn and Catherine Rossiter."

Gertie was alarmed. "What are they saying about Catherine? Poor woman, she's only been here five minutes."

Betty laughed. "All sorts of things. Somebody told me she's after Frank, would you believe? And only this morning Bertha Fillingham was in and said she and May Dickens had seen her up on the cliff tops singing her heart out like Julie Andrews in *The Sound of Music*."

"Oh no! What are they like? By the time that story's done the rounds it'll be claimed she was up there singing complete with a full orchestra and dressed in a nun's outfit. I hope they don't say anything malicious though cos she's ever so nice. On the other hand, I can see why that Freddie chap is causing a stir. He's really weird and a bit freaky but at the same time he's quite dishy."

"I'll say! He was in here the other day for a hair-do. He won a prize voucher at the Barn Dance, you see. Although I'm not quite sure how as I didn't think he was even there. Anyway, he had a perm, would you believe?"

"A perm! You're joking," said Gertie, as Betty began to rinse her hair. "But he was at the Barn Dance, Bet, cos I remember seeing him, and Percy said he'd been talking to him too. They bumped into each other outside apparently. Freddie probably couldn't take the heat in the hall cos it was very warm, wasn't it? Especially dancing. I'm sure I ought to have lost a stone."

"That's not very likely is it, Gert. I mean, how many glasses of cider did you drink because the heat made you thirsty?"

"Okay, too many. Anyway, remind me before I go to look in the phone box on my way home as I'd love to see Freddie's hair."

"The phone box?" queried Betty.

"Yeah, he always seems to be in there when I walk by, although come to think of it, he wasn't this morning. God only knows who he's phoning all the time. He must have lots of friends."

Betty reached for a towel to dry Gertie's hair. "I expect you didn't see him this morning because he's going home today. He told me so when he was here. Shame really, I think we'll all miss him."

As Dorothy and her female helpers drank coffee in the kitchen of the Inn, waiting for the imminent departure of guests due to leave, they heard footsteps on the stairs. Anticipating it would be either, Edward Tucker, Freddie Short or Pauline Pringle, for the Gibson sisters had already gone, Dorothy went into the hall to investigate. It was Freddie who stood at the foot of the stairs, carpet bags in hands, wistfully glancing around the hallway.

"I'm gonna miss this place," he said, as Dorothy approached him. "And I'm gonna miss you too, Dotty. And Frankie, of course. In fact I'm gonna miss you all."

Freddie put down his bags as Dorothy offered her hand for him to shake. "Well, you know if ever you want to come back for another holiday then I'm sure the new people will be more than pleased to see you, assuming of course, that we find a suitable buyer."

Freddie took her hand, squeezed it hard and then pecked her on the check. "I hope I do get the chance to come back one day.

Meanwhile take care of yourself, Dotty, and enjoy your retirement." He glanced back towards the stairs. "Pauline will be leaving shortly too. I'm giving her a lift to the station in Redruth and I said I'd wait for her in the car. After that I think you'll find we'll all have gone."

Dorothy blushed, surprised by his unexpected kiss. "Mr Tucker is still here, but with you and Pauline gone we'll have enough to keep us going for a while. Bed changing and cleaning, that is."

Freddie laughed and opened the door. "Well, I don't think I've left too much mess. God bless you, Dotty." He picked up his bags and humming *A Whiter Shade of Pale* closed the door and was gone.

Before Dorothy had time to return to the kitchen, she heard more footsteps on the stairs and Pauline Pringle came into view. Both women smiled and shook hands warmly.

"Where's your luggage?" asked Dorothy, aware that Pauline had only a travel bag and her handbag.

"Freddie's already put it in the car. He did it a while back. Oh, Dorothy, I've really enjoyed my stay here. I've met some lovely people, it's been really wonderful and I feel it's done me the world of good. Perhaps when you see him you'll say goodbye to Mr Tucker for me, as I've not seen him this morning."

"Of course," said Dorothy, touched by Pauline's enthusiasm. "I hope you have a pleasant journey home and that the future holds everything you might wish for."

Pauline smiled. "Thank you."

When Pauline closed the door, Dorothy returned to the kitchen to tell the ladies they could make a start on the rooms, she then went to Pauline's room to collect the first of the bed linen. Just as she had expected, Dorothy found the room clean and tidy with the dirty bed linen already removed and folded neatly beside the pillows. As she dropped the washing into her cane clothes basket and turned towards the door, she noticed a brown paper bag on top of the window sill. Thinking perhaps Pauline had left something behind she crossed the room to take a closer look. She was surprised therefore when she saw her name written on the bag. Intrigued, Dorothy opened it up. Inside was a note saying:

Freddie won this dear little gonk in the Barn Dance raffle and gave it to me as we swapped our prizes. Please don't be offended, but

there's something about it this little fellow that reminds me of Frank, and for that reason I thought you might like to have him.
Regards and best wishes, Pauline.

Dorothy sat on the bed and rested the gonk on the palm of her hand. "Well, that'll teach me not to meddle with prizes in the future," she laughed.

But in a funny sort of way she was pleased to have the gonk back, for since his departure she had felt guilty for having taken a dislike to something which resembled her husband, although she was a little perturbed that following her reunion with the unprepossessing object, she found the resemblance even more striking than before.

The morning was overcast as Percy and Peter chugged along the coastline towards the old mine where they had two strings of pots lying on the sea bed. As he steered the boat, Peter gazed up at the dark clouds rolling across the grey sky from the south west and groaned. "Looks to me like we're in for rain."

Percy glanced up from the old cupboard door on which he was cutting up bait. "Well, hopefully it'll hold off 'til we get back. I don't want to get a soaking as I've a feeling I've got a sodding cold coming on and I'm taking the wife out tonight."

"Hmm, I've heard there's a cold doing the rounds, so don't give it to me. I 'spect the kids will all come down with it though when it's time to go back to school."

Percy sniffed. "When do they go back? Can't be much longer now."

"Not sure. Probably this week, cos Betty's been flapping around for a day or two sorting out uniforms and suchlike. Oh, that reminds me. Matthew said last night he wants to be a fisherman when he leaves school. I'm not sure whether to encourage him or tell him to think of something more reliable, as I'm inclined to think by the time he's learned the ropes the best days might be over. What do you think?"

Percy wiped his running nose on the back of his hand. "I dunno, it's just not possible to say. I think there'll still be plenty of fish for a good many years yet. Having said that I reckon it'd be as well for any newcomer to have something else up his sleeve, cos as we both know only too well, it's the winter when times are hard, and it's then all the ruddy bills come in."

Peter sighed. "Don't they just? Have your lads decided what they want to do for sure? They've only got another twelve months left at school, haven't they?"

"Yeah, but neither of 'em seems to be drawn towards fishing. John definitely wants to go into building and I've had a word with Harry Richardson about that. Tony, I reckon might go into farming like Gert's old man, as he often goes up and gives the old boy a hand. You never know, if he's keen enough he might be able to run the farm when Cyril retires. That way the old boy wouldn't see the place go into the hands of strangers. I think that's what Gertie wants and I know she's discussed it with her mum."

"Wise choice for both of them," said Peter, veering slightly to the left. "Although I suppose farming like fishing has its ups and downs and is reliant on the weather. Still, at the end of the day all outdoor occupations beat being stuck in an office, hands down."

"Hear, hear," laughed Percy, putting the last of the bait into a box. "And we're beholden to no-one. I don't think I could tolerate being told what to do."

"God, me neither, and imagine having to start and finish work at the same time every day and having to grovel to your boss for a day off. I'm so glad I'm not part of the rat-race."

As Peter steered the boat towards a dahn denoting the spot where their first string of pots lay on the sea bed, Percy leaned over the side and washed his hands in the salty water. When he stood he was facing the cliffs outlining the coast beneath the old mine. He squinted as he dried his hands on an old rag and looked towards the rocky shore. "Hey, what do you reckon that is?" he asked, pointing towards the coast. "Look, Pete, over there on the rocks."

Peter let go of the tiller, crossed the deck and stood by Percy's side.

"Blimey, it looks like somebody's lying up there. No, surely not! Perhaps it's just a bundle of old clothes that someone's thoughtlessly discarded hoping they'd get washed away with the tide." He wrinkled his nose. "I suppose we ought to take a closer look. What do you think?"

Percy sighed. "Yes, I suppose so. It'd be irresponsible not to."

Peter quickly returned to the tiller, changed course and headed inland through the bobbing waves as far as it was safe to go without risking damage to the bottom of the boat on rocks beneath the surface of the water.

Percy stood in the bow of the boat, attempting to focus on the bundle of clothes. "Christ, I think it's a body," he gasped. "Look, Pete, there's a hand dangling over the edge."

Peter brought the boat to a standstill and moved to Percy's side. He nodded on seeing the hand. "You're right, and judging by the clothes, I'd say it's a bloke."

Percy pulled off his boots and thick sea socks. "Whoever it is he hasn't moved a jot since we first spotted him. I mean, unless he's stone deaf he must have heard the boat. I know it sounds negative but I'm going to take a look to see if he's alive, Pete."

Percy leapt into the water and swam with the in-going tide. When he reached the cliffs he clambered onto the rocks and climbed upwards to where the body lay, face down and motionless. Percy paused and held his breath, afraid the casualty might be known to him. He then knelt, apprehensively, and slowly turned the man's head, his heart thumping in his ears. To his relief, although the man's features were battered and bruised, it was clear that the face was that of a stranger, although Percy felt sure he had recently seen the victim around somewhere and guessed he was probably a holiday maker staying in the village or surrounding area.

Comforted by the knowledge that the man was not known to him, Percy listened for a heartbeat, but none was present. The body was cold and stiff. Its wounded face, white, its eyes, wide, staring and lifeless. Percy was unsure what his next move should be. He looked to the cliffs above. A quick appraisal of the situation suggested the man must have fallen from the cliff path, for his clothes were torn, stained with dry blood, and one of his shoes was missing.

Percy rose to his feet, confident beyond any doubt that the injured person was dead, and as he was well above the high water mark he decided it was quite safe to leave the corpse where it lay, satisfied it would not get washed away with the incoming tide. With a heavy heart he swam back to the boat to tell Peter what he had found.

After a brief discussion the two fishermen decided Peter should return to Trengillion alone, to report the accident, although it was obvious the arrival of the emergency services, would be too late to do anything to resuscitate the deceased stranger.

Percy watched from the rocks as the boat chugged back along the coast round the corner and out of sight. With the knowledge his wait might be a considerable length of time, he pulled his airtight baccy tin from the soggy pocket of his trousers, rolled a cigarette and leaned back on the rocks to smoke it and to watch the rolling, grey clouds increase in volume until no blue was visible at all.

Percy shivered as he threw his cigarette butt to the rocks below. He was wet through, his bare feet were numb with cold and his throat felt more sore with every passing minute. He stood and flapped his arms in an attempt to get warmer, but the exercise made him feel worse. As he sat back down his nose began to tickle, he felt a sneeze coming on. He pulled a handkerchief from the pocket of his sodden smock, but it was dripping wet and useless. He looked at the corpse and wondered whether it might have a handkerchief about its person. With reluctance he leaned forward and tried both pockets in the jacket. They were empty. Percy felt flustered, as though he were robbing the dead. The tickle got worse. He hesitated briefly and then tried the trousers. To his relief he found what he wanted tucked deep inside.

Percy pulled out the handkerchief and shook it. From its middle a piece of paper dropped by his feet. He bent, picked it up and began to unfold it, but as he did so, he sneezed and it fluttered away in the wind.

Percy cursed, conscious that the paper might have contained information which may have been useful to the police in their quest to identify the mysterious man. But the only words he could be sure of having seen, were those of a house name, Chy-an-Gwyns.

CHAPTER FOURTEEN

After what seemed to Percy like several hours, help arrived and identification of the corpse was established. Fred Stevens recognised him as one of the Inn's guests and for that reason, once back ashore, Fred himself went to the Inn to inform Dorothy and Frank of the unfortunate accident and to seek permission to search the room of the deceased, Edward Tucker. Dorothy was distraught, and sat at the kitchen table to stop her legs from shaking, whilst Frank, shocked and white faced, asked Fred what had happened.

"We can't be too sure yet, but all the signs indicate he fell from the cliff path. We'll have to make further enquiries, of course, but our first priority is to inform his next of kin."

"He wasn't married," sobbed Dorothy, pulling a handkerchief from the sleeve of her cardigan. "That I do know because I heard him say so to Miss Pringle after she'd explained that she was still a spinster having spent the last fifteen years looking after her invalid mother who has since died. Edward, I recall, was very sympathetic, they seemed to get on quite well. I believe it turned out that they lived not far from each other. Not that that has anything to do with his misfortune. Poor man, he was very quiet and unassuming, although a little nervous and often he only spoke when he was spoken to."

Fred placed his helmet on the table and pulled a notebook from his pocket. "Oh dear, what a shame, but at least if he's not married then perhaps he never has been. I'd hate to think some poor kids might have lost their dad."

Frank agreed. "It's funny you turning up just now, cos Dot and I were only saying a while back that we wondered where Mr Tucker had got to. Not that we were too worried as he paid up front for his lodgings. He's due to go home today, you see, but he wasn't in for breakfast this morning, which we thought was a bit odd. We knew he was still around somewhere though because his things are still in his room and his car's outside parked in the same spot he always parked in."

"I see, and was he in for dinner last night?"

Dorothy nodded. "Yes, definitely and he sent word through Alice to say the pie was delicious."

"So he died sometime between dinner last night and breakfast. Do either of you recall seeing him in the bar last night?"

Both shook their heads. "It was really busy," said Frank. "I don't think he was in but then again I couldn't swear to that."

"Oh dear. Well, the poor chap won't be going anywhere today other than the mortuary. Have you got someone else wanting his room? We'll have to get a move on if you have."

Frank shook his head. "No, no, we're not quite full this week. The busy spell's done now, thank goodness, so luckily we can make do without Mr Tucker's room. Come on, I'll show you where he's been staying." He led Fred into the hall and towards the stairs.

"If you can't find what you're looking for amongst his possessions," called Dorothy from the kitchen doorway. "We've his full name and address in the register."

"Brilliant," said Fred, "I'll take a look at that when I've had a browse through his possessions. He didn't have any identification on him, you see. No wallet or anything like that."

Dorothy was surprised and hoped there might have been a mistake. "Oh, so how do you know it's him?"

Fred sighed. "I recognised him, myself. I spoke to him when I was in for a pint the other day, you see, and he asked me then if it was alright to walk through Bluebell Woods. Apparently he was fond of walking."

"Hmm, yes he was," said Frank. "I don't think he's been out in his car more than a couple of times since he's been here."

"So, do you think he fell during one of his walks, Fred?" Dorothy asked.

"Looks like it, as I've already said, all the indications to me point to an accident. Oh, and before I forget, I'd better take details of everyone else that was staying here at the same time as Tucker, just in case the necessity arises for us to ask them a few questions."

Frank nodded. "They all went home today but of course we have their addresses and so forth."

"I'll copy them out," said Dorothy as Frank escorted Fred up the stairs.

Once Frank had let Fred into Edward Tucker's room he went back downstairs where he found Dorothy sitting at the kitchen table, crying, with a sheet of paper in her hand telling the previous guest's details.

"Are you alright, Dot? You look ever so pale. Would you like me to give Madge a ring to see if she can come and help with tonight's dinner? I don't want you having an accident with all those damn great pots and pans."

Dorothy half smiled. "You're a good kind hearted man, Frank, but I'll be alright, and we mustn't bother Madge, they're very busy on the farm at present. I just feel very sad. Poor Edward! What a horrible way to die. He probably lay there for some time in great pain and suffering before he finally died from his injuries."

Frank leaned forward and patted her hand lovingly. "Don't dwell on it, Dot. He may well have died instantly, not that that's much of a consolation for the poor bloke. Come on, dry those pretty eyes and I'll make you a nice cup of tea."

"That'd be nice, and while you're about it you'd better make one for Fred. And I think if it's alright with you, I'd like a drop of brandy in mine."

Gertie was admiring her new hair-do in the mirror prior to deciding which of her favourite dresses to wear for her birthday treat, when Percy arrived back at Coronation Terrace. On hearing him call from the kitchen, she ran down the stairs to welcome him home. She was dismayed, however, when she saw the bedraggled, wet state he was in and the tired look of anguish on his pale face. He smiled half-heartedly and wished her a happy birthday again.

"Whatever happened to you?" she asked, not hearing his good wishes. "Don't tell me the boat capsized."

Percy smiled. "No, thank God. Nothing that drastic. At least not for me and Pete." He took off his boots and wet socks and threw them outside the back door. "We found a body today, Gert, and it turned out he was some poor bloke staying at the Inn called Edward Tucker. It looks like the silly sod fell from the cliff path and killed himself stone dead. It's been a bit of a shock, but not as awful as when we dragged up poor Rosemary Howard with our pots. This poor bloke was on the rocks and had probably been there for quite a while."

The colour drained from Gertie's face, "A body. How horrid. Where was it? I mean, which rocks was it on?"

Percy sneezed and wiped his nose on Edward Tucker's handkerchief. "The rocks beneath the old mine. He was lying on a ledge there. Poor bugger!"

Gertie reached out and touched Percy's arm. "Oh no, I am sorry. Poor you and poor Pete. You're drenched too and you're shivering. Come on, get those wet things off before you catch cold and I'll go upstairs and run you a nice hot bath."

When Percy was clean, warm and dry, he sat with Gertie by the electric fire in the living room each with a mug of coffee.

Gertie was clearly anxious. "If you'd rather not go tonight we could always cancel our table. I wouldn't mind, honest. I don't want you taking me out if you'd rather have a quiet night in. You look awful and your voice sounds hoarse."

"I wouldn't dream of it, Gert. It's been a shock to say the least but staying in won't change anything, will it? It does make you wonder how long any of us have to live though. I mean, that poor bloke should have been going home today having had a nice holiday. What rotten luck for him to lose his footing like that. He must have got too near the edge and stumbled somehow cos he lost his shoe in the fall. I reckon that's been washed out to sea by now."

Gertie stood up. "I'm going to give Mum and Dad a ring and tell them what's happened. Then I'll ask if they'll drive us to the Talk of the West and pick us up later. I don't want you driving tonight but we'll go cos I think you need a drink as it'll help you unwind. Mum and Dad won't mind because when I told them where we were going they offered to drive us anyway. They've some friends out that way so they'll go and see them to pass the time."

While Gertie was on the phone, Percy remembered the piece of paper that had fallen from Edward Tucker's handkerchief. He had not mentioned it to the police because he felt guilty for having rummaged through the deceased's pockets in the first place. He wondered if he ought to say anything to his wife, but concluded as identity had been established then he could not see that the note was of any importance, so he chose to push it from his mind for all time.

Two days later, Madge drove into the village in Albert's Land Rover to deliver eggs, a job she did every Monday. When she had first gone to live on the farm she had found the prospect of looking after the chickens very daunting, but Dorothy had diligently shown her the ropes and in no time at all Madge began to regard the hens as her friends and was very much amused by their antics.

She had several customers in the village, many of whom had bought their eggs from the Treloars for many years, hence Madge enjoyed Mondays. It gave her a chance to get out and meet people, hear a bit of gossip and still be able to class her morning as work. And as the death of some poor chap called Edward Tucker was the gossip on the lips of most as she travelled around the village she became quite knowledgeable on the subject and eagerly looked forward to calling at The Police House where she might find out the very latest news from Annie Stevens. When she arrived at The Police House, however, she found that Annie was not in, but a note lay in the front porch along with money for the eggs. Madge cursed. Annie was usually in. What a week to choose to be out!

Madge's next call was the post office, where she always left two trays of eggs for her daughter to sell in the shop, and as usual Madge chose to park directly outside, fully aware that to do so would obstruct the bus stop. But as she was confident no bus was due until the middle of the afternoon, she considered it to be of no consequence and proceeded to park the vehicle in as near perfect a manner as possible without the need to reverse. Once done she slipped down from the driver's seat, removed the eggs from the back of the Land Rover, quickly glanced at the notices in the post office window and then carefully carried the trays inside the building and placed them on the counter.

"Hello, Mum," smiled Milly, taking the eggs and placing them on a shelf near the window. "You're a lot later than usual. Have you time for a cuppa? I'm just about to close for lunch."

Madge looked at her watch. "Yes please. I didn't realise it was quite that late, but I don't need to get back to feed Albert cos he's helping out his cousin in Polquillick today, so Bill's wife will feed him."

Milly took money for the eggs from the till and tucked Madge's invoice at the back. She then turned around the closed sign on the shop door, pulled down the blind, turned the key in the lock and led her mother into the kitchen.

Milly filled the kettle. "Would you like a sandwich, Mum? I've a nice bit of ham, or corned beef if you prefer."

"Yes please, that'd be lovely. I'll have ham if that's alright. I've not been able to face corned beef since that typhoid outbreak a few years back and I am rather peckish, I must admit. It must be all that talking, you obviously know all about that Tucker chap from the Inn."

Milly nodded as she buttered four slices of bread. "Yes, dreadful, isn't it? It's all anyone is talking about these days. And fancy him being a reporter."

"A what?" said Madge, dropping her handbag onto the floor. "I know nothing about that."

Milly laughed. "Ah, then you've not heard the latest. Annie Stevens was in a little while back, she called in for some humbugs on her way into town. She's gone to buy a new pair of slippers cos her big toe's poking through her old pair. Anyway, she told me he's a reporter and he works, or should I say worked, in Fleet Street for one of the big national newspapers…"

"…What?" interrupted Madge, eyes like saucers. "So why was he staying in Trengillion, I wonder? Oh, the plot thickens!"

"Cos he was on holiday," laughed Milly, surprised by her mother's over dramatic reaction. "Reporters have holidays just like everyone else, although in this case it's possible he was also on the run. Would you like mustard?"

"Really! What? Yes please. On the run! How exciting! Tell me more."

"Well, apparently he'd been having an affair with a woman in the office where he worked. At least he was until her husband found out, and that only happened because the husband had an anonymous phone call from an unknown woman telling him. He was livid apparently, and threatened to kill Mr Tucker. I don't expect he meant it, but the poor bloke was scared stiff. Tucker that is, not the husband. So you see, the holiday he'd already booked at the Inn came at a very opportune moment. There's a question now though as to whether or not he was pushed from the cliff path, but I think it's unlikely, although I doubt that the wronged husband will shed any tears over Tucker's passing. Isn't it nice to have a policeman's wife who likes to share the news?"

Madge sat open-mouthed and speechless as she digested information received.

Milly spoke again. "Mind you, I expect it'll be in all the papers tomorrow anyway, so Annie hasn't revealed anything confidential."

"Well, this is a turn up for the book," said Madge finding her voice. "And it makes it all a bit more exciting. Thank Goodness I still have a few more calls to make to pass on the news. So now the big question is, did he fall, was he pushed, or did he jump?"

Milly arranged the ham sandwiches on two tea plates. "I expect he fell. At least I hope he did. I've heard he spent most of his holiday walking along the coastal and bridal paths, so there's no reason to think his being near the old mine is at all suspicious."

"Thanks," said Madge as Milly handed her a plate. "I suppose you're right."

Milly sat down. "Oh, I've just remembered Annie did mention one more thing. Apparently Edward Tucker is his real name, but for his gossip column he writes under the name of Teddy Tinsdale."

CHAPTER FIFTEEN

"I can't believe we have to go back to school again already," groaned Matthew Williams. "I wish lessons went as quickly as the time does when we're in these woods."

"You're lucky, at least you'll be going back to the school here," said Anne, sulkily. "I have to start at Grammar School tomorrow and I'm dreading it. I'm the only one from Trengillion going this year."

"At least you passed your Eleven Plus," said Susan, with admiration, "so you can claim to be clever, cos although I like our Secondary Modern School and I've lots of friends there, I'd much rather have gone to Grammar School and then I wouldn't feel I'd been labelled a dunce."

"Oh, don't be silly, Sue, no-one thinks children who fail the Eleven Plus to be dunces," said Elizabeth, pulling a packet of Spangles from her pocket, "especially Dad. He considers it to be a very unfair test as everyone has off days. Although even he has to admit there has to be a way of separating youngsters and sending them along the right path. But then I suppose it all depends what you want to do with your life. I mean, there's not much point spending years being educated with subjects that will never be of any use to you if you intend to, say, work in a shop or a factory. It's much better to get out to work as soon as possible and start earning money and learning about the real world. On the other hand, if you want to do something that requires qualifications, like teaching, law, or medicine then you need to be educated at a Grammar School. Having said that, I've no idea what I want to do with my life, although of course Mum and Dad both want me to go into teaching. Anyone for a Spangle?"

"You'd make a good teacher," grinned Tony Collins, taking a sweet from the proffered packet. "Because you're bossy as well as clever."

"No, she's not bossy," piped up young, Stephen Pascoe, casting a sheepish glance at his guardian. "She's gentle and kind."

Elizabeth stuck out her tongue at Tony, gave Stephen a quick hug and asked him what he wanted to be when he grew up.

"A shop keeper like Dad," he answered, without hesitation. "Then I'll be able to eat sweets whenever I wanted to."

"But you'd still have to pay for them," said his brother David. "Mum and Dad always put money in the till when they get sweets for us."

"I want to be a nurse," said Anne, dreamily. "What do you want to do, Susan?"

"Work in an office and type," she replied. "Grandma has an old typewriter which she lets me use when I go up to the farm and I'd love to learn to type properly and quickly."

"There you are then," said Elizabeth, referring to her earlier opinions. "If you want to do office work you just need to stay on at school an extra year, get some decent CSE results, and then spend a year or two at tech learning shorthand typing, and Bob's your uncle. Much better than being stuck at Grammar school doing GCE O-levels and then, God forbid ghastly A-levels."

"That's what Mum says," said Susan, uplifted slightly. "But I still feel that I'm a failure."

"Stop being so hard on yourself, Sue," frowned Tony. "John and I both failed our Eleven Plus and we're not bothered by it, and you'll have the chance to prove yourself clever if you really want to when you do your CSEs, although I can't really see the point in taking them and I'll be glad to leave school at fifteen."

"Come on, let's not waste our last day," said Diane, jumping to her feet. "I'm tired of talking about school, we'll have enough of that tomorrow. Let's go and see if Danny's working."

"I second that," said Elizabeth, also rising, and the rest of the girls agreed.

"Danny, Danny, Danny," mimicked John. "I suppose we might as well go and take a look though, lads, you never know we might be entertained by precious Danny falling off a ladder or something similar."

The boys laughed, and followed the girls, giggling and joking about any catastrophe that might befall the unsuspecting builder who was completely unaware of his small band of admirers. When they reached the Lodge, however, they found men busily taking down the scaffolding. The new roof was finished, its slates shone in the sunlight.

"Oh no," gasped Jane, peering through parted hydrangea leaves. "Don't say they've finished already."

"It looks like they've only finished the roof," said Tony, with an air of knowledge. "They've yet to do the pointing and they can't really do that until the scaffold is out the way."

"Pointing?" frowned Anne, a note of question in her voice.

"Pointing's the mortar mix between the granite stones. It keeps out the damp," said John, proudly.

"How do you know that?" asked Anne.

"Because I'm definitely going to be a builder when I leave school next year. In fact Dad's already had a word with Harry Richardson about taking me on as an apprentice and Harry has agreed, although he'll be retiring very soon and the business will then go over to his son, Dave. Which is great cos Dave's a good laugh."

"I wonder why Harry and Dave aren't doing the Lodge job for P.C. Stevens," said Elizabeth.

John answered her question. "Because they have a big job on in Polquillick and Mr Stevens couldn't wait until they'd finished because he wanted the roof done this summer before winter sets in."

As they watched the builders busily working, Fred Stevens drove his car between two large granite pillars, fixation points for a pair of rusty, dilapidated iron gates, marking the entrance and driveway of Penwynton House. He pulled up outside the Lodge, and as he emerged from his car to view the progress of his future home, one of the men switched off the grubby transistor radio playing from the rooftop of a green Morris Minor van. The girls groaned simultaneously, for the first few notes of Gooseberry Pie's *Crazy Maisie*, had just begun to drift through the air waves.

Fred stayed talking for about ten minutes. He then climbed back into his car and continued up the driveway towards Penwynton House.

"Where's he going?" whispered Susan, watching the car disappear around a bend.

"To check that the big house is alright, I suppose," said Elizabeth. "I heard Mum telling Dad recently that he checks it every time he visits the Lodge to make sure there's been no vandalism."

"Let's go and have a look for ourselves," said Diane, turning away from the hydrangeas. "We've not been near the big house for ages. I wonder if anyone's bought it yet."

Jane giggled. "Hopefully Danny has. The real one that is, not the builder. Wouldn't it be brilliant if he had?"

The girls all agreed and even the boys considered it would bring a bit of excitement to the village.

When they arrived at the house Fred had already gone.

"Oh dear, it looks so sad and neglected with some of its windows cracked and broken," said Anne, dismayed. "Poor house! I hope someone buys it soon."

They walked all around the house marvelling at its size, the height of the numerous chimneys and the far reaching views from the back.

"I wouldn't want to live here," said Jane, with a shudder. "Not with all those trees in the woods so close. It feels very spooky even in daylight and I'd always feel someone was watching me."

Graham laughed. "What like Anne's bogey man?"

"Well yes," said Jane. "We never did find out who he was, did we? So there's no reason not to suppose he might turn up again."

"Oh, come on, Jane, I thought we'd all agreed he must have been some poor bloke just taking a walk. He might even have been someone who'd been looking at Penwynton House and was curious about the woods so took a quick peep. I'm sure he was completely harmless and I expect Anne's forgotten what he looked like now, anyway."

Anne giggled. "Well, I have sort of. But I did a sketch of him the night after we, or rather I, first saw him, so if the face ever crops up again I'll have something to refer to."

"I bet it doesn't look anything like him," scoffed Elizabeth, who had seen the picture on numerous occasions.

"Well no, it doesn't really, but seeing it reminds me of the face I saw if that makes sense."

"I know what you mean," said Diane. "Something about it jogs your memory, an *aide memoire*."

Susan giggled. "A what?"

"An *aide memoire*," smiled Diane. "It is what it says, an aid to the memory."

They wandered over to the stable block but did not go inside as a large notice warned of danger.

"I'd love to live here," said Anne, dreamily. "If it was all painted and nice. I'd have horses in the stables, flowers in the gardens, a tennis court and a swimming pool. Then on hot summer evenings I'd have parties for my friends and we'd watch the sun go down drinking champagne."

"Shush," whispered Diane, amused by Anne's yearnings of affluence. "I can hear a car. Perhaps Mr Stevens is coming back."

They ran back around to the front of the house and hid amongst the rhododendron bushes, just as a car emerged from a bend in the driveway. The children watched as a well-dressed couple stepped out of the car and stood looking up at the three storey building before they climbed the front steps, unlocking one of the large double doors and then disappeared inside.

"If they have a key they must be looking at the place to see if they want to buy it," whispered Tony. "Because the keys are with a London agent now."

The children watched impatiently, eager to know what thoughts and comments the mystery couple might have regarding the old house. They saw and heard nothing, however, until Graham spotted the woman looking from one of the upstairs windows. She appeared to be struggling with the catch which eventually gave way enabling her to slide up the huge, rattling sash panes until it jammed part-open. Not deterred by the small gap revealed, she lowered her head, peeped beneath the dirty panes and pointed to the woods and the surrounding countryside. The man came and stood beside her. They then closed the window, with difficulty, and disappeared back into the house.

The children crept a little closer to the driveway as they were eager to hear what the visitors had to say when they emerged outside. They were not disappointed. The couple stood not far from where they hid and extolled the virtues of the house with enthusiasm.

"It would be perfect, darling," said the woman. "Our clients would benefit enormously from the fresh air here and they could ramble in the woods and we could even keep horses as there are stables and fields. What do you think, sweetheart?"

"I think it would cost an arm and a leg to get it up to scratch and could take up to a year to get it fit for purpose. But it does have huge potential, I'll give you that. In fact, it's by far the best we've seen this year. If we could knock down the price a bit then our project would be more than feasible. I suggest we go back and do a bit of negotiating, that is of course unless we like the one in Devon better."

"Alright, but I don't think we'll like the one in Devon as much as this and remember the sea is not far from here either. In fact this place has everything a good health farm needs."

"A health farm!" spluttered Elizabeth, in disgust, as the couple returned to their car.

The boys laughed at her indignation.

"Well, they probably won't buy it anyway," giggled Diane. "Let's hope they like the place in Devon more. Either that or the trustees won't drop the price."

"I think we ought to keep an eye on the place and scare off any buyers we don't like the look of," said Susan, earnestly.

Tony laughed. "You mean anyone that isn't Danny Jarrams. Come on Sue, be realistic. Danny's not going to move down here and neither are any other pop stars. Anyway, we can't keep much of an eye on the place as we're back to school tomorrow, worse luck. Come on, let's go back to the den, it's nearly two o' clock and I'm starving."

Dorothy picked up the afternoon post from the doormat of the Inn as she walked down the stairs having been up to the bathroom hanging a clean shower curtain from the rail above the bath. All was addressed to Frank except for one letter which was addressed to both Mr and Mrs Newton.

Dorothy took Frank's post to the bar where he was clearing up after lunchtime opening, and the letter to the two of them she took into the snug bar and sat on the window seat where the sun shone onto the table. To her surprise the letter was from Sharon and Lynne Gibson. After reading it, she called Frank to her side and read to him what the two sisters had written.

Dear Dorothy and Frank,
We've just read in the paper an article telling of Edward Tucker's death which looks and sounds as though it might have been an

accident. We feel, however, that we ought to tell you what happened on the night we got back from the wedding, that being we heard noises in Freddie Short's room but we knew he wasn't in at the time because we had seen him outside the village hall where the Barn Dance was taking place. Being a little curious, we waited to see who came out of the room by hiding, and it was Edward Tucker. We've no idea what he was doing in there but thought we ought to tell you in case it's of interest to the police, as it might be that the two men did not like each other for some reason.

Thank you for our lovely holiday. We thoroughly enjoyed it.

Our very best wishes, Sharon and Lynne Gibson.

"How the devil did he get into Freddie's room without a key?" asked Frank, nonplussed. "Surely he didn't pick the lock."

"I've no idea," said Dorothy, clearly agitated. "But I think we'd better show this to Fred, just in case it is of any significance. Because I've just remembered, the other day, Annie mentioned that one evening when Sally was working here, she heard Edward Tucker on the phone and he too made reference to Freddie, asking whoever he was talking to, to make enquiries about him. What's more, she also heard Freddie on the phone earlier that same evening and he was speaking in a normal non-hippie type voice. Oh dear, I do hope Freddie wasn't a bad person because I rather liked him."

Frank shook his head. "Well, it looks like one of them was up to something. What a turn-up! We'd better start the ball rolling and find out which of them it was."

CHAPTER SIXTEEN

The following morning, a group of school children waited outside the post office for the first bus into town, and judging by the laughter and noise which emanated from their mouths, there was very little evidence to endorse their claims that school was hated as much as they professed.

"Don't they look smart with their shiny shoes and new blazers?" said Joyce Richardson to Milly, as she viewed the gathering through the post office window. "It seems like only yesterday that my two were that age. They just don't stay children for long."

"Hmm, they don't stay dressed like that for long either," said Milly, weighing out half a pound of bacon for her customer. "I wonder how long it will be before things get lost and go missing, my two are bad enough still being at primary school, but I dread to think what they'll be like by the time they're that age."

"How old are your boys now?" asked Joyce, eying the lean ham on display in the post office chiller.

"Nine and seven. So I have both of them in the village for a couple more years yet."

Inside the village school, Meg and Ned greeted pupils new and old, especially the new, whose tear stained faces would melt any heart as they came to terms with being parted from Mum. But, as was usually the case on the first day of school, it wasn't long before smiles replaced tears and Mrs Reynolds became a substitute for mother and someone with whom secrets could be shared. New little classmates, strangers at first, gradually became friends and for many those early friendships would last a lifetime.

The village school consisted of just two classrooms, one for the infants the other for the juniors. There was no staff room, hence Ned and Meg took tea during the morning break in Meg's classroom, where, if the sun was shining they could sit in the brightness and discuss their pupils, lessons and the forthcoming term. Many of the children went home at lunchtime, but for those requiring school dinners, meals were brought in from a neighbouring school where kitchen facilities were of the highest standard and the meals produced from them, plain cooking, but good value for money, and even the children rather enjoyed them. Ned loved his work and so did Meg, and most people agreed that the day Ned Stanley was offered the job of headmaster was probably one of Trengillion's brightest.

With the children safely packed off to school and Percy out, having gone fishing in spite of a streaming cold, Gertie left her house in Coronation Terrace and walked through the village to Chy-an-Gwyns. She was now nearing the end of her second week and very much enjoying her little job. The work was not arduous, her surroundings were very pleasant and a nicer person than Catherine Rossiter Gertie could not wish to meet. She only worked three mornings a week, Monday, Wednesday and Friday for three hours each day and Catherine did not mind at what time she finished and started, the choice was Gertie's. But usually she arrived at half past nine and finished at half past twelve and this earned her the grand total of one pound eleven shillings and sixpence a week and Gertie relished having a little money which she felt she could call her own.

The beach was quiet as Gertie passed it by, all the fishing boats were out and the only person visible was someone walking a dog. Gertie pushed her hands deep inside the pockets of her jacket, for there felt a distinct nip in the air and there was a fresh breeze blowing up from the sea. In the gardens of the two holiday cottages overlooking the beach, shrubs were still in full leaf and dahlias and Michaelmas daisies bloomed in perfusion, their vivid flowers adding a welcome splash of warm colour against the plain, cold white-washed walls of the cottages.

Gertie continued her walk up the steep hill and round the bend. By the green five bar gate where the name Chy-an-Gwyns was engraved on a brass plaque and fastened to the top bar, she turned and walked across the field towards the house alongside a hedge where blackberries, plump and ripe, hung in clusters amidst the thorny stems. Gertie stopped to pick a handful, they were sweet and juicy. She made a mental note to bring a bag another day so that she might make some bramble jelly like her mother had done for as long as Gertie could remember.

When she arrived at the house, Gertie walked through the back door and into the kitchen. There was no sign of Catherine or her friend whom Gertie had not yet seen. Assuming the bathroom might be in use, she started work in the living rooms. First she dusted the drawing room, and then the dining room: lastly the sitting room, where she pulled back the heavy drapes to let in the morning sun. When all three rooms were neat and tidy, she went back through the hallway to the utility room for the vacuum cleaner. From above Gertie heard voices; she was relieved, for if both ladies were up then the vacuum cleaner could not wake or disturb them.

When the floors were finished Gertie went upstairs to do the bathroom. No-one was inside and so she quickly cleaned out the bath and the wash basin, polished the taps and the mirrors and straightened the towels. As she turned to leave she was aware that someone was walking across the landing. Gertie peeked outside the door expecting it to be Catherine, but to her surprise she came face to face with a woman whose features were hidden behind a thick layer of buff coloured cream and whose hair was not visible beneath a large, blue towel wrapped around her head like a turban. Gertie screamed, the stranger laughed and Catherine ran from her room to see what was wrong.

Gertie felt her face redden. "Sorry, I shouldn't have screamed like that. It was very silly of me but you gave me a bit of a scare."

Catherine smiled. "Gertie, this is my friend, Margaret. And Margaret, this is Gertie to whom I am very grateful for the work she so dutifully does for us."

Margaret offered her hand. It was cold and thin with blue veins visible beneath the white skin like streams on a snowy mountain side. Reluctantly, Gertie shook the proffered hand.

"Please don't be alarmed by Margaret's appearance," said Catherine, aware of Gertie's hesitance. "She puts on this thick cream every morning to soothe her skin. She's had a bit of trouble you see, but it's only for ten minutes each day so your timing was just a little unfortunate."

"I've finished your bathroom," said Gertie, at a loss as to what else to say. "So I'll just pop back downstairs now and start on the kitchen."

Catherine nodded her approval. "Excellent, and put the kettle on when you get there, I'll be down in a minute then you and I can have a nice cup of coffee and a chat while Margaret takes a bath."

"So what did you think of them?" asked Frank, as he closed the side door of the Inn after the departure of potential buyers.

"They were alright," said Dorothy, obviously glad they had gone. "But I don't somehow think they'd suit this place. They lacked enthusiasm and drive, her in particular, miserable creature, she seemed a right sour-puss and I didn't like the way she criticised the wallpaper in our sitting room."

Frank laughed. "Well, there's bound to be some things that anyone who looks at the place won't like. Her old man moaned about the cobbles and said they were uncomfortable to walk on, but I just laughed and told him they'd been there for a couple of hundred years. But you're right, she needn't have said anything about the wallpaper. I thought he seemed alright anyway, at least he took a bit of interest in the business side of the Inn and looked past the fixtures and fittings. But I don't expect they'll buy it as your sour-puss let it be known quite clearly, that they had other businesses to look at and she was more interested in having a shop from what I could make of it."

"Good, well I hope they find one to suit them, but I think undertaking would be a more suitable line of business for a misery like her."

After school Ned popped into Rose Cottage to see his mother who was busy in the garden pulling up annuals which had gone-over.

"Ned, I didn't expect to see you today," she grinned, tossing yellowing snap dragons into the wheelbarrow. "What's it like to be back at work? I should think you're glad, the summer holidays are far too long in my opinion."

"Yes, it's good to be back," said Ned, offering his hand so that Molly could step from the flowerbed onto the lawn without losing her footing. "It's time I had something worthwhile to occupy my thoughts again. I've been a bit lazy this summer, I must admit, and I've put on a few pounds too."

"You need a hobby, Ned," said Molly. "Everyone should have an interest in life other than work. I don't know where I'd be without my garden."

"And it's a credit to you."

"Thank you."

"It's also a lot more reliable than fortune telling and suchlike. I'm delighted you don't do that much anymore; having said that it's thinking of people who have passed over to the other side that brings me here today."

Molly's eyebrows rose. "Tell me more."

"Well, I know it sounds daft, but I don't suppose by any chance you've been thinking about Sylvia lately, have you?"

"Sylvia!" spluttered Molly, taken aback by the unexpected question. "I can't say that I've thought of her at all. Why on earth do you think I might have?"

"I don't know really. It's just that she's been on my mind a lot of late and it all started when I brought up her name while talking to Catherine Rossiter in the churchyard. Mentioning her name stirred up old memories and now I can't get her out of my head. I was thinking perhaps you might say the same."

"But why should I? I've not spoken of her to anyone."

"I know it sounds daft but I just thought that maybe her spirit was around for some reason, and I knew if anyone was to pick up those sorts of vibes, it would be you."

"I'm flattered, Ned, but honestly I've not thought of Sylvia for ages." Molly removed her gardening gloves and dropped them into a bucket with the withering annuals. "Not deeply, anyway."

Ned sighed, clearly dejected.

Molly reached out and touched his arm. "My not thinking of her doesn't mean her spirit's not lurking around for some reason, Ned. But she has been dead for fifteen years, so at a guess I'd say it's all in your head and maybe this latest incident up by the old mine has dug up old memories. I mean, this Tucker chappie fell very near to where Sylvia's ashes repose and I daresay it has triggered off thoughts in your sub-conscious."

"Well yes, Tucker's death certainly hasn't helped; it's all anyone seems to talk of at present: death and mysterious happenings. It's really frustrating though, Sylvia that is. You know what it's like when something gets stuck in your head like an annoying tune or a famous quote."

Molly smiled. "I think you've got back to school in the nick of time. Having said that it could be that the Inn being for sale has brought back memories of our late landlady too. They were very harrowing times weren't they, Ned? I mean to say, whoever would have thought that Sylvia would turn out to be a double murderer. But for all that I still can't claim that her name leaves a nasty taste in my mouth, although I wouldn't say so to Doris as she's never really got over the loss of her niece."

As they spoke, Doris walked up the garden path clutching a large, brown, paper bag. Ned and Molly turned to greet her both hoping she had not heard any of their conversation.

"Would you like a few daffodil bulbs, Molly?" asked Doris. "Jim dug up a load from his garden the other day to make way for wallflowers and as he didn't want them he gave them to me. I've planted several but there are far more than I've room for."

"Now that is good timing. I was wondering what to put in place of my annuals, and daffodils would be perfect."

Doris handed over the bag and Molly took a peep inside.

"Are they all the same variety, do you know?"

"Yes, they're all King Alfred's according to Jim and I expect that's right, he's very fussy about knowing the names of everything."

"Fancy a cuppa?" asked Molly. "You too of course, Ned. I could do with one and then I'll plant these bulbs out later."

Ned declined the offer, saying he really ought to get home, but Doris readily accepted and the two women went into the house chatting about their respective gardens.

Elizabeth and Anne were at home raiding the biscuit tin when Ned walked through the back door and into the kitchen.

"Hello girls. Where's Mum?"

"Post office."

"I see. So how did you like your first day at big school, Anne?"

Anne smiled. "It was good. There are some really smashing girls in my class and I've already made friends with some of them. The teachers are nice too."

"Humph," said Elizabeth. "They're not all nice. In fact some of them are downright horrid, especially Knobbly Knees Nixon. She's ghastly, bossy, and mean."

Ned grinned. "I take it you're not too happy about being back, Liz."

"Well, I suppose it was nice to see my old friends again. Some of them anyway. But not Marianne, she's getting to be a right pain in the ar…"

Ned wagged his finger. "…Elizabeth, that's enough."

Anne giggled. "I thought you liked Marianne."

"I did, cos she has a really nice house and lots of fashionable furniture, but she's getting to be a right bighead now."

Ned sighed. "Oh dear."

Elizabeth's lips tightened. "Do you know what her latest boast is?"

Ned and Anne shook their heads.

"Her dad's going to get a colour television set. Colour! Imagine that! *Top of the Pops* in colour! It's not fair."

Ned laughed. "Well, I consider it a bit early to think of getting a coloured set yet as I believe the only programme so far broadcast in colour was Wimbledon tennis back in the summer. It was also the first ever service in Europe. It'll take a while for everything to be recorded in colour, Liz, so don't feel hard done by."

Elizabeth sat up straight. "So, if *Top of the Pops* is still recored in black and white, then that's how Marianne will see it. Just the same as us."

Ned nodded. "Absolutely, *Top of the Pops* and almost everything else as well, but don't worry, because when nearly all programmes cease to be made in monochrome, and the price of colour sets comes down, then we shall have a colour set too. Your mother and I have already discussed this and we, like you, have no intention of getting left behind."

"Wow! That's fab, Dad. Perhaps you're not such an old square after all."

Later that evening Ned, tired after the first day back at school, dozed on the settee, leaving the book he was reading to fall onto the floor. He was woken after fifteen minutes by Stella, who shook his shoulders and informed him that George was on the phone wanting a chat. Ned sleepily rose to his feet and stifled a yawn, annoyed that he had been asleep. Unsteadily he stumbled into the hallway where Stella handed him the phone.

After greeting George, the latter told of a funny incident that had taken place at school that day involving another teacher whom neither particularly liked. Ned listened, amused until the word 'hurt' triggered off memories of a dream he had had during his brief sleep. When the phone call was over, Ned returned to the sitting room, sat back down on the settee, picked up the book and tried to recall details of the dream. It was not difficult, he had dreamed of Sylvia. She looked just as he remembered her and was standing as he had seen her many times in the past, behind the bar of the Ringing Bells Inn. Her dress, however, was as he'd never seen her before except in an old photograph taken during the War before she had ever set foot in Trengillion. She was dressed in Women's Land Army uniform. But it wasn't the outfit that alarmed Ned nor even seeing her in his dream, it was her apparent state of mind and what she said. She was clearly distressed, tears rolled down her cheeks and dripped like heavy raindrops onto the bar and into a pint of beer she had poured especially for him. She spoke in a broken voice, her chest heaving back and forth with painful sobs. As Ned neared the bar she reached out, touched his arm and croaked, "I'm worried about Frank, Ned. I'm worried that he'll get hurt. They mustn't upset him, they mustn't. It would be too cruel."

Ned stood up, walked over to the window and looked across the village. The sun was setting in a blaze of colour above the stable rooftop on the side of the hill where Sylvia's two horses, Winston and Brown Ale still lived. Thoughtfully, he watched as the colours dispersed, her words echoing in his mind. Nothing made sense, and he had not the slightest inclination as to the identity of the *they* she referred to in the dream.

CHAPTER SEVENTEEN

"Did you ever get that film developed?" asked Diane, as the children travelled home from school on the bus during the second week of the new term. "You know, the one with us all on at Chy-an-Gwyns."

Elizabeth looked up after putting her bus pass safely back inside her wallet. "Not yet, the film needs finishing off and I just haven't got round to doing it, simply because I don't know what else to take."

"How about Danny the builder?" giggled Susan, turning round from the seat in front. "Then I can borrow it and show it to big headed Brenda. She's sending everyone up the wall at school with her boasting. She went to Plymouth to see Gooseberry Pie in concert this summer, you see, and she just keeps going on and on about it. She's driving us crazy, but if I could show her a picture of our Danny and pretend it was the real thing, then it might shut her up, cos although she hung around for ages, she didn't actually get to meet him."

Elizabeth laughed. "Alright, that's a good idea, we'll pop along to the Lodge on Saturday morning. Hopefully the weather will stay fine 'til then."

Diane, sitting beside Elizabeth, shook her head, unconvinced. "The picture won't look very authentic, will it? I mean our builder won't be wearing the sort of clothes the real Danny wears, will he? He'll be in his scrags."

"No, but he'll be wearing jeans and a T shirt cos he always does, which is better than the gear he wears when on stage and posing for photographs anyway, because then I can claim to have met him at home when he was just slobbing around." Susan giggled and clapping her hands gleefully.

Diane shook her head. "No, it won't work because you won't be able to get close enough to take a good picture without him seeing you."

Susan frowned. "Humph, that is a good point. I think Liz will have to go up to him and ask if she can take the picture, that way we should be able to get him smiling too."

"What! I'm not doing that," squeaked Elizabeth, horrified by the prospect. "It'd be far too embarrassing, and what if he said no?"

"In that case I'll do it," said Susan, licking her lips. "That way I can really claim to have taken the photo."

"But what on earth will you say?" asked Diane, amazed at her friend's pluck.

"I don't know yet. I shall have to spend this evening thinking about it, as well of course, as to what I'm going to wear. But I won't be able to get too dressed up or Mum will think I'm crackers. You never know, I might even be able to persuade him to let one of you take a picture of me standing next to him, or better still, take one with his arm around my shoulder. Oh wow, I can't wait! Roll on Saturday!"

"Humph, I don't think that's fair, after all it is my camera," said Elizabeth, feeling left out and envious. "I think instead we must ask one of his builder friends to take a picture with all of us on."

"I second that," said Diane.

"Fair enough," said Susan. "In which case we must all dress with care."

Giggling, the girls then discussed the contents of their wardrobes, each relishing the prospect of being able to fool their collective school friends in turn.

During lunchtime opening, a stranger drove into Trengillion, parked outside the Ringing Bells Inn, walked into the bar and asked Frank if he had any vacancies. Frank told him they had, but did not mention the only vacant room had previously been occupied by someone who had had the misfortune to die whilst staying at the Inn, and the room had only the day before been given the all-clear by the police.

"Splendid," said the stranger, glancing around the bar. "I'm on my own and would like to stay for a week to ten days if that's alright."

"You can stay as long as you like. Things are getting quieter now, although we're now full this week if you're going to stay."

The stranger grinned. "Must be my lucky day then. I'll go and get my things from the car."

Frank called Dorothy from the kitchen to speak to the new arrival as he had several customers in the bar. Dorothy quickly removed her apron and was in time to greet the new guest as he entered the Inn with his luggage. Once his details had been entered in the register, she showed him the dining room and the side door of the Inn used by guests. She then took him upstairs to view the allocated room, on the front of the Inn facing south. He was delighted. "A sea view, wonderful, it's enchanting, thank you very much, Mrs Newton. It's exquisite."

"My pleasure," she smiled, overwhelmed by his admiration. "Do you know Cornwall at all, Mr Briggs?"

"No, first time I've ever been here, but I like what I've seen so far."

"Good, and may I ask if your visit is business or pleasure?" asked Dorothy, eying his luggage.

"Pleasure," laughed Bill Briggs, gazing from the window with both hands resting on the sill. "I need to take a break from work and city life before the winter sets in. I've been working too damn hard lately, you see, and I think I deserve a few days to myself."

Dorothy frowned as she retreated towards the door. "Dinner is at seven. I hope you enjoy your stay with us and get all the rest you want."

"I'm sure I will. But before you go, Mrs Newton, tell me. What's the name of that fine looking house up there on the cliff tops?"

Dorothy crossed to the window and looked in the direction of his outstretched hand, although she knew instinctively to which house he was referring.

"That's Chy-an-Gwyns. It belongs to Mr and Mrs Castor-Hunt, but they're in America at present so they have let the house during their absence," said Dorothy, in a very matter-of-fact manner."

"Hmm, I'll no doubt be able to take a closer look when I go for a stroll up there. What a wonderful location!"

Back downstairs Dorothy went into the bar to help Frank wash the glasses so that he could clear up and close on time.

"New bloke seems alright, don't he?" said Frank, as he filled a gap on the shelf with new cigarette packets.

Dorothy nodded thoughtfully. "Yes, he seems pleasant enough, although perhaps a bit too pleasant. His name is Bill Briggs by the way." She frowned. "There's something odd about him, Frank, and I can't quite put my finger on it. He's too enthusiastic and he says he's here on holiday, yet he has a bulging brief case with him and a hard black case, which isn't a suitcase. He was also keen to know the name of Chy-an-Gwyns. Something doesn't ring true. Call it female intuition or whatever you like, but he makes me feel uneasy, though at present I can't quite see why."

"Oh, come on, Dot, don't let Edward Tucker's death make you suspicious of everyone. There's nothing odd about guests asking about Chy-an-Gwyns, it's a place most folks are inquisitive about. In fact, I'd think someone was odd if they didn't ask."

She smiled. "Yes, I suppose so, but I still have an inkling that he's up to no good. Still, time will tell. I just hope he doesn't cause any trouble, that's all."

As Frank walked from behind the bar to wipe down the tables and empty the ashtrays, Fred Stevens strolled into the Inn.

"Don't worry, there's nothing wrong," said Fred, noting the alarmed look on Dorothy's face. "Your guests are all safe, as far as I know."

Dorothy sighed with relief. "That's good, but we've just had another one arrive and he seems a bit odd, I thought you might be coming in to say there was a wanted man in the area."

"Oh, come on, Dot, that's not fair," said Frank. "The poor bloke's only just got here, you can't possibly have him labelled as up to no good without any justification."

Dorothy didn't answer as she lined up the clean glasses neatly on the shelf.

"Actually, it's because of one of your guests that I'm here," said Fred. "But fear not, he's not one of your current lot. It's Freddie Short. I've just had word from the Met that he's alright, no police records or anything like that. I thought you'd like to know to put your minds at rest, cos I know you were a bit bothered by the letter you got from the Gibson sisters."

"Oh, thank goodness, that's wonderful," smiled Dorothy, with genuine enthusiasm. "I always knew he was alright in his own peculiar way."

"So, why do you think Edward Tucker was going through Freddie's things?" asked Frank. "That's assuming the sisters didn't imagine the whole thing."

Fred wrinkled his nose. "I've not the foggiest idea. I only know what I've been told and that's what I've just told you. But I suppose if anyone was in the wrong then of course it would be Tucker, and as he's dead there's not much as can be done. We certainly can't ask him, and when all's said and done, Freddie Short never reported anything missing, did he? So goodness only knows what that was all about."

That same evening shortly after darkness fell, as Cyril Penrose sat in the bar chatting to Bill Briggs and telling him about his newly purchased farm on the cliff top, brought about by the demise of Charles Penwynton, Molly and the major put in a rare appearance. Frank, delighted as always to see his old friends, served the major with drinks and enquired after the couple's wellbeing, while Molly tried to make out why Dorothy was frantically winking and nodding towards the end of the bar. After quickly assessing the situation, Molly concluded the strange behaviour could only indicate that Dorothy had something of importance to say, hence she made her way quickly towards the designated spot where Dorothy likewise was heading.

"Try and find out what that chap sitting over there talking to Cyril is up to," Dorothy said, delighted at having successfully compelled Molly to her side. "He's called Bill Briggs and he says he's here for a break, but with his luggage he has a bulging briefcase and a large black case, which isn't a suitcase. I've been thinking about it and I reckon he might a private investigator or even the husband of the woman with whom Edward Tucker, God rest his soul, had an affair. It must be something like that. He asked me about Chy-an-Gwyns too. I'm sure I smell a rat, he looks shifty. See what you think."

"Leave it to me," said Molly, thrilled at the prospect of subtle scrutiny. "I'll point the major in his direction and he'll find out all you need to know without either of them knowing anything about it."

"Thanks, Molly, I know I can rely on you."

A little later Molly approached Dorothy with the waited for news. "He's a twitcher," she yawned, wearily placing her gin and tonic on the bar. "The black case must hold his camera, binoculars and suchlike."

Dorothy wrinkled her nose and frowned. "A what?"

Molly laughed. "A twitcher. I know, I'd never heard the word either. It means a bird watcher, only they don't watch just any old birds, they track down rare species and tick them off lists or something like that. He wouldn't tell us what he's hoping to see or where he's hoping to see it and I don't expect we'd have heard of it, anyway. The major's fascinated but I'm bored stiff."

Dorothy was clearly disappointed. "I see, but what about the brief case? What pray, might he have in there, do you think?"

"I've no idea. Bird magazines perhaps or maybe pages and pages of information about birds, birds, and more birds."

Dorothy sighed. "That figures, but what about his interest in Chy-an-Gwyns?"

"I don't know, but up on the cliffs is probably the place where he's expecting to see his bird or birds, so at a guess I'd say when he looked up there he saw the house and most likely asked out of curiosity. It is after all a fine looking place. I know it interested me when first I came here."

"Yes, I suppose you're right. Oh dear, I am sorry to have lumbered you like that. I tell you what, since it's quiet tonight, I'll take a little break. Frank will be alright on his own for a while and then you and me can have a little chat. I've not seen you since Pauline Pringle's disastrous hair-do, so we've lots of gossip to catch up on. I don't even know your thoughts on the death of Edward Tucker and I'm sure you must have a strong opinion about that."

She poured herself a Dubonnet and lemonade and topped up Molly's gin and tonic.

"Do you know," said Molly, as she followed Dorothy carrying their drinks to an empty table, "there was a time when I'd have labelled you as someone who'd have no interest whatsoever in gossip, but now you're competition for Madge and Albert."

"Well, we are related and I'm just a late developer, but it peeves me to think how much I must've missed over the years. Working here has shown me people in a different light, and when you look deeply they're all a damn sight more interesting than I'd ever have thought possible."

CHAPTER EIGHTEEN

On Saturday morning the children wandered along the main street of Trengillion calling for each other in preparation for the pre-planned visit to Bluebell Woods. Not all children were able to participate in the excursion. Jane helped her mother with the hairdressing salon on Saturday mornings and didn't want to miss out on the four shillings she was paid for her help. Likewise, Tony and John were also absent: Tony having promised to help his grandfather, Cyril Penrose, on the farm, and John to meet up with school friends in town, arrangements for which in both cases had been made before the trip to Bluebell Woods was planned.

Spirits were high as they walked down the lane by the school with the girls eagerly expressing their hopes and desires regarding the outcome of their meeting with Danny. And during the course of the rowdy conversation, each confessed to wearing a favourite top beneath their normal, everyday clothes. For the prospect of Danny agreeing to have his picture taken alongside the girls meant it was absolutely essential to look as pretty and attractive as possible.

They approached the woods with an air of excitement. They had not been to their den since the beginning of the new term and it would be good to pretend they were on holiday again. They followed the path by the stream through the trees until it reached the opening where their den was hidden. Everything was as they had left it, except a few, sporadic golden leaves now lay in the earth.

"Come on," said Diane, her voice tinged with impatience. "Let's not hang around here, let's go and find Danny.

"No, hang on a minute," said Susan, fumbling around in her pocket. "I have to put some make-up on first."

Elizabeth was impressed. "Wow, did you bring some with you? I didn't think of that."

"Only lipstick, mascara and scent," said Susan, with pride. "You can borrow some if you want."

Elizabeth, Susan and Diane each successfully managed to apply mascara to their eyelashes and lipstick to their lips, despite the absence of a mirror. Anne, on the other hand, was not allowed to partake in the girl's beauty routine, for Elizabeth emphatically informed her that she was too young to use cosmetics and to do so would make her look silly.

The girls, once satisfied they looked as good as was possible under the difficult circumstances, dashed through the woods with renewed enthusiasm towards the Lodge, leaving behind the strong scent of Lily of the Valley. They stopped only when commanded to by the boys, who wanted to see if any of the conkers dangling from the horse chestnut tree were ripe. A brief glimpse above soon established they were not, and so they continued on through the undergrowth until they reached the hydrangeas edging the drive behind which they normally hid. However, when they parted the leaves and eagerly looked towards the Lodge, jaws dropped with bitter disappointment. For the cement mixer was quiet, no vehicles stood in the driveway and no radio played pop music from Radio Caroline. The house stood empty and silent.

"Oh, sod it, it's Saturday," Susan groaned, pushing through the shrubbery and walking towards the house. "I don't believe it. Builders don't work at the weekends, do they? We should have thought of that. How annoying!"

The others joined her and stared at the Lodge in disbelief.

"But then that means we'll probably never see Danny again," Diane croaked. "They'll have finished off all their jobs by half term. It's not fair us having to go to school."

Susan sighed, her thoughts elsewhere, as she pondered how best to make something of the unfortunate situation. "I know school's a pain, but let's not get too down-hearted and waste our visit. I think we should take a look around the Lodge. I'm sure Mr Stevens wouldn't mind and I'd love to take a peep in the downstairs windows."

Elizabeth nodded. "Yes, so would I. Mr Hughes told Dad there's a well in the garden much like the one at the Inn. I'd like to see that too and make a wish. In fact we must all do that. We must wish that somehow or other we'll see our gorgeous Danny again."

Around the back of the Lodge, the large gardens were overgrown with brambles and nettles several feet high, their stems entwined with convolvulus, whose white flowers peeped sporadically through the dense wilderness. In the distance the stonework of a high boundary wall was part visible beneath the creeping tendrils of thick ivy.

Outside the kitchen door, a large area had been cleared of weeds and from it led a path to an impressive well, built of granite, with a wooden pitched roof. Beneath the roof, over a seemingly bottomless void, a piece of frayed rope, wound loosely around a rusty spindle, swung in the breeze.

"It looks awfully dark and deep," said Anne, peering over the side. "Creepy too. I'm glad we don't have to use wells nowadays."

Graham searched for a stone and dropped it over the wall. They heard a distant splash.

"Blimey, it's deep. I wouldn't fancy anyone's chances of survival if they fell down there."

Elizabeth shuddered, unnerved by the image conjured up following Graham's suggestion. Meanwhile, the other girls, hunted around for small stones and in turn dropped them into the water while making a heart-felt wish. Elizabeth then did likewise.

Once all wishes were made, they walked around the house peering in the windows. There was very little to see, for the rooms all stood empty, the floors were bare and in places, loose plaster had fallen from the walls leaving unsightly holes.

"Let's go back to our den," said Anne, nervously. "I feel we shouldn't be here because we're trespassing now that it belongs to Mr Stevens, aren't we?"

Diane agreed and so they left the Lodge and ambled back into the woods.

Back at their den, Elizabeth despondently sat down on the fallen tree trunk. "What shall I finish the film off with? I was really looking forward to having pictures of Danny."

Susan shrugged her shoulders. "I suppose you could always take more pictures of us."

"Hmm, I don't really have much choice, do I? We'll have to go somewhere else though because there's not enough light here."

Diane sprang to her feet. "Let's go back into the village and see the horses in the pub's paddock. You can take pictures of us sitting on the old wall, Liz, and then we can take a look in the old tunnel to see if Maggie Nan's been hidden down there."

"Are you mad?" laughed Graham, flabbergasted by his sister's sudden proposal. "You know Mum said we're never to go inside the tunnel. It's dangerous. Besides, whatever makes you think Maggie Nan might be in Cornwall? It's highly unlikely and even if she was, she's hardly going to be in Trengillion? You're crazy!"

"Don't get so stroppy," said Diane, offended by his harsh words. "I'm only trying to think of something slightly exciting to make up for the disappointment of not seeing Danny."

"I'm not going to the tunnel," said Anne. "I heard some old ladies talking about ghosts and they said the spirits of two murdered girls are down there."

Elizabeth shivered. "I hope not, but we can't go in there anyway, 'cos I heard Dad tell Mum, that Mr Richardson has taken the ladder away so no-one can get inside now."

"Humph, what a spoil-sport," muttered Susan. "Not that I want to go down there. Mum says it's an evil place but she won't tell me why, so perhaps Anne's right about the ghosts of murdered girls."

"Oh, this conversation's silly," said Graham, kicking a lump of earth and watching it disintegrate as it hit the trunk of a tree. "There are no such things as ghosts, everyone knows that."

"Oh, but there are ghosts," said Diane, sulkily, and angry that Graham had made her feel small. "And your granny can talk to them, can't she, Liz?"

Elizabeth nodded. "Yes, but it's something we never talk about at home and Granny has been forbidden by Dad to mention it to us. He said he doesn't want us frightened by some of her tales."

"Let's go over to the big house," suggested Anne, feeling uncomfortable. "It's much nicer there and we'll be able to see if it's any different."

"Well, of course it won't be any different," scoffed Elizabeth. "No-one has bought it yet, silly!"

"I'd still like to see it," said Anne, rising to her feet. "I like it there and I like going in the gardens and it's all so much more open. These woods feel claustrophobic today."

"It'd be a good place for hide and seek," said Graham, nodding with enthusiasm. "It's so overgrown there'd be loads of good hidey holes. Come on, let's go, it'll be light enough for you to take some pictures too and it's starting to feel quite chilly in the shade."

They wandered through the trees towards the house, but when they reached the edge of the driveway they stopped, for in front of the building a gleaming red Mercedes was parked on the gravel.

"Oh bother," said Anne, placing hands on hips. "I expect that's somebody else looking at the house. I hope they won't be long."

"Gosh, I'd like to take a closer look at that Mercedes, it's a beauty," said Graham. "It's pretty new too and what a fab colour."

"You mustn't go out there," said Diane, pulling him back behind the rhododendrons. "The people in the house might see you from one of the upstairs windows."

"But it doesn't matter if they do see us," groaned Graham, freeing his arm from her grasp. "We're not doing any harm."

"Well, they're not to know that," said Diane. "Strangers might think we're responsible for the broken windows and report us to the agents or something like that. Anyway, we don't want them to know we're here because we want to listen to what they say when they come out."

"Perhaps the car belongs to a pop star," said Susan, dreamily. "An ordinary person wouldn't drive a car like that, would they?"

"They would if they could afford it," said Graham, with awe. "I'm going to have flashy cars like that when I'm grown up. Take a picture of it, Liz and then I can show it to the boys at school."

Elizabeth removed her camera from its case. "Okay."

"Too late," said Diane, leaping back. "Someone's coming. Quick, duck."

They heard the front door of the house close, followed by rapid footsteps running down the steps.

"Can you see anyone?" Susan asked Elizabeth, who was nearest the driveway.

"No, but I can just see the front of the car. As long as no-one jogs my arm I should be able to take a picture of your car as it drives off."

They heard the car door open and close. The engine started and the vehicle roared off scattering gravel under its spinning wheels. As the sound of its engine faded in the distance the children crept from their hiding places and stretched their legs.

"Did you get a picture, Liz?" Graham eagerly asked.

"Yes, I snapped it before it went round the bend. Hopefully it'll come out alright."

"Wow, thanks, you're an angel."

Elizabeth smiled. "You're welcome. Right, come on, let's finish off this film before we get any more interruptions. Everyone on the steps in an orderly manner and say cheese when I tell you."

The children clambered onto the steps and sat down in front of the large double doors. Elizabeth took five pictures to finish off the film and then carefully placed the camera back in its case.

"Brilliant," said Diane. "Now let's play hide and seek round the back of the house and the last one to reach the old stable block is *it*."

On Saturday afternoon, with stick in hand, Pat Dickens walked across his land to the meadow through which ran the coastal path where his herd of dairy cattle grazed. Once there, it was his intention to round them up and move them onto greener pastures nearer to the farm. For with the days getting shorter and the mornings darker, to have the cows closer to the house, would be beneficial to both himself and his wife, May, for early morning milking.

Pat climbed over the stile with the agility of a much younger man, but as he set foot on the grass he heard and sensed movement nearby. He stopped to listen, expecting to witness the sight of a fox or a rabbit fleeing across the fields, but neither materialised. He stood perfectly still, listening for any further sounds. For a minute or two all was silent and then he heard a rustle. Quickly he turned his head and was surprised to hear the hearty laugh of a man followed by the uttering of the words 'got you'. Pat was puzzled. The voice had clearly been audible, yet he could see no-one in close proximity to where he stood. Intrigued, he climbed onto the top of a stile and looked to his right, towards the Witches Broomstick, and then along the deserted coastal path towards Chy-an-Gwyns standing proudly on the cliff tops. There was no sign of life anywhere other than a few seagulls drifting over the sea, and the air was devoid of sound other than the wind and the distant rumble of waves crashing onto the rocks far below.

Pat climbed down from the stile, but as he strode into the field he saw a flash of light, like sunlight reflecting on a piece of glass. Quietly, he ambled in the direction from which the light had shone and with a feeling of excitement climbed on top of a dense, granite wall. In the next field Pat observed a man, dressed in dark clothing, lurking in the bushes. Beside him was a large black case and in his hands he held a pair of binoculars. Pat was baffled. Was the man a bird watcher, a butterfly enthusiast, a country lover or a peeping Tom?

Suddenly, the man stood up and Pat, not wishing to be seen, jumped quickly down from the wall and fell awkwardly onto his ankle. With his hand over his mouth he managed to stifle a painful cry, he then hurriedly stood and peeped through the foliage sprouting from the top of the wall. The binoculars were no longer in the man's hands but now hung from a thick strap around his neck and in his hands he held a camera, large and impressive with a huge lens. Pat heard a series of rapid clicks and a cry of satisfaction. He scratched his head. The stranger had obviously taken pictures which had fulfilled his purpose, but what were they of? In front of him lay nothing of any significance. Just grass, rocks, sporadic gorse bushes and Chy-an-Gwyns, where Pat could just about make out two people standing in the grounds. The farmer watched as the man packed his gadgets back inside the black case, after which, carrying his cumbersome equipment, he headed along the coastal path towards Trengillion, tunefully singing *Waterloo Sunset* at the top of his voice.

Later in the afternoon, Stella arrived back from town where she had been for the weekly shop, to find Ned helping Elizabeth with her history homework and Anne moping around the house claiming she was suffering from extreme boredom.

"In that case," said Stella, dropping her bags onto the kitchen table, "perhaps you'd like something to do. Pop these secateurs round to Grandma. She asked me to get her a new pair as hers have gone missing."

"Oh, alright," said Anne, without enthusiasm, as she took the secateurs from her mother's hand. "Then when I get back can we have tea, cos I'm starving?"

"Food must never be a remedy for boredom," retorted Stella. "Tea will be at the usual time."

Anne left the house, secateurs in hand and ambled down the road towards Rose Cottage. The afternoon was quiet and no-one was about except for a man, whose back she could see as he read notices on a board outside the village hall. Anne gave a cursory glance as she passed by assuming he was a stranger, a holiday maker perhaps as there were still several in the area.

A car approached from behind as she continued to walk along the footpath. Instinctively she turned her head to see who it was, but before the car came into view her eyes became transfixed on the man by the village hall. He also had turned and his face was clearly visible. Anne felt giddy. Her heart thumped loudly. For without doubt, he was the man, the stranger with thin, longish hair tucked behind his over-large ears. The stranger who had watched her in Bluebell woods.

Without hesitation, Anne took larger and quicker steps. Voices in her head told her to run. She approached Rose Cottage with exceptional haste and nervously glanced back over her shoulder to determine the man's whereabouts before she made the final dash to the safe haven of her grandparents' home. But much to her alarm the man was following close behind at a steady pace.

Automatically, Anne's steps turned into a sprint and she heaved a sigh of relief when she reached for the latch on the gate of Rose Cottage. Without stopping further to ascertain if she was being followed, she ran up the garden path and round to the kitchen door, but when she pressed the latch to let herself in, she found the door would not open. It was locked. Deeply alarmed that no-one was home, Anne's forehead broke out into a cold sweat. Her hands turned clammy and sticky, but in spite of her fear she was still able to think clearly and without hesitation quickly stooped to reach for the key she knew would inevitably be hidden beneath the flower pot. With key in hand she unlocked the door, let herself in, slammed it shut and then locked the door from inside.

Trembling and fighting back the tears, Anne threw the secateurs onto the kitchen table and went into the living room where she saw two pairs of slippers tucked neatly beneath the sideboard. Knowing it would be futile to call out to see if anyone was home, she crouched behind the settee and prayed that the stranger had not followed. Minutes passed by as Anne listened to the clock ticking on the mantelpiece. No sound could she hear from outside and fear prevented her from approaching the windows, lest she be seen, hence she was unable to establish the whereabouts of the strange man.

Eventually, hopeful that her pursuer had abandoned the chase, she slowly emerged from her hiding place and crept out into the room. Keeping well away from the window, she pondered over her next possible move.

On an occasional table beside her grandmother's chair, she spotted the telephone. Anne breathed a sigh relief. Of course, she must phone home, explain the situation and get one of her parents to rescue her. With a quick glance over her shoulder, she ran to the phone, but before she had time to lift the receiver, a noise startled her and sent her into another panic. Someone was trying to get in through the back door, for the latch could be clearly heard clanking up and down. Anne fled back to her hiding place behind the settee and put her hands over her ears to muffle the sound. When no-one entered the room she withdrew her hands and listened hard. From around the front of the house the sound of voices met her ears. Angry voices, arguing, each making accusations as to the inefficiency of leaving a key beneath a plant pot. Overwhelmed with relief, Anne sprang to her feet, left her hiding place and dashed into the hallway where she opened the front door and with tears streaming down her flushed face, ran into the arms of her surprised and totally bewildered grandmother.

CHAPTER NINETEEN

With Ned and the children back at school, Betty busy hairdressing, Gertie working and Meg teaching again, Stella felt surplus to requirements and wondered if perhaps she ought to think about finding herself a job to justify her existence. On reflection, however, she decided to do so would bring little benefit other than to satisfy her whim to feel needed, for Ned's earnings more than covered the cost of living and the family were not in want or need of anything they could not afford. Hence, with a beautiful autumnal day stretching before her, Stella decided to go blackberrying, for Gertie had said at the last drama group meeting, that many berries were ripe and ready for picking.

Stella left The School House with a basket hanging from her arm and strolled down the hill towards the stream. At the bottom she stopped, sat on the bridge and dangled her legs over the wall above the flow of sparkling clear water. The scent of woodbine entwined through the branches of a hawthorn bush filled the air as its petals tussled with the breeze gently blowing through the valley. She sighed, content, and blessed the day Rose had suggested Ned apply for the headmaster's job at the village school, for Stella could not imagine living anywhere other than Trengillion and without doubt the past fourteen years had been some of the happiest of her life.

She sat for a while relishing the view and enjoying the babble of trickling water flowing over stones before it disappeared beneath the bridge. In the distance, the trees in Bluebell Woods had lost their vivid green appearance, the leaves were darkened with age and some were already turning brown ready to fall in the next strong wind. Beyond the trees, the tall chimney pots of Penwynton House stood proud and prominent in spite of the general decay of the house over which they towered, for the children had told her that some of the downstairs windows were broken and the place looked neglected, forlorn and unloved. Stella wondered who had first had the house built and tried to imagine how splendid it must have been in the early days. She made a mental note to do a little research and decided her first interview must be with Jim Hughes, for Ned had told her that before his retirement, Jim had been the estate's gamekeeper, a job he had done for most, if not all, of his working life.

Stella climbed down from the wall, her basket still empty, and walked up the hill, past a row of cottages towards Long Acre Farm. In one field, bales of straw lay ready to be collected and stored to feed Cyril's cattle during the winter, and in the next, rows and rows of healthy, young cauliflowers spread out their leaves to take in the warmth of the sun.

On the edge of a meadow where sheep grazed, Stella placed her basket on the grass and began to pick the berries growing in profusion from intensely entwined brambles. Soon her hands were stained with the juice. She was glad she had not worn her best clothes for the thorns on the briars snagged her cardigan sleeves and caught on the skirt of her dress. With her basket half full she moved on, a little peeved that the best berries were out of her reach.

In the next field, berries were plentiful and she was able to fill her basket to the brim, and as the day was pleasant, she decided rather than take the same route home, she would carry on walking towards the old mine and venture back to Trengillion by way of the coastal path.

As she approached the five bar gate leading away from the fields and onto the cliffs, Stella saw something white peeping up through the grass. Thinking perhaps it might be a mushroom, she put her basket down and eagerly walked across the meadow to identify the object, but to her dismay it was a screwed up, white paper bag. With a laugh she turned and walked back towards the spot where her basket lay, but then something else caught her eye, a shoe, partly hidden amongst tussocks of grass around the edge of the field. Stella bent, picked it up and glanced around to see if another lay nearby, but there was no sign of its mate. Intrigued, Stella walked towards a gateway and looked into a lane, partly overgrown through lack of use. It led to the back of the old coastguard cottages. Puzzled as to why someone would throw a perfectly good shoe into a field, she tucked it beneath the hedge and then resumed her walk. But she felt a little uneasy. Anne's story of the man who twice had frightened her, sprang to mind, even though it had been agreed by all, that the stranger had done nothing at all to justify the fear he had injected into her daughter and Molly and the major had seen no-one at all hanging around their house when they had returned from their walk.

Once back in the village Stella felt safe and at ease. She walked up the road back towards The School House with a renewed spring in each step, and as she passed Ivy Cottage, Jim Hughes emerged through Doris's garden gate.

Stella smiled. "I was thinking about you a while back. I've been blackberrying you see." She held up her brim-full basket. "I thought of you whilst sitting on the bridge at the foot of the hill where I could see the chimney pots of Penwynton House through the trees. I was hoping you might be able to tell me a bit about its history, one day."

"I'd be delighted to, have you time now? I've nothing to rush home to of course, just an empty house."

"Oh, yes please. Come on, Jim, back to The School House and I'll make us each a cup of tea. I'll be glad to get home as this basket is beginning to feel rather heavy."

Jim reached out to take the blackberries from her hand. "Allow me."

Stella happily passed over the basket and rubbed her hand where the handle had left its indentation.

"So, what makes you want to hear about the Penwyntons?" Jim asked as they strolled along the road.

Stella wrinkled her nose. "Well, no reason in particular, it's just that as I glimpsed it through the woods, it suddenly struck me I knew nothing about the place and even less about the families who've lived there and I thought it a little remiss of me to be so ignorant when I've been living here for nearly fourteen years."

Jim stopped walking. "Have you really been here that long? My, how time flies. But then poor old Flo's been gone for nearly twelve months."

Stella paused. "Yes, I know. It was bonfire night, wasn't it? How are you coping? It must be very hard to be left alone when you've been with someone for so many years."

They resumed walking.

Jim nodded, thoughtfully. "It was dreadful at first. I just couldn't get used to Flo not being there. But I've sort of got used to it now and of course Doris has been a great help. Soon after Flo died she said that if ever I'm lonely then I must pop round and see her regardless of the time. So I often do. We've known each other since we were nippers, you see. We went to the village school together and both left at the same time when we were thirteen."

They reached the School House and Jim opened the gate to let Stella through. "That's really nice," she said, as they walked up the garden path. "And what about Flo? Was she from Trengillion too?" Stella stooped and retrieved a key from beneath the doormat. She then unlocked the back door. Once inside, Jim took a seat at the kitchen table and Stella filled the kettle and switched it on.

"Flo came from Gunwalloe," said Jim. "I met her when she came to work at the big house. She were only a gel then and as pretty as a picture. She worked as a kitchen maid and that's how I got to know her, cos I often went into the kitchen for a mug of tea and a bite to eat. Well, actually the kitchen was as far as I ever went. We knew our place in those days, you see. They were good times though. Old Cedric Penwynton were still alive then, of course, and he treated his staff well. Flo stayed on working there after we were wed and until she had our first child, then she stopped and became a full time mother. By then she's learned a lot about cooking from Winnie Bray. Winnie's pasties were the best in the world. She often made them for the staff, and the master he liked them too. In fact he told us once he preferred a good old pasty to all the posh stuff he had to eat at dinner parties and such like."

Stella placed a mug of tea on the table in front of Jim. "How fascinating. I'd no idea Flo worked on the estate."

"Thank you." Jim stirred a heaped teaspoon of sugar into the steaming mug. "Lots of people worked there once upon a time and then of course many others worked in the mines. That's how the Penwyntons made their money, you see. In fact, that's how most wealthy Cornish folks made their money. Cornwall had three industries, tin mining, fishing and farming, but mining was by far the most profitable. At least it was for the owners."

Stella opened a packet of chocolate digestive biscuits and placed half on a plate. "So the Penwyntons must have had the big house built, in which case only that family will ever have lived there."

Jim nodded. "That's right. They built the big house and all the others on the estate. The Inn too, of course, but they sold that back in the thirties."

"Is that when Frank bought it?"

"Yes, and a right state it was in too."

"And was it an inn then?"

Jim nodded. "It was, but it hadn't been used since mining was in its heyday. Cedric Penwynton closed it during the First World War because it was unsafe and it stayed empty, falling more and more into disrepair, for years until Frank bought it."

"Sounds much like the story of Penwynton House," said Stella. "I refer to the state of disrepair."

Jim nodded thoughtfully. "That's right. I think it's a real shame that the estate has been split up. But then the same thing is happening everywhere. It would have been nice though if the name of Penwynton had lived on in the village."

Stella put the plate of digestives on the table and sat down opposite Jim. "Please help yourself to biscuits, Jim." She stirred an artificial sweetener into her tea. "So who were the first Penwyntons, the ones that had the house built?"

"Well, that was Henry Penwynton, great, great, great, great grandfather of Charles who died recently. He was born in the 1720s and married Anne Stapleton. On Henry's death the estate went to their son, Henry. Then Henry left it to his son, George. Then from George it went to his son, Charles, who left it to his son, George. It then went to Cedric who left it to his son, Charles. Needless to say the sons all had wives, except for the last Charles, that is. He never married of course, more's the shame."

Stella laughed. "How on earth do you remember all that? It sounds most confusing."

Jim took a biscuit and dunked it in his tea. "I learned it years ago. It were all part of the job knowing a bit about the family: good and bad."

"And was there any bad?" asked Stella, with hope.

"Well, there was back in the days of the second George. He was born in 1820 and married Charlotte Grenville. They had two sons, Grenville in 1850 and Cedric in 1852. And it were during the birth of Cedric that poor Charlotte died."

Stella sighed. "Oh dear, but then sadly death during childbirth was a common occurrence back then."

Jim nodded. "Yes, it was. Anyway, a couple of years later George took a second wife. She was Talwyn Nancarrow, from down Penzance way. And in 1854 she produced a son they named Gorran and in 1856 a daughter called Kayna. I think I've got that right. Yes, I'm sure I have, but then the dates don't really matter, anyway, do they?"

Stella shook her head and smiled as Jim paused and took a huge sip of tea. "So who were the bad family members?"

Jim wiped his mouth on the cuff of his sleeve. "Well, the story handed down through two generations of employees says that Talwyn, the second wife, wasn't up to much. She didn't like Charlotte, the first wife's boys, you see, especially Grenville, who she knew would inherit the estate on his father's death, him being the oldest and all that. And it's said, because of this, they, the staff that is, thought it odd that he, Grenville, suddenly went off without saying goodbye. But he did leave a note which said he wanted to live a more simple life and he asked his father not to try and find him, ever. Well, needless to say, George did try to find his son, but he never had any luck and so to this day no-one knows where he went and what happened to him."

Stella frowned. "That sounds rather odd."

"Hmm, that's what folks said back then and because it seemed so out of character it was suggested that Talwyn was behind his going. She had money of her own, you see, although it were nowhere near as much as the Penwyntons had. Anyway, it's thought that she gave him enough dosh to start a new life elsewhere, and folks reckoned he would a bin only too glad to accept cos she made his life hell."

"Made his life hell! In what way?"

"Mental cruelty," said Jim. "Nag, nag, nag. You know what some women are like."

Stella smiled. "That all sounds rather ominous, but surely if it were true, then Grenville would have told his father. I mean, I can't believe his father, George didn't know what was going on. Not if it was so obvious that even the servants picked up on it."

"Well, maybe he did know or maybe he didn't. Perhaps he didn't really care. Grenville wasn't his favourite, you see. Cedric was. Grenville didn't like, hunting or shooting. He didn't like riding either and was afraid of horses. It's said he was a bit frail like his poor late mother, Charlotte, the first wife."

"I see. So when George died, the estate went to the younger brother, Cedric, of whom you speak most highly. So perhaps in a way, Gronville leaving was a blessing in disguise."

"Ah, yes, but it's said that after Grenville's departure, Talwyn tried to get Cedric to leave as well. But he had his eyes on the estate and would have none of it." Jim laughed. "She's got her wish now, though. Talwyn, that is. Her daughter might not have inherited the estate, but in the end her great grandson did."

"Now I'm really confused," said Stella. "I thought the whole estate had been left to a nephew in Canada."

"It has. Well, not a nephew he'd be more likely a second cousin. It's a bit complicated, let's see if I can explain it." He closed his eyes and screwed up his face deep in concentration. "Talwyn's daughter, Kayna, married a London banker. I can't be sure of his name but I think it was something or other Reeves. Anyway, they had a son called Geoffrey who moved to Canada and married a Canadian girl, after which they had a son who they christened Bernard who'd be in his fifties now, and he, Bernard, is the lucky relative."

"Oh, I see, I think. But what about Gorran, Kayna's older brother. Didn't he have any family? Because surely his family would take precedence over Kayna's?"

"Ah, now that's another story. Gorran died in his early twenties, you see. In a shooting accident, it was, and on the estate too. Well, it's always been claimed it were an accident but there were many as had their doubts."

Stella raised her eyebrows. "I'm intrigued. Tell me more."

"Well, there were a young gel working at the house and she were a chambermaid. Florrie Ham she were called as I remember. Anyway, when it were discovered that she were gonna have a little 'un, and that Gorran were likely as not the father, Talwyn promptly sacked her and sent her packing. Gorran denied having been anywhere near poor Florrie, you see, which broke the poor girl's heart." Jim tut-tutted. "It seems to me Gorran were just as cold hearted and conceited as his money-grabbing mother Talwyn."

Stella's eyebrow's narrowed. "Are you suggesting that Gorran was shot deliberately then?

Jim nodded.

"But by whom?"

"Florrie's father, it's reckoned. He were a fisherman over Polquillick and he were also a poacher. Everyone knew he had a rifle, so folks put two and two together and in the eyes of many made four. But of course we may be doing Gorran an injustice, although many said the child Florrie bore had Talwyn's eyes."

"So, in a way, if it's true, Talwyn got her comeuppance when she lost her beloved son. But what became of Florrie's child. Do you know?"

"Poor thing died when it were just a few months old. So it didn't live to have any descendants, who might have claim on the estate, if that's what you're thinking."

"Stella smiled. "You can read my thoughts. But what about Charles who died recently? Did he not have any siblings?"

"He had a twin sister but she died in the late 1940s. 1948 I think it was, not long before I retired. But she, like her brother never married and that's why the estate has gone into foreign hands. At least the proceeds from the sale of the estate will have gone overseas, but there will be a fair bit of death duty to pay first."

Stella and Jim both sat quietly each with their own thoughts until Stella broke the silence.

"Jim. If Grenville who disappeared married and had children elsewhere, then surely his descendants would take precedence when it comes to inheriting the estate over the descendants of his half-sister. I mean, Grenville was the rightful heir in the first place."

"You're right, but sadly because no trace of him was ever found, Charles, who died recently, left everything in his will to his cousin's son. So even if a descendant of Grenville was to turn up now, it'd be too late, and it's not likely to happen anyway. I've given it a lot of thought lately and reckon it was just kitchen tittle-tattle. The bitterness between George's second wife, Talwyn, and the boys that is. Folks like to have something to gossip about and I suppose they found it difficult to believe that anyone could turn their back on life in Penwynton House. I must admit, I would like to know what happened to him though, but I don't expect I ever will now, not after all this time. After all it's nearly a hundred years since young Grenville disappeared."

When Ned arrived home from school he found Stella sitting on the floor surrounded by photographs and an upturned empty drawer.

"Having a turn out?" he asked.

"No," Stella replied, smiling at a picture of the girls when they were little, "I'm trying to make a start with my new hobby. It's genealogy, you see. Jim Hughes has been round today telling me all about the Penwyntons. Jim knows details of the recently deceased Charles' ancestors going back to when the big house was built in the 1700s and it's made me realise just how little I know about my ancestors and yours too for that matter, and I think it will be a nice little hobby to find out."

"I see," grinned Ned, "but those photographs won't help much, will they? They only go back as far as our wedding."

Stella laughed. "I know, but it's a good excuse to have a look at them again. Meanwhile, while it's all still fresh in my mind, I shall write down details of the Penwynton history otherwise when Jim has gone it will be lost forever and that would be a great shame."

Ned nodded enthusiastically. "That's a lovely idea and I'm sure Jim would be only too happy to put you straight if you've forgotten some of the details."

Stella jumped up. "Would you like a cup of tea? It's time I got back in the kitchen anyway as I've a mountain of blackberries to deal with."

"I would, so I'll put the kettle on and make the tea while you deal with the blackberries and then you can tell me all about the Penwyntons."

CHAPTER TWENTY

Gertie was very quiet at the Drama group meeting on Tuesday evening and clearly had something on her mind, therefore Stella was not completely surprised when at the end of the rehearsal, Gertie asked if Ned was home because she needed to ask his advice. Stella, intrigued, was more than happy to invite Gertie back to The School House and eagerly looked forward to finding out what had caused her friend to forget her lines with alarming regularity.

It was dark with not a single star visible in the overcast sky when the two women left the village hall and walked the short distance along the dimly lit road. Stella, while wound up with curiosity, tactically refrained from asking any questions regarding Gertie's melancholy mood and chose instead to comment on the weather forecast which predicted rain for the following day and the possible success of the drama group's concert, thanks to the excellent choice of two one act plays selected by Joyce Richardson. Gertie made little response other than the occasional hmm and yes, her mind was clearly elsewhere.

The kitchen was in darkness and empty when they went in through the back door. Stella switched on the light and offered to take Gertie's coat after she had removed her own. She then led Gertie down the hall and into the sitting room where Ned sat at the table marking sums.

"Gertie," he said, looking up as she and Stella entered the room. "What brings you to our humble abode? A spot of learning lines perhaps?"

Gertie smiled feebly. "No, although I think I could do with it. What I actually want, Ned, is your advice. That's if you don't mind."

Ned was both flattered and curious. "Of course not. It's something everyone likes to give but no-one likes to receive. I'm all ears."

"Well, the thing is, I know in the past you've experienced weird goings on and such like. I mean things like Emily Penberthy and then before that the mystery of Jane's murder. It's because of those things

I need your help as I don't know who else to turn to or what else to do."

Ned's eyebrows rose sharply. Had Gertie been having thoughts of Sylvia too? Intrigued, he removed his reading glasses, closed the half marked arithmetic book and pushed it to one side. "Sit down, Gertie, and tell us what's wrong. After all a problem shared is a problem halved."

Gertie sat on the settee and Stella sat down beside her. "It's Edward Tucker or should I say Teddy Tinsdale. I know the police think his death was an accident or if it wasn't then he might have been bumped off by his ex-lover's husband, but I know of another motive and I don't want to say anything unless you think I ought as I don't want to lose my nice little job at Chy-an-Gwyns as I enjoy it very much and Catherine is ever so nice. Oh dear, I just want you to tell me my theory is silly so that everything can go back to being normal. You see, I've been worried sick about it for a week now, especially after hearing May and Bertha telling Madge that they had seen Catherine behaving in a very strange manner on the cliff tops by the old mine, directly above the spot where it turns out Teddy Tinsdale's body was found."

Ned baffled and confused, sat on the edge of his chair. "You have my undivided attention, Gertie. Whatever is it that you've found out?"

"Well, one day when I was at work a car pulled up outside, I don't know what sort it was because I could only see the top of the roof and I'm useless at car names anyway so I'd be none the wiser if I'd seen it all, but for what it's worth it was black. Anyway, out of it got a man who I'd never seen before and I watched as he walked along the path towards the front of the house. Catherine answered the door and I listened in the hallway simply because I wanted to know who he was. I don't know why, I just did, because I'm like that. Anyway, he said his name was Teddy Tinsdale and he showed Catherine a little card. She looked at it and then told him to go away. I didn't think anything of it much at first cos I didn't know what the card said and I thought he must have been selling something, you know, like insurance, but now I know he was a reporter it makes more sense. You see, I think he thought that Catherine's friend was Maggie Nan, and he went to the house after a story. Catherine's friend is called Margaret you see, so it sort of makes sense, doesn't it?"

Before Ned had a chance to reply Elizabeth burst into the room.

"Mum, did you collect my photos? Dad said you did but I can't find them anywhere."

"Elizabeth, don't interrupt when your elders are in conversation," snapped Stella, appalled by the behaviour of her daughter. "It's very rude, but yes, I did collect your snaps and they're still in my handbag because I forgot to take them out."

"Yippee," shouted Elizabeth, leaping up and down. "Can I get go and get them, please?"

"Yes, but then make yourself scarce and don't you dare interrupt us again."

Elizabeth hastily left the room and a few seconds later was heard running up the stairs calling to Anne.

Stella sighed. "I'm sorry about that, Gertie. My, how things have changed. I would never have dared enter a room like that without first knocking if my parents had someone with them."

"I know," said Gertie. "My mother was quite strict too. Still is in fact, and I'm not sure if the invention of the teenager was such a good thing. Having said that, I don't suppose Liz even knew I was here."

Ned didn't comment on the subject of behaviour as he was trying to make sense of the rigmarole he'd just heard.

"Okay, I can see where you're coming from with your theory, Gertie, but I can't see what evidence there is to back it up other than the fact that Catherine Rossiter has a friend called Margaret. I mean, surely you don't think Mrs Rossiter pushed Edward Tucker-cum-Teddy Tinsdale from the cliff path?"

Gertie raised her hands and then slapping them down on her knees. "I just don't know. I certainly hope not and I don't think she'd do anything like that, but police do like to know the movements of people who have died if the circumstances are at all suspicious, don't they? And she was certainly not pleased to see him and, as I've already said, May and Bertha both saw her on the cliffs behaving strangely the day before his body was found."

"So, let me get this straight," said Stella, trying to make sense of Gertie's information. "You think that Maggie Nan has not been kidnapped in America but is staying here in Cornwall with her friend, Catherine Rossiter, and that Teddy Tinsdale, staying at the Inn under his real name, Edward Tucker, got wind of the fact and went to Chy-an-Gwyns to confront her with his supposition?"

"Precisely," said Gertie, with delight. "You've got it in one. Now, do you think I'm crackers or should I go and tell Fred?"

"I think you ought to tell Fred," said Ned, his voice hesitant. "But surely by now someone must have seen the Margaret staying at Chy-an-Gwyns. From what I've heard Catherine Rossiter was a frequent visitor to the Inn when she first arrived here so someone must have seen her friend, and if she is the missing fashion designer surely she'd have been recognised. I mean to say, her face is plastered all over the papers often enough to quash any confusion."

"Well, actually I saw Alice the other day," said Gertie, "and I asked her, subtle like, if Catherine had been to the Inn lately and she said she hadn't seen her since the friend had arrived. But the thing is I've seen her myself. Margaret that is. Only once mind you and her face was smothered in cream which Catherine says she needs to put on every day. Oh dear, I should have mentioned that before, shouldn't I? Silly me! But I couldn't have identified her from what I saw cos as well as the cream on her face she had a towel on top of her head covering every bit of her hair. Needless to say, when I realised Teddy Tinsdale was a reporter, it occurred to me that the cream might be treatment for her gone-wrong face lift."

"Good heavens," said Stella, with alarm. "Then you definitely must see Fred, Gertie. That certainly sounds very odd."

"But surely if Maggie Nan was in hiding, Mrs Rossiter would have made sure that you never saw her, Gertie," said Ned.

"Well, that's another thing, I saw her quite by accident as I'd never seen her before and I haven't seen her since."

The sound of two sets of footsteps running down the stairs echoed through the house. When they reached the bottom, the sitting room door opened slowly and Elizabeth peeped in.

"Hmm, sorry to interrupt, but I thought you might like to see these photos," she said, waving five pictures above her head. "They're really odd, you must see them."

"Later," said Stella, exasperated. "Can't you see we're very busy?"

Ned noticed a look of disappointment on Elizabeth's face. "Bring them here, love," he said. "It'll not take a minute for a quick peep, come on."

Elizabeth meekly entered the room closely followed by Anne. She handed the photographs to Ned. The pictures were almost identical, each portrayed Anne and friends sitting on the steps of Penwynton House simultaneously saying cheese.

"Very nice," said Ned, feeling he'd done his duty. "But only five, didn't the rest come out?"

"Oh yes, the others were taken at Chy-an-Gwyns and they're fine, in fact they're really good cos Mrs Castor-Hunt took them, but it's these I wanted you to see. Put your specs on, Dad, and look again, then you'll be able to see what I'm getting at."

Ned picked up his reading glasses and perched them on the end of his nose. He looked again and then handed one each to Stella and Gertie. Both women stared at the pictures, nonplussed.

"Look at the downstairs window nearest the doors," said Elizabeth, impatiently. "There's a man looking out. Anne and I have looked at him through the magnifying glass and we recognise him from the pictures we've seen in the papers. He's the man that fell from the cliffs. Edward Tucker or whatever he's called."

She handed the magnifying glass to her father.

"Good heavens, you're right," said Ned, amazed. "How odd, but whatever was he doing in there? I'm surprised your young eyes didn't spot him when you took the pictures, Liz."

"I didn't spot him because he wasn't there," said Elizabeth, emphatically. "And that's because I took these pictures on the Saturday morning *two weeks* after his body had been found. Which means by then he was long dead. That face staring from the window must be his ghost. There's no other explanation."

CHAPTER TWENTY ONE

The following afternoon, when she knew he would be home from school, Gertie called for Ned and asked him to go with her to see Fred. He readily agreed and they walked down the road to The Police House in the rain, eager to hear if there had been any developments regarding Catherine Rossiter's possible concealment of Maggie Nan. Gertie had already visited the police constable that morning and told him of her theory. He had listened with interest and said he would call on Catherine himself before reporting anything to his superiors and suggested she called again later in the day, and if possible, bring with her the photos showing the face of Teddy Tinsdale at the window of Penwynton House. For although the photos would in no way implicate Mrs Rossiter he was keen to see them.

"What was Fred's reaction when you first mentioned the Maggie Nan and Catherine Rossiter connection?" asked Ned, as they walked down the road together huddled beneath Gertie's umbrella.

"He wasn't surprised because May and Bertha had already been round to see him to tell of the bizarre goings on they witnessed by the old mine involving Catherine. He conceded that nothing should be ruled out at this stage, although he has already dismissed as irrelevant the tale of the two old ladies. What's more, the husband of Tinsdale's ex-lover has cleared himself of any wrong doing by coming up with a rock solid alibi, so they've no reason to suspect him anymore, although of course he could have hired a hit man. On the other hand it could quite simply have been an accident and I hope it was: not that that will bring the poor man back. Percy said he was battered black and blue. What a horrible way to die, especially if it was a lingering death."

Ned smiled. "And is there a nice way to die before one's time is up?"

"Oh come on, Ned, you know what I mean. And yes, to die peacefully while sleeping would be a nice way to die, but let's chance the subject, it's too depressing!" She giggled, "You should have seen the look on Fred's face when I told him about Elizabeth's photos. He said, 'Ned and his bleedin' ghosts', then he apologised for swearing. I think he wants to see them so that he can make out it's a reflection or something like that. I hope you've remembered to bring a magnifying glass just in case he doesn't have one."

Ned grabbed Gertie's arm to avoid a puddle. "Oh yes, I know what Fred's like. He's probably Cornwall's greatest sceptic, when it comes to visions of the departed that is. "

Annie greeted them when they reached The Police House. She took their coats, put Gertie's umbrella in the kitchen sink and showed them into the living room to wait for Fred who was on the phone in the spare bedroom which he used as an office.

"Would you like a cup of tea?" Annie asked, as Gertie and Ned sat down beside each other on the settee. "I've just put the kettle on."

They spoke in unison. "Yes, please."

When Annie arrived back she placed the tea tray on the coffee table and sat down to let the tea brew.

"Do you have the photos with you?" she asked, a twinkle in her eyes. "They sound most intriguing."

Ned passed them to her along with the magnifying glass as she put on her reading spectacles. "They're all much of a muchness but some are a little clearer than others."

Annie crossed to the window to make use of the brighter light and looked at all five photographs. "Well, well, it's him without doubt. How fascinating." She handed the pictures back to Ned and then sat down. "And when was it they were taken?"

Ned lay the photographs down on the coffee table. "On the Saturday, two weeks after Edward Tucker's body was found. And as Stella reminded me, there's no doubt about that because the jacket Anne is wearing was only purchased in town the day before, as Stella met the girls from school especially to buy it as her old one was getting a bit on the small side."

"I see. Well, I don't know what Fred will make of this, you know what an old sceptic he is. Have you shown them to Molly yet?"

Ned nodded. "Yes, I popped round with them at lunch time as I'd taken them to school with me. She's convinced it's him and is emphatic that if his ghost is around then he was murdered and his spirit cannot rest, but I think that's probably wishful thinking."

They heard the sound of footsteps descending the staircase, and then Fred entered the room.

"Ah, Gertie, I'm glad you're here as I can now put your mind at rest. Catherine Rossiter's friend is not Maggie Nan. I've met the lady in question, without face cream I might add, and it was plain even to an old man like me that they're nothing like each other, and I would say that Margaret at Chy-an-Gwyns is a bit older than the dress designer too, although I didn't like to ask her age, so it's only guess work."

Gertie fidgeted nervously. "Did you tell Catherine that it was me who reported Teddy Tinsdale's visit to Chy-an-Gwyns?"

Fred nodded. "I'm afraid I had to but she wasn't cross, in fact if anything I think she was quite amused and flattered that you thought she had friends in such high places."

Ned tilted his head to one side. "Did she say why Tinsdale had called on her then? If she told him to go away she must have had good reason to do so. In fact, why did he call on her in the first place?"

"She says she saw him in the post office one day and realised it was him even though he was wearing a wig. She also knew by the look he gave her that he'd recognised her as Captain Rossiter's wife. Her husband, Henry, is quite a well-known figure in up-country circles and he was most likely wanting to know why she was in Cornwall when her husband was at sea. Teddy Tinsdale apparently has a gossip column, so she assumes he jumped to the wrong conclusion and thought she was having an affair with a Cornishman or something like that. She's very wary of the media, she doesn't like the way they pry into people's lives and that's why she was a little off hand with him."

"Well, that's a relief," said Ned, leaning back on the settee. "So if Tinsdale's ex-lover's husband has a good alibi and Catherine Rossiter has nothing to hide, then it looks as though it was an accident, and I suppose even if it is him on the photographs it proves absolutely nothing."

"Ah, the photos," grinned Fred, glancing at the ceiling. "Let's have a look at them."

Ned handed over the pictures, which the police constable studied with a puzzled expression.

"Well, as much as I would like to disagree with you, this chap certainly looks like Edward Tucker." He lay the photos down on his lap. "The thing is, I got a colleague of mine, who has a friend in the Met, and he agreed to have a chat with the estate agents in London who are handling the sale of Penwynton House, to see if either Edward Tucker or Teddy Tinsdale had viewed the house, bearing in mind you'd need a key to get inside. And no-one of either name has been to, or made enquiries about the place, which makes me believe that he wasn't inside the house at all, but it was his reflection looking into the house from outside."

Gertie giggled. "But ghosts don't have reflections, do they? she impishly said. "And aren't they supposed to be able to walk through walls and doors? Cos if that's the case he wouldn't have needed a key."

"Humph, don't ask me," Fred grunted. "Ask Ned, he's the expert. Anyway, if what I know about ghosts is true, and I can't believe I'm even saying this, then their spirits are supposed to haunt the place where they died, aren't they? In which case, Tucker's ghost should be on the rocks by the old mine and not inside the old house at all."

"Jane died at the Witches Broomstick," said Ned, without hesitation. "But her spirit popped up in all sorts of places, so I don't go along with that theory. But I can see what you're trying to say. If Tucker had never been inside the house, then there's no reason for his ghost to be there."

"Precisely, whereas he could quite easily have walked through the grounds of Penwynton House, as many people do, especially Bluebell Woods, and in this case I know he was interested to go there, as he asked me about public access a day or two before he died. And that theory's also backed up by a statement from Frank and Dorothy, who said Mr Tucker was very fond of walking. So at the end of the day, even if it is his ghost, then it proves absolutely nothing. And if ghosts are free to come and go as they please, their presence doesn't indicate foul play. Which I must admit, thrills me greatly, as I didn't want to have to inform my superiors of more spooks in Trengillion. Nevertheless, I'm told by my colleague's mate in the Met, that a couple interested in viewing the old house are coming down next Tuesday, and they've been instructed to drop the key in to me when they've done so then I can take a poke around.

And then after I've done that, I'll post the keys back to the estate agents in London. I'm hoping that little move will keep everybody happy."

"Don't go round the old house on your own Fred, you mustn't, not if it's haunted," said Gertie.

Fred laughed. "Don't worry about me young lady. I don't really believe in ghosts and I'm sure that if I was in a room full of them I wouldn't even notice."

Ned called at Rose Cottage to see his mother after he had escorted Gertie back to Coronation Terrace, as he had promised to let her know if there were any new developments. He found her in the kitchen preparing sandwiches for supper, while the major watched a documentary about battles on the television in the living room.

"Any news?" she eagerly asked, as he took a seat at the kitchen table.

"Not really," said Ned, helping himself to a pickled onion. "Not interesting news, anyway. Catherine's friend is definitely not Maggie Nan, and Edward Tucker's, lover's, husband has an alibi for the day Tucker died, so really it's all a bit of an anti-climax."

"Oh dear, how disappointing," said Molly. "I've been thinking about the photos, by the way, and as we agreed at lunch time, there's no way that face at the window is anything other than a ghost, which I find most exciting, as it's the proof I've always wanted to flaunt at the 'doubting Thomases' of this world. The trouble is I can't see that it bears any relevance to the poor man's death and I think a more likely indication as to what's going on might be found in your dream about Sylvia."

"Sylvia!" said Ned. "Whatever do you mean?"

"Well, I don't really know. But Dorothy is convinced that a chap staying at the Inn called Bill Briggs is up to no good, although I couldn't detect any insincerity about the man when I met him. I just thought him boring. He's sleeping in the room previously occupied by Edward Tucker, not that that was his doing, it just came about by chance. But I can't help but wonder if there might be something dodgy going on and Sylvia was trying to tell you in a dream, so that perhaps you could warn Frank."

Ned frowned. "But surely if that were the case she would warn Frank herself. I mean to say, how can I say anything to him if I've no idea what the danger might be?"

"She probably couldn't go to Frank direct cos he's not susceptible to voices from the spirit world, whereas you are. How was it she said Frank was in danger again? Tell me her exact words, if you can remember them."

"She didn't say he was in danger, she said she didn't want him to get hurt, which I suppose is the same thing. But in retrospect, I'm sure that was nothing more than a dream brought about by my thinking of her a lot lately. Dreams are after all, a mishmash of each day's events and thoughts."

Molly agreed. "Well, yes, I suppose they are and perhaps I'm just grasping at straws."

The door opened and the major walked in from the living room.

"I thought I heard voices, but it was a job to tell over the telly. My hearing's not what it used to be. Any news about that chap Tucker, Ned? I think it was suicide myself. Newspaper blokes are a bit highly strung and if he'd been threatened it wouldn't take much to push him over the edge, if you'll excuse the pun. I met several newspaper men during the War and believe you me, they weren't like normal folks."

"Oh come on, Ben, that's a bit unfair," said Molly. "Sid Reynolds is perfectly normal and he's a reporter."

"But he wasn't born to it, Moll, not like some of them are, and he only works for the local rag anyway. I'm talking about the Fleet Street lot. I've heard they can be quite ruthless when the opportunity arises for them to make a name for themselves. Why, there's no doubt about it, but some of them would sell their own grannies to get a good story."

CHAPTER TWENTY TWO

The third Friday in September brought with its dawning, great excitement amongst the younger members of Trengillion, for it heralded the beginning of weekly discotheques to be held in the village hall, and as Jamie Stevens was to be the DJ, the girls held long discussions on the bus returning home from school, as to what they would be wearing on the off chance that Jamie might notice them on the dance floor. The fact he had a girlfriend of twelve months with whom he was going steady was no deterrent to the giddy girls. Day dreaming was all part of growing up, therefore with Jamie taking on the role of DJ, when he already belonged to a local pop group, statistics made him the obvious idol on whom to focus their undivided attention. For the departure of Danny the builder from their leisure time activities, had left a void which the girls urgently needed to fill, otherwise, they considered life had no meaningful purpose at all.

The Village Hall Committee had approved the discotheque providing no alcohol was consumed on the premises, for they wanted the events to be occasions where the youngsters could enjoy themselves without trouble which might occur if alcohol were involved. They chose also, not to put a lower age limit on admission and instead left that decision to the discretion of parents, who it was considered would know how responsibly their children would behave when out of parental supervision. Elizabeth had the blessing of Ned and Stella to go to the first discotheque under the premise that should they hear any unfavourable reports about her behaviour then her first would also be her last. Anne on the other hand was deemed far too young and would have to wait until she was thirteen.

"It's so unfair," Anne complained, as she watched Elizabeth getting ready to go out. "Susan and Jane are both going and they'll not be thirteen 'til next February and April. Mum and Dad are so mean."

"Yes, but at least they'll be thirteen next birthday, you'll only be twelve and then not until June. You're far too young: the discotheque's for teenagers, not children. Anyway, I'll tell you all about it tomorrow, so that'll nearly be as good as being there."

"It won't!" said Anne, bitterly, and she stormed off to her room, slammed shut the door and wrote in her diary about the unfairness of life with such anger that the harshness of her words left their indentation, deep throughout the following blank pages of her book.

Shortly after Elizabeth left for the discotheque, the telephone rang in The School House. Stella answered. It was Rose, a note of excitement in her voice.

"You'll never believe what," she said, before Stella had time to greet her properly. "I've been dying to ring you all day, but didn't like to use the phone at work."

Stella sat down on the hall floor eager to hear the exciting news. "Fire away Rose, I'm all ears."

Rose giggled. "Right, well, George and I went to a party last night, it was the fortieth for one of my work colleagues and she held it in a small hotel nearby. It was a really good do, fantastic food and a great group played too, not a well-known one of course, just a few local lads. Anyway, you'll never guess who was there."

"Hmm, I've no idea," said Stella, thoughtfully racking her brain for names. "Unless it was Maggie Nan."

Rose chuckled. "Good guess, but nowhere near right. It was Freddie Short. You remember, the hippie bloke staying at the Inn when we were down the other week."

"No! Well I never. Was he dressed like he was down here?"

"Sort of. He still has long hair, but it's curly now and he's grown a fabulous, droopy moustache which really suits him. I have to admit he actually looked quite dishy. Anyway, his clothes, while still very way-out, were not quite as extreme as back in Cornwall and he certainly didn't have flowers in his hair."

"He had his hair permed while he was down here," said Stella. "After you'd gone home. Betty did it for him. Apparently Miss Pringle, staying at the Inn won a hair-do in the Barn Dance raffle or something like that and she and Freddie swapped prizes. So did you get to talk to him?"

"Absolutely! As soon as I saw him I knew I had to speak and I must admit I was dead chuffed because he recognised me instantly."

"Well, fancy that. It really is a small world."

"Oh yes, but the amazing thing is he's a copper in the Drug Squad, and his dress is all part of his uniform, so to speak."

Stella gasped and leaned back on the wall. "Good heavens! Well then it all makes sense now, doesn't it? It explains why, on occasions, he used to forget to say groovy, fab, babe and suchlike, and why he was a bit vague about his profession as a teacher at Art College."

"Absolutely! He no more teaches than I do, and that's why he recognised the smell of cannabis, of course."

"Brilliant," said Stella, with a girlish laugh. "That also means I know a bit more about him than Fred. He knew that Freddie was alright, but that was all."

"What on earth do you mean?" asked Rose, clearly baffled by Stella's remark.

"The letter Dorothy and Frank had from the Gibson sisters who stayed at the Inn this summer. Surely I must have told you about that."

"No, I've not the foggiest idea what you're talking about. I know who the Gibson sisters are because they were down for a wedding the same time as us, but as for what you're talking about, I'm completely in the dark."

"Oh, well it's a bit of a non-story really, but Frank and Dorothy had a letter from the girls, or should I say women, saying they'd seen Tucker coming out of Freddie's room at the Inn one night when he wasn't there, because he was actually at the Barn Dance. Apparently, they didn't say anything at the time, but when they read in the papers that he was dead, they felt they ought to let someone know. Anyway, Fred reported it, and he had word back that Freddie had been investigated and was not involved, but he wasn't told any more than that, which makes sense if he works undercover. We got this all from Molly who gets on well with Dorothy."

"So what was Tucker looking for?" Asked Rose. "Drugs do you suppose?"

"No idea, and I don't expect we ever will know now he's dead. So do you reckon he was working while down here or was he on holiday?"

Rose giggled. "He wouldn't say but I've a sneaky feeling he was working. I was really surprised when I first saw him and then I half expected to see Miss Pringle at the party too and find she was also worked for the Drug Squad."

"But surely she wasn't! That would be too hard to imagine."

"No, she wasn't. I asked Freddie about her though and he said they just got on well. He felt sorry for her, being on her own, and I'm sure he helped make her holiday a happy one. We talked about Edward Tucker, alias Teddy Tinsdale too, and Freddie was surprised he'd not realised who he was when he was in Cornwall. Although he said he didn't take Teddy's paper so his face wasn't familiar and of course he was wearing a wig as well, wasn't he?"

"Hmm, so I'm told."

"Anyway, don't say anything to anyone about Freddie's job will you? Although I think it's unlikely he'll be seen in Trengillion again. Unless of course it's for a holiday, which it may well have been this time. I hope that makes sense."

"Yes, of course, and I won't say anything about Freddie's job. I'm a bit concerned over his visit here though. I mean, I hate the idea of drugs being available in Trengillion, especially having two young daughters."

"I think you'll find drugs are pretty easy to come by in most places if you know where to go, but your girls are sensible and I'm sure they'd never do anything daft. Anyway, how is everyone?"

"Everyone's fine. Elizabeth's out, she's gone to Trengillion's first discotheque, so we've a very grumpy Anne at home because Ned and I both said she was too young to go. I don't think she likes us very much at the moment."

"Oh dear, poor Anne, but she is too young. Although I doubt it would really matter in a village. I mean, there's hardly likely to be any trouble, is there?"

"Probably not, but we have to draw the line somewhere and we don't want her to think she can do just as she pleases. How's the job? Anything interesting happening in your area, apart from finding Freddie is a work colleague that is?"

"No, it's been pretty humdrum lately and I've lost interest in the Maggie Nan story too. It's gone on for too long so has lost its intrigue and I'm beginning to think, like the media, that she's sunning herself on foreign shores somewhere, waiting 'til she looks presentable again."

"Hmm, I think I agree, because I thought it very odd that after her husband handed over the ransom money, her kidnappers didn't reveal her whereabouts. Although someone else could have got in on the act, I suppose. An imposter perhaps, and it was he who sent letters to the American police. But whatever goes on it all sounds very fishy and I don't think anybody knows or cares now."

"Just remembered. I keep meaning to ask if Frank has found a buyer for the Inn yet; it must have been on the market for several weeks now."

Stella shook her head. "Not as far as I know. They've had several people look and they didn't like one couple in particular. At least Dot didn't like the wife, according to Molly. I don't get down there much, but if a buyer had been found then I'm sure I would have heard on the grapevine; we've some very active gossips in the village as you'll well remember."

After the phone call, Stella picked up the Radio Times to see what was on the television and as nothing in particular seemed of interest in her current state of mind she opted instead to pursue her quest for information regarding her family history.

"Who are you writing to?" asked Ned, peering over Stella's shoulder as she sat on the settee with note pad on her lap, busy scribbling away with her fountain pen.

"Mum," she answered, tapping the end of the pen on her teeth. "I've written out a questionnaire for her asking the full names and dates of birth of her parents and grandparents, aunts, uncles and so forth and I've written out one for Dad too. If they can give me the details I want then it might be enough to get my family tree started. I think it's really exciting and it'll be something I can hand down to future generations."

"Hmm, it should be interesting, if you can get anywhere with it," said Ned, looking at his watch.

"I've written out the same questionnaire for your mum too, but I don't know what to do about your dad's side of the family. Do you think your mum would be able to fill it in?"

Ned laughed. "I doubt it. Mum likes to pretend Dad's family don't exist, but if you'll let me have one of your questionnaires I'll send it to Dad myself. It's about time I dropped him a line, anyway, as I don't think I've done so since his birthday, which is very remiss of me."

"Well, I've nearly finished my letter to Mum and Dad, so I'll be finished with the writing pad in a minute. You can do your letter then, as there's no time like the present."

"Well, actually, I was thinking of popping down to the Inn for a pint, if you've no objections. But I promise I'll do the letter tomorrow as I've nothing else planned."

"Of course I've no objections as long as you don't drink too much or cast an eye on any female in there you consider to be prettier than me."

"Oh, for God's sake, Stell, you know I'm no womaniser, my intention is purely to have a chat with the lads."

Stella grinned. "I know, but it doesn't hurt to remind you from time to time. Anyway, since you'll obviously see Frank try and find out if they've a buyer for the Inn yet. Rose asked me when she phoned tonight and I had to say I didn't know."

"Good point, someone asked me the same question the other day, but I can't remember who it was."

He bent down and kissed her cheek. "I'll not be long, about an hour I suppose. See you later."

Stella suppressed a smile, looked at the clock as he left the room and made a bet with herself that he would not be home before closing time.

CHAPTER TWENTY THREE

On Saturday morning, Molly went into her pantry for eggs to make a cake and found only one left in the box. She cried out with frustration. She and the major had had omelettes for lunch the previous day and Molly had completely forgotten she needed to make a cake for the harvest festival. She did, however, remember that Milly sold eggs in the post office from Treloars' farm, because Madge had told her that if ever she ran out, either to give her a ring or go and see Milly, and as Molly had already creamed together the margarine and caster sugar, time was of the essence, and so she opted to pop over the road to the post office before they closed at twelve thirty.

Without bothering to brush her hair or put on her shoes, Molly grabbed her purse from her handbag and ran over the road in her slippers without bothering to lock the door. But when she reached the post office she found it empty: neither Milly nor Johnny was behind the counter and the door was wide open. Molly waited patiently, thinking whoever was looking after the post office had perhaps slipped into the living quarters to spend a penny, although she thought it seemed odd that they should bother so near to closing time.

Three minutes went by and Molly began to feel agitated by the tedious wait. Drumming her fingers impatiently in the counter she glanced at the main headlines on the front pages of the unsold newspapers, and then to pass the time, counted the polystyrene tiles covering the shop's ceiling. But still no-one appeared to serve her.

The clock on the wall struck half past twelve. Frustrated and perplexed, Molly's eyes darted from the clock to the open post office door. She mumbled a few words of dissatisfaction, sighed deeply, and then held her breath in order to listen for any sound of life emanating from the Pascoes' living quarters. When she realised all was silent, she felt slightly ill at ease. Her heart began to race, as with a quick glance over her shoulder, she walked, apprehensively towards the door that led out into the hallway. By a table on which the telephone sat, she called out Milly and Johnny's names. There was no response. Molly's unease turned to panic and then fear. Her throat went dry. She knew something was wrong, terribly wrong. For in retrospect neither Milly nor Johnny would ever leave the post office unattended. Both were sensible and responsible adults.

Molly tapped her fingernails on her teeth and pondered over what action she should take. A bus pulled up outside and as it pulled away it suddenly occurred to her that the post office might have been robbed and Milly and Johnny may be somewhere out the back lying bound and gagged.

Conjuring up a little confidence, Molly decided to look inside the till to see if any money was missing. Feeling like a criminal, she stepped into forbidden territory behind the post office counter. As she reached for the drawer, her foot kicked hard against something soft on the floor. She stopped dead and her heart sank as she forced herself to look down. She screamed. Milly lay in a heap, her clothing soaked in blood. Panic-stricken and terrified, Molly shouted for help, locked the door in fright and ran back into the hallway where she grabbed the telephone receiver and dialled 999. She then phoned Fred at The Police House.

Molly was relieved when she heard Fred rapping on the post office door. Eagerly she unlocked it and let him in, thankful to hand over the situation to a wiser and more composed human being than herself. Fred put his hands on Molly's shoulders in a reassuring manner and then dashed across the floor and knelt by Milly's side. "Thank God, she's still breathing, Molly. You have phoned for an ambulance, haven't you?"

Tears streamed down Molly's face. "Yes, I have. Oh, I'm sorry Fred, I'm completely useless. I should have looked behind the counter before I did, but my silly old brain doesn't think as quickly as it used to."

Fred brushed a strand of hair away from Milly's face. "I wonder where the rest of the family are. They obviously aren't here or they'd have heard the commotion."

Molly dried her eyes. "The boys are probably up at the farm. Madge was saying only the other day how much they like to visit, especially this time of the year when there's so much going on. I don't know where Johnny's likely to be though."

When the ambulance arrived, Fred rang the Treloars' farm. Madge, who was busy making sandwiches for lunch, answered the phone. "Yes, David and Stephen are both here and so is Johnny. They are out gathering straw to decorate the church for the harvest festival. Why do you ask?"

Madge was shocked to hear of the attack on her daughter and too stunned to speak. She passed the phone over to Johnny who had just entered the kitchen to wash his hands.

"I'm on my way," said Johnny. He dropped the phone down and turned to Madge. "Come on, we'll drop the boys off at the Inn with their Auntie Dorothy."

"No," said Madge, trying to keep calm. "No, we'll leave them here with Albert, then we'll not have to tell them what's happened. We'll pretend we've gone to get something. I'll quickly tell Albert while you make up excuses to the boys. The sandwiches are all made so they'll probably not sense anything is wrong. We mustn't frighten them."

Madge and Johnny followed the ambulance to the hospital where Milly was taken unconscious with serious head injuries, while in the post office, police officers from town questioned Molly and searched the premises for clues as to the identity of the attacker. Robbery had already been established as the motive, for Johnny had checked both drawers in which they kept their takings. The shop drawer was empty, except for small change, but the post office drawer had not been touched. So either the robber was not aware the takings were kept separately or he didn't have time to look thoroughly. They also found the blunt instrument which had been used to hit Milly on the head. It was an old fashioned clothes iron, used to prop open the shop door on sunny days. Fred found it outside in the long grass, one side of it smeared with dry blood.

"You can go now, Molly," said Fred, gently taking her hands in his. "You're looking very pale and there's nothing more you can do. Would you like me to give the major a ring so that he can come and get you?"

"No, thanks, Fred, I'll be alright, but it's been such a shock. I'll go and see Doris, I think. The major's out, you see. He's at the golf club, so he'll not be back 'til teatime."

Fred took Molly's arm. "Then I'll escort you to Ivy Cottage. We can't have you passing out in the street."

Doris made Molly a cup of strong, sweet tea, even though she did not take sugar, and then wrapped a blanket around her shoulders, for she could see that Molly was still in shock.

Molly sobbed as she sipped her tea. "I feel so silly, so stupid. Poor Milly's lost a lot of blood and if I'd had the sense to look behind the counter earlier then she'd have got medical help sooner which would have boosted her chances of survival. I'll never forgive myself if she doesn't make it. I'm a fool, a silly, silly old fool and I'm thoroughly ashamed of myself."

The following day the church was packed for the harvest festival, although the vicar did not doubt for one minute that many of the faces not usually seen in the congregation were there purely to find out the latest gossip regarding the horrendous attack on Milly Pascoe. For although questioning by the police had established a motive, the identity of the attacker was a complete mystery. The last person to see her prior to the robbery was Joyce Richardson who had called at the post office just after midday for some stamps, and in her statement to the police she reported Milly's behaviour had been perfectly normal. She had told Joyce the costume she was making for her part in the Drama group's play was almost finished. Joyce did not recall seeing any suspicious characters in the vicinity of the post office or any unfamiliar cars.

Prayers were said for Milly, and the harvest hymns, well known and favourites with many, were sung with less enthusiasm than previous years, for the voices of Trengillion lacked lustre and even the choir sang with muffled tones.

Many of the villagers found it incomprehensible that such brutality could happen in a quiet Cornish village and they keenly expressed their views after the service.

"It couldn't have been anyone local," said Betty, as she chatted to her contemporaries outside the church in the September sunshine. "Pete said they only took the takings from the shop drawer, but all local people know Milly and Johnny had a drawer for the post office as well."

"Yes, but it might have been someone who wanted it to look like it was done by a stranger, although I find it difficult to believe that anyone from Trengillion would harm Milly," said Meg. "I reckon it was someone passing through, who went in the post office, found Milly on her own, and he took his chance. But whoever he was I'd like to get my hands on him and wring his neck."

Gertie was alarmed. "Christ! Don't let your dad hear you talk like that, you're supposed to be forgiving."

Meg half smiled. "I don't think you'll find Dad very forgiving today, he's absolutely livid. He would have postponed the harvest festival had so many people not already made preparations and gathered stuff in."

"I reckon someone wanted the money for drugs," said Gertie, thoughtfully nodding her head. "There's been some right weird people about this summer. Remember that bloke who stayed at the Inn recently? Freddie something or other. I bet he was up to no good. I mean, no-one could really be like that, could they?"

Stella heard the comment and bit her lip, knowing she could say nothing in Freddie's defence.

"Between you and me, it's really upset Fred," said Annie Stevens, who had caught the end of the conversation. "He's wondering if Milly's attack is in any way linked to Edward Tucker's death. I mean, it does seem odd to have two such incidents so close together, although there's nothing at all to link the two."

"I thought Fred was only too happy to rule out anything suspicious regarding Mr Tucker," smiled Meg. "That's what I'd heard, anyway."

Annie nodded. "And so he was, but as I said, now he has his doubts. So many ends need tying up and he was only saying a couple of days ago that by now Tucker's shoe ought to have turned up."

Betty wrinkled her nose. "Shoe. What shoe?"

"Apparently one of Edward Tucker's shoes was missing when his body was found and it was assumed it came off in the fall, but Fred said he didn't really see how that could have happened, cos if it had come off in the fall surely it would have landed near to the body."

Gertie nodded. "Percy mentioned that, but he assumed it had fallen into the sea."

Stella listened to the conversation dumbfounded, looking from one woman to another until the chatter ceased.

"Why on earth has no-one mentioned a shoe before?" she asked, when finally she found her voice. "I was out walking, a while back now, in fact I was blackberrying, and I found a shoe in a field near the lane at the back of the Coastguard Cottages. I thought it odd that it should have been discarded as it was almost new."

Annie gasped. "Really! Come back with me Stella and tell that to Fred, he'll be most interested, and between you perhaps you'll be able to establish whether or not your find fits the description of the missing shoe."

Fred was cutting the escallonia hedge in the back garden when Annie and Stella arrived at the Police House. Annie tapped on the kitchen window and beckoned him to join her inside.

"Stella has something to tell you," she blurted, as he put his head around the kitchen door.

Fred lay down the shears on top of the dustbin. "Really!" What have you been up to, young lady?"

Stella blushed. "Nothing, but thank you, Fred, it's nice to be called young again after all these years."

"You'll always be young in my eyes."

"Thank you."

Fred entered the room and closed the back door. "Right, shall we sit down?"

They each pulled out a chair and sat around the kitchen table. Fred cast a questioning glance at Stella. "So, what is it you want to tell me?"

"It's probably not the right one, but I found a shoe up on the cliff tops a while back, in a field by the lane leading to the Coastguard cottages, and Annie thinks there's a chance it may have belonged to Mr Tucker."

Fred leaned back and scratched his chin. "Really! Can you remember what it was like?"

"Yes, I can, because it was much like a pair Ned has, but Ned's are black and this one was a brown. It was a brown, Lotus lace-up, size eight and nearly new. I found it in a field when I went to see what turned out to be a screwed up white paper bag. I'd thought the bag might have been a mushroom, you see. As for the shoe, I assumed it must either have been thrown into the field or that it had fallen from someone's foot as they had walked across the field, although in both cases it didn't seem feasible. So, is it the missing shoe do you think?"

Fred firmly nodded his head. "Without question. Can you remember what you did with it, Stella?"

"Yes, I tucked it in a hedge thinking perhaps it'd keep dry there, should anyone go looking for it. But I suppose in retrospect that was a silly thing to do."

"If I drove you up there could you show me where you put it?"

"I'd be delighted to," said Stella, feeling a pang of excitement.

Fred stood up. "The sooner we go the better, because if there has been any foul play it might still have finger prints on it, if it's been protected from the weather that is."

Stella also rose. "Can I just pop home first and tell Ned what's what or he'll wonder where on earth I've got to."

"Of course," said Fred, reaching up for the car keys hanging from a hook on the back of the door. "You can pop in as we drive up that way."

A fresh wind was blowing across the cliff tops as Fred parked beside the gate in the lane near to where the shoe had been found.

After closing the car door Stella pointed towards a hedge "It's in this field here, but I went into it from the other side as I was on the bridal path."

Fred nodded. "I guessed this was where you meant."

They walked through long grass towards a dilapidated five bar gate. Fred rested his hand on the top. "Let's see if we can get this wretched thing open. Might be tricky though because it looks to me like these ropes haven't been disturbed for a while."

"Hmm, and I think the grass beneath it is a bit too long to drag the gate over anyway. I don't know about you, but I can climb it." Stella put both feet onto the bottom bar of the gate. "It'll be a lot quicker than trying to undo it."

Fred laughed. "Well, I should hope I can climb over too. I don't think I'm completely senile just yet."

Both climbed the gate and jumped down into the field below.

"It's funny you thought you saw a mushroom in this field, cos when I was a boy, this was known as the mushroom field, although I don't think there have been any in here for a good many years now."

"Who owns it?" asked Stella.

"Cyril Penrose, it's part of Long Acre Farm. It really pleases me that Cyril was able to buy the farm in the end. He's worked hard enough for it over the years. I've a lot of time for farmers; they do a damn good job."

"Absolutely," agreed Stella, as they walked through the grass. She pointed as they neared a hedge. "The shoe's over there by the elder bush."

"I haven't been up here for years," said Fred, stopping to take in the scenery and the view across the ocean. "That's the trouble with living in a place like this, you're inclined to take it for granted and not make use of what it has to offer."

Stella was puzzled. "But didn't you come up here when Mr Tucker's body was found?"

Fred shook his head. "No, we didn't. We approached the spot from the sea in Percy and Peter's boat. We couldn't have got to him from up the cliffs as he was too far down."

"I see." Stella knelt and parted the leaves of the hedge. "This is the place, I remember it because of the clump of nettles. I tucked it in here."

But when she looked the shoe was not there. Thinking it might have slipped, she and Fred then searched the undergrowth but it was nowhere to be seen.

Stella was frustrated and cross. "This is crazy. Where can it be? I mean, surely no-one has taken it. One odd shoe is of no possible use to anyone."

"Hmm, I reckon it's gone because someone knew it could be used as evidence," said Fred, scratching his chin. "You know what, Stella? I reckon Tucker was brought through this field, either dead or unconscious and he was chucked over the cliff. And it was while he was carried through here that his shoe fell off. But then if I'm right, I'm mystified as to why that gate hasn't been opened for a while, cos there's no other way in from the lane."

"Perhaps whoever brought the poor man here threw him over the gate and then climbed over himself as we did," suggested Stella. "In which case, during the fall, Mr Tucker could quite easily have lost his shoe."

"You know, I think you could well be right, young lady," said Fred, with a satisfied grin. "Well done! Now we better get back, because this whole to-do needs a lot more attention than it's had so far. I don't know about you, but it looks very much to me, like we're faced with a sickening case of murder."

The post office remained closed throughout Monday and in the evening the church held its annual harvest sale, when produce donated for the Harvest Festival was auctioned. Usually the proceeds from the sale went into church funds, but following an emergency meeting held by the Parochial Church Council, it was unanimously decided that all money raised should go to Johnny Pascoe and the boys.

The sale was better attended than usual and the produce fetched high prices as all were keen to show that the Pascoe family were high in their thoughts. There was also an air of excitement as word got round that the police regarded the death of Edward Tucker as suspicious. Bertha and May let it be known that they thought Catherine Rossiter was somehow involved, while many others pointed fingers at one of the other guests staying at the Inn the same time as Edward Tucker, namely Freddie Short. It was even suggested that Miss Pringle was probably not as sweet and innocent as they recalled.

CHAPTER TWENTY FOUR

On Tuesday afternoon, Bill Briggs carried his luggage out to his Ford Cortina, packed it in the boot and then returned to the Inn to thank Frank and Dorothy for their hospitality."

"Did you see the bird you were looking for?" asked Frank, spotting a cobweb in the corner by the door as they stood in the hall.

"Yes, I did. It was up on the cliffs where I'd anticipated it would be. I've taken several pictures and now I want to get back, develop them and show them off to my colleagues."

"Lovely," said Frank. "And now you've found what you were looking for, are you willing to tell us its name, not that I expect we'll have heard of it."

Bill Briggs paused and then laughed. "I don't expect you have. It was a Black-throated Yellow Spotted Gillygot, a close relative of the wagtail. A friend told me one had been spotted down here and I was determined to get a picture, so needless to say, I'm delighted."

"A Black-throated Yellow Spotted Gillygot!" spluttered Dorothy, when Bill Briggs had gone. "I reckon he's just made that up. I told you he was up to no good."

"Don't start that again, Dot. Anyway, even I've heard of a wagtail. I even know there's a black and white variety which looks a bit like a miniature Magpie."

"Well, I know that too. You're referring to the Pied Wagtail," scoffed Dorothy. "But I'd be very much surprised if its relative the Black-throated Yellow Spotted Gillygot variety exists."

As Dorothy left the hallway to get fresh bed linen in order to change Bill Briggs' bed, the bell by the side door of the Inn rang.

Dorothy scowled. "Damn, that'll be the Withers. They're early, I was hoping to get the phoney twitcher's room looking tidy before they arrived." She slammed the linen cupboard door shut.

With a tired sigh, Frank answered the door. On the doorstep stood a couple in their late thirties or early forties. Frank offered his hand. "Mr and Mrs Withers, I assume."

"That's right, chum. I'm Raymond and this is my other half, Gloria."

"Come in," said Frank, unimpressed by his first impression. "I'm Frank Newton and this is my wife Dorothy."

The two couples shook hands in the hallway.

Frank closed the door. "Now, where would you like to look first, in the bars or in the guest rooms upstairs?"

Mr and Mrs Withers both spoke at once. He opted to view the bars and she the upstairs rooms. All four gave a false laugh.

"I'll show Gloria upstairs and the guest's rooms, and you take Raymond to the bars," said Dorothy. "That way everyone will be happy."

"Quick thinking, Deidre," said Raymond. "I like to see a woman with her wits about her. Come on, Frank, show me where you make all the lolly."

Dorothy smiled sweetly to hide her annoyance and led Gloria up the stairs.

"I like it here," said Gloria, before they even reached the landing. "There's a nice feel about the place. The walls seem to exude happiness. I'm very susceptible to the way houses feel, especially old ones."

"Hmm, I know just what you mean. I've been very happy here, although the old place has seen sad times too, of course," said Dorothy, thinking of Sylvia, Jane, and now Edward Tucker. "But thank goodness, the good times far outweigh the bad."

Gloria peeped inside and nodded her approval of the bathroom as they passed it by. Dorothy then opened the door of the first bedroom on the front of the Inn. Gloria stepped inside and clasped her hands with joy.

"There are sea views," she cried, rushing to the window. "How exciting! This room is a good size too. I think I'm falling in love with the Ringing Bells Inn. It's better than I ever dared imagine. You see, I've always wanted to live near to the sea. I think it's wonderful!"

Dorothy nodded her head thoughtfully. "I'd have to agree with you there. Some people think it can get boring after a while, but I've never got tired watching it. Having said that, I've never had time to look at it for long so I suppose that was rather a silly thing to say."

Gloria smiled warmly. "Where do you and your husband sleep? Judging by the lack of personal things this is obviously a guest room."

"Yes, it is. All the upstairs rooms are for guests. We sleep downstairs. I'll show you in a minute. We have our own living room down there too, but not a kitchen. We use the main kitchen next to the dining room for all our needs."

"I see. Well, we would have to use one of these rooms for the boys," said Gloria. "We have two sons, you see, but that's not a problem. In fact they would probably like it up here away from us."

"Oh, that would be nice," said Dorothy, sincerely. "This Inn hasn't had children living in it for as long as I can remember and I've been in Trengillion all my life. There have of course been children with some of the guests, but that's not quite the same, is it?"

"Well, our children aren't very young, they're sixteen and fourteen, so they consider themselves to be grown up, but they're still children in my eyes."

When they had viewed all the rooms on the upper floor, Dorothy led Gloria down the small back stairs, its entrance concealed behind an un-numbered door, to view their living quarters below.

Gloria giggled like a school girl as they emerged through the small door at the bottom where they had to duck to avoid banging their heads. "How quaint, and what a delightful room, it's so cosy and warm, and oh, I do like your choice of wallpaper, Mrs Newton. It's very pretty."

"I'm glad you're liking what you see," said Dorothy, much heartened by Mrs Withers' impassioned enthusiasm. "Let's hope your husband is equally happy with his wander round the bars."

"Hmm, well, it certainly seems that you have a good little business here," said Raymond, after briefly viewing the Inn's takings for the previous tax year. "And I know Gloria and I could make a go of it after we'd made a few improvements here and there. Nothing drastic like," he added quickly, noticing Frank frown. "Just a lick of paint in the neglected corners and a bit of modernisation to bring the place into the twentieth century. Ah, there you are, Glore," he boomed as his wife entered the bar with Dorothy. "What do you think? Do you like what you've seen?"

"It's lovely, charming and oh, these bars are well-proportioned too. And the plates," she sighed, hands clasped, looking at the beams in the snug bar, "they look so perfect, what a novel idea."

"Humph! If we left them up you'd have to wash the damn things," said Raymond. "I can't see much point in having things like that. I take it they'd be included in the sale price, Frank?"

"Well, yes, everything's included except the furniture in our living quarters."

"What are the upstairs rooms like, Glore? Did you like them?"

"Yes, very much," she replied, with enthusiasm. "In fact, I like everything about this place. The location, the size, the..."

"...well don't get too carried away or you'll have Mr Newton here putting the price up. It's not perfect, not by a long chalk, but it has great potential, I'll give you that. And I know with my talents we could make a go of the place. Anyway, if you've seen enough, Glore, then we'd best make a move and go and chew things over between the two of us."

"Don't you want to see the upstairs rooms, love?" asked Gloria. "They're very..."

"...no, no, the bed and breakfast side of things would be up to you. Women's stuff like that doesn't interest me. The only thing here that matters as far as I'm concerned is selling the beer, lots of it and I don't see a problem with that." He slapped his hand on top of the bar. "And look at this Glore, long, smooth and straight. Perfect for sliding the old whisky glasses down."

Looks of bewilderment flashed back and forth between Frank and Dorothy. Gloria noticed and quickly jumped in to explain.

"Raymond is fanatical about the Wild West, that's why he wants a pub in the West Country. He's got loads of cowboy outfits and he wants his party trick to be sliding glasses of whisky down the bar to his customers. We've looked at several pubs but this if the first one with a suitable bar."

Dorothy felt a sudden desire to laugh, but the look on Frank's face prevented her from doing so.

"Come on, Glore," boomed Raymond. "We've kept these good folk long enough. It's time for a serious chat."

He led the way to the side door and let himself out. Gloria meekly followed behind.

"We'll most likely be in touch through the agents," said Raymond, with a hearty laugh. He turned to his wife. "Look there's a cobweb, come on, Glore."

"Thank you for showing me round," said Gloria, giving Dorothy's hand a quick squeeze. "I'm sure you're going to see much more of us."

"So what did you make of them?" asked Dorothy, as she gently closed the door.

"Don't interrupt, Dot, I'm still counting to ten," said Frank, as his face reddened.

Dorothy smiled. "Pompous ass, blithering idiot, obnoxious prat, arrogant oaf, are they some of the names you're looking to avoid? Shame really, because I've a feeling deep down in my stomach that Gloria and Raymond Withers will be the next landlord and landlady of the Ringing Bells Inn."

CHAPTER TWENTY FIVE

On Wednesday morning a letter arrived at The School House addressed to Elizabeth and Anne, postmarked Florida. Elizabeth found it on the doormat as she went downstairs for breakfast.

After squealing with delight she ran into the kitchen waving the blue airmail envelope above her head, she then sat down at the table to open it. Anne peered over her shoulder as she enthusiastically read the neat handwriting telling news from the other side of the Atlantic.

"Wow, do you think they might come home early?" asked Anne, as Elizabeth thoughtfully folded the delicate sheets of lightweight paper.

"With any luck, yes," said Elizabeth, hope shining in her eyes. "Wouldn't it be brilliant if they were back for Christmas?"

"Why should they come home that soon?" asked Stella, amused, as she poured her daughters each a cup of tea.

"Because they all miss England, even their mum and dad. They say the weather's good but everything's so different, and the crocodiles keep giving Lily nightmares."

"Crocodiles!" gasped Stella. "But surely there aren't any out there that are a threat to the public?"

"Well, no, they don't exactly have any in their garden or anything like that, but there are some nearby and Lily is terrified of them and so expects every bit of water to be infested with them. She's even afraid to go swimming in their pool."

"Who wrote the letter?" asked Stella.

"Lily," said Elizabeth, "but Greg has added a bit on the end. He said he dreamt we were all in our den one night and was bitterly disappointed when he woke up and realised he was thousands of miles away. I shall take this to school with me today and show it to the others on the bus, and then tonight I'll write back and tell them to come home."

"I'll write as well," said Anne, enthusiastically, "and remind them that there are no crocodiles here. We must tell them about David and Stephen's mum and the robbery too."

Elizabeth nodded. "And about the murdered man who fell off the cliff path and whose ghost is on our pictures."

"We must send one of the pictures of us all at Chy-an-Gwyns as well, because that will make them homesick."

Stella smothered a smile. "I hardly think stories of murder and robbery are going to endear Mr and Mrs Castor-Hunt to the idea of returning to Cornwall. Quite the opposite in fact."

"Gosh, you're right, Mum," said Elizabeth, surprised by her mother's perspicacity. "We'll just tell them about the ghost called Teddy, but not say who he was or why he's dead and we'll say David and Stephen's mum's in hospital, but we won't tell them why."

Anne tilted her head to one side. "And do you think we ought to tell them that the woman staying in their house is potty?"

"Certainly not," spluttered Stella. "I'm sure the stories about Mrs Rossiter have been grossly exaggerated and it would not be fair to the Castor-Hunts to cause them unnecessary worry, especially when they're so many miles away."

Elizabeth scowled at Anne. "Anyway, I thought we'd all agreed that Mrs Rossiter is alright. Susan said her mum likes her and that's good enough for me."

"Look at the time," said Stella, glad of a reason to change the subject. "Get a move on both of you or you'll miss the bus."

Amongst the post was also a letter for Stella from her mother. Stella opened it eagerly once the girls had gone off to catch the bus for school, hoping it might be the completed questionnaires. It was and so she poured herself a second cup of tea, lit a cigarette and then sat down to study the papers.

"Any post for me?" asked Ned, coming in from the outhouse where he had been polishing his shoes.

"No, but look at this. My granny on Mum's side of the family was a Penn. Do you think that by any chance she may have been married to a Penwynton and he dropped the Wynton bit to avoid being traced?"

Ned laughed, "When was your granny born, then?"

"1880," said Stella. "And her parents were George Penn born in 1850 and Grace Penn nee Watson born in 1852. See, the years add up and I've probably just missed out on a family fortune without knowing it."

"Oh, come on, Stell, you don't surely believe that, do you?"

"Not really," grinned Stella, "but I shall pretend that I'm a Penwynton from now on until my enquiries prove otherwise."

In the afternoon Frank received a phone call from the agents handling the sale of the Inn, who were delighted to inform him that they had received a very good offer from Mr and Mrs Withers, which they strongly advised him to accept. Frank thanked them and promised to ring back within the hour once he had discussed the offer with his wife.

"You look awfully pale, Frank," said Dorothy, concerned, after he had told her the news. "Are you alright?"

"I'm fine, Dot, and I should be blissfully happy, but that phone call has brought it home to me that I really am going to leave this place and to that dreadful man of all people. I've been here such a long time. The place holds so many memories. Suddenly I just feel sort of empty, like it's all been for nothing."

"Oh, Frank, you're bound to feel like that, but the longer you stay the worse it'll be. You have to make that move now and the offer is very, very good." She put her arms around him and gave him a hug. "And as for Raymond Withers, he might not be as bad as he seemed when he was here. It might all have been a bit of an act and he was trying to impress you. She was nice anyway. Gloria that is. Come on Frank, it's time to move on."

"I know and I couldn't go if I didn't have you, Dot. I couldn't leave and live on my own. I know it's the right thing to do, but an awful lot of water has passed under the bridge since I first came here and it's just going to take an awful lot of courage to pick up that phone and let it all go."

Dorothy squeezed his hand tightly, smiled and beckoned him to stand. "Come on, it's time for a new beginning, Frank. It's time you had some time for yourself."

"Alright, let's get this done, and then I'll ring one of Godfrey's boys and tell them we're ready to go ahead with buying the bungalow. That pleases me, thinking about the bungalow, I mean. Cos I really am looking forward to doing some gardening there and the major says I must join the golf club too. You're right, Dot, there's a big wide world outside these walls and it's time I got out and about a bit. Why, we could even have a holiday. I've not had one for over thirty years. Good God, I'd never really thought about that. I've not had a holiday since I've been here."

But in spite of Frank's positive thinking, after he had made the necessary phone call, he sat on the chair in the hallway and shed a tear for old memories, old friends, and a long, lost love.

The following afternoon a middle aged couple called at The Police House with the front door key to Penwynton House.

"We were asked to drop these in to you," said a man, with greying hair. "The estate agents said you wanted to look over the place."

"Ah, yes," said Annie, taking the key. "Thank you, although I'm sure it's not necessary. How did you like the place?"

"We liked it very much, it has great potential, but we're a little concerned why the police might want to check it over. Has there been a problem with vandalism or anything like that? We didn't see any damage other than a few broken window panes, but that's quite common in empty houses."

Annie opened the door wide. "Come in and join me for coffee and I'll explain."

"Thank you, you're most kind."

Annie showed the couple into the house, made them coffee and then joined them in the sitting room.

"Before we go any further I must introduce myself. I'm Annie Stevens, and my husband, as you'll probably have gathered, is Police Constable, Fred Stevens."

"And I'm Dick Cottingham, and this is my wife, Mary" said Dick.

They shook hands and then Annie explained about the recent death of a holiday maker and his mysterious presence on the photographs taken after his death.

Mary clapped her hands with glee. "So you want the keys to go ghost hunting? That's wonderful, I'm liking the house more every minute."

"Well, not exactly ghost hunting," said Annie. "Fred wants to see if there is any evidence that the deceased had been on the premises, really just to keep local gossips at bay. Did you see anything unusual?"

"Sadly, no," said Mary, unable to wipe the smile from her face. "There was evidence that people had looked around, you know, fingers had been run through thick dust on the mantelpieces and that sort of thing, but we didn't see any mysterious movements or feel any ice cold blasts, and we certainly didn't see a ghost, I'm sorry to say."

"Better luck next time, if there is a next time," smiled Annie. "So may I ask if there's a possibility that you might be interested in buying the place?"

Mary looked at Dick. "I think the answer to that has to be yes. It's actually just what we're looking for. We would be turning it into a hotel, you see, with the necessary permissions of course. Do you think there would be a need for a hotel in this area?"

Annie answered with enthusiasm. "Yes, I think there would. Trengillion is growing in popularity because of the beach and at present there is only the Inn and one or two houses doing bed and breakfast that provide accommodation, so it would almost be a necessity, but don't quote me on that. It would also provide employment for local people, which is always a good thing."

"Brilliant, and do you know if there are any plans to put caravan and camping sites in the area?" asked Dick.

"Camping sites on farmland are a probability, but permanent caravan parks will never be permitted, the local council have put down their feet firmly on that issue. Trengillion is a beautiful spot which everyone here believes must not be spoiled."

"Perfect," said Dick, wringing his hands. "We've been looking at property all year. We want something we can all invest in as a family, that's Mary's sister, Heather, and her husband, Bob, and our own daughter, Linda, who says she wants to be part of the project too. We've not been too fussy, anywhere in the West Country would have suited us, but this is the best we've seen by far. Do you know if there's been much interest in the place?"

Annie shrugged her shoulders. "I really can't say. With it being in the hands of London agents and them having the key we don't hear anything unless it's through local gossip and then of course it can be wrong."

"What are the people like at the pub?" asked Mary. "Does it have a good trade?"

"Well, actually the Inn is shortly to undergo a change of ownership, as only this morning I heard that Frank, the current landlord, had accepted an offer from potential buyers. But yes, it does have a good trade, both with accommodation and the bar at present, but naturally I can't speak for its future."

Mary nodded. "Of course. Sorry about all the questions, but there is just one more. How many guest rooms does the Inn have?"

"Hmm, I'm not sure whether it's four or five," said Annie, trying to recollect the layout of the Inn's upper floor, "but certainly no more than that."

"Well, in that case there'd be more than enough room for the two establishments in the area," said Dick, with delight. "I think we'll pop in the Inn this evening, Mary, to sus the place out."

Annie nodded. "I think you'll approve of it. It's a lovely old place and very welcoming."

"May I ask what the pub's called?" said Mary.

"The Ringing Bells Inn."

Dick nodded, thoughtfully. "I've just remembered, there is one more question I'd like to ask. As we were driving here we both felt for some reason the name Trengillion seemed vaguely familiar. We felt we'd heard mention of it on the news or something like that. We're probably wrong, of course, but can you shed any light on it?"

Annie bit her lip. "Well, yes, Trengillion was in the news some fifteen years ago, back in 1952. It was all very sad. You see, the landlady of the Inn was arrested for the murder of a local girl, Jane Hunt, but it turned out she not only murdered poor Jane but the politician William Wagstaffe as well."

Dick Cottingham slapped his thigh. "Of course, it's all coming back now. Wagstaffe! You remember, Mary, he was murdered by his lover, the housekeeper, Grace something-or-other."

Annie winced. "Bonnington. She was called Grace Bonnington."

Mary nodded. "I remember. She buried his body in a spinney, didn't she? And then came to Cornwall using a different name."

Annie felt light-headed. "She used the name of a friend she had made in the Women's Land Army who was killed during the War. Sylvia Spencer was her name."

Mary noticed Annie's pale face. "Sorry, we're being very insensitive, aren't we? You no doubt knew everyone involved."

Annie nodded. "Yes, I did, and Grace, whom we all knew as Sylvia, married Frank, landlord of the pub. It was very shocking."

"Poor you. It must have been very distressing especially with your husband being involved in the whole ghastly business."

"Yes, and it's something you'll find most local people reluctant to talk about. You see, as daft as it might sound, we all liked Sylvia." Annie laughed sardonically. "Sylvia, we'll always think of her as Sylvia but of course that wasn't her name as you know. But in all these years I've never heard anyone refer to her as Grace Bonnington."

Dick shook his head. "Dreadful! It must have been an awful shock for your landlord."

"It was, but thankfully time healed and he has since remarried. Not I suppose that his first marriage was legitimate, with his wife not being who she said she was."

"And is the pub's current landlord the same as back in 1952?"

Annie nodded.

"Ah, in that case," said Mary, "we shall not make any reference to the past whatsoever."

"Very wise," said Annie, "it's all best forgotten.

Mary smiled. "Well, in spite of what you've just told us I think this little venture is still very exciting and we'll have to get the rest of the family down as soon as possible. If, and once we get their approval, we can then put in a realistic offer. I do hope they like it, there's something about this village, despite its dubious past, that makes me think I'd like to spend the rest of my days here."

Annie half-smiled, feeling perhaps she also ought to say something about the dreadful attack on the postmistress and confess that the ghost in the pictures had probably been murdered, but after a brief reflection she thought better of it. She liked the Cottinghams and did not want to frighten them off.

CHAPTER TWENTY SIX

On Friday evening the youngsters of Trengillion made their way through the village for the second discotheque, but much to the disappointment of the girls, when they arrived in the hall they found the DJ was not Jamie. After asking around they discovered Jamie had a streaming cold, hence chatting into the microphone in his stead was a friend from the Midland Bank.

"Hi guys and gels. Get on the dance floor and getta groovin'. My name's Desmond, but you can all call me Dezzy. Now get those limps swinging, sway those hips, pop pickers, and let's dance the night away."

"Oh, my God," spluttered Elizabeth, with gaping mouth. "What's an old man like that doing in Jamie's place? He's ancient. He must be as old as Dad or even older."

"Oh shut up," scolded Tony, tapping his feet to the rhythm of the music. "I think he's really cool. Age doesn't matter these days, Liz. The important thing is his choice of music and it just happens to be great. His girlfriend's a cracker too. Just look at those legs!"

Elizabeth turned up her nose. "Humph! Mutton dressed as lamb, if you ask me, and Crimplene would be a more appropriate dress fabric for a woman of her age." She turned to Diane who was by her side. "Come on, Di, let's go and get something to drink."

The two girls linked arms. "I can't see the point of having a DJ if he isn't going to be someone we can't drool over," said Diane, as they headed towards the cloakroom where refreshments were on sale.

"Absolutely right. I suppose boys can't understand that, can they? In fact when I think about it, they've no idea about anything that matters."

Susan and Jane, already in the cloakroom, agreed with their friends' unflattering criticism and to show their disapproval, all four girls went outside and sat on the bench in front of the village hall to eat crisps and drink lemonade. When everyone had finished their snacks, Jane took the rubbish back into the hall and tossed it into a bin. As she stepped back outside Susan leapt to her feet. "Let's not stay here. Let's go to the big house and see if we can see Teddy's ghost. It'd be much more exciting than having to listen to old man Dezzie's soppy chat."

Diane was horrified. "But it'll be dark soon."

"All the more exciting," said Susan, urging the girls to stand. "Come on. No-one will know we've gone as we'll be back before the discotheque ends."

Jane giggled. "I'm for it, but won't your brothers notice you've gone, Sue?"

"Humph! I doubt it. They're both too busy ogling the legs of Dezzie's old dear. It's dark in the hall, anyway, so they'd only suspect I was missing if they were actually looking for me and that's not likely to happen."

Elizabeth said nothing. She was horror-struck by the thought of seeing Teddy's ghost, for she knew if he were walking in the grounds of Penwynton House, then she would be the one to see him. For like her father and grandmother, she was afflicted with the gift to see that which others were unable to see, but whereas her grandmother regarded ghosts and spirits as harmless souls to be helped and pitied, the thought of seeing one made Elizabeth want to run for her life.

"You'll come too, won't you, Liz?" said Jane, tugging at her sleeve. "You must, after all it was your camera that spotted him in the first place so he must like you."

Elizabeth laughed feebly. "Of course I'll come," she heard herself say. "I wouldn't dream of being left behind and missing all the fun."

"But what if the chap who attacked Mrs Pascoe is in the woods?" asked Diane, very unhappy about the impending excursion.

"Safety in numbers," retorted Susan in a matter-of-fact manner. "He wouldn't dare attack us all. Besides we've nothing to steal except our refreshment money and that wouldn't get him very far."

The girls left the hall and ran through the village keeping very quiet as they passed by their respective homes, but once they were in the lane going down the hill and away from the village they resumed their chat and girlish laughter.

At the foot of the hill they climbed down the bank and followed the familiar path alongside the stream and into Bluebell Woods, where the canopy of trees obscured the fast fading light.

"We should have gone the other way," said Diane, frequently looking over her shoulder. "Down the main drive, I mean, at least we'd be able to see better then."

"But it would've taken too long, this way is much quicker," said Jane. "Besides, going the other way would mean passing the Lodge and Mr Stevens might be there, and the last thing we want is for him to see us and tell our parents."

"It's much spookier this way," added Susan, with a feeble laugh. "I must admit I'm actually beginning to wish the boys were with us."

"You're very quiet, Liz," said Diane, noticing her friend was lagging behind. "Are you alright? You look very pale."

The others stopped and turned.

"You do," said Susan. "Shall we stay here for a while so that you can sit down and rest?"

Elizabeth forced a smile. "No, I'm alright and I want to carry on so that we can get out of these woods."

Jane looked at Elizabeth quizzically. "Have you seen something scary and you're not telling us?"

Jane gasped. "Surely not Anne's big-eared man."

"No, no, it's just…"

"What?"

"It's just, well, the other day I overheard Mum and Dad talking about the Penwyntons. You know, the ones from long ago."

Susan drew her breath. "What dead ones, you mean?"

"They're all dead, silly," scoffed Jane. "Charles was the last."

"So what did they say?" Diane asked, eagerly.

"Well, recently Mum's been talking to Mr Hughes, you know who I mean?" They all nodded. "Well, he worked here on the Penwynton Estate for years and years and so knows lots about its history and apparently some chap called Gorran from long ago was murdered in these woods while he was out shooting pheasants."

"Serves him right," said Susan, dispassionately. "Poor pheasants."

Diane looked panic-stricken. "So, who murdered him and why?"

Elizabeth looked over her shoulder. "It's thought he was shot by Florrie Ham's dad. She was pregnant, you see, and Gorran was the baby's father."

Three jaws dropped heavily.

Jane spoke first. "But that's silly. To shoot the baby's father, I mean. Why on earth did he do that?"

"Because he said the baby wasn't his. That's what he told his mum anyway and because of that his wicked mum sacked poor Florrie."

Jane frowned. "Sacked her! I don't understand. Sacked her from what?"

"Her job. She worked at Penwynton House."

Susan looked shocked. "You mean, Florrie wasn't Gorran's wife?"

Elizabeth shook he head. "No, they weren't married. Florrie was just a chambermaid."

Diane blushed. Jane gasped. Susan giggled.

Without speaking the girls quietly resumed their walk and followed the stream path, frequently looking over their shoulders until they reached their den. By the fallen tree they veered off to the right through dense woodland towards the house, keeping close together and occasionally putting their hands over their ears to obliterate strange noises which emanated from the undergrowth and the swaying branches of rustling leaves.

As they neared the house all sighed with relief, the tall trees were behind them and the rhododendron bushes, whilst huge, did not obscure the light.

"Oh God, the house looks really spooky in the half light," muttered Jane, as the girls stood on the drive way and gazed up at the house. "And look at the size of that moon. All it needs now is a few bats flying around the chimney pots and Dracula to jump out of his coffin."

Diane clutched Elizabeth's arm. "Don't say that. The thought of seeing a coffin makes me want to run."

Susan laughed. "Come on girls, we're not likely to see any coffins. A ghost maybe if we're lucky, and we've two to choose from now Liz has told us about Gorran the pheasant shooter, but coffins, definitely not."

"Let's go round the back," said Jane. "We could play a game of hide and seek. It would be really thrilling now it's getting dark."

"What! Are you crazy?" screeched Diane. "I'm not going off anywhere on my own. You can call me a coward, but I don't care."

"I agree," said Elizabeth. "I think we ought to stick together."

"But why?" screeched Susan, suddenly feeling ebullient. "There's nothing here to harm us and the boys will be impressed when we tell them how brave we were."

"The strange man that Anne saw might still be around," said Elizabeth, promptly.

"Or one of us might get lost," said Diane, searching for a reason which did not sound cowardly. "After all, scrambling about in unfamiliar grounds is a bit stupid when it's nearly dark. I'm not saying we shouldn't play though, but I think it'd be better if we went in twos. One couple could hide and the other couple look for them. It'll still be fun, but a lot less scary."

"Yes, that's a good compromise," said Elizabeth, much relieved. "But we mustn't hang around for too long, it'll be really dark soon and I don't like the idea of trying to find our way through the woods when we can't see a thing."

"It won't be completely dark," said Jane. "The sky is clear and the moon will light our way."

Susan laughed. "Even better, we might see a werewolf."

Diane's heart sank. The thought of listening to old man, Dezzie's soppy chat, suddenly seemed the perfect way to spend an evening.

With linked arms, the four girls left the drive and walked round the side of the house and through the long grass.

"Jane and me will hide," said Susan. "And you two can come and find us."

"Alright," said Diane, glad that she would have Elizabeth as a partner. "But you must promise not to leap out from somewhere and make us jump and don't you dare make scary noises either."

Susan giggled. "We won't. Hide your eyes by the old stables and count to fifty."

Elizabeth and Diane leaned on the side of the stable wall and began to count, and as they heard their friends' fading voices, they listened hard to try and establish in which direction they had gone.

"Ready," shouted Diane, when they reached the specified number.

"I think they went away from the house towards the paddock," whispered Elizabeth. "But then knowing them they probably doubled back. What do you think?"

Diane nodded. "I agree, but look they've left a trail, the grass is battered down here where they have walked. This could be a doddle."

"Hmm, but it might not have been them that went this way. People viewing the house could have walked around the grounds and don't forget we played here the other day ourselves."

Diane shuddered. "Do you think it's possible they might have gone all the way down to the buttercup field?"

Elizabeth shook her head. "No, they might be braver than you and me but they're not that brave. It's much too far away."

Nevertheless, the two girls crept along the path of flattened grass in search of their friends, hoping they were going in the right direction, and eventually they reached a five bar gate, beyond which lay a paddock.

"I don't think they'll be in there," said Diane, slowly shaking her head. "There's nowhere to hide, and look the grass has not been disturbed at all. I think if they did come this way, then they'll have done as you said and doubled back towards the house."

With the trail having gone cold the girls turned and retraced their steps back towards the stables.

"Do you think they might have gone through there?" Elizabeth asked, pointing to an open wrought iron gate leading away from the main gardens of the house. "I can't remember whether or not it was open before and I've no idea where it might lead."

Diane's face lit up. "It probably leads to the walled garden. Mum told me her great uncle was head gardener here in its heyday, and the walled garden is where they grow vegetables, or should I say grew. And judging by the state of the grounds, I shouldn't think it's been used for donkey's years."

The two girls made their way through an area where once a sunken lawn had flourished, they then followed a narrow path towards the gate and peeped through the twisted iron bars into a garden, where long grass, nettles and brambles colonised large beds, once occupied by prize winning vegetables, herbs and flowers for the house. The high walls, granite and tumbledown in places, looked gloomy and forlorn, and at the bottom, greenhouses with broken panes of glass, framed with decaying wood, leaned against tall, ivy covered walls.

Nervously the girls walked round the outside of the gardens, past a rose bed where one solitary flower bloomed amidst an array of weeds. Further on, they tiptoed beneath a broken wooden archway, heavy with honeysuckle, the strands of which reached the ground and ran off through the undergrowth.

"Do you think they're in here?" whispered Diane, kicking a wooden wheelbarrow, which promptly collapsed into a pile of rotting wood. "It seems too quiet, I think we'd have heard them giggling by now if they were here."

"Hmm, you're probably right, but we mustn't give up yet."

As they turned a corner, Elizabeth pointed to a granite building with part of the roof missing. "Look, they might be in that barn or whatever it is, over there. I think we should take a look before we go from here."

The building contained a sparse collection of rusty tools, a broken chair and a table. On the walls, moth eaten coats and an old leather apron dangled from large rusty nails.

"Oh, this is really weird," said Diane. "My great, great uncle must have sat in here and perhaps drank tea from a flask and ate his sandwiches. I feel all goose pimply. Do you ever feel like that?"

Elizabeth nodded. "Yes, *déjà vu*. You feel as though you've been in the same place sometime before. I know just what you mean."

From the trees around the front of the house an owl hooted, causing both girls to scream. Its sudden screech also had the same effect on Susan and Jane, who squealed and then laughed helplessly at their own foolishness.

"They're over there," shouted Diane, turning quickly. "I heard them and look that bush is moving."

They ran across the garden to where elder bushes, dripping with berries, occupied a dark corner. Hidden behind the foliage and fruit, they found their two friends.

Elizabeth heaved a sigh of relief. "Can we go home now?" she asked, trying to sound casual. "I feel quite drained."

"Oh, but don't you want a turn to hide?" asked Susan, disappointed. "You ought, there are so many brilliant places to choose from, especially here in this old walled garden."

"I think we should be getting back," said Diane, looking at her watch. "It's a quarter to nine. What's more I think we ought to go back the long way rather than go through the woods and that'll probably take nearly an hour. But we must go carefully when we pass the Lodge in case Mr Stevens is there, although I don't think he will be now that it's dark."

"I suppose you're right," sighed Jane. "And we don't want to be late and get into trouble as we'll probably not be allowed to go to the discotheque next week and that would be awful as Jamie should be better by then."

The girls made their way back through the walled garden towards the gate and off in the direction of the house. From a paved area almost hidden by weeds, ran a large, wide, flight of granite steps leading up to the back of the house. As they passed it, Elizabeth abruptly stopped and beseeched the others to do likewise.

"Look up there," she whispered, pointing to the upper floor of the house. "In that small window there's a glimmer of light."

The girls huddled together behind a huge Grecian urn and watched, open-mouthed as a dim light moved slowly around beyond the window panes of an upstairs room.

"If the light's moving," squeaked Susan, her courage having deserted her. "It must be a torch or a candle."

"But then that means there's someone in there," screeched Jane. "Come on, let's go. I don't think I want to hang around and find out who it is."

As she spoke, a figure came into view at the window, its arms appeared to reach upwards and then disappeared altogether.

"Oh, Christ, I bet that's Gorran. The back wing would have been the servant's quarters. He'll be in there looking for Florrie Ham," screamed Susan, trembling with fright. "Come on, let's run. I've gone off the idea of ghost hunting."

Jane was already running along the path. "I'll second that. What with Teddy's ghost round the front and Gorran's round the back this place is too scary for words."

When the girls reached the side of the house, they crouched, clutching each other for moral support and then crept on their knees towards the front driveway, continually looking in all directions to ascertain the coast was clear.

"I can hear a car," screamed Jane, with alarm, as they were about to step onto the drive. "Oh no! Who can it be? I can't take much more."

"It's alright, it's probably Mr Steven's leaving the Lodge," said Susan, trying to sound calm. "On a clear night such as this, we'd hear him easily from here."

They listened, but the sound of the engine grew louder instead of fainter.

"No, it can't be him going. Whoever it is, is coming this way," screamed Diane. "What on earth shall we do?"

"Quick, the rhododendrons," commanded Elizabeth. "We mustn't be seen."

The four girls dashed across the driveway and leapt behind the rhododendron bushes just as the headlights of a car turned the corner. They heard the car door slam, followed by the sound of someone running up the front steps to the house. The front door creaked open and then closed. Petrified, the girls peered around the bushes. A car gleamed in the moonlight, a sleek, impressive car. A red Mercedes.

Jane gasped. "Surely that has to be the one we saw here before." The girls looked at one another and nodded, and then without uttering another word, all ran through Bluebell Woods and back to the village faster than they had ever run before in their lives.

CHAPTER TWENTY SEVEN

"You look a bit tired, love," said Ned, watching his wife over the top of his newspaper as she poured boiling water into the teapot. "Didn't you sleep very well last night?"

Stella sat down at the kitchen table and sighed deeply. "Yes, well, no, not really. Oh dear."

"What's wrong?"

"Well, probably nothing, but then again I can't be sure. You see, I couldn't sleep because I was worried about Elizabeth."

Ned's eyebrows rose sharply. "Elizabeth! What's wrong with her?"

"There's nothing wrong with her, it's just, well, there was something strange about her when she came in last night. She seemed distant, even perhaps guilty and she looked untidy, her dress was dirty and her hair was a mess."

Ned folded the newspaper and dropped it onto the floor. "And you suspect what?"

"Well, I don't really know but it crossed my mind that maybe she went off somewhere with a boy. What I mean to say is, do you think it's possible she was out in the fields last night with a lad, when she should have been at the discotheque?"

Ned frowned. "Why didn't you mention this last night when I came in, Stella, you know we always share our problems and misgivings?"

"I didn't like to bother you, you looked tired, and a little drunk." She smiled.

"Oh dear, was it that obvious? I didn't intend to stay for more than one pint, but Sid was in, we got chatting and before I knew it Frank was ringing last orders and my brain had lost contact with my feet. I'm sorry, that's two weeks running, isn't it? Are you cross?"

"Of course not," said Stella, amused by his penitence. "But what do you think about Elizabeth, should I say something or leave well alone?"

"Leave it to me," said Ned, after a little thought. "I've not seen her since the discotheque, but when I do I'll ask her how it was and see if I perceive a sense of guilt."

Stella jumped up and took two mugs from the kitchen cabinet. "Thanks, Ned. That's a great weight off my mind. Now, how many aspirins would you like with your tea?"

He laughed. "Is my sore head that obvious? Oh dear, I'd better have two please."

Elizabeth and Anne never left their beds very early on Saturday mornings, therefore Stella was surprised when she heard voices in Anne's room and found Elizabeth's bed empty when she went upstairs to get their dirty school uniforms from the linen basket. The girls' talk, however, was not loud. Their voices were hushed and little more than a whisper. Intrigued, Stella crept towards Anne's bedroom door and listened with her ear close against the wood. When she realised Elizabeth was telling Anne about the previous evening, her heart skipped a beat. She listened, holding her breath, dreading what was to follow the story of Jamie's illness and his DJ replacement being an old chap called Dezzy. She gasped and fell to her knees when she heard the words 'Don't tell Mum or Dad'. But her anguish was short lived and turned to amazement when Elizabeth proceeded to convey to Anne, the trip to Penwynton House, the game of hide and seek and the terrifying spectacle the girls witnessed at the back of the house.

Forgetting to be quiet, Stella sighed, much relieved that her earlier misgivings regarding Elizabeth's movements the previous evening, were unfounded, although she had been right to perceive that all was not well.

The girls, sitting on Anne's bed, heard their mother's cry of alleviation. Elizabeth leapt across the room and opened the door.

"Err, good morning girls," Stella said, trying to sound as normal as possible while scrambling unsteadily to her feet. Her eavesdropping, however, had not passed unnoticed.

"You were listening, Mum," said Elizabeth, in disgust. "And you have the cheek to go on to me and Anne about bad manners. Snooping is sneaky."

"Anne and I, not me and Anne," said Stella, trying to sound dignified. "Really, don't they teach you anything at school these days?"

"Don't change the subject," said Elizabeth, crossly.

"And don't you be so cheeky, young lady," snapped Stella. "I want you downstairs, now, and you can tell your father exactly what you just told Anne."

Elizabeth repeated her story and answered numerous questions fired at her by her surprised parents.

"I think we ought to tell Fred," said Ned after digesting the facts. "The owner of that car may have been up to no good, although there haven't been any reports of strange happenings at the old house and there's nothing to steal if the place is empty."

Anne's eyes were like saucers. "But what about the person at the window? Do you think it was Teddy's ghost?"

"Or even Gorran's ghost?" Added Elizabeth.

"No, sweetheart," laughed Ned, patting her head. "I've never heard of a ghost carrying a torch or a candle. The image you saw must have been a real person, no doubt an associate of the man with the red Mercedes." Ned looked at his watch. "Right, Liz, go upstairs, get dressed, have a quick bit of breakfast and then we'll pop down the road to see Mr Stevens."

Fred and Annie were both in when Ned and Elizabeth arrived at The Police House. Annie showed them into the sitting room where Jamie was lying on the settee feeling very sorry for himself. Elizabeth was horrified. She was wearing an old pair of trousers, a jumper her grandmother had knitted, and because she was sulking she had not brushed her hair properly. Jamie stood, when he saw his parents had visitors.

"I'll go upstairs out of the way," he sniffled. "I don't want you catching my germs." He noticed Elizabeth. "How did last night go? Did Desmond do a good job?"

"Yeah, yeah," said Elizabeth, with an awkward smile. "He was great, really great, and his girlfriend's very pretty."

"Good," croaked Jamie. "I knew he wouldn't let me down. He was a bit worried that you'd all think him too old, but I assured him that youngsters these days are a lot more tolerant of the older generation than when he was a lad."

He left the room as Fred entered. Elizabeth felt her heart sink as she sat down with her father on the settee vacated by Jamie.

Fred and Annie were surprised by Elizabeth's story and confirmed there had been no reports of suspicious behaviour at Penwynton House. Besides, Fred himself, who spent a considerable amount of time at the Lodge, had not seen any stranger people or strange cars in the driveway.

"I'll check your story out though, but it could be that the Mercedes was just someone interested in buying the house taking a second look, not many people buy a place after a first inspection and especially not when there's such a huge amount of money involved."

Elizabeth scowled. "But if that was the case, how could there have already been someone in the house when the Mercedes arrived?"

Fred shrugged his shoulders as he considered Elizabeth's question. "Hmm, well I suppose they could both have been there already and the car driver popped out for some fags or something like that. I mean, if they were viewing the house and had the keys, then they'd have all the time in the world."

Annie frowned. "But we've still got the keys. They're on the sideboard."

"Crikey, good point, love," muttered Fred. "There must be two sets of keys then."

Elizabeth was not convinced. She and the girls had been in the grounds of the house for quite a while before the Mercedes had pulled up and it most certainly had not been there when they had arrived.

"I know it's unlikely, but I don't suppose by any chance, any of you took a look at the number plate, did you?" asked Fred, drumming his fingers on the side of his head. "It'd be a tremendous help if you did."

Elizabeth gently shook her head. "I doubt it. I certainly didn't. We were hiding behind a bush at the time and the only light was from the moon, but I'll ask the others when I see them."

Later in the day, Fred called at The School House to report that according to the estate agents handling the sale of Penwynton House, no-one had the keys to view it and the only set was with him.

Ned was astonished. "So, the owner of the Mercedes must have broken in. Either that or he has his own key, but that seems rather unlikely."

Fred nodded. "Something like that, but this morning, shortly after your visit with Elizabeth, I went over there to take a look. Well, I didn't go on my own, I asked Dick Remington to go with me. You remember him don't you, Ned, a colleague of mine from Polquillick? Anyway, we found no sign of forced entry, in fact there was no evidence of anyone having been there at all. Nevertheless, we're trying to check out the red Mercedes but it's difficult, almost impossible, without the registration number. I don't suppose Elizabeth's had any luck with her friends on that point, has she?"

"She's out with them now," said Stella, glancing at the clock. "She should be back soon but she doesn't hold out much hope."

As they were drinking tea, Ned observed a very excited Elizabeth running up the garden path waving something in her hand. With a crash the back door opened and she stood breathless on doormat.

"Oh, I'm glad you're here, Mr Stevens," she gasped. "It's the Mercedes. The red Mercedes. I'd forgotten, I took a picture of it when we saw it the first time so that Graham could show it to his friends at school. It was Diane who remembered while I was at her house, and here's the photo I took with the number plate clearly visible."

Fred leapt up and took the picture. "Well done, young lady. Now we'll be able to find out who this wretched car belongs to."

Later in the day Fred was able to report that the car belonged to a Percival Archibald Clayton who lived in Reading and that Reading police had called at his home and found no-one in. On Monday, however, the local police would be contacting the estate agents again to see if anyone of that name had ever visited Penwynton House. Meanwhile, as no criminal damage has been done and nothing stolen, it was to be treated as a low profile case.

Elizabeth was disappointed that Percival Archibald Clayton was not a wanted man. Her imagination had labelled him as a crook, a bank robber perhaps, who, along with his accomplice, had stashed away vast amounts of used bank notes in the upper rooms of Penwynton House. Nevertheless, she met up with her friends in the recreation ground at the back of the Inn, where in the heat of golden September sunshine, they digested the police news and came up with their own theories.

As Stella drew the curtains to shut out the impending darkness, the telephone rang in the hall. She cursed, her favourite television programme was due to start, the girls were in Elizabeth's room and Ned had popped down to Rose Cottage to see his mother, hence she would have to answer it herself. With fingers crossed that it would be a wrong number, she picked up the receiver.

"Hi, Stell, it's me."

"Rose, what a surprise. I was going to ring you this afternoon but somehow never got round to it. How's George?"

She groaned. "Driving me mad. He sprained his ankle last night, dancing would you believe? I'm sure it's painful, but what a fuss he's making, he wants waiting on now, hand and foot. You'd think he was on death's door."

Stella laughed. "Where is he then? I don't think you'd be talking like that if he were in earshot."

Rose lowered her voice. "In the bath, so I have a few minutes respite and I feel better already for having had a little moan."

"Oh dear. Well tell him we send our love and wish him a speedy recovery."

"I will. Anyway, how are Ned and the girls?"

"Fine. We're all fine. We had a bit of excitement earlier though. Elizabeth and some of her friends went up to Penwynton House last night when they should have been at the discotheque, and while they were there they saw the figure of someone in one of the upstairs rooms. Of course they thought it was Teddy Tinsdale's ghost, you remember me telling you about the image of him on one of the photos Elizabeth took?"

"Yes, but surely it wasn't, was it?"

Stella laughed. "I shouldn't think so, but they also thought it might be the ghost of a long dead Penwynton called Gorran."

"Why would they think it's the ghost of a long dead Penwynton called Gorran? I don't get that. Not that I've ever heard of him."

"Because he was allegedly murdered in Bluebell Woods by the father of a girl he'd got into trouble. You know the old theory ghosts are the spirits of the dead who cannot rest."

"Hmm, anyway, what happened?"

"Ah, yes, well we assured them the image they saw wasn't Tinsdale or Gorran, but the thing is, while they were there a car arrived, a red Mercedes, which they'd seen there before. They didn't see the driver because they were hiding behind the rhododendrons, but apparently he went into the house. Actually, this is a bit of a none-story cos he probably had every right to go in, but the police know who he is anyway because they've traced his name and address through the car's registration number. He lives in Reading, but when they called on him he wasn't at home, but then he's not likely to be, is he, if he was in Cornwall last night. Sorry Rose, I'm rambling and you've probably not the foggiest idea what I'm talking about."

Rose laughed. "Well, it sort of makes sense, even if it was a bit garbled. So out of curiosity what's this mysterious chap with the red Mercedes called?"

"Percival Archibald Clayton," said Stella with precision. "Gosh, I'm surprised I remembered a mouthful like that, it doesn't exactly slip off the tongue."

"Really? That name rings a bell. Where on earth have I heard it before? No, I've not heard it, I've read it. Come on brain, think."

"Perhaps it's the name of a wanted criminal you've heard mentioned at work, but no, it can't be because the Reading police don't have him down as a wanted man. Perhaps he's a work mate of Georges then."

"No, I shouldn't think so. I can't imagine George's work colleagues driving a Mercedes."

"Maybe he's an actor then."

"Oh God, I remember now. Yes, it was in a magazine. I bet it's him. You're never going to believe this, but Archie Clayton is the name of Maggie Nan's publicity agent."

CHAPTER TWENTY EIGHT

Ned's jaw dropped when he arrived back from Rose Cottage and Stella told him of Percival Archibald Clayton's possible identity.

"Good heavens! Is Rose sure?" he asked, dumbfounded by her information. "I mean, she's not mistaken?"

"No, she's positive," said Stella, clearly agitated. "I think you should tell Fred straight away. If this Clayton is Maggie Nan's agent, he may have her hidden somewhere in the old house."

Ned sat down. "Yes, of course, but why on earth would he kidnap his own client? That's if he has. It's silly and just doesn't make sense."

Stella shook her head. "I wouldn't be surprised if the whole story is fabricated and nothing less than a publicity stunt. Maggie Nan meanwhile is probably in hiding at Penwynton House and Clayton visits her there with food, although I have to admit it does sound a little far-fetched."

Ned frowned. "Oh, come on, Stella, surely with the sort of money she must have, they could have found a nice remote place for her to hide in with a lot more comfort than Penwynton House."

Stella nodded. "I agree, in which case perhaps Clayton himself kidnapped her because he's short of money. That's if she's there of course. What do you think?"

Ned rubbed his forehead. "I must admit I don't know what to think."

"Hmm, and I suppose our thoughts are of no importance anyway. What does matter is that you must go and see Fred. This speculative chat is wasting precious time, and as I said, we don't even know that she's there."

Fred was flabbergasted.

"But, but, Dick and I searched the place," he stammered. "We searched it from top to bottom."

"What every room?" Ned asked. "Weren't there any that you could not get in?"

"None," said Fred, shaking his head to emphasise his conviction. "There were no locked doors or anything like that and there certainly weren't any signs of anyone living there."

"Then perhaps we're mistaken," said Ned. "After all I suppose Maggie Nan's agent has as much right as anyone else to view Penwynton House, but Rose said according to the media, Clayton is on holiday abroad, but we know for a fact that he's been in Cornwall, so there's definitely something fishy going on."

"Actually, we didn't look everywhere," said Fred, slowly and thoughtfully. "We didn't check the cellars and I'd imagine they'd be pretty huge. We saw the door leading down to them and peeped round it, but we couldn't go any further because it was dark down there, and being daylight neither of us had thought to take a torch."

Ned sprang to his feet. "Then they must be searched. You'll have to go again, Fred. Maggie Nan may be hiding in the cellars during the day and then she goes wandering through the house at night."

Fred looked uncomfortable. "I suppose you could be right."

"Whether I'm right or not doesn't really matter, does it. The fact remains the cellars must be searched and the sooner the better."

Fred stood and patted Ned's back. "You're right. Do you fancy coming with me? I don't want to inform the Force in town if it's likely to be a wild goose chase, but at the same time, I don't much like the idea of going on my own, and it seems unfair to disturb Dick Remington again, especially on a Saturday night."

Ned spoke without hesitation. "Yes, why not? I'm always up for solving a problem. But if you don't mind, first I'll pop home and get my jacket as the night air's a bit chilly, and I would imagine the cellars in particular will be cold. I also want to ask Elizabeth which upstairs window it was they saw the light from."

Fred removed his slippers and reached for his shoes. "Okay, I'll pick you up in twenty minutes. Meanwhile, I'll look out my sturdiest pair of handcuffs."

Ned laughed. "That's what I like to hear, optimism. And make sure your torch has good batteries in it too. I'll bring one as well, then we can split up if needs be."

There was no sign of life as Fred's car approached Penwynton House. The building was in total darkness but its silhouette was clearly visible in the strong moonlight.

Before they went inside Ned and Fred walked around the back to view the upstairs windows from the outside.

"That'll be the one," said Ned, pointing upwards. "The one on the end. Elizabeth mentioned it was directly beneath a small window with a piece of broken guttering hanging above it."

"Right, well there doesn't appear to be anyone there tonight, unless of course they're sitting in the moonlight."

The two men made their way back round to the front of the house and let themselves in using the key Fred still had in his possession, handed to him by Mary and Dick Cottingham.

"God, it smells musty," said Ned, sniffing the stale air, "and this hallway's huge, it'd cost a fortune to heat a place like this. Surely no-one will ever buy it to live in. It would have to be someone with a commercial interest."

Fred closed the door. "The last couple to view it, would like to run it as a hotel. I hope they're successful. Annie liked them, and she's always been a good judge of character. She said they seemed honest and level headed, not that it's always possible to make people out straight away, but I think first impressions are often the most accurate."

Ned flashed his torch over the ornate, high ceilings in the hallway. "A hotel! Hmm, how many bedrooms does it have?"

"Twelve," said Fred. "Dick and I counted them. Twelve upstairs, anyway, and then there are a further half dozen attic rooms. It's in two parts as you'll have seen out the back. This is the main part where I assume the family always lived and the wing jutting out at the back has smaller rooms and a separate, smaller staircase, which I assume would have been the servants' quarters and perhaps the nursery. It's a pity it's dark. Dick and I came in daylight of course and we were able to have a good poke round."

"Well, as you temporarily have the key, perhaps you could show me round sometime in daylight, and Stella too, she'd love to see it. We could pretend we were potential purchasers."

Ned shone his torch through the open double doors into one of the rooms. "Not that I'd want to take on this place even if I did have pots of money, but then I'm not very adventurous."

"Same here," said Fred. "Come on, we'd better investigate, let's start with the back wing, since that's where this Nan woman or Teddy Tinsdale's ghost is alleged to be. Although in the picture your daughter took Teddy Tinsdale's ghost was here in the front, rooms, wasn't he?"

"Teddy Tinsdale's ghost!" laughed Ned, as the two men walked through the passages to the rear of the house and into a large kitchen. "Do I detect a note of cynicism in your voice?"

Fred grinned. "Maybe. Anyway, we get to the cellar door through here, it's next to the walk-in larder."

Ned paused in the kitchen doorway. "Christ, this place looks as though it's out of the Ark. I've only ever seen rooms like this in museums."

He crossed the cold stone floor, peered into one of the three huge sinks and turned on a large brass tap. "Well, at least it has running water but I bet it's not on the mains, is it?"

Fred flashed his torch into the dark corners. "No, there's a very deep well out the back and the water's pumped in from there somehow. It does have electricity though, but of course it's all switched off now, so our intruders won't be making use of that if they're here."

Ned opened one of the old solid fuel oven doors and peeped inside. "Wow, Winnie Bray must've baked her pasties in here. The very thought makes me feel all goose-pimply." He turned towards the table. "And she'd have rolled out the pastry on here most like. I wonder why it wasn't sold at the auction."

"I would imagine they didn't think anyone would have room for a damn great table like this," said Fred, kicking one of the huge solid legs.

"I suppose so. It is rather enormous. It feels really weird being here. Gosh how I'd love to go back in time and see this place in its heyday."

"Me too, but how come you know about Winnie Bray? She were a bit before your time, mine as well for that matter, although as a boy

I do remember seeing her briefly but she was a very old woman then."

"Jim told Stella all about the history of this place and of course she passed lots of it on to me. It's given her the incentive to research her own family history too and now she fantasises about being a descendent of the Penwyntons."

Fred laughed. "I see, she's heard the old yarn about Grenville Penwynton then. Well, anything's possible, but she'll not be the first to try and connect herself to the family. Many have over the years but none have had any luck. Come on, are we going down these cellars or not?"

They opened the door and shone both torches onto the steep steps which lead into a passage at the bottom.

"Well, perhaps we ought to go a little way," said Ned, with an obvious lack of enthusiasm. "But I really don't think anyone has been down there for years. You lead."

"Okay, but you stay close by me."

Both men descended the staircase with great caution. The steps were solid granite. Ned counted them, thirteen in all. At the bottom a long passage disappeared into the darkness. They flashed their torches to the far end. Oil lamps hung along the walls, the floor was flagstone and the passage was lined with several closed doors.

"Err, shall we go any further?" asked Ned, hoping Fred would say no. "I mean, looking at those oil lamps tells me there isn't even any electricity down here and I shouldn't think this place has been used for donkey's years."

"I agree, but as we're here perhaps we ought to just take a peep behind one or two of the doors, although I can't see much point in checking them all. No-one in their right mind would hide in this God forsaken place and there are no footprints in the muck on the floor."

Behind the first door lay the remains of a few old logs, no doubt once used as fuel for the many fires. Behind the second, coal dust covered a cobbled floor and dirty, long cobwebs stretched across the bare, blackened walls of a small room. The third door was huge, solid, and reinforced with bands of metal. In the lock a large key protruded. Fred turned it with force and pushed back the door. The light from his torch showed walls with deep, arched alcoves built two high on three sides. Ned was impressed. "Wow, this was no doubt the wine cellar. I take it the Penwyntons weren't tee-totallers then."

Fred grinned. "Some of them might have been but I think it unlikely."

The other rooms were empty, except for a few pieces of broken furniture and a dysfunctional mangle, all long forgotten and of no use to anyone.

Ned pulled up the collar of his jacket. "Christ, it's freezing down here. Come on, Fred, it's obvious we're wasting our time, as fascinating as it might be."

Fred agreed, and both men left the cellars, returned to the kitchen and then headed for the staircase leading to the rooms above.

The stairs were steep, straight, and with no windows to let in natural light. Upstairs the rooms were empty and devoid of furniture. Fred and Ned looked in each one and flashed their torches into every corner, determined not to miss anything that might indicate the presence of human life.

Systematically, they passed through each room until they reached the end of the narrow corridor and the room where the girls had seen the mysterious vision. The door was slightly ajar. They opened it with caution, but the room, just like all the others, was empty. Ned was puzzled, he really had expected to find something.

Fred on the other hand was amused. "Well, perhaps Teddy and Maggie complained to the management that their rooms out here at the back weren't up to scratch and they've been moved to finer quarters."

Ned grinned. "Probably, but now we'll have to search the whole house cos I can't believe there's nothing here at all."

Fred pointed to the ceiling. "There are the attic rooms above here, so we'd better do a thorough job and look at them before we go back to the main part of the house."

The attic rooms were reached by a very narrow winding staircase.

"Mind your head in the doorways, Ned, they're not very high and beware of the beams too, poor Dick banged his head and it came up in a lump."

The rooms in the attic were very small, the walls and ceilings sloped and damp patches above their heads indicated spots where the roof leaked. In places the floorboards, stained with heavy varnish, wobbled."

"I suppose these rooms are where the servants slept," said Ned, looking up at the cracked ceiling. "They look pretty grim and I can't imagine them ever offering a jot of comfort."

"Hmm, depends how many were crammed in here," said Fred, "but it was probably no more uncomfortable than your average cottage."

Ned fumbled with the catch on one of the small windows and looked out.

"I reckon we must be above the room where the girls saw the light which we found to be empty," said Ned, looking out. "See, the piece of broken guttering is just above my head."

Fred leaned from the window and looked above his head. "I'm so glad I didn't report any of this to that lot in town, they'd have been suggesting I take early retirement on the grounds I'm getting senile.

"Ah, but we may well find something yet," grinned Ned, confused but still determined. "Don't give up hope, Fred."

They returned downstairs, left the back wing and walked through the passages to the main part of the house.

The Penwynton family rooms were large and in spite of the damp smell, they felt airy. Fred and Ned wandered from room to room but their search proved inconclusive. There was no sign of anyone living in the house.

They went upstairs by way of a wide, curved impressive staircase. At the top, Fred and Ned separated and meticulously searched the bedrooms individually, but again the rooms were all empty. When they met on the wide landing, Ned opened one of the windows and peered outside. From where he stood, the back wing of the house was clearly visible. He looked across to the window of the room where the children had seen an image. Above was the small window, tucked beneath the piece of broken guttering. Ned blinked, momentarily convinced he saw a flash of light pass across the glass panes. He looked again. Without doubt, a dim light was slowly moving across the surface of the window. Excitedly, he called to Fred.

"But we've just been in there," spluttered Fred. "What…"

Ned closed the window. "Come on, let's get back there quick, before it disappears again."

The two men raced down the staircase into the large hall and along passages back into the servant's wing. Both stopped at the foot of the back stairs.

"You alright, Fred?" asked Ned, breathing heavily.

Fred puffed to catch his breath. "Yes, but I'm not sure which is having the biggest impact on my heart, fatigue or fear!"

At the top of the stairs they crept along the long narrow corridor, glancing in each room but not stopping until they reached the last one. The door was ajar as they had left it and no light shone through the gap. Ned pushed the door gently, it swung open, he then flashed around his torch, but the room was quite empty.

"Oh, this is ridiculous," said Ned, with a deep sigh of frustration. "We both saw a light and the kids saw it last night too. Whatever goes on?"

He marched across the room opened the window and looked above his head. To his surprise the small window directly beneath the piece of broken guttering was not there. He looked to his left and was mystified to observe yet another window indicating there was another room beyond the room where they stood. Ned looked up, he could not believe his eyes. For above the next window was the small window directly beneath the piece of broken guttering.

"What!" said Ned, scratching his head. "This is crazy, there must be another room after this one."

Fred also took a look outside. "But there can't be, and if there is, where the Devil's the entrance? The corridor ends here and there are no more stairs."

Fred closed the window and looked at the walls. "The panelling?" he whispered with raised eye brows. "What do you think?"

"You mean there might be a secret room behind it?" said Ned. "I hadn't thought of that, but I suppose many of these old houses had them to hide people for political and religious reasons. As someone who used to teach history I should have thought of that."

The panelling ran along all four walls of the room. The two men nervously began to tap, fully aware that someone must be on the other side for they had seen torchlight, but their tapping revealed no obvious place for a secret door, the walls sounded solid.

"I give up," said Ned, baffled and annoyed. "I mean, we can't have missed another staircase, can we? So how on earth do you get into that wretched room without a ladder from outside?"

"I wonder if it's possible to get to it from above," said Fred, thoughtfully. "I'm thinking about the attic rooms. Remember the wobbly floorboards? I wonder if they wobble because they're not nailed down, and the reason for that, is so they can be lifted up with ease."

"It's possible," said Ned, intrigued at the prospect of finding the secret hidey hole. "Come on, let's go and see."

The two men crept up the narrow winding stairs like very excited school boys, and once inside the room directly above the room where the torchlight was detected, they stopped and searched for the wobbly boards.

"They're here," whispered Ned, standing in the corner.

They felt around the lose boards and found several could be raised. They lifted them with caution, not knowing who, or what, lay in the room below. Fred shone his torch into the hole finally revealed; a steep, wooden open staircase came into view. Without saying a word, he lowered himself onto the first tread. He reached the bottom and shone his torch around. Ned watched from above. Both men gasped. In Fred's torchlight the shape of a body appeared, curled in the corner on the floor beneath an old grey blanket. Ned quickly slipped through the gap and hastily climbed down the stairs. The body was a woman, she appeared to be sleeping or unconscious, and in her limp hand lay a torch, its dim light casting shadows across the bare floorboards.

"Good God! It's her Fred, isn't it?" muttered Ned. "It's Maggie Nan. I recognise her from the television coverage."

Fred knelt by her side, rested his head on her chest and listened for a heartbeat.

"She's alive, thank goodness. Oh, this is daft. I feel as though I'm in a daze. I never dreamt we'd find her or anyone else here for that matter. Poor soul! If that Clayton man is keeping her prisoner here, he's left her nothing to eat or drink so she must be in a pretty bad way."

Ned shivered. "Shall I take your car, go home and phone for an ambulance? Or do you think it would it be better if you went?"

Fred rubbed his chin. "Hmm, I think you'd better go. I feel it's me who should stay, after all this is a crime scene and so I should take full responsibility over anything that happens." He thrust his hand into his jacket pocket. "Here are my car keys, Ned. Good luck, and please get back as quick as you can. I don't much like the idea of being here on my own."

Ned hurriedly climbed the staircase and ran through the attic room, along the passage and down the narrow back stairs and into the main part of the house. But before he left the building he felt compelled to peep into the drawing room where Teddy Tinsdale's ghost had stood. The room was bitterly cold and felt airless. Ned slowly turned and shone his torch across the papered walls. Dark patches outlined the position where large pieces of the furniture had once stood. Ned shivered. He was wasting time. He ran back into the hallway and out through the large double door.

Outside Ned looked up at the house. Above its rooftop a huge golden moon beamed from a clear bright, starry sky. He shuddered. The house looked eerie, forsaken, sad, and to quote Anne 'unloved'. With haste Ned unlocked Fred's car, climbed inside and started up the engine.

Fred looked at his watch, it was half past ten. He wished he had left Annie a note to say where he was going, but he'd expected to be back long before she had finished baby-sitting for Sid and Meg. He looked at Maggie Nan, she was in another world and there was nothing he could do for her, except pray. He decided to leave her in peace until help arrived. The room she was in was small, claustrophobic and smelt musty. He climbed the staircase and sat on the floor of the attic room above with his legs dangling through the gap made by absent floor boards. He lit a cigarette, smoked it and then threw the butt into the corner having first made sure it was out. Fred stood up, his back ached. He looked at his watch again. It was twenty minutes to eleven. He reckoned Ned would be home and dialling 999. He sighed, a little comforted by the knowledge that help would soon be on its way.

Fred walked across the room to stretch his legs. By the door he stopped. Far below, deep inside the house, he heard a jingling noise echoing through the empty rooms and passages. Fred put his head around the door and listened again. He heard a distant door slam. He jumped. Surely Ned wasn't back already? He listened. Nothing. Fred decided the slamming door was caused by a draught blowing in through a broken window or maybe down a chimney.

With confidence he crept along the passage to the top of the narrow stairs. He looked from the window. Something was moving in the long grass below. Quietly he released the catch, raised the lower half of the window and shone his torch onto the garden. The light reflected on four bright eyes and two cats ran down the flight of granite steps and off towards the stables.

Fred laughed, closed the window and slowly shuffled down the stairs to the bedrooms in the back wing. As he peered into one of the rooms he heard the jingle again. Fred felt his heart thumping against his ribs. Surely, surely, the ghost of Teddy Tinsdale was not walking through the house. Fred wished he had not mocked its existence. It was unwise, especially when he had seen a picture of Teddy with his very own eyes, taken after the poor man had died.

Fred felt for the handcuffs in his pocket. A fat lot of good they would be when confronted with a ghost. Quietly he turned and crept back up the stairs to the attic rooms. Perhaps Teddy only haunted the lower part of the house, if so he would be safe at the top of the back wing.

He returned to the hole in the floor and once again sat with his legs dangling through the gap in the floorboards. He froze. The jingling was getting closer and he could hear footsteps on the attic stairs. Quickly Fred climbed onto the wooden staircase and pulled the floorboards into place above his head. He then fled down the stairs and flashed his torch across the room. Maggie was still sleeping, her breath very shallow. Fred listened, from the room above he heard a cough. He gasped. The cough convinced him the presence was not a ghost, but that knowledge was of little comfort.

Fred switched off his torch and stepped back into the shadows as the floorboards above began to move and two large feet appeared through the open staircase. Crouched down in a corner he kept very still, and watched the silhouette of a tall man stop in front of the window, his outline was clearly visible in the strong moonlight. Dangling from his right hand, a bunch of keys jingled. Fred kept very still as the man approached Maggie Nan and kicked her hard. Fred stiffened. Maggie groaned.

The man bent down. "Aren't you dead yet, bitch?" he spat.

Fred felt his heart thumping and the torch heavy in his hand.

"Die woman, die. Then I won't have to come to this God forsaken, evil dump ever again. Bloody horrible place!"

The man turned away from Maggie, rested his hands on the window sill and peered through the dirty, cobwebby glass. "Ghastly Cornish scumbags."

Fred felt his blood begin to boil. His face was burning. He wanted to shout. He slowly stood up and raised his arm. With enormous force he brought down the torch hard on the back of the man's head. The man fell sideward onto the floor with a loud thud.

Fred stepped forwards, grabbed the man's hands and locked handcuffs around his wrists. He then stood up and kicked him in the back.

"That's from her," he said, nodding his head towards Maggie Nan, and don't you ever insult this house or Cornwall's people again!"

But Percival Archibald Clayton did not respond. He was out cold.

CHAPTER TWENTY NINE

On Sunday morning, Stella and the girls went to church. It was the first day of October. Ned did not join them for two reasons, first, he was emotionally exhausted by the previous night's events and secondly, he did not feel mentally prepared for the inevitable barrage of questions inquisitive churchgoers were likely to ask.

Fred Stevens likewise opted to refrain from cleansing his soul, and instead walked around to The School House to tell Ned the latest news. Ned greeted him warmly and both men sat in the kitchen with mugs of steaming coffee to chew over the latest developments.

"So, how's Maggie Nan?" asked Ned, offering Fred ginger biscuits straight from the tin.

Fred took one. "Thanks. She's still out cold but she's stable, thank goodness. They're going to transfer her to a London hospital later today. Her husband's down apparently and he insists she's sent nearer to home."

"And what about Clayton? Has that cad come round yet?"

Fred grinned. "Yep, and they've nicked the bugger. He's still in hospital but is likely to be discharged later today and transferred to a nice cosy police cell."

Ned dunked a biscuit in his coffee, something he only did when Stella was not around. "Good! Well, I don't know about you but I've thought of little else since last night but I'm still mystified as to why the man kidnapped his own client?"

Fred nodded. "Same here. I've tried to fathom it out but haven't been able to come up with anything, unless he needed the money. But if that was the case why did he want her to die. It makes no sense whatsoever."

"Well, hopefully he'll confess since he was caught red-handed."

Fred yawned. "And if he doesn't I'm sure we'll still have enough evidence to nail him. As you say, he was caught red-handed and then of course we'll soon be able to hear Maggie Nan's story. That should be very interesting listening."

Ned grinned. "I still can't get my head round the fact that Maggie Nan ended up here of all places. Trengillion has certainly put itself on the map one way or another with well-known personalities. What with Wagstaffe and now Maggie Nan, the village will soon become a tourist attraction for reasons other than the sea."

Fred nodded but his eyes looked tired and sad. "I don't know about you, Ned, but I found last night mentally confusing. What I mean is, I've been in the Force for nearly forty years and much of that time I spent clipping youngsters around the ears for scrumping and ticking lads off for letting off bangers in the street on Bonfire Night. I've seen very little real crime, although of course, there have been a few serious cases, like Jane Hunt's death and the attack on poor Milly Pascoe, not that I played any part in solving those crimes. In fact I've made very few arrests. In my younger days I yearned to be the hero, you see, and catch wanted criminals, but now I've done it I feel sort of hollow, does that make sense? I feel I've seen a side of life I'd rather not have seen. What's more, it brought out something in me that I'd rather not witness again, either. Anger, Ned! I was so angry when he kicked that poor woman and told her to die. Please don't repeat this as it'd get me into trouble, but when he was out cold, handcuffed and defenceless, I kicked the bastard. I shouldn't have done it, I know, but I did and I felt better for it. But surely my display of bad temper makes me as worthless as him."

"Worthless!" Ned cried. "Oh, come on, Fred, you can't compare yourself with him, and if I'd been in your shoes I'd probably have done the same. Besides, he's alive and likely to be discharged from hospital today, so you've not harmed him at all. You're a good man, Fred, you've done a good job during your years in the Force, and if there's been very little crime while you've been the village bobby then you can take the credit for it. The youngsters here look up to you and respect you. Your presence here has kept generations of kids on the straight and narrow, so don't let me ever here you say again that you're as worthless as a no-good like Clayton."

On Monday morning, as Elizabeth ran down the stairs, two at a time, doing up her school tie, the daily newspaper dropped through the letterbox and onto the doormat. Elizabeth bent down, picked it up and tucked it beneath her arm before looking into the hall mirror to check her tie was straight. She then went into the kitchen to join the rest of the family who were already eating breakfast.

"Ah, good, the paper," said Ned, taking it from his daughter. "It'll be interesting to see what they have to say about Trengillion's latest incident."

He unfolded the newspaper and lay it on the table over his cereal bowl.

"Aha, there he is, girls," said Ned, pointing to a picture on the front page. "Percival Archibald Clayton. What a rotter! Let's hope he's never given the chance to set foot in Cornwall again."

Stella and the girls moved towards Ned and peered at the paper with interest. Stella tut-tutted. Elizabeth hummed a noise of acknowledgement, but on Anne, the picture had a more dramatic effect. The colour drained from her face and her lips quivered. She pointed at the picture with a shaking hand. "It's him," she whispered. "I'd know him anywhere. He's the horrible man I saw in the woods, who later followed me to Grandma and Granddad's house."

"Humph, it can't be," said Elizabeth, disparagingly. "He doesn't have long hair."

Tears formed in Anne's eyes. "No, but he has big ears."

Ned looked closely. "Anne's right, Liz. I saw him, remember, and he did have long hair but it was pulled back in a ponytail, just as it is in this picture."

Shortly before teatime the telephone rang in the School House. Stella answered it as she passed through the hallway. It was Rose. Grinning, Stella sat down on the rug with her back against the warm night-store heater. "I bet I know what you're phoning about. I was going to ring you but I've been waiting to hear which weekend Frank and Dot will be having their leaving do so I could invite you and George down. It'll definitely be this month and hopefully will coincide with half term so that you can come down for the week, if you can get the time off work that is."

"Wow, yes, I'm sure I'll be able to do that even if I have to swap some shifts."

Stella tucked a wisp of hair behind her ear. "Anyway, you were right about Archie Clayton and your quick thinking probably saved Maggie Nan's life."

Rose giggled. "Oh yeah, I hadn't thought of that. So in a funny sort of way that should counteract the guilt I felt all those years ago when poor Rosemary Howard died. Do you remember her, Stella?"

"Of course, how could I ever forget her? What a crazy honeymoon that was! Anyway, how's George?"

"Oh, loads better. I think he got fed up with being incapacitated and so he started to think more positively."

"That's good."

"I keep meaning to ask if you've listened to Radio One, yet."

"Yes, we were right in at the beginning and had it on at seven for Saturday's launch. How about you?"

"Same here. What do your girls think of it?"

Stella laughed. "They think it's alright but weren't impressed that Ned and I listened to it. Apparently old-timers like us should be glued to Radio Two."

"Ugh, old timers, and George and me are even older than you two."

"Not at heart, you're not. By the way, I owe you an apology. I must admit I've always sneered at your love of what I considered to be trashy magazines and worthless newspapers, but had it not been for them and your thirst for news of the rich and famous, then this crime might not have been solved quite so successfully."

"Ah, thanks, Stell. That's a real compliment and I appreciate it. It's nice to know I've done something useful."

"You're welcome."

"You know, it was really weird reading about Trengillion in this morning's papers, and that picture of Fred was a few years old, wasn't it? Where on earth did they get that from?"

Stella laughed. "A reporter came knocking on the Police House door yesterday asking for an interview with Fred, but he wasn't in cos he was here with Ned, and Annie was at church. Jamie was home though and he gave them the picture from the sideboard taken twenty years ago. Fred's dead chuffed by some of this morning's headlines, he even thinks it's funny to be called P.C. Plod."

"Ah, bless him. What does Ned make of it all?"

"He was alright yesterday, but today's papers and the television News has upset him a bit. He doesn't like reference being made to the Wagstaffe case and he hates to read about Grace Bonnington or

Sylvia as he always calls her. He feels the press paint a very ugly picture of her and it's unjust. It's a pity they had to dig that all up, after all there's no connection between the two cases."

"Yes, I agree," said Rose, "and it can't have pleased Frank much either. How about Milly, is there any news there yet?"

"I've not heard anything lately, as far as I know she's still in a coma and the boys spend a lot of time on the farm with Albert and Madge. That was a nasty business and they've still no idea who did it."

Rose sighed. "Oh dear, how sad, and I suppose Molly's still fretting over it?"

"Yes, I'm afraid so and I pray Milly recovers. If she doesn't, it's likely to kill Molly. God everything's so topsy-turvy at the moment!"

"But had Molly not gone in the post office when she did then Milly would surely have died, so in a way she saved her."

"That's what we keep telling her, but she says she was too slow, she wasted precious time and that time was vital. At least she can't blame herself for Teddy Tinsdale's death or Edward Tucker, whichever you like to call him."

"Did they ever establish the cause of his death? I mean, I know he fell from the cliff path, but is that what killed him? And did the shoe you found provide any clues as to whether or not he was murdered?"

"He died from injuries caused by the fall," said Stella. "At least that's the case as far as I know. I don't think the shoe episode proved to be of any help at all, and its disappearance after I'd put it in the hedge really means nothing, cos anyone could have found it by chance and tossed it somewhere else. Although the police did do quite a thorough search. Why on do you ask?"

"Because you mentioning Teddy, has just reminded me that he had an affair a few years back with Archie Clayton's wife, Angie. Teddy was a shocking womaniser, so plenty of men had a motive to kill him including Archie, and I've just realised, Archie was probably in Cornwall when Teddy died."

Molly rushed down the road to the post office on Monday evening to buy a bar of her favourite chocolate. The major was away for the night, he had gone with George Fillingham and fellow members of his golf club to a tournament in Devon and would not be back until Tuesday evening, hence, since she would be spending the evening alone, she decided chocolate would be a nice accompaniment for a glass or two of elderberry wine.

Molly found Johnny in the post office removing unsold newspapers from the news rack. She was surprised, for when she had been there of late, Fran Bray, Betty's mother, who had once worked in the main post office in town, had served her. Molly's guilt re-emerged seeing Johnny and she asked, nervously, if there were any news regarding the state of Milly's health.

Johnny shook his head. "No, she's still in a coma and deteriorating slowly. I regret to say we're preparing ourselves for the worst."

Molly paid for the chocolate and dropped the change into her purse. "I'm so sorry, Johnny," she whispered, fighting back the tears. "So very, very, sorry."

Molly left the post office in a daze and walked home as rain drops fell from the heavens. Quickly she ran as fast as she was able for the last few yards. Once inside she locked the door and drew the curtains to shut out the impending wet and windy night.

Molly felt low, but made herself a pot of tea and a ham sandwich, took them into the sitting room and switched on the television for the News. The News showed intrusive footage of Maggie Nan leaving the hospital in Cornwall, still unconscious on a stretcher. Molly was shocked, Maggie had lost a lot of weight and she looked tired, drawn and in spite of the face lift, older.

Molly finished her sandwich, drained the pot of tea and then took her dirty crockery into the kitchen. She did not bother to wash up as it did not seem worth it for such a small amount. From the pantry she took a half full bottle of elderberry wine and from her coat pocket she pulled the bar of rum n' raisin chocolate. She then returned to the sitting room, stoked up the fire and sat back to watch *Coronation Street*. As the sombre music of the programme faded away, Molly rose from her chair and peeped through the curtains into her front garden. The rain was lashing hard against the window panes and the silhouette of plants and shrubs could be seen fighting to stand upright in the strong south westerly wind.

A sudden flash of lightening made Molly jump. Swiftly she pulled the curtains back together. Simultaneously, from above, a loud clap of thunder shook the house causing the window panes to rattle. As Molly turned back into the room, the lights flickered and then went out, leaving the room in darkness except for the orange glow from the fire.

From a drawer in the sideboard, she took three candles and lit them from the flames in the hearth. She then switched off the television set at the wall and pulled out the aerial. With no television to watch and insufficient light to read or sew by, Molly had nothing else to do but listen to her thoughts, drink the wine and eat her chocolate.

Molly tried hard not to think about Milly and attempted to avert her thoughts by mulling over information received regarding Maggie Nan, but the saga made no sense and her thoughts continually drifted back to Milly. Slowly, Molly sipped her wine and recalled the morning she had found the young post mistress, and again her sense of guilt united together with her feelings of grief. In her deepest, darkest thoughts, she recalled Johnny's words saying they were preparing themselves for the worst. Molly cried out with frustration. Life was too cruel!

The flames in the fire flickered sleepily and cast eerie shadows across the walls and ceiling, Molly watched, mesmerised, she knew she was not alone. There were faces in the shadows and voices whispering in the wind. She finished her wine and threw the chocolate wrapper onto the fire. A brief burst of energy sent a coloured flame high above the rest, it then withered and died and the blackened wrapper rolled from the bed of coal into the hearth.

Molly slipped off the settee, picked it up with the shovel and flung it back into the flames. As she knelt, the wind whistling down the chimney, begged her to pray. Obediently, she clasped her hands together, wept and asked God, her trustworthy guardian angels and the spirits of long departed family and friends, to join together and not let Milly die. She remained on her knees repeating her prayers, until her knees felt numb, her back ached and her throat was hoarse from crying. And then finally, when she felt she could do nothing more, she crawled across the room back to the settee, climbed onto it, removed her slippers, curled up into a ball and fell fast asleep. Shutting out the storm, the torment and the pain.

When Molly woke the room was quiet and the morning was still. She shivered, slipped off the settee, crossed to the window and pulled back the curtains. The grey clouds had gone and the sky above was blue, the rain had stopped and the wind had abated.

In the garden, flowers were attempting to raise their heads and dry their faces in the warmth of the sun. Molly went into the hallway and opened the front door. The air smelled fresh and clean and spider's webs sparkled in the September sunlight.

She left the house and walked with bare feet onto the wet lawn. The morning was beautiful. Hope hung in the air and she knew, without any doubt, that Milly Pascoe would live.

CHAPTER THIRTY

On Wednesday morning, Maggie Nan recovered consciousness and the following day doctors deemed she was strong enough to be interviewed briefly. A full report was made of the interview and a copy of it was passed on to the Cornish police, even though the case was out of their hands and Percival Archibald Clayton was safely under lock and key in London.

On Saturday afternoon, Fred Stevens, with his copy of the report, went to The School House on his return from town to show it to Ned. Stella was out, she had gone over to Polquillick to drop off Elizabeth at a school friend's house for a birthday party and Anne was out shopping with Molly.

When Stella returned she found Ned deep in thought, elbows on the kitchen table with his head resting on his up-turned hands.

"Are you tired, Ned?" she asked, as she removed her coat. "You're very pale."

"No, just shocked, sad and I don't know, muddled, I suppose."

Stella went into the hall to hang up her coat, she then returned to the kitchen. "I'll make us a cup of tea and then you can tell me what's bothering you. If you want to, that is."

Ned leaned back in the chair. "Of course I do. Is the fire in the front room lit?"

"Yes, love. I lit it before I went to Polquillick." Stella took two mugs from the kitchen cabinet. "I thought it seemed a bit chilly today, but then we are in October now."

"Good, let's go in there, I feel in need of a little comfort and there's nothing like a blazing fire to make one feel relaxed and at ease."

Once the tea was made, with mugs in hands, they went down the hall and into the front room where Stella removed the fire guard.

Ned sat down on the settee. "Fred came round today, just after you left, with a report on Maggie Nan's statement to the police up-country. It made interesting reading and because of it, Archie

Clayton will go on trial at the Old Bailey for murder, and two cases of attempted murder."

Stella sat down in her favourite chair by the fire. "What! But who did he kill? Oh God, it must have been Teddy Tinsdale. Rose said he had a motive cos Teddy'd had an affair with his wife. And one of the people he attempted to kill was of course Maggie Nan, but who on earth was the other?"

"Milly," hissed Ned, through gritted teeth. "Our poor Milly. Thank goodness she's on the mend otherwise the village would be up in arms when they found out, but at the same time, they'll no doubt be relieved to know her attacker is under lock and key."

"So the attack on Milly obviously wasn't robbery, in which case, what was the motive?"

"Apparently Clayton went to the post office for some fags and there was a picture of him on the front page of one of the magazines, condemning him for soaking up the sun while his most famous client was still missing. Unfortunately, he saw Milly glance at it, realised she'd recognised him, grabbed the old clothes iron from beside the door, bashed her over the head with it, grabbed some money from the till to make it look like robbery and left her for dead."

Stella's jaw dropped. "The bastard!"

"Hmm, and then he boasted about it to Maggie. You see, his plan was to starve her to death, so he knew she'd never be able to tell. Some poor copper in Reading's in big trouble for not spotting the link when the name Clayton first cropped up."

"How do you mean?"

"Well, when the Cornish police asked for Clayton to be checked out regarding a possible unlawful sighting, the case should have received more attention. Apparently the poor chap who dealt with it was new to the area and didn't even know who Clayton was, so it sort of slipped through the net."

Stella sighed. "Oh dear, another tale of woe. But I'm mystified as to why Archie Clayton wanted Maggie dead. I mean, was it him who kidnapped her in the first place? Was it him who asked for the ransom money? Just what was it all about, Ned?"

"I'll start at the beginning, it's the only way and you can ask questions when I've finished, not that I'm sure I'll even be able to answer them all."

Stella leaned back in her chair. "Okay, I'll try not to interrupt."

Ned half smiled. "Right, well it all began with the face lift that went wrong, which of course we first heard about from Rose. As we know, the media gave her a lot of stick and her popularity plummeted because of it, and so Clayton hatched up a plan to win her sympathy and get back her status as one of the country's top fashion designers. He didn't give her a chance to not go along with his plan, because he told her if she didn't, he'd tell her husband about some bloke she'd had a brief fling with whilst in Paris for a fashion show."

"Humph," muttered Stella, "according to Rose, Maggie Nan's old man is a shocking philanderer and so I very much doubt if he'd have given a toss about a brief affair anyway."

Ned nodded. "I agree."

"And the plan was obviously to say she'd been kidnapped."

"Yes, at least that was the plan as Maggie knew it and to make it sound more glamorous they decided to have her kidnapped in the States."

"What do you mean by the plan as Maggie knew it?"

Ned sighed. "I'll tell you later. First things first."

"Okay."

"Right, now where was I? Ah yes, they decided to claim Maggie had been kidnapped in the States and so Clayton flew out to Los Angeles with his sister, who with the aid of a wig, dark glasses and make-up looked enough like Maggie Nan to get her through the airports. The following day his sister flew back under her real name and a couple of days after that Clayton reported Maggie missing. Meanwhile, she was here in Cornwall, mixing with holiday makers, would you believe? But to avoid detection she also wore a wig, sunglasses and stayed in a caravan under a false name. Clayton had already been in Cornwall before the kidnapping, you see, to sus the place out."

Stella tut-tutted. "Well, fancy that."

Ned frowned.

"Sorry, I won't interrupt again."

"Okay. While Clayton was in America he sent a ransom letter to the Los Angeles Police and to make it sound authentic he included a tape on which they'd staged Maggie begging for mercy. As we know, the media here didn't believe it, they claimed she was really in the States to get her face sorted out and that the kidnapping claim was a publicity stunt-cum-hoax, which of course it was. Clayton left America a couple of weeks later, saying he had to return home as he had other clients needing his attention, and to keep the story going he paid some crook several hundred dollars to post letters he'd already written to the Los Angeles Police Department, from time to time. And before I forget, the ransom note sent to the American television company asking for money wasn't sent by him, so that must have been a copy-cat villain trying to cash in on the case."

"Not surprised by that."

"Me neither. Anyway, once back in England, when he thought it was safe to do so, Clayton came down here to Cornwall again, after first telling everyone he was off to Italy, on business, to take a well-earned break. Meanwhile he had made enquiries about property for sale down here, but the only one he was really interested in was Penwynton House, which he knew was on the market because he'd read about the death of Charles Penwynton. And the reason he knew, was, and this is the bit that will interest you, is because his great granny was none other than Florrie Ham, the chambermaid who was sacked by Talwyn Penwynton for falling for a baby of which her son Gorran was the father."

Stella sat up straight and gasped. "No, surely not."

"Yes, he was, well, he still is. Anyway, through his great grandmother he knew about the secret room, because one of her duties was to keep it clean, but I'll come back to that part of the story in a minute. Anyway, once Clayton had established which estate agent was handling the sale of Penwynton House, using a false name and address, he asked to view it and he was given a key by the estate agents. He then came down for a look round. He told Maggie he needed a good place for her to hide, saying he was worried she might get recognised one day if she mingled with the public despite being incognito."

"She was still in Cornwall then?"

"Yes. Anyway, after Clayton had viewed the house and found the secret room, he went to Truro and got another key cut. He then went back home and called in at the estate agents with the original key, and told them the house needed too much spent on it to make it habitable, but to make him seem a genuine purchaser, he took away details of other properties. He then came back to Cornwall and Maggie Nan made the secret chamber her home, while her appearance, which never had been as bad as the media made out, slowly improved."

"I'm with you so far."

"Good. The next part of Clayton's plan was, when the time was right, to send word to Maggie's husband, revealing her real whereabouts, so that he could come and get her. Although of course to make it look authentic a ransom was to be asked for. And so for a week or so Maggie hid in the secret room by day and crept out at night to stretch her legs and wash in the old kitchen sink. Clayton meanwhile brought her food and drink and everything seemed alright. Then one day, as the sun was setting, Maggie and Clayton were looking from the windows on the front of the house when they saw Edward Tucker furtively walking along the drive. Tucker stopped by Clayton's car, the red Mercedes, looked at the registration number and then tried the front door, which was unlocked at the time. Maggie said she hid in one of the bedrooms, but at that time she didn't know where Clayton went. She remembers hearing Tucker climbing the stairs and shouting Clayton's name, saying he guessed he wasn't alone in the house.

Maggie doesn't know quite what happened next but there was a lot of noise and shouting, and then a scream followed by several loud bumps. When all went quiet she came out of her hiding place and saw Tucker lying at the bottom of the stairs, not moving. Clayton stood over him going through his wallet, a look of satisfaction on his face.

That night when it was dark, Clayton drove to the cliff path with Tucker's body in the boot of his car. We assume he drove up the old lane leading to the coastguard cottages as you and Fred had surmised, and took a short cut through the mushroom field to the old mine, where the shoe must have fallen from Tucker's foot. Incidentally, the police have since found that shoe, hidden in the boot of Clayton's car."

Stella sighed. "If only I'd had the nous to bring it back when I found it."

"Humph, maybe, but it wouldn't have helped solve the crime any quicker, would it?"

Stella slowly shook her head. "No, I suppose not. Anyway what happened next?"

"After the Tucker incident Maggie got really scared. She always knew she would be in big trouble if the truth behind Clayton's plan ever came to light regarding her kidnapping, but when it came to the murder he'd committed, she knew she was guilty by association even though she played no part in it. And she was right to be afraid because after that he began to treat her badly, saying she needed to be in a poor way when she was found, otherwise the kidnapping claims wouldn't look authentic. And so he went to the house less often and brought her very little food. She thought about trying to escape and going to the police, but she was too scared of the consequences. Then one day he arrived and told her he'd killed a nosy bitch at the post office and at that moment Maggie knew she would be his next victim."

"Oh God, I've gone all goose-pimply," said Stella. "But surely she didn't really think her life was in danger. She was after all his meal ticket, and would prove very little use to him dead."

Ned half smiled. "He was and still is pretty well-off, Stella, and so money is, was, no object really."

"I suppose not. So what happened next?"

Ned shuddered. "On the evening of the day on which he'd attacked Milly, he sat on the stairs in the secret room and calmly told Maggie it was time to prepare for the end. She was to be starved to death and then after her demise, he intended to send word to her husband telling him she was now in England and demanding ransom money in exchange for the address as to where she was hidden. Except, he planned that when her husband and the police arrived, there'd be nothing left to find. Just a fire. A huge fire. Penwynton House in flames with Maggie's dead body inside."

Ned took a breath and drank the remains of his tea. Stella opened her mouth to speak, but Ned raised his hand to stop her.

"Wait, let me finish, for the most astonishing is yet to come. You see, the real reason for the whole kidnapping farce and why Clayton wanted Maggie dead, was to get revenge for his great grandmother, Florrie Ham, as she bore resentment to the Penwyntons 'til the day she died at the grand old age of eighty eight. At the time Clayton was a lad of twenty two. Actually, that's not quite true, her real resentment was towards the Nancarrows, and if you cast your mind back to your chat with Jim, Nancarrow was Talwyn's maiden name."

Stella nodded. "Yes, Cedric Penwynton married Talwyn Nancarrow from Penzance. I remember that fact clearly, but I'm completely confused."

"Maggie Nan was a Nancarrow, Stella, but she shortened her name to Nan because she thought it tripped off the tongue more easily. But Clayton didn't know that, not at first, anyway. He knew nothing of her connection to the Penwyntons or Nancarrows until Maggie read in the newspaper of Charles' death. She then told him, with great amusement, that her distant cousin, Bernard Reeves, was about to become a wealthy man. In retrospect she recalls the revelation had a strange effect on Clayton. He went very quiet and thoughtful, but she thought nothing of it and assumed his mind was elsewhere and he wasn't really interested."

"Good heavens! I'm actually speechless."

"I know how you feel. Poor Maggie. After Clayton revealed her fate she remembers very little other than lying on the floor in her prison, drugged so that she could not escape or alert anyone should they view the house." Ned's eyes filled with tears. "But on one occasion she heard the voices of children and switched on her torch and dragged herself to the window to warn them of the danger, but she was too weak to stand and fell before she'd had a chance to open the window. She remembers Clayton came that night and she prayed that he'd not seen the children, for she knew what happened to people who saw what he didn't want them to see."

"Elizabeth," muttered Stella. "Our Elizabeth, and Susan, Jane, and Diane. That's too close for comfort."

"I know. After that Maggie has no memory. She doesn't remember Fred or me, and she doesn't remember her rescue either. But she must have heard us in her sub-conscious and shone her torch to see from where our voices were coming. Had the poor soul not done so, then she would probably still be in her secret chamber with no chance of ever being found and the fate of Penwynton House was to become a pile of burnt out rubble."

When Ned looked away from the fire he saw that Stella was crying. He rose from the settee and gave her a hug.

"What'll happen to Maggie?" she asked. "Surely she can't be charged with her own kidnapping."

"I don't know," said Ned, softly, "in my opinion she's as much a victim as poor Milly and Tucker. I'm so glad they have Clayton and I shall follow his trial closely when it comes up, but it's a shame they've done away with the death penalty."

"But you don't agree with Capital Punishment," said Stella. "You've always said it was barbaric."

"I know," said Ned, "but that was because if Sylvia had not taken her own life then she would have hanged. But things are different now and this has made me less forgiving, and if Milly has a relapse and dies and he lives, then I shall spend the rest of my days campaigning to get it back."

"You'll think differently after a day or two," said Stella, gently. "It's just all been a bit too much for you. But at least you can be proud of the fact you helped to save Maggie Nan's life, and Milly is on the mend too, so not everything is gloomy. And I suppose, although I could never condone Clayton's action, I can't help but feel a little sorry for him. He must after all have loved his great-grandmother very much to have behaved so outrageously."

Ned shook his head. "But two wrongs don't make a right, do they, Stella? And the thought of Penwynton House being burned to the ground makes me feel very sick."

"Yes, I'd have to agree with you there. For although he may have felt the destruction of the house where his great grandmother was seduced might right a wrong, in reality it would prove to be nothing less than a woeful act of arson."

"Revenge can never be justified," said Ned, "no matter how severe the injustice. I tell you what though, of one thing I am really glad. That being my dream of Sylvia's concern about Frank's welfare has come to nothing. I did think for a time that somehow he'd get hurt by all this, but thankfully there's no connection."

"And what about poor Catherine Rossiter," sighed Stella. "I bet she'll be glad that this has all been solved and her name cleared. The poor woman has been the subject of many a gossiping tongue of late and for no just reason at all.

CHAPTER THIRTY ONE

With less than two weeks to go before she and Frank were due to leave the Inn, Dorothy Newton allocated one day each to thoroughly cleaning out the guest rooms as they became vacant in order that Gloria and Raymond Withers could in no way make scathing comments about the standard of cleanliness at the Ringing Bells Inn. In each room she moved the wardrobes, chests and dressing tables and pulled out the beds so that the carpets could be scrupulously vacuumed underneath and any discoloured paintwork on the walls and skirting boards, touched up. She also fixed loose pieces of wallpaper with a generous layer of thick paste. It was a laborious job but Dorothy rather enjoyed it and it gave her plenty of time to think about the past and with unreserved optimism, the future.

On Monday morning it was the turn of one of her favourite rooms to undergo a spring-clean, the single room on the front of the Inn which had previously been occupied by Edward Tucker and later, Bill Briggs. Dorothy liked that room, it was bright and airy and as the sun was shining it made her task more of a pleasure than a chore. She opened the window to let in the fresh air and then moved the wardrobe with ease and wiped over the skirting board with a damp cloth. She was pleased to see that the walls were still in a good decorative order, but had half expected that would be the case as they had been freshly papered earlier in the year, just before Easter. The dressing table and bed likewise concealed little dirt other than a thin layer of dust, so Dorothy could see that the room would be finished and the windows cleaned before Frank was ready to close the Inn after lunchtime opening, as the only piece of furniture unmoved was a cumbersome chest of drawers in the corner. Dorothy eyed the drawers and contemplated their fate. Should she leave well alone or should she struggle to move them when the only dirt was likely to be dust on the skirting board? She opted to leave them and cleaned the windows instead. She then vacuumed the floor and began to polish the furniture. When she reached the chest of drawers however her conscience began to prickle. "No, I can't leave the job half done."

With a tut she stood the furniture polish and duster on top of the dressing table, removed each drawer from the chest and piled them neatly on the floor, she was then able to pull away the chest from the wall with ease. As expected there was very little dust other than a thin layer on the skirting board, but there was something else, a piece of paper which must have fallen from the chest and become wedged between the wall and the back of the drawers. Dorothy picked up the folded piece of paper. Judging by the pictures of military ships, it looked as though it was part of a Royal Navy newspaper and the date at the top indicated it was a couple of years old. She looked at it with very little interest until a picture caught her eye, a picture of Captain Henry Rossiter with his wife, Catherine. With her curiosity slightly roused she began to read the article but soon became bored with naval terms, facts and figures. Deeming it of little or no interest she tossed it into the bucket containing her cleaning jars, tins and clothes and continued to clean behind the chest prior to replacing the drawers and finishing off the room.

Half an hour later the room was spotless and smelled clean and fresh. Satisfied that she had done a good job she returned to the kitchen to prepare lunch for herself and Frank. Nothing special, just sandwiches, as they always had a hot meal in the evening whenever they found the time.

Dorothy ate her sandwich and put Frank's in the refrigerator; she then made a pot of tea and when it was brewed took a mug through to the bar for Frank, where she found him doing the crossword in a newspaper. There were very few people still drinking as it was nearly closing time.

Dorothy returned to the kitchen and poured a mug of tea for herself and took it through to their little living room to drink. Once seated in the chair by the fire, though no fire was lit, she surveyed the furniture in the room which they would be taking with them to the new bungalow, and tried to visualise where each piece might go.

"Well, there'll be no shortage of pictures to go on the walls," smiled Dorothy, glancing around the room where pictures almost obscured the wallpaper. Even the mantelpiece was cluttered with photos, all of which belonged to Frank and were of him and his first wife, Sylvia.

Dorothy laughed, how many women would permit their husbands still to keep pictures of their first wives on such prominent display. But Dorothy conceded in Frank's case there was room for lenience, after all, he and Sylvia had not divorced, she had died or rather taken her own life. Dorothy thought about her predecessor. She bore her no malice, for like many in the village she had liked Sylvia Newton in spite of her heinous crimes.

"Anyway," grinned Dorothy, "we have a picture of us on our wedding day in the bedroom and that seems far more intimate than on a dusty old mantelpiece."

Nevertheless, she could not help but wonder where Frank would want the pictures of Sylvia put once they had moved.

Dorothy finished her tea, and then picked up the drama group's programme which she'd purchased at the concert the previous week. It had been, as always, a very entertaining evening and Dorothy was impressed by the ladies' efforts not only to show off their talents but in some cases to make complete and utter fools of themselves, something, in spite of being on show behind the bar, she felt she could never do.

Laughing, as she recollected Gertie's face when the teapot she was holding came apart from the handle and fell onto the stage floor where it smashed into several large pieces, Dorothy put down the programme, stood up and returned to the kitchen with her empty mug, she then began to empty out her cleaning bucket in order to wash the clothes and rags. In the bucket was still the newspaper page found behind the chest of drawers. She opened it up again wondering whether or not it should be kept.

"Oh, we can't keep everything," she said. "I don't expect whoever left it will want it back again anyway, and it's of no interest to us, besides, we've enough clutter of our own."

She began to screw it up, but then a familiar name caught her eye. Dorothy frowned, conscious she was shaking, and slowly unfolded the paper to make sure it was not a trick of the light or her imagination playing tricks. No, the name she saw was correct. She sat down and lay the paper on the kitchen table. It was the article she'd seen earlier about Captain Henry Rossiter and the name which shocked her was at the end of the very last paragraph. Dorothy read the print in disbelief.

Captain Henry Rossiter and his wife, Catherine, have both been married before. Captain Rossiter's first wife, Ellen, was an officer in the W.R.N. corp. and died from injuries inflicted during the Second World War, and Catherine is the widow of the late William Wagstaffe, MP, who was murdered by his housekeeper, Grace Bonnington. Mrs Bonnington evaded arrest by fleeing to the West Country where she took refuge in Cornwall at the Ringing Bell Inn, using the identity of a deceased friend.

Dorothy felt sick. She panicked. She was terrified, and had no idea what to do or what action to take. Breathing heavily, she tucked the offending article inside the sleeve of her cardigan, walked as calmly as was possible down the passage and peeped into the bar.

"I'm just popping round to Rose Cottage to see Molly for a little while," she said in a voice that was not her own. "I won't be long, there's a sandwich in the fridge."

"Jolly good, Dot. No need to rush back," said Frank. "Give my regards to Molly and the major."

"I will," Dorothy squeaked, her voice hardly audible. "I will."

Outside, Dorothy took in a deep breath of air and let out a cry of despair. Molly and the major would be able to give her good advice. They were after all very close to Frank. Dorothy ran along the road as fast as she was able, intending not to stop until she crossed the threshold at Rose Cottage, but as she got closer she saw the major's car was not parked outside on the road. She paused by the gate to catch her breath and then walked up the garden path with a heavy heart. To her dismay the back door was locked and the cottage was silent. Confused and unhappy she lowered herself onto the backdoor step and pondered over what on earth she should do.

As the last customers left the Inn, a yellow sports car pulled up on the cobbled area and from it stepped two women. With slight hesitation they entered the Inn and with arms linked addressed Frank who was drying glasses behind the bar.

"Frank, I know you're just about to close, but this is my friend, Margaret, and we both need to talk to you. That is, we want to get something off our chests because we owe it to you," said Catherine Rossiter, with a less formal tone than all were accustomed to hearing.

Frank was taken back. "Hello Margaret, I'm pleased to meet you at last. You'd better come in ladies and tell me what's troubling you."

As Catherine and Margaret crossed the threshold, Frank locked and bolted the door behind them.

"Would you like to stay in here or would you rather we went into our little living room?" he asked. "I don't think there's a fire lit but I've done all the clearing up now."

"Whichever suits you," said Catherine, smiling sweetly. "We don't want to keep you from your afternoon rest, so we'll not be long."

"We'll pop into the living room then. I don't like to stay in here after we're closed in case folks think we're still open. You'll have to excuse the mess though. We're trying to get things sorted and packed up, you see, ready to move."

Catherine raised her hand. "Of course, we understand, please lead the way."

Baffled as to what two relative strangers might have to say to him, Frank led the two women out of the bar, past the dining room and kitchen and down the passage into the living room.

"So ladies, what's the problem?" asked Frank, as they all took a seat. "Nothing serious, I hope. I'd offer you a cup of tea but Dorothy has just popped out to see her friend, Molly. Although if you really wanted one I could always do it myself. I've done so enough times in years gone by but I've sort of got out of the way of doing it over the past fourteen years."

"No, no, please," said Catherine, with hands raised. "Please, we insist you don't go to any trouble. As I've already said we don't want to detain you, but we feel we owe you an explanation as to what's been going on these last few weeks, and we want to tell you ourselves before you read or hear about it from someone else. Oh dear, you go first Mag, I feel quite flustered and my thoughts are muddled."

Margaret reached out and touched Catherine's hand in a reassuring manner. She then turned to Frank.

"I don't really know where to start," she said, nervously twiddling her fingers, as she glanced at the pictures on the mantelpiece. "It's sort of a bit delicate."

Frank was intrigued. "How about the beginning. I find that's usually the best place to start. Come on, love, I don't bite."

Margaret smiled and coughed to clear her throat. "Right, well, during the War I was in the Women's Land Army on a farm in Northamptonshire, but for years afterwards I remembered nothing about it, in fact I had no memory at all."

The colour drained from Frank's face as he recalled Sylvia had also been in the Women's Land Army in Northamptonshire. Margaret noticed his expression and nervously bit at her thumb nail.

"The thing is," she stammered, "I mean, what I'm trying to say is. Well, you see the lines and marks on my face?" Frank nodded. "Well, they are not all entirely due to age. Many were caused by fire, a ferocious fire, not that I remember it. I suffered during the War, you see, with burns. Oh dear, what I have to tell you will shock you badly and I'm so sorry to open old wounds, but I must."

"Shock me!" laughed Frank, more confused by the minute. "I doubt it. I'm bomb proof."

"Bomb proof," sighed Margaret, with a sardonic laugh. "What an unfortunate turn of phrase. You see it was a bomb blast that caused the fire. A bomb dropped on Adastral House. I don't remember what happened or know why I was there, that part of my memory seems to have been lost forever. Anyway, that's where they found me, in the wreckage of Adastral House with no identity papers or any personal possessions. For many years after I couldn't remember anything at all and then one day I saw a picture of Grace Bonnington in a magazine and lots of memories started to come back. Slowly at first and then in great waves, although I still can't remember why I was in London. Mr Newton, Frank. My name's not Margaret. It's Sylvia. Sylvia Spencer, and your late wife used my name and identity."

For the first time in his life Frank was speechless. Margaret went on.

"I was given the name Margaret at the nursing home where they cared for me. One of the nurses said I had eyes like Princess Margaret, and so they started to call me Margaret as I had no idea who I really was."

"Two big tears rolled down Frank's cheeks. "You were waiting to meet your boyfriend," he said, recalling the details of the letter left by Sylvia before she died. "He were home on leave. But she thought you were dead. Really she did. She wouldn't have pinched your name if she'd known you were still alive. You left your identity papers in her little red tin, you see. I didn't know anything about it at the time cos she kept it hidden. People have said lots of hurtful things since she's been gone, but deep down she was kind hearted and considerate. Please don't think badly of her, she wasn't wicked and she wouldn't have done those awful things if she hadn't been pushed into it."

Margaret rose from her chair, quickly crossed the room and put her arm around his shoulder. "I know," she sobbed. "I know she was a good person. Memories of those days on the farm are slowly coming back. She was my best friend and that's what I wanted to tell you. Why I'm here. I wanted to put flowers on her grave, but I take it she was not buried in the churchyard."

"No," said Frank, drying his eyes. "She was cremated and her ashes were scattered by the old mine on the cliff tops. She liked it up there, you see, so we thought it only right. Oh dear, I can't believe what I'm hearing. You're the first person I've ever met that knew Sylvia when she was someone else. It's a pity you didn't know her in the days when she were larking around with that Wagstaffe bloke, though. I should like to have known what he was like. I mean he must have been a bit of alright for her to have fallen for him in the first place, but I take it he was obsessed with power."

"Yes, he was," said Margaret, glancing towards Catherine. "I'm told he was like Dr Jekyll and Mr Hyde and Grace fell for Dr Jekyll. He was power crazy behind his caring disposition, you see, and was desperate to get to the top of his political career. And in the end, he was prepared to trample over anyone who got in his way, even his own family."

"Good God," said Frank, turning his head towards the door, aware of quick footsteps in the passage. "How do you know that?"

The door flew open and in ran Dorothy. Hair ruffled, face flushed and eyes ablaze with anger and fear. Dorothy waving a carving knife, and ready to attack, pointed her weapon angrily at Catherine Rossiter. She snarled in a very un-Dorothy like manner. "I saw your car outside, Mrs Rossiter, and so knew you were here. Frank, Mrs Rossiter is the late William Wagstaffe's widow."

CHAPTER THIRTY TWO

News of Catherine Rossiter and Margaret's identity caused many Trengillion jaws to drop as they struggled to get the facts straight and pass on their learnings to others with an air of knowledge, for it was, by Trengillion's standard, an unprecedented occurrence. So deeply shocked and taken back was everyone by the news that no-one even dared profess, as on many other occasions, that they had known since the very beginning who the two women staying at Chy-an-Gwyns really were. And none were more shocked than Molly, who found on her return from a ramble over the cliff tops, a torn out page from the old Navel newspaper laying on the door mat of Rose Cottage.

"So, how did Catherine Rossiter and this Margaret-cum-Sylvia woman first meet?" asked the major, emptying his pipe into his large glass ashtray. "It must have been by sheer chance if Margaret didn't even know herself who she was."

Molly, having just returned from the Inn where she had received the latest information from a still deeply shocked Dorothy, sat down on the settee removed her shoes and put on her slippers. "Well, apparently she, Margaret that is, saw an article in an old magazine at the nursing home about William Wagstaffe and Grace Bonnington, and the name, along with a picture, jogged her memory. So one of the nurses made enquiries and wrote to Catherine asking if she would be prepared to meet Margaret. You see, it was hoped that her hearing about Grace from someone who had known her, might have a therapeutic effect and help refresh her memory. When Catherine got the letter, she agreed to meet Margaret purely out of curiosity, because as unlikely as it might sound, Catherine was actually very fond of Grace, and it turns out that she had every intention of visiting her when she returned to London, following her arrest and before her trial. But as we all know that didn't happen."

"Well, at least Frank's not upset too by it all," said Ned, who with Stella had called at Rose Cottage to make sure they had all the facts right. "From what I've heard he seems quite chuffed now he's had a chance to come to terms with it."

Molly nodded. "And I'm told that he and Margaret have agreed that she will continue to call herself Margaret, and Frank will continue to refer to Sylvia as Sylvia. Oh dear, if anyone didn't know what I was talking about they'd think me quite mad."

Stella smiled. "And I suppose Teddy Tinsdale's visit to Catherine, as witnessed by Gertie, was to get a story about why she was in Trengillion, it being the place where her husband's killer had taken refuge. I wonder how Gertie is feeling now she knows the truth."

"I knew Catherine was alright," Gertie gleefully said to Betty as they sat drinking coffee at number two, Coronation Terrace. "All those horrid rumours about her being mad and up to no good, how silly they were. Poor woman, can you imagine what she must have been through, one way or another?"

Betty tried to smother a smile. "Of course, but there were times when you doubted her a little yourself. After all you ended up seeking help from Ned and then going to see Fred."

Gertie blushed. "Well yes, but at least my worries were about something real and not a figment of my imagination, although I'm glad I didn't find out the truth at the time or I'd have been really scared, a bit like poor Dorothy must have been." Gertie's eyes misted over. "It was funny talking to Catherine this morning, knowing now who she is. I mean, she used to be Sylvia's boss and then Sylvia used to be our boss, didn't she? And now she's my boss. It's a bit weird really. Neither of us mentioned Jane, of course. Isn't it strange, and sad, how we've all chosen to forget what happened to her? I suppose it's a fact of life though, that the memory blocks out bad things that have happened."

"Yes, I know what you mean, like when we were young it seems the sun shone every day and no-one was ever in a bad mood." Betty frowned. "There is one other thing that still mystifies me: May and Bertha. Why do you think Catherine was acting in such an odd way when they saw her by the old mine? I mean they're not the sort of people to tell lies, are they?"

A huge grin stretched across Gertie's face. "Well, you're never going to believe this, but Catherine was talking to Sylvia, or rather Grace as she calls her, I keep forgetting that. She told me so herself, about talking, that is, and singing. You see when she came across

Ned in the churchyard he innocently told her Sylvia's ashes were scattered by the old mine. It's really bizarre. You see Catherine liked Grace even though she was having an affair with her husband, but she didn't really mind because she was already besotted with the extremely handsome Henry Rossiter."

Betty was dumbfounded. "No, surely not."

Gertie giggled. "Yes, it's true, but please don't tell anyone, will you? She told me in confidence, you see, as everyone else assumes their relationship didn't start until after William Wagstaffe's death, or should I say disappearance, because if you remember, everyone assumed he was still alive for the two years following to the incident that New Year's Day."

The colour drained from Betty's face. "Oh, my God! Then in a funny sort of way, Sylvia, by Sylvia of course I mean our Sylvia not the Margaret one, did Catherine a favour by bumping off her old man."

"So, Bill Briggs was a gossip columnist just like Edward Tucker-cum-Teddy Tinsdale or whatever you want to call him," said Dorothy, rubbing in the fact, as she packed her best dinner service into a tea chest. "I told you he was up to no good, Frank Newton. Black-throated Yellow Spotted Gillygot indeed, and it must have been his newspaper cutting I found down the back of the chest, although I suppose it might have been lost by Mr Tucker-cum-Tinsdale, him being a nosey so and so too."

Frank laughed. "I suppose in a way he wasn't lying. He told us he'd spotted a rare bird on the cliffs and was probably making reference to Catherine. Wagstaffe and Wagtail are after all, very similar names."

"That's not funny, Frank," snapped Dorothy. "Oh well, we won't have to endure lies and deceit from anyone else now as all our guests have gone."

"Cheer up, Dot. Most of our guests over the years have been really nice people, even the odd ones like Freddie Short. Don't let Bill Briggs mar your memories of this place, cos I expect in time you'll laugh about him and the events that have taken place these last few weeks."

Dorothy placed the lid on the tea chest. "You'll be greatly missed here, Frank Newton. I know I've said so before, but it's true. You've time for everyone and the patience of a saint. I can't see people getting the same consideration from Raymond Withers."

Frank, not wanting to discuss Raymond Withers, as he found it very difficult to like the man, quickly changed the subject. "Do you think Catherine and Margaret will come to our farewell do on Saturday, Dot?"

"I hope so," she replied, with sincerity. "I really do. I'm sure they think I don't like them and to be honest, to say I didn't at first, would be an understatement. But I think they've helped you in a way and for that I'm very grateful."

Frank grabbed Dorothy's arm and pulled her onto his lap. "And you say I'm the one with time for everyone and the patience of a saint. You should look at yourself more often in the mirror, Mrs Newton. You'd be surprised by what you'd see."

"Do you fancy going to Frank and Dorothy's last night do?" Catherine asked Margaret as they sat on grass beside the cliff path outside Chy-an-Gwyns, watching the sun set. "I'd like to go but I'm not sure that we ought."

Margaret folded her arms, for the late afternoon felt chilly. "But they did ask us and I really think they meant it. Well, Frank did, anyway, I'm not so sure about Dorothy. I think she's a little wary of us. It's really sweet the way she tries to protect him, isn't it?"

Catherine looked down at her hand and twisted the wedding ring on her finger. "And who can blame her. We're all victims of a very peculiar chain of events, Margaret."

Margaret nodded. "We most certainly are and I'm so glad we came to Trengillion. I feel as though I've found myself again in the time we've been here, even though much of my past is still very vague."

"I know what you mean. There's a tranquillity about this village that seems to brush one's troubles aside. I'm not at all surprised that Grace fell in love with this place."

"Just look at that sunset. How I wish I could paint."

Catherine sighed. "Beautiful indeed." She turned and clutched Margaret's arm. "Returning to my question, do you think we should go to the party?"

Margaret nodded. "Well, what do you think?"

"I think we should go, if for no other reason than to show there are no hard feelings." She glanced back across the village towards the old mine in the distance. "And do you know what? I think if it was possible to ask her, then Grace would agree."

Margaret smiled, her eyes misted with tears. "I'm glad you've said that because I should like to go, but let's hope there won't be any newspaper men there, not national ones, anyway. I don't mind chaps from the local rags, but the big boys are a pain in the neck."

"Hear, hear. They wrote some pretty scathing articles about William when he was missing, and assumedly on the run: many dreadful and most without just cause. He may not have been perfect, and how many of us are, but he was my husband and I dearly loved him once."

Margaret reached out patted Catherine's arm affectionately. "Do you think Bill Briggs will still publish his story or do you think because you've confessed he'll not bother?"

"I think he'll not bother," said Catherine, with an air of confidence. "I rang his office yesterday and told him I knew he had been in Cornwall, thanks to our chat with the Newtons, and I got the impression he had already heard on the grapevine that that was the case. Telling Briggs of my temporary residence here must have been one of the last things Tinsdale did before he died. What rats the two of them are, or in the case of Tinsdale, were. As far as I'm concerned they are as worthless as each other, but having said that I don't wish Briggs to go the same way as Tinsdale." She laughed. "Not at the moment, anyway."

Margaret smiled. "And it seems they weren't the only rats in Trengillion this summer. I refer of course to Archie Clayton, not that I've ever met the man."

"I met him once," said Catherine, "at a fund raising event or something like that. It was a couple of years ago and I can't say that he was my cup of tea." She laughed. "I heard a well-spoken chap in the post office yesterday refer to him as a cad. I think that adjective just about sums up not only Clayton, but Tucker and Briggs also."

Saturday, October the twenty eighth dawned as on any other day. The morning was overcast and the autumn air fresh, cool and tinged with the smell of bonfires burning away summer's debris. In Bluebell Woods the leaves which had shaded the woodland floor for several months, were slowly turning from green to varying shades of yellow and orange. Some had already fallen and been swept by the wind into small heaps where they would slowly decay over the long winter months. Others had fluttered down into the stream to be taken by the gentle flow of water on a journey towards the sea.

Around the village, beneath the dull sky, a hint of sadness hung in the atmosphere, combined with a buzz of excitement. For the day brought with its dawning, the last day that Frank and Dorothy Newton would ever serve drinks at The Ringing Bells Inn.

In the early afternoon, Ned and Stella drove to Penzance Station to pick up Rose and George, who had opted to travel by train so as not to be tired for the big night. And everywhere in Trengillion, where people met, the words 'see you later' rang out with marked enthusiasm. Even teetotallers were keen to show their gratitude and be there for the last night to thank Frank who for more than thirty years had supported the village on many occasions.

The sale of the Inn was not due to be finalised until Monday morning, but Frank and Dorothy had decided to make Saturday their last day, so that on the Sunday they could devote their time to packing the last of their belongings ready for the big move, leaving the staff to look after the bar whilst they did so.

The evening got off to an early start with people arriving shortly after opening time to ensure they had a seat, and Frank, eager that his customers and friends should not be kept waiting for their drinks, had plenty of staff waiting to cope with the anticipated turn-out. Alice and Sally worked alongside Gertie and Betty who volunteered to work for old time's sake.

The first arrivals were greeted by the warmth of an open log fire and a glass of punch with Frank and Dorothy's compliments. Thereafter, drinks were sold at lower than usual prices to clear the stocks prior to the Withers taking over the Inn on Monday. Hence by nine o'clock most people were feeling slightly inebriated, both by the drink and the intoxicating atmosphere.

It was an evening of speeches, compliments and announcements, the most unlikely being, Jim Hughes standing to tell the crowd, silenced by the ringing of the Inn's bell, that Doris Jones, his lifelong and very good friend had agreed to become his wife. Molly was flabbergasted. She knew Jim and Doris were old friends but had no idea there was any romance in their relationship.

"Jim and I were sweethearts many moons ago," laughed Doris, when Molly tackled her over her secret. "But we fell out over something really trivial, then he met Flo and that was the end of that."

"You dark horse," said Molly, kissing Doris on the cheek. "Is that why you never married?"

Doris nodded. "That and the fact no-one else ever asked me."

"Oh, Doris, I don't think you can imagine just how thrilled I am, but there is one thing that bothers me. Will you be moving in with Jim after you're wed or will he be moving in with you?"

"He'll be coming to live with me at Ivy Cottage. That's something I insisted on, as I couldn't possibly leave my garden or the house that I've lived in all my life. It's where I brought up Jane. What's more, I rather like my neighbours."

Once it was deemed that all likely to put in an appearance were tucked within the walls of the Inn, the major made a speech which brought tears to the eyes of everyone present. He thanked Frank and Dorothy for the wonderful service they had provided to Trengillion over the years and the warm hospitality that was always to be found at the Ringing Bells Inn. Frank and Dorothy were then presented with gifts, bought from money raised in a collection for the couple's retirement. For Frank a rocking chair and a book titled, 'Gardening for Beginners' and for Dorothy a pair of slippers, chocolates and a beautiful lead crystal vase.

The children of Trengillion, in order that their parents could attend the last night party without the worry of baby-sitters, had a party of their own in the Newtons' living room. Frank and Dorothy left them with a large supply of fizzy drinks, bags of crisps and a record player on which to play the records they had been invited to bring along for the occasion.

"I wish Greg and Lily were here," said Elizabeth, dreamily opening her second bag of crisps. "It seems like they've been gone for ages already but it's only eleven weeks."

"Eleven weeks and counting. I think you fancy Greg," said Susan, burping loudly due to the consumption of too much orangeade. "You often mention him."

"I do not," spluttered Elizabeth, with indignation. "I miss Lily just as much as him."

"Ha ha, you're going all red," laughed Anne. "Do you want to marry him?"

"Don't be so silly, you stupid girl," snapped Elizabeth, squirming on the sofa. "Of course not. Please will someone change the subject?"

Susan giggled, "What shall we talk about then?" Anyone got any suggestions?"

"Blimey, that's a first, you stuck for words, Sue," said her brother, John.

"Our Auntie Rose had a letter from Maggie Nan," said Anne, always glad of an opportunity to speak. "She showed it to us when she arrived this afternoon. It's quite long."

"What! But why was that?" asked Diane. "I didn't know they knew each other."

"They don't, but Maggie Nan heard it was Auntie Rose's quick thinking that probably saved her life," said Anne, with pride. "Auntie Rose knew the name of Maggie Nan's agent, you see, or something like that."

"What with fashion designers being kidnapped, Teddy Tinsdale's ghost, and a pop star look-a-like at the Lodge, it's been a funny old summer, hasn't it?" said Jane. "Not to mention the time you saw Archie Clayton's face in the bushes, Anne? It still gives me the creeps thinking about that."

Anne shuddered. "Please don't mention him. I'll never be able to forget the scare he gave me, but at least he's safely locked up now and so he can't harm anyone else."

"I expect you've all heard that the big house is going to be a hotel," said Diane, glumly. "So that rather puts an end to our dreams about Danny living there."

The boys laughed at the looks of disappointment on the girls' faces.

"Don't worry, if you want any dashingly handsome company then Tony and me will still be here," teased John, putting his arm round the shoulder of his twin brother.

Jane giggled. "Ah, but you two might have competition for our attention soon. I've heard that the new people coming to the Inn have two sons. Teenage sons, and hopefully, they'll be quite dishy."

"Wow, really," said John, throwing his crunched up crisp packet into the empty fireplace. "Now that is good news. It looks like the days of us older boys being outnumbered by you girls will soon be over then."

Elizabeth, seated on the settee, leaned back. "I wonder if the new owners of Penwynton House will still let people walk through Bluebells Woods when it's a hotel," she said, thoughtfully.

Susan looked aghast. "God, I hope so. If not what on earth will we do next summer? I mean, all this year's excitement was centred around the estate, wasn't it? I'd hate not to be able to go down there again."

Anne groaned. "I agree, it's a horrid, depressing thought. It's bad enough knowing we'll soon not be allowed in the grounds but to be barred from the woods as well would be too cruel."

"And there's nowhere else around here with good trees to climb or ones for making dens in," added Matthew, equally fed-up.

The joyous atmosphere had changed dramatically and Elizabeth, feeling guilty for mentioning access to the woods in the first place, was determined they should regain the party spirit, especially as they were all together under one roof. She sprang up from the sofa. "Come on, let's stop moping and dance instead. Did anyone bring a copy of *Crazy Maisie*? I should really, really like to hear it, as it will always remind me of the nice things about this summer and especially spying on our gorgeous Danny."

Diane reached for her bag. "I did." She took the record from its sleeve and dropping it onto the turntable.

They all stood, and to Gooseberry Pie's music ringing out from the record player, they danced until their legs ached.

Mary and Dick Cottingham, back in the village for the weekend in order to attend Frank and Dorothy's last night because they wanted to get to know local people, were talking to Annie Stevens when Ned accidently knocked Annie's arm and spilled a little of her dry Martini onto her sleeve.

"Oh, Annie, I'm so sorry," Ned said, taking a handkerchief from his pocket and gently dabbing her arm.

"Don't worry, Ned. It doesn't matter. I should think by the time the evening's out I'll have had quite a few drinks splashed on my clothes; there's hardly room to move."

Ned nodded. "'Tis a bit of a crush, isn't it? But please, let me get you another drink."

Annie shook her head. "That's very kind, Ned, but very little was spilt. Besides, I mustn't drink too much because I want to remember everything about tonight even though it's all very sad."

"Hmm, I reckon there will be quite a few tears shed before the evening's out. The end of an era and all that."

Annie smiled. "And the beginning of a new one. Ned, may I introduce you to Mary and Dick Cottingham, they are in the process of buying Penwynton House, along with Mary's sister and her brother-in-law."

Ned grinned. "Ah, I had wondered who you might be. I'm delighted to meet you." He shook their hands in turn.

Annie took a sip of the remains of her dry Martini. "Needless to say Fred and I are delighted about the sale and think it's wonderful because when Fred retires and we move to the Lodge, then Mary and Dick will be our nearest neighbours."

"Yes, of course." He turned to the Cottinghams. "Well, I must say I think you're very brave to have taken on the project, considering the state the old house is in."

"It looks a lot worse than it is," said Dick. "We've had structural engineers give the place a good going over and they say it's sound. Of course the interior will need dramatically up-dating, lots more bathrooms and so forth but we're looking forward to the challenge, aren't we, Mary?"

Mary nodded, clearly excited. "Absolutely, I can't wait."

Ned was impressed by their enthusiasm. "Well, good luck to you all and I hope it's a roaring success."

Dick raised his glass. "I'll drink to that."

Ned chinked his glass against those in his presence. "Of course, my daughters are a little disappointed that Penwynton House is to be a hotel. The giddy girls live in a world of fantasy and were hoping that some pop star called Danny Jarrams would buy it to live in."

A broad smile crossed Mary's face and her eyes twinkled. "Really! Well they might see him yet. Danny Jarrams is our nephew."

THE END

Printed in Great Britain
by Amazon